Praise for the novels of Leslie Glass . . .

"This series [is] a winner."
—*Mystery News*

"Detective Woo is the next generation descended from Ed McBain's 87th Precinct."
—*Hartford Courant*

"I'll drop what I'm doing to read Leslie Glass anytime."
—Nevada Barr

"Fast-paced, gritty . . . [April Woo] joins Kinsey Millhone and Kay Scarpetta in the ranks of female crime fighters."
—*Library Journal*

More praise . . .

"An intense thriller . . . Glass provides several surprises, characters motivated by a lively cast of inner demons and, above all, a world where much is not as it initially seems."
—*Publishers Weekly*

"Deft plotting and strong characterization will leave readers eager for further installments."
—*Library Journal*

"Glass not only draws the reader into the crazed and gruesome world of the killer, but also cleverly develops the character of Woo . . . and her growing attraction for partner Sanchez."
—*Orlando Sentinel*

"If you're a Thomas Harris fan anxiously awaiting the next installment of the 'Hannibal the Cannibal' series and looking for a new thriller to devour, you'll find it in *Burning Time*."
—Ft. Lauderdale Sun-Sentinel

"A suspenseful story in which those who appear to be sane may actually harbor the darkest secrets of all."*—Mostly Murder*

"Sharp as a scalpel. . . . Scary as hell. Leslie Glass is Lady McBain."—*New York Times* bestselling author Michael Palmer

LESLIE GLASS

JUDGING TIME

A SIGNET BOOK

SIGNET
Published by the Penguin Group
Penguin Putnam Inc., 375 Hudson Street,
New York, New York 10014, U.S.A.
Penguin Books Ltd, 27 Wrights Lane,
London W8 5TZ, England
Penguin Books Australia Ltd, Ringwood,
Victoria, Australia
Penguin Books Canada Ltd, 10 Alcorn Avenue,
Toronto, Ontario, Canada M4V 3B2
Penguin Books (N.Z.) Ltd, 182–190 Wairau Road,
Auckland 10, New Zealand

Penguin Books Ltd, Registered Offices:
Harmondsworth, Middlesex, England

First published by Signet, an imprint of Dutton NAL,
a member of Penguin Putnam Inc.
Previously published in a Dutton edition.

First Signet Printing, February, 1999
10 9 8 7 6 5 4 3

Printed in the United States of America

PUBLISHER'S NOTE
This is a work of fiction. Names, characters, places, and incidents either are the product of the author's imagination or are used fictitiously, and any resemblance to actual persons, living or dead, events, or locales is entirely coincidental.

For my mother, Elinor Gordon,
whose passion was justice

Acknowledgments

First I want to thank all the good people at NYPD who risk their lives around the clock to make New York City a safe place to visit and to live. My goal with this, as with all my books, was to create characters in realistic situations, who are true to life but do not resemble any real people in the precincts and other agencies I describe. This is a work of fiction.

I want to thank former commanding officer of Midtown North, Inspector Diane Prizutti, for letting me visit, and commanding officer of the 30th Precinct, Inspector Jane Perlov, for letting me sit at her desk, metaphorically speaking. Thanks to Pam Delaney and all my friends at the Police Foundation, who do so much to help in so many ways. Thanks to the good people at New York University School of Law—Jim Jacobs, Steve Zeidman, Debra LaMorte, and of course, Dean John Sexton, who educated me relentlessly. Thanks to the Glass Institute Fellows and Dr. Wilma Bucci for dedication above and beyond. Thanks to Dr. Richard C. Friedman for the vital help in psychology that makes such a difference, and to my favorite cousin, Dr. Deborah Loeff, who brought me the murder weapon from Chicago and taught me how to kill.

Thanks to my agent, Nancy Yost, for deliverance and to Dutton Signet for everything else, especially good judgment and other editorial excellences, by Audrey LaFehr, and leadership, by Elaine Koster.

Last, kudos in order of their appearance to Edmund, Alex, Lindsey, and Peanut, my very best friends this and every year.

We should be careful to get out of an experience only the wisdom that is in it—and stop there; lest we be like the cat that sits down on a hot stove lid. She will never sit down on a hot stove lid again—and that is well; but also she will never sit down on a cold one any more.

—Mark Twain
Pudd'nhead Wilson's New Calendar

1

At fifteen minutes after midnight on January sixth, when Merrill Liberty took a phone call at her table in Liberty's Restaurant, she had thirty minutes to live.

"It's the boss." Patrice, the cocoa-colored maître d' from Haiti, smiled and handed her a mobile phone.

Merrill tensed and made a face before reaching for the phone. "Where are you?" she asked in a low voice.

"Just got in." Her husband's voice sounded as strained as hers.

She nodded at her companion—*he's back*—then leaned forward in her wicker chair with its high fan back. "What took so long, Rick?"

"Hey, don't start, baby. Haven't you noticed it stinks out there? My flight was canceled. I just squeaked in on another airline. I'm lucky to be here tonight at all."

"Same old story." Merrill's voice, so often sweet and silky in her TV roles, took on its less famous offstage sulk. "You didn't have to go," she muttered.

Frederick Douglass Liberty—known as Liberty in his football days—sighed his martyr sigh. "You know I had to go."

"No, I don't." Merrill glanced at Tor, who was shaking his head at her, smiling and pouring himself the last of the wine.

"Say I said hello," Tor murmured.

Merrill ignored him.

He shrugged.

"If the weather was so damned bad why risk your life?" Merrill demanded.

"For you, baby. I risked it for you."

"How's your head?"

"The head's all right, but I'm exhausted. How was your evening?"

Once again Merrill fixed her deep green eyes on Tor. He was sipping wine and smiling. "First rate."

"Time to come home, then."

Merrill drummed her fingers on the table. "You've been away all day. You in any particular hurry now?"

"Fine. Patrice said you just got your dessert, enjoy it."

His voice had taken on the bitter edge she hated, so she gave him a lighthearted laugh. "Nothing's secret here, I see."

"You better believe it."

Suddenly Merrill smiled at Tor. The lusty way he'd begun attacking almost at the same moment both her spiced apple cobbler and his fried bananas with crunchy toasted coconut was characteristic of his approach to life. It made her want to laugh again.

"Merrill—?"

"Yes?"

"Just remember I love you." They were the last words Rick Liberty said to his wife.

"And I love you, too," were her last words to him.

Tor rolled his eyes as she punched the off button and handed the phone to Patrice, who had drifted over to the table to retrieve it. "You two."

"Thanks, Patrice," Merrill said. "Will you tell Jon everything was great?"

"I'll tell him, but he won't believe it from anyone but you. Anything else I can get you tonight?"

Tor raised his eyebrows, questioning. Did they want anything else? Merrill shook her head. No, they did not. Patrice smiled and drifted away.

"Rick's cool?" Tor asked.

Merrill frowned for a second because with Rick one could never be absolutely sure. "He's cool," she said.

Then her mood lightened. "Hey, Tor. Leave me a bite, will you."

"Go ahead, dig in."

After thirty-five years in America, Tor still had a bit of a Scandinavian accent, a feature Merrill found charming. She picked up her fork and tasted the spiced apple cobbler that was one of Rick's mother's recipes. "Amazing, as usual," Merrill pronounced it.

Tor gazed at her. "So are you."

"Well, thanks. But I know you say that to all the girls."

He laughed. "With you, though, it's the truth."

"Well, I think you're pretty terrific, too." Merrill's face shone with the wine, food, and other pleasures she'd enjoyed that evening. At that moment she did think Tor Petersen was terrific. For a second she wondered whether Tor had told his wife where he was going, and what the dizzy Daphne herself might be doing with the free time. But only for a second.

"I've always been crazy about you, you know that."

At six one, Tor was an inch shorter than Rick and had almost as sturdy a build. Fourteen years older, however, Tor now had to fight in earnest the spreading abdomen of middle age, affluence, and complacency. And where Rick had the mixed blood of African, American Indian, and Caucasian, Tor was pure Nordic, with an ample head of hair more flaxen than silver and eyes as blue as the Vikings of his ancestry. Tor's second wife had been the daughter of an Arabian princess, and when the two couples had gone out together, people were always confused because the two blonds were married to the two people of color and not each other.

"If I'd married you, we'd still be together."

Merrill considered the declaration with a twinkle. Tor was marching out onto a limb that couldn't hold him. "Which time?"

"Any time. How about this time?"

"Well, maybe later this week after you've dumped this one."

"Oh, you know." He looked surprised.

"Darling, you're an open book." Merrill laughed and took a bite of the "fried 'nanas" with the drop-dead crunchy coconut. "I don't know how you get away with it. Let's go home."

Tor finished his last bite and looked up. "Okay, okay. Time for bed?"

Merrill nodded and pushed back her wicker chair. At 12:38 A.M. on a cold January night, the stylish restaurant was not yet empty. There were still a few people drinking exotically flavored coffees at the bar and finishing their desserts at their tables. Suddenly she was sorry that Tor was always so solicitous of his driver, sending him home every time the man complained about the weather. Earlier, it had been no big deal to walk a block from the theater to the restaurant. Late at night though, when every street corner was a deceptive snow-covered slush pit that sucked the unwary into a frigid ankle-deep lake and it wasn't always so easy to get a cab, she didn't relish the possibility of having to walk home. Merrill grabbed her fur-lined black suede coat off the chair beside her, draping it over her arm as she headed for the dazzling stainless-steel kitchen to say good-night to Jon the chef. Then she shrugged on the coat, waved at Patrice, who was busy at a table, and went out the front door where Tor had preceded her some minutes before to get a cab.

Liberty's had a tiny garden in front with a step up to the street and a gate on the sidewalk level. The dwarf fir trees in planters surrounding the space were crusted with snow and still wore their Christmas lights. Merrill closed the two doors of the restaurant and stepped out into the garden. Tor and another person were standing close together, as if in deep conversation. Merrill hesitated. Something was odd about them. She heard the sound of car wheels slapping through the slush just slightly above them on the street, but not the sound of voices. The other person drew closer to Tor as if to embrace him. He had his broad back to Merrill, and she couldn't see what was happening. Suddenly, without a sound, Tor slumped to the wet pavement. Merrill lurched forward, crying his name "Tor—!"

Almost instantly she was at the place where he had fallen. "What happened? My God, what is that thing? What are you doing? Not you! No! Tor, Tor—?" Merrill's voice became frantic as the shiny thing she'd seen disappeared into a coat sleeve, and Tor tried to raise himself from where he'd fallen, facedown on the freezing cement.

Merrill lunged forward to help, but a black-gloved hand grabbed her arm and prevented her from sinking to her knees. She became hysterical at Tor's desperate struggle and the hideous noise that erupted from his mouth as he tried to speak, tried to breathe, and failed at both.

"What are you doing? Let go. Tor—Tor—?"

Suddenly Merrill felt a little dizzy from the wine. She was further confused by the powerful fingers digging into her arm that wouldn't let go. Tears stung her eyes as terror for him—not herself—overcame her. She formed the word *help* in her head, but all that came out of her mouth was a whimper. "You?"

She couldn't get to Tor, couldn't help him. "Don't—please!" Two powerful hands held her arms so tightly the throb in her biceps felt like screams.

"Tor!"

He'd stopped moving. "Oh, God, what did you do to him?" Panicked, Merrill finally wrenched her head around toward the restaurant door and started to scream.

Her body jerked against the vise that gripped her arm. "Let go, *please*." The coat she hadn't had time to button flew open.

"Stupid *bitch*! Can't you see it's too late now."

One hand released her arm. Merrill thought she was finally being freed. Then she saw the shiny thing again, felt a pressure on her neck, heard her assailant grunt the way tennis champions did when they leaned into a 110-mile-an-hour serve. "Uh."

"Oh, God, no!" In that grunt, Merrill heard something give in her neck. The grip on her arm loosened and was gone. Blood bubbled out of her throat like a fountain. She put her hand up to stop it. "Oh God." Her mouth filled with blood. She staggered, unable to breathe.

The gate to the street opened and closed. Her vision blurring, Merrill Liberty saw Tor's killer melt out into the street. She turned to the restaurant door, but couldn't stand up. She collapsed on the body of her friend. Her head lolled on Tor's shoulder, her blood soaked his back. Her eyes were wide open in horror. By the time the restaurant door opened and Patrice came running out, Merrill could no longer tell anyone anything.

2

The autumn that NYPD Detective April Woo made sergeant a winter sky socked in over Manhattan on the first day of November and stayed there, relentlessly frigid and unforgiving to the light-sensitive—all through the holiday season. It had rained the four days preceding Thanksgiving, then hailed on the parade. It snówed three times before Christmas, thawed, then froze again half a dozen times in the days before New Year's. As the old year wound down in bone-chilling cold, so did crime in New York.

New Year's Day came on Wednesday. By the first weekend in January the celebrating came to a dreary halt as Manhattan's tourist season ended and thousands of visitors returned to their homes around the world, leaving the city looking tired and empty. Residents of New York were staying off the streets, holed up inside and waiting for a break in the winter misery.

On Thanksgiving, April Woo had not been on duty in the 20th Precinct on Eighty-second Street and Columbus Avenue for the Thanksgiving Day parade. She'd made sergeant ten days before and was reassigned twenty-seven blocks south to a supervisory position in the detective squad of Midtown North. When April reported for duty at 8 A.M. on her first day, there had been a lot of activity going on, but not one of the six detectives working the phones at that time had looked up and said, "Hi, how are ya," given her a high five, or done any of the friendly guy things they usually did when a new fellow came in. The thing they did when she arrived new to the job was pointedly ignore her.

Five five, 116 pounds slender. Perfect oval face and almond eyes, rosebud lips, swan neck. As usual, April had been wearing her own personal cop uniform of navy slacks and navy blazer, and that first day, a thick red turtleneck for warmth and good luck. Only the 9mm strapped to her waist gave her away as a cop. That and the fact that there were no earrings in her ears, no jade ring on her finger, no gold necklace around her neck, and she was wearing no makeup except for the barest frosting of *Gingembre doré* on her lips. The lack of these items cost her quite a bit because she valued her femininity as much as her job. She enjoyed her jewelry, craved her makeup, and felt both ugly and stupid without them.

Midtown North was a bigger and more important house than the Two-O, but the detective squad rooms were all broken up and gave the effect of looking smaller. As April had stood there on her first day taking in the empty holding cell and the backs of her colleagues in her new home, the guy with the big office and an actual name plaque on his door, LT. HERNANDO IRIARTE, frowned and wiggled a finger at her.

Come in here.

Ah, a frowner. April opened the lieutenant's door with the glass window and went inside. "Sergeant April Woo, reporting for duty, sir," she said.

Lieutenant Iriarte was a good-looking man with a carefully clipped mustache that was much shorter and thinner than that of her would-be lover, Detective Sergeant Mike Sanchez, whom she hadn't seen in almost two weeks because of their ill-timed days off. Iriarte also had a more serious short haircut than Mike's and very classy clothes, like those of a businessman who considered himself a success. A pair of half glasses were tucked in his jacket breast pocket, along with a snowy handkerchief. The lieutenant took the glasses out, hung them low on his nose, and peered at April over them as if he were going to interview her about her qualifications.

She waited, eyes slightly lowered in the Chinese pose of modesty and self-denial that she had learned at birth and had to unlearn over and over to be a good cop.

Iriarte finished looking her over. "I won't say women can't be good cops," he said at last. "We happen to have a woman commander in this house. You might take your cues from her."

"Sir?" April hadn't met the commander and was unsure what this meant.

"It is not difficult to ascertain that men and women are not the same," Iriarte said. "They are very different . . . in fact."

"Yes, sir."

"I want those differences clearly defined."

"Yes, sir," April repeated, still uncertain where he was going with this.

"I don't like women who act like men, talk dirty, and sleep in the men's dorms. We had one like that, claimed she was a professional and had a right to stay in the dorm. We got rid of her."

April nodded. Uh-huh.

"You can sleep in the women's dorm," he added.

"I go home on my turnarounds," April told him.

"Good. Keep to yourself and keep your femininity." The lieutenant folded his glasses and tucked them back in his pocket. He pointed at an empty office catty-corner to his. "There's your office, then. I run a tight ship."

"Yes, sir. That's what I've heard."

"I have a good feeling about this." He showed her the back of his hand in dismissal. That was six weeks ago. Since then she'd covered a couple dozen burglaries, couple of rapes, two homeless deaths from exposure. A "justifiable" homicide involving a cop apparently threatened by a suspect flashing a "knife" (shiny object). But who knew. She did the best she could. She was the one who had to explain the situation to the seven members of the dead man's family who came to the precinct to find out what had happened to him. They had arrived without knowing he was dead.

In six weeks not a lot had changed. At 12:45 A.M. on the Monday that began the first full week of the new year, April caught sight of her new boss Lieutenant Iriarte through the window in the closed door of her first office. Lieutenant Iriarte exited his own exceptionally clean and tidy office wearing his dove gray (probably cashmere blend) overcoat. The commanding officer of the detective squad plopped his dark gray fedora on his head, tilted it rakishly, then crossed the squad room to the locker room where all the detectives except for April ate their meals. Lieutenant Iriarte passed from April's view. A few seconds later he passed her door again, showed her the back of his hand without looking at her, and left the precinct house for the night. For the next fifteen minutes until 1 A.M. when she could go home, April was in sole charge of the detective squad. All was quiet. She sighed and started cleaning up her desk.

At 1 A.M. she glanced at her watch. "Time to go," she murmured. No one to talk to so now she was talking to herself. She pulled on her coat, grabbed her shoulder bag, and left the squad room.

She took the stairs to the main floor, where a uniform getting ready to go off duty was busily mopping into a single grimy film all the dirty puddles of melted snow and ice that had pooled in worn spots on the green linoleum floor. At the forbidding front desk the desk crew (not the most cheerful she'd known) worked the phones and signed in everyone who entered the building.

Over the desk a sign, hand-lettered with red marker and decorated with gold garlands, read MIDTOWN NORTH WISHES YOU A HAPPY NEW YEAR! On the wall nearby a cartoon showed a hand slipping into a jacket pocket with the words WATCH YOUR WALLET in several languages. Sitting at a table below the front desk, an irritated female uniform spoke rapid-fire Spanish to a sulking Hispanic male.

As April headed for the front door, the bald sergeant at the desk put his hand over the receiver and called out to her. "Where you going, Woo? There's been two homicides at Liberty's Restaurant. Get over there ASAP or night watch will fuck it up." At two minutes after 1 A.M. April caught the call.

The crime scene was at Forty-fifth Street between Eighth and Ninth Avenues. Midtown North was on Fifty-fourth Street between Eighth and Ninth Avenues. From the front desk April called the detective squad room upstairs for a detective to go with her. The only one still around was Charlie Hagedorn. April had nothing against Hagedorn, but nothing for him, either. Hagedorn was a white male, early thirties. Five nine, weighed about 190. Didn't appear to work out. His pale, light brown hair was baby fine and soft. It lay flat on his crown as if lacking the energy to stand up like a man's. His lips were thin and chapped, his nose was thin and red. He had chubby cheeks and brown baleful eyes.

April's mother, Sai Woo, who was old Chinese to the core, would diagnose Hagedorn as "not in harmony," too much yin, not enough yang. A person in perfect harmony had to have the right amount of yin and yang. Yang was male—intellectually strong and action-oriented. Yin was female—passive, receptive, relaxed, pleasing, generous. Extreme yin, of course, made for a person who was passive and vague, physically soft and weak, emotionally anxious and vulnerable, intellectually indecisive and uncertain. A yin was not the kind of person you'd want in the alley with you when that 250-pound man (the one the males were always throwing at female cops to try and make the point they couldn't do the job) cornered you in an alley with a chainsaw and two assault rifles blazing. Could be April was wrong about Hagedorn, though, and just didn't know him yet. There were a lot of people around who said the same of her.

Hagedorn took the time to wait for an elevator to carry his chunky body down the one flight of stairs to the precinct lobby where April was impatiently cooling her heels. One of the problems being a boss was you couldn't always move at your own speed or deviate from protocol, which was different from procedure. With protocol, in every situation there were about ten thousand or more things that one just *couldn't* do. In this case April couldn't go get a car. She had to wait for Hagedorn to lumber out into the lot for an unmarked unit to drive her to the location. What a sorry idiot. Turning the very first corner on old tires and a patch of ice he spun out the forest green Pontiac. In the passenger seat April held on and said nothing even though she'd probably have to take the blame if one of her men cracked up the unit while she was in it.

Hagedorn said nothing as they pulled up to the address of the call and stopped behind a line of blue-and-whites where the first officers at the scene were not having a lot of luck securing the area. They'd taped off a hundred or so feet of sidewalk on either side of Liberty's Restaurant, but already a half a dozen people were inside the tapes tramping around.

Right away April started having a bad feeling about this. But that was not so unusual. Every time she went to a scene her skin tingled, almost as if she developed a whole new layer of antennae around her body to take in as much information through as many channels as possible. Sometimes, no matter how much evidence was collected by the Crime Scene Unit, or how many witnesses and suspects told their false stories about what happened, it was April's first impressions that led her through the maze to the true story.

This was the time of yin in a new case, the time when the door to a puzzle of huge dimension—something new and altogether unknown—opened to a vast space of churning, primal chaos. And she had to enter it. Yin was the time of discovery, before the forceful action of yang must be taken. Hagedorn cut the motor. April felt anxious. Despite all the people around who were supposed to be on her side supporting her actions and authority, she knew she was alone. From the number of cars and the attitude of the people standing around, it looked as if this was going to be the Big One every detective both wanted and feared. She shivered, afraid of messing up.

From the car she couldn't see the bodies. They appeared to be on a lower level, down two steps in a tiny yard enclosed by a row of dwarf conifers that twinkled merrily with dozens of white Christmas lights. A number of uniforms hung over the outside railing in a clot, stamping their feet and blowing steam as they looked down. Opening the car door, April was hit with a blast of killing winter air that felt even more penetrating than it had only a few minutes earlier. A single snowflake smacked at her cheek. Great, it was beginning to snow.

In the street, ice was crusting over the slush. On the sidewalk, snow powdered between patches of ice. These were the worst possible conditions for a crime scene. The temperature was dropping. And with a dozen people walking the area since the murders, it might well be impossible to determine if the perp had left anything of himself behind.

The sight of the thickly padded uniforms brushing the snow off the railing and stamping the sidewalk to warm their feet gave April a flash to the mirror in the Bed-Sty precinct that had been her first house. The mirror had been inside a closet, was dappled with ancient grime, and had a jagged piece broken out of one corner. All the patrol officers had been complaining about her—the skinny Chink, probably a dike, talked so soft no one could hear her.

Steve Zapora had been her supervisor at the time. About six foot four, red-faced, the size of a minivan. Every day in roll call this red-faced giant yelled at her that her hair was too long, had to be higher than her collar. Insisted that she shave her neck and personally checked to make sure it was done. And every day he took her downstairs. He made her stand in front of the stupid filthy mirror and he made her growl like a dog, made her raise her voice saying, "Hey you, there on the stairs, stop. Hey you in the red jacket, stop. Hey you, stop" over and over until she could say *stop* loud enough to command attention.

Then Zapora got the biggest guy in the house and told her to take him down. April took the guy down so fast he was on the floor before he was aware she'd made a move. Then, like a complete idiot, she'd put her hand to her mouth and said, "Gosh, I'm sorry." Things changed for her in the house after that, though.

April got out of the car. Her breath made great clouds of steam. Right in front of her two guys with black knit caps were busy rigging spotlights out of a van. "What are they doing here?" she demanded.

Hagedorn shrugged. "TV crew. They must have picked up the call. I know these guys. They hang out around here." Five networks had studios in the area. Hagedorn's baleful eyes were full of scorn that his new supervisor didn't know that.

"I know what they are," April snapped. "Get them out of here."

"Huh?" He looked shocked at her change of tone.

"Now." She ducked under the tape, hating him for making her have to act like one of them. The clot of uniforms turned around to stare. One said, "Lady, you can't come in here."

Then they caught sight of Hagedorn, who jerked his head at her. "Sergeant Woo," he explained.

April nodded brusquely to them. "Anybody ever tell you what the procedures are for protecting a crime scene? Would you like me to tell you now?"

No one said anything. The uniforms just edged away to let her take over, as if they were glad there was someone else to take command of the situation. April moved into the other space in her mind, began to concentrate on all the things she would have to remember when she was back in her office and had only photos to remind her of what she'd seen. Her former boss, Sergeant Joyce, had not always bothered with a notebook. She'd relied on other people's notes; but old habits were dying hard with April. She pulled out her regulation steno pad that the DAs always called Rosarios and began taking everything down. Who was there when she got there, what they had done so far, what they were doing now. She would follow the sequence for the rest of the night, noting the times from that moment through the Crime Scene Unit's work, the investigator from the ME's office pronouncing the deaths, right up to the end when the bodies were bagged and everybody went home for what was left of the night.

She leaned over the railing, her fingers already so stiff from the cold she could hardly hold her pen. The front yard of the brownstone that housed Liberty's Restaurant was about twelve feet square. Partially camouflaged by the twinkling hedge on the side closest to the steps, as if they had been caught while leaving, a man and a woman lay, eyes open, on their backs. The man's muddy hands were palms up on either side of his blond head. He looked puzzled, as if he had raised them with a query and then died before he had a chance to frame the question. His camel-colored coat and black sport jacket were flung open on a nubbly gray turtleneck sweater. Like his hands, his face and hair were scum-streaked, but there appeared to be no blood on him, no sign of an injury that might have killed him. Could be something under the hair, April thought.

The violence done to the woman was an unnerving contrast. In the twilight of a thousand tiny shimmering lights, inky-looking blood streaked her hands, her face, her long blond hair, the front of the tan sweater dress she wore, and the cuffs that peeked out beneath her fur-lined, black suede coat sleeves. All April could see was one small hole piercing her throat. Unless there were other stab wounds she couldn't see, somebody had known just where to strike. April studied the shocking sight from above, not wanting to add her own footprints to the mess below. Her teeth began to chatter.

Sometimes she could tell right away what happened. She could see in the arrangement of the scene how the preceding events must have played out. A mugging gone wrong, guy got scared and used his knife, used his gun. Over in a second. Sometimes he got away with a few dollars. Sometimes he didn't get away with anything. Or a guy killing his woman. There were always precipitating events. You could find out what they were. But this was ambiguous-looking, hard to tell what had happened. It was creepy. Two well-dressed people dead in front of an expensive restaurant where plenty of people must have been passing by, even late on a freezing January night. Except for the hole in the woman's throat, they didn't look as if they'd been interfered with. The woman's clutch bag was closed, wedged under her right foot. The scene didn't feel right. For what reason would someone have taken such a chance in such a public place?

A warm animated voice made April turn around. "Well, this looks like my first double of the year. Know who they are?"

The black woman peering over April's shoulder was taller than she, probably over six feet with the three-inch heels she wore, heedless of the snow. Only a wisp of the woman's hair had escaped her severe French twist that showed off her perfect jawline, the white even teeth behind her magnetic smile, her nose more Caucasianlike than April's, and eyes both curious and bold. Large gold earrings glittered with major red stones in her ears, a black mink coat draped her body, and a frothy cut-velvet-and-silk scarf swathed her shoulders. More than just stunning and dramatic, she had presence. Even in the treacherous snow, April could feel the strut in her walk. She had seen the woman before and thought at first she was one of the famous models that appeared on the covers of magazines. Until the woman introduced herself.

"I'm Dr. Washington. Are you in charge here?"

"Yes. I'm—Sergeant April Woo." It took April a few seconds to remember she wasn't just a detective anymore.

"I've heard of you," Dr. Washington said.

April had heard of her, too, and was surprised to see her there. It wasn't common anymore for the deputy medical examiner to come to crime scenes. They'd changed things in New York. Now most of the time an investigator from the ME's office who wasn't even an MD came to the scene. Dr. Washington cocked her head inquisitively at the two corpses, then at the black sky overhead now whitening with snow. "If CSU doesn't get here pretty soon, those bodies are going to be covered with snow in the photos. We better go take a look. Know who they are?"

A tall black man with a down jacket thrown over his shoulders who'd been talking quietly with a uniform just outside the restaurant door started to wail. "Of *course* I knew who they were. I knew right away who they were. They'd just left, mon. It's Liberty's wife and his best friend. The owner's *wife,* I'm telling you. Of course I tried to help them. Why wouldn't I?"

The officer said some things that April couldn't hear, causing the man to protest even louder. April shook her head and went down the steps to calm things down.

"I'm Sergeant Woo." April introduced herself to the agitated black man being badgered by an officer half his size whose uniform tag identified him as Matthew Hays.

The officer drew himself up and spoke first. "This is the man who found the bodies. Apparently he moved them around quite a bit."

The tall black man responded angrily. "They'd only been gone a few minutes. I thought they might be alive." His face was wet with tears. He swiped at his cheeks with the back of his hand.

April dug into her shoulder bag for a tissue, handed him the package, then waited while he blew his nose.

"Are you Chinese?" he asked softly after he'd done so, carefully avoiding the eye of Officer Hays.

April nodded, gathered he was asking if she was in charge.

"I've never seen a Chinese cop."

"Well, I was born here." She didn't say most Chinese would rather iron shirts than walk a beat in this system.

The man thought over her country of origin and didn't appear to understand how that should enlighten him. He glanced at Hays, then turned to April again, revealing his confusion over whom he was supposed to address—the white man in uniform or the Chinese woman in plain clothes.

It happened all the time. April gave him a smile of encouragement. "I'm the one in charge. You can talk to me."

"I'm the manager of the restaurant," he said grudgingly.

"And your name is?"

"Patrice."

"Patrice what?" April was shivering but didn't want to go inside yet and leave the bodies.

"Patrice Paul," the man replied impatiently. "Please let me go inside. I have to call my boss and tell him—he has to know."

"Who is that?"

He pointed at the sign. "Liberty. You know who he is? Don't you?"

April hesitated, unsure of exactly who he was. She didn't want to lose face in front of a possible witness if the victim's husband was someone any educated person should know. Since leaving the 5th Precinct in Chinatown, not a single day went by when April wasn't made painfully aware of all the things she had never even considered until she came uptown. At the moment she had all the credits for a college degree and would graduate in June from the John Jay College of Criminal Justice. But she was beginning to suspect that one degree didn't prove a thing and was not going to be enough in the long run.

Patrice Paul didn't press her. Now that he had someone else to talk to, he glowered at the uniform.

"I'm going inside and use the phone."

"We'll get to that," April said, not wanting to tell him that was not his job. "Can you describe what happened, Mr. Paul?"

"What happened was I tried to help them. I didn't do more than any decent human being would do," the man insisted. "Someone attacked my friends. They were my *friends*. They were my *patrons*. What was I supposed to do, leave them there to die if they were still alive and I could help them?"

"No one's accusing you, Mr. Paul," April said gently. "We're just trying to establish what happened here, that's all. What caused you to come outside?" She glanced at his hands working in his jacket pockets.

"What do you mean? What caused me to come outside? Two people were attacked."

"Uh-huh. How did you know? Did they call out, was there a struggle?"

"How did I know?" he asked blankly.

"Yeah. What made you come outside?"

April noted that the light-colored jacket hanging on Patrice Paul's shoulders was speckled on the front and on the bottoms of the sleeves with spots that looked like blood. His eyes were puzzled. He was not responding well. He was confused. It was not an uncommon reaction.

"I looked out the window," he said finally. "I wanted to make sure they got a taxi."

"What did you see?

He whimpered. "I saw them lying there."

The officer shook his head. "That's not what you said a minute ago."

"I'm upset, mon. I'm crazy upset. Can I go inside and call my boss now?"

"Officer, would you go and take down names of the

people inside, but don't let anybody out here until I say so. Mr. Paul, where is Mr. Liberty now? We will need to reach him, and the next of kin of the other victim."

"Oh, God, it's Tor Petersen. He's a very important mon, too. You've heard of *him,* haven't you? I have his home number somewhere."

April nodded. "Thank you, Mr. Paul. Why don't you go inside and warm up. We'll talk in a moment."

"Can I call my boss?"

"Where is he?"

"I'm not sure, somewhere out of town," he answered quickly. "But I can beep him, and he'll call me right back."

"As soon as we clear a few things up, Mr. Paul."

April turned away, distracted by the sight of Dr. Washington hunkering down on her high heels in the bloody slush as easily as a Chinese peasant in the fields. The tall woman had gathered up her coat and now the shimmering fur was suspended out of the wet, trapped under her bottom as she flexed her fingers, then casually extracted rubber gloves from her evening bag and snapped them on as if it was something she did at the end of every evening outing. April, too, carried a wad of rubber gloves in her shoulder bag for occasions just like this when she had to root around in something horrid that might contaminate her, or she it. She'd never met anyone else off duty who was so prepared. She was fascinated by the professionalism of the deputy ME as Dr. Washington expertly examined first the female and then the male corpse. Standing beside April, Patrice Paul choked back a sob.

"My, my, this is interesting," Dr. Washington muttered to herself as she worked. "Sergeant, come and take a look at this—" A wail of sirens swallowed the rest of her words.

The wail reminded April of something. She frowned. Where was EMS? Shouldn't a team have arrived by now? Snow thickened in the air. April's exposed skin burned as the wind picked up. Under her jacket she was flushed and sweating, terrified for some reason that wasn't completely clear to her. Her heart felt ready to burst because she was alone with this. Her supervisor, Lieutenant Iriarte, hurrying to beat the snow, was probably halfway home to Westchester by now.

Dr. Washington pulled off the gloves with a loud *thwack*. "Sergeant, would you come here for a moment?"

April took control of herself. She hurried toward the deputy ME and stepped into a puddle. Icy water sloshed over the toe of her boot and leaked through the vulnerable place where the rubber sole was joined to the leather. She shuddered as it soaked her sock. Rosa Washington, however, still apparently heedless of her evening clothes and the cruel conditions, pointed at the mouth of the man the restaurant manager had identified as Tor Petersen. "Blue," Dr. Washington said.

"Blue?" April looked at the man's grimy face, fixed in its puzzled expression. Where blue?

"See that blue around his mouth?"

The corpse's face looked gray to April, but she figured that was a result of the poor light. "What does it mean?"

"Looks as if the poor bastard saw his date stabbed in the neck and had a heart attack."

Washington straightened gracefully, shaking her fur coat out around her. "As for the woman, she must not have known what hit her. It doesn't appear as if she even tried to fight off her attacker. Someone took her by surprise. You're looking for a guy with a sharp knife or possibly a pick, maybe an ice pick, possibly someone she knew." The ME gazed at the door of the restaurant musingly, then shrugged. "I'll know more tomorrow. Meanwhile, see what kind of sharp instruments they have in the bar and in the kitchen. Someone might have put it back. Then again, he might have thrown it out."

"Thanks." April was grateful for the input.

3

It did not look like a sentimental postcard of winter at 2:30 A.M., which was when Sergeant Mike Sanchez, after less than an hour of sleep, showered, dressed, and stumbled out in the storm to scrape snow and ice from the front and back windows of his red Camaro, which turned out not to be fully protected by the roof in the parking lot provided by his building. The job only half done, he tried the ignition key and discovered that the battery still had life. Then, with the windshield wipers noisily squeaking their protest, he slowly limped out of the borough of Queens, grateful he had been awakened now instead of three or four hours later when he might have had to dig the car out, or worse, resort to public transportation.

For the last several weeks Sanchez had lived on the twenty-second floor of a building complex less than ten years old. His new apartment consisted of an L-shaped living room with a terrace the width of the picture window, from which the magnificent skyline of Manhattan alone was worth the rent; a bedroom with a view of the parking lot where his car had its own designated spot in all weathers; a bathroom with faucets that didn't drip and pipes that didn't clank when the water was turned on; a kitchen with both a dishwasher and a window.

There wasn't much more in it than the queen-sized bed he'd yet to share with anyone, a table he'd eaten at once, and a quite new secondhand sofa covered in beige tweed he'd gotten from a detective whose wife decided to take him back after a year's separation that didn't end in divorce. The Garden Towers, as it was called, was seven minutes from the Midtown Tunnel, which in turn was close to the precinct on Twenty-third Street where Sanchez was now headquartered in the Homicide Task Force. The Twenty-third Street location put him around the corner from the Police Academy building where many of the labs were still located pending the completion of new and better facilities in Queens.

One advantage of Mike's new life was that his hours were now a civilized 10 A.M. to 6 P.M. five days a week unless he was working off the chart on a major case. As a specialist he covered the whole city and was no longer confined to whatever came down in a single house. He worked out of one of the cubbyholes each precinct provided for Special Cases, was one of those people he used to resent when he was in a precinct detective squad and an outsider came in to "help" them. So far he hadn't had those kinds of problems of too much hostility directed at himself and liked the constant change of scenery. On the personal front, he now had a home of his own in which to spend time with the woman of his dreams, but hadn't gotten her there long enough for the *amor ardiente* he'd had in mind. Mike Sanchez never thought he'd fall big-time for a cop. But he had, and the woman he loved still worked the killer four-and-two schedule with days off that never coincided with his.

Night for a cop was not supposed to be downtime. These days Mike had more downtime than he was used to and it was driving him nuts. That night he had asked himself how he could possibly get through his second day off with nothing to do but relax. It seemed as if he hadn't been asleep for more than a minute or two when the phone rang and he was apprised of the situation at Liberty's Restaurant. Double homicide. He understood there was nothing official on his possible involvement yet—the call was just a tip in case he got assigned the case later—but if he wanted to see the scene before the bodies were removed and to stake a claim, he'd better head into Manhattan right away despite the inclement weather.

Mike's head cleared of all his miseries and doubts as he drove as quickly as his car would take him through the storm. He had something else to worry about now. Frederick Douglass Liberty had been a hero of his, always came across in the press and his TV interviews as a really upright kind of guy, the thinking man's athlete. Mike had been impressed by him every time he saw him, but then everybody had been impressed by Liberty. Even when he was only twenty-two, he'd had class. He'd been in another stratosphere from the other players. Rick Liberty had never shaved wedges into his hair, tattooed his arms, or pierced any part of his body. He hadn't been a brawler. He hadn't made a franchise of himself when he left football and didn't appear in movies or commercials. He'd explained that he didn't want the celebrity life. He'd wanted to be a regular working guy—some regular guy! He'd become a rich banker. Sanchez knew because Liberty was quoted in the newspapers in the business section now. He was married to a soap opera star, and she was apparently one of the victims. Mike wondered where Liberty was when his wife was murdered. He hoped it was far, far away.

No other car was either in front of him or behind him in the mile-long tunnel. He couldn't remember another time when his had been the only car in the Midtown Tunnel. It felt eerie, almost as if the tunnel had been shut down in preparation for the end of the world. On the other side of the river in Manhattan, the streets were almost deserted in the sheeting snow. It took nearly thirty-five minutes to get across town.

Mike was relieved to see that the ambulance and Crime Scene station wagon were still at the site. And not so happy to see that farther down at the end of the block two news vans were set up to film what they could of the removal of the bodies. Spots lit up the street. He left his Camaro behind the ambulance and ducked under the Crime Scene tapes to take a look at the restaurant garden. A makeshift tent had been erected over the area to protect it from the weather as it was being photographed and sketched and gone over by the CSU. Saul Bernheim, the skinny criminologist who claimed that he didn't eat much because food was bad for you, was gnawing on a hunk of what looked like cornbread.

"Ah, Mike. I'm glad to see they've sent in a big gun. We're going to need a razor brain on this one. How ya doin', man? You come in from the Bronx? I hear it's real bad up there."

Mike smiled at the compliment. "I live in Queens now. It's fine in Queens."

"No kidding. Well, take a look. You're in luck, they're about to bag 'em." Saul waved what was left of the bread at the bodies.

Mike crouched down under the heavy plastic that had been suspended over the two victims and now was covered with snow. He stared at the corpses for a long time. Both looked like large, very well-dressed mannequins that had been carelessly dirtied and mangled. Mike particularly noted how big both were. Two big people who looked to be in good shape. His first thought was that it was an odd setup. Death had come to these two swiftly, and was the more shocking for it. The front of the woman's body was covered with blood. It was smeared everywhere. At first he couldn't see its source.

"Gunshot wound?" he said.

"Naw, take a look at her neck."

"Jesus."

Saul frowned at the precise placement of a small hole above the woman's jugular vein, which must have been pierced in one blow.

"Any other wounds?"

"Might be. Can't tell."

Mike cocked his head, looking sideways at the male lying faceup but not bloody like the other victim. Head wound? he wondered. Two attackers, maybe, one with an ice pick, the other with a blunt instrument. He straightened up and heard some bones crack. "What do you think we have here?"

"A mess, a real mess." The skinny criminologist had finished the bread and was blowing on his bare fingers. A beaver hat with flaps came down low on his forehead and covered his ears. His nose was running and he needed a shave.

"Another weird one," he added. "There's something . . . intimate about this hit, know what I mean? Doesn't have the feeling of a stranger thing. Ice pick killing, maybe only one strike—" Saul shook his head, activating the beaver flaps around his ears. "Usually a guy that works with a pick, he'll choose an isolated location, then stab the victim more than once. It's a rage weapon, know what I mean? I saw one once—female resisted a rape, guy stabbed her with a screwdriver sixty times, maybe more. It was hard for the ME to count because the guy was in such a frenzy he hit in the same place over and over. One strike just right, that's not something you see every day, especially when there are two victims. Doesn't look like either one fought back. . . . Stinking weather, too," he mused. "Someone had to want to hit her pretty bad, wouldn't you say?"

Mike shrugged. It was too early for speculation.

Saul pointed to the door of the restaurant. "Your girlfriend's in there." He moved away from two guys with a body bag and stretcher.

"Huh?"

"Woo, April, is the OIC. Didn't anyone tell you?" Saul pulled a grimy handkerchief from his pocket and wiped his nose.

"No. No one told me a thing." Mike shook off the snow collected all over him and slicked back his hair. He stamped his feet and headed for the door, thinking this was indeed his lucky day. He'd asked for relief from the piles of boring paperwork due on his last case, cleared a few days ago, and here he was, getting it. He'd wanted to see April and here he was seeing her. April was always talking about luck and how it could be changed by a person's behavior. He must be living right.

Inside the restaurant most of the lights were off, but Mike could make out a kind of Caribbean theme. Palm trees, whitewashed boards, crudely carved, brightly painted fish on the walls. Fan-backed chairs around tables with wicker bases. Overhead a dozen ceiling fans were ghostly still. The large bar was dark and the room was empty except for April, a black man who wasn't Liberty, and an ADA Mike had once worked with named Dean Kiang. The three of them were in deep conversation that stopped abruptly when he came out of the shadows.

"Hi," he said. "Mind if I join you?"

He had the satisfaction of seeing the young assistant district attorney freeze into one of those Chinese masks of wariness he'd seen so often on April. And April clearly hadn't been expecting him. The woman of his dreams almost fell off her chair at the sound of his voice.

An hour later they sat in the red Camaro in front of the now locked and dark Liberty's Restaurant, waiting for the car to warm up. The crime scene tapes were still up around the garden, but the plastic tent and the bodies of the victims were gone. So was Hagedorn with the green unit and the Chinese ADA, who had not seemed happy when Mike sat down at the table uninvited. April finished telling Mike everything she'd found out about the case before he'd arrived. She closed her notebook with a cold smile that tried to cover a bad taste she couldn't deny was bitterness. She wasn't even three hours into this difficult investigation and already the cavalry had galloped in to take it away from her. Mike was good, very good, but she couldn't imagine anything more annoying than having him there to second-guess her.

If Homicide had sent anybody but Mike, her desire for independence and the need to prove herself would have outweighed any other consideration. She wouldn't exactly have obstructed, but she would have revealed only the major facts and kept the details to herself. After all, who knew at this point what was going to be important in this case and what was not? Why spill too many beans and confuse people? Sometimes a stupid detective became invested in a certain bean too fast because it offered the easiest outcome, then tried to bully everybody else into seeing things his way. April had handled everything just right, she'd called an ADA instantly, and she was gratified that the one she got was Chinese. Dean Kiang was good-looking, seemed very professional, and she'd been pleased at the team they made. Then Mike had to stick his nose in and raise the tension level by claiming her loyalty.

"I'm kind of surprised to see one of you people here in the middle of the night," she said after a pause in which Mike didn't thank her for coming through without an argument, or for telling him the story on what they had so far. "Isn't that kind of unusual?"

He raised the eyebrow that was crooked with burn scars from the previous June, when he'd jumped in front of April and the hostage they'd been trying to liberate just before an explosion that almost killed all three of them. Whenever he raised that eyebrow, April felt a thousand times less worthy than she was. She felt double and maybe triple stupid in ways she didn't begin to understand. Loyalty and love had gotten her all mixed up. And now they weren't even on the same team.

"What is this 'your people and my people,' *querida*?" Now both of Mike's dark eyebrows shot up.

April's cold fingers became still in her lap as she wrestled with the problem. Sanchez glanced at her hands speculatively. "I thought we were all one people," he murmured, resisting the impulse to take one hand and squeeze it.

Outside, the snow was beginning to falter. The flakes were smaller, not so puffy and dry. It seemed to be warming up as suddenly as it had gotten cold;

it might even turn to rain soon. The wipers squeaked over melting snow on the windshield.

With a shrug April relented. "Sorry, I didn't mean to be territorial."

Mike laughed. "Yes, you did. Always have to do everything yourself, don't you?" he teased.

She opened her mouth, then closed it. Only a few weeks ago, when Mike had been in a similar position in a precinct squad, he'd been every bit as territorial about *their* cases. But why argue? She breathed in the familiar cologne that permeated his clothes and even the upholstery of his car. Mike's perfume—one couldn't get away with calling it anything else—was unlike anything April had ever smelled before or since. On the surface it was sweet and spicy, but underneath it had a pungent sort of kick that kept her off balance as long as he was around.

In the early days of their relationship this almost palpable aroma used to give April a headache. The squad room of the Two-O had reeked of it. In fact, it was Mike's smell that had first gotten her attention. She hadn't known where the powerful essence originated. Then she realized that when Sanchez wasn't around for a while it would disappear, only to return when he did. After that she noticed the pirate's smile with which he studied her and his interesting hair that was different from Asian hair. Mike rolled up his sleeves when he worked, revealing the hair on his arms. He had a fine layer of hair on the backs of his hands, and most likely on his chest, too. In spite of the prevailing taste among April's relatives on the subject, hair on a man's body did not seem altogether barbaric to her.

Jimmy Wong, April's last lover, had one lone hair on his chest growing from a mole near his left nipple, had never smelled of anything but garlic and beer. He'd never said he loved her, or called her darling. He had enjoyed torturing her by telling her anybody who was her partner was guaranteed to die in a shootout since he ranked her the worst shot in the entire department. Jimmy didn't approve of ambition in women and went so far as to threaten not to marry her if she made sergeant. Lucky for her she'd broken up with him before his threat could be tested. In addition to all this, a five-days' growth of beard yielded a very sparse display on his face. Why she'd ever liked him in the first place was now a mystery to her.

In comparison, Mike encouraged her to enjoy life, to advance in her career as far as she could, and called her darling in Spanish in front of everybody whenever he felt like it. His thick and luxuriant mustache was long enough to skirmish with his top lip and often quivered with emotion, causing palpitations in her stomach. During moments of deep concentration he sucked pensively on the ends of it. After April had started working with him, she learned that he was also the best detective she knew.

"You have a problem with my being here?" he asked now.

"Uh-uh. It's just your day off . . . so I wondered who called you," she said.

"You're in my thoughts, so you must have," he murmured. That sounded good to him so he smiled. This was going to be a really big case, after all, and no one liked being left out of big cases. "Oh, come on, you're glad to see me, admit it."

She shook her head, didn't want to.

"Fine, don't admit it," he said cheerfully, with every appearance of confidence in his ability to win all his battles with her in the end.

"I could handle this myself," April insisted.

Mike hummed some Spanish love song. At her level of mastery of the Spanish language April was able to make out the words *somos novios,* which mean "we are boyfriend/girlfriend. We are lovers." She bit back a smart remark. They were not lovers. They were not engaged. They were hardly even speaking to each other. Then he seemed to remember the awful task in front of them and fell silent as he put the car in gear and pulled out without spinning the tires.

4

The Park Century was twelve blocks north on Fifty-seventh Street. Mike and April headed up Eighth Avenue without speculating whether Frederick Douglass Liberty would be at home to receive them at four in the morning. Patrice Paul had told April that Mr. Liberty was out of town. The restaurant manager had been in tears, almost hysterical the whole time April questioned him. Over and over he had begged her to let him try to reach Liberty on his cellular phone and inform him of what had happened. He didn't want Liberty to hear about the tragedy on the news. Though it might have seemed a reasonable request, April could not let him contact Liberty. She needed to cover some ground about precipitating events. What had happened during the evening. How was the restaurant run. What were the relationships of the people involved. She did not give Patrice a single opportunity to be alone. Even now he was getting a ride home to Brooklyn in a squad car.

April would not have let him make the call and give away any information under any circumstances. But in this case there was something worrying about the nature of the restaurant manager's extreme distress. April wondered why he was so eager to be the first one to reach his employer, as well as someone he called his friend, with such devastating news. Informing relatives was the worst job anyone could have. April hated those moments more than any other in her job.

But maybe Patrice Paul was glad Merrill Liberty

was gone forever. April didn't have to remind herself that she had to be careful here. Really careful. The race issue made her uneasy. Sure, it was always there, and it always complicated everything. The chemistry of every case was affected by what sort of person was the primary detective managing it and what sort of people were the suspects. Class made a difference, as did the level of education people had and their attitude toward the police. Cops didn't even know they were adjusting the circumstances in each case to fit their own particular prejudices. It wasn't conscious. And color probably made the most difference of all. Color made people nervous, made them jump one way or another, changed the way they acted or didn't act. Color raised the stakes on the possibility of political repercussions. It guaranteed deeply emotional and often dangerous responses that were camouflaged or not depending on the parties involved. Anybody who said only the facts mattered was dreaming.

Patrice Paul was a witness. It was more than likely he knew more than he was telling. Maybe he was more involved than he would like to admit. What if Petersen had died of other causes? They'd been in a restaurant, had eaten and drunk. Maybe he'd been poisoned somehow and been stricken when he got outside. It would explain how two people had been taken out so suddenly without a fight. Maybe the death of Merrill Liberty was an employee/boss's wife thing. Maybe it was a boyfriend/girlfriend thing. Maybe it was a race thing. Maybe it was a random act of violence, which would make it the worst possibility of all—a mystery. No one liked a mystery.

April wanted to handle this correctly. She knew this was an explosive situation no matter who had killed the victims or what the motive had been. Even if the perpetrator turned out to be a white homeless person who didn't even know them—which everyone who had seen the victims tended to doubt—there would still be plenty of battles fought over this case. The two victims were white, rich, and celebrities. The husband of one victim and the employee who went out to help them were black. It wasn't supposed to make a difference but it would.

It was a visceral thing. A lot of people of all colors and ethnic backgrounds didn't like each other. And they especially didn't like mixed marriages of any kind—people like her mother and her father who were otherwise fine people. But Sai and Ja Fa Woo didn't stop at disliking blacks. April's parents didn't like anybody—not whites, not Hispanics, not Pakistanis or Native Americans or Koreans. Chinese were best people to them. That was it. Nobody else counted. It was hard to take, especially considering April's current not-so-secret passion for a Latino. She sneaked a look at Mike.

Very few cars were out to challenge the snow on the street. The Camaro was low, and it plowed through some fresh inches, making grumpy, straining car noises. Mike seemed concentrated on his driving. She could tell he was in his waiting mode. He knew all about male sexual jealousy and how lethal it could be, but he would not make anything of Merrill Liberty's having been out with her husband's best friend, a white man, and the possible implications of *that* until there was something to make of it.

April couldn't help remembering the speculative way the ME had looked at Patrice, and then the way Dr. Washington's gaze had returned to the restaurant door more than once, as if she thought the killer might have come from inside the restaurant with an ice pick and not from the street. Why did the medical examiner think that? April made a mental note to ask Dr. Washington what her suspicions were. But April also had her doubts that Rosa Washington, well known for her rigid correctness, would tell her anything unless she knew April really well and trusted her. And the doctor had seemed extremely professional, not the kind of person to speculate about things she couldn't prove.

The Camaro took the turn through six inches of

slush on Fifty-seventh Street like a small motorboat heaving through a mighty swell. It pulled up in front of a building that was splendid even at four in the morning on a storm-ravaged January night. Mike crossed himself. Whether in gratitude for getting there without mishap or in comment about the place itself April couldn't tell.

Like a sentry on either side of the front door was a topiary that looked like a lollipop with Christmas lights. Green letters on a white canopy importantly declared the building's name: PARK CENTURY. Race came back to mind again as April wondered how many other blacks lived in this building, how many Latinos, how many Asians. Cops were trained not to make assumptions. In the department they were supposed to be all one color, blue. On the street they were supposed to look at everybody the same. But they didn't. In confusing situations, black cops in plain clothes who ran with their guns unholstered in pursuit of bad guys risked getting shot in the back by their white colleagues.

At 4:12 A.M. Sergeants Sanchez and Woo entered the Park Century, where Liberty had shared the penthouse with his wife Merrill. The doorman was a large sleepy-eyed man who smelled of cigarettes and didn't like the sight of them.

"You're sure Mr. Liberty is here?" Mike asked after identifying himself and April and hearing that the former football star was at home.

"Of course I'm sure. I got to write everything down, don't I? Mr. Liberty came in before midnight." A black pin on the doorman's jacket gave his name as Earl.

Earl checked the clipboard on his porter's desk under the intercom board. "But Mrs. Liberty is still out. Is that what you're here about?" He wore green and gold livery even this late on the graveyard shift. A gleaming black top hat sat on the credenza along the wall. "Is she all right?" Earl suddenly looked concerned.

"Would you ring the apartment for me?" Mike asked.

"Mr. Liberty won't like it."

No one ever did. Mike jerked his chin at the intercom. It wasn't his problem.

April pursed her lips. Instantly they'd fallen into their usual routine. Mike being the authority figure. The man. She would have been more conciliatory with the doorman because they would need his cooperation later. But hey, who was complaining? Mike always got the job done.

Three minutes later they got out of a gleaming, dark wood-paneled elevator on the twelfth floor. There was only one door on the floor, but they wouldn't have confused the apartment anyway. The famous quarterback who'd been known as Liberty (and whom April recognized now that she saw him) stood there bleary-eyed in his doorway. In spite of the lateness of the hour, he was dressed. He wore a pair of gray slacks and was pulling a gray cashmere sweater into place as he frowned at them.

"What's going on?" he demanded.

"I'm Sergeant Sanchez. This is Sergeant Woo." Mike pulled out his ID, but Liberty turned his head away without looking at it.

"Do you mind if we come in?" Mike asked.

The impression he gave was not one of alarm. Liberty looked wary, eyed them with distrust. "All right," he said evenly. "Come in here." He led the way across a tan marble floor, then hit the light switch in the living room, stunning the two detectives with its splendor.

For a second, Liberty seemed shocked by it also, for he gripped his forehead, shielding his eyes from the great expanse of room and windows heightened by lengths of soft white sofas, white throws, miles of textured white rugs on a white marble floor, and white gauzy curtains, all of which were offset by many pieces of striking African art. Chieftains' stools served as coffee tables. Masks hung on the walls and were suspended above ebony columns by long metal rods. Ceremonial objects, cups, tobacco boxes, brass figurines were arranged on shelves. Particularly arresting were several large wooden statues of women with outsized breasts and men with outsized penises. Some were decorated with small shells, colored cloth, raffia, and many bits of mirror. April knew the contrast of primitive and ultrasophisticated decorating was done for a particular purpose. She didn't want to guess what it was.

Liberty waved his hand at one of the spans of sofa but didn't go so far as to invite the two detectives to sit. April noted his demeanor carefully. The man was clearly annoyed by their intrusion, but she couldn't attribute a meaning to the tension in his jaw. He looked as if he were about to, or just had, bitten off the end of his tongue. As men often did, Liberty concentrated on Sanchez, stared at him challengingly as if he did not want to lower himself by asking again what was the reason for their predawn visit.

As she watched the set of Liberty's powerful clenched jaw that was so photogenic and had daunted so many opponents on the playing field, April flashed back to the story she'd heard several years ago of the middle-class man who claimed his wife had thrown herself from the fifteenth-floor window in their bedroom. Simple case. The husband gave a great performance, weeping, telling the detectives how the tragedy occurred—what the distraught woman had said, how she stormed out of the living room where he had been sitting reading the evening paper. Everything. Problem was it didn't add up. For one thing, there had been no sign of an evening paper. For another, the woman's makeup was carefully laid out on the dressing table, and only one of her eyes had been completed. The picture was of a woman interrupted in the middle of an activity. In addition, one of her slippers had snagged on the claw foot at the end of a leg on her dressing table. The other slipper was on her foot when she was found. When confronted with the question of the unfinished makeup and the snagged slipper, the man calmly confessed that after thirty years of his wife's boring conversation he couldn't face another dinner with her and threw her out the window as she was getting ready to go out.

"I'm sorry to have to bring you bad news," Mike said now.

Liberty swallowed. "What kind of bad news?"

Mike glanced at April.

Liberty closed his eyes. "Is it my mother?"

"It's two people," Mike said slowly.

The man looked hostile. "Who?"

"Your wife. And the man who was with her."

"That's not possible. You're mistaken."

"I'm sorry, sir," April said. "Would you like to sit down?"

"No." Liberty spun around as if there were a sound at his front door. "My wife's fine. She's on her way."

He stared at the door, waiting for it to open. Nothing. The tan gallery was dark and silent.

Mike and April watched him watching for an elevator that wasn't going to come.

"I'm sure you've made a mistake. They're fine. I know they are," he said again, concentrating on the front door.

Mike shook his head. "I'm sorry, sir."

Suddenly Liberty's face contorted. He put his hands to his forehead and gripped it with both huge paws, shielding his eyes.

"Do you want me to get you something?" April murmured.

"I get migraines. My doctors say they come from an old football injury. But I've always had them."

Mike glanced at April.

Liberty's hands dropped to his sides. "I have to call the restaurant. My wife is there."

"It's four in the morning," Mike said. "There's no one there."

"Four?" Liberty lifted his arm to check his watch. He wasn't wearing it. He frowned. "I just spoke to her. Four in the mornings—? I must have fallen asleep." He stared at them. "What happened?"

"We're not sure yet. Mr. Petersen may have had a heart attack."

"A heart attack?" Liberty cocked the head he said was hurting him. "A heart attack? Where's Merrill? Did she go to the hospital with him?"

"No, she was assaulted in front of the restaurant."

"What?" Sweat glistened on his forehead. His two-hundred-pound physique still looked like solid muscle. He towered over them. April would not like to fight him in a dark alley.

"She was struck as she left the restaurant," April said, taking up the slack.

"Struck? That just can't be true—" Finally Liberty sat down.

Mike and April remained standing. After a second the big man got up again. "Tor had a heart attack and my wife was attacked? How could such a thing happen? Where were they? I—"

"They were leaving the restaurant. Somebody attacked your wife in the yard. She's dead. I'm sorry," April said softly.

"Dead—?" Liberty clutched his head. "In the yard?" His face was ashen. "Oh Jesus. This can't be happening. He was a thief. I didn't think he was a killer. No, no."

"Who?" Mike said sharply. "Who's a killer?"

"I told Tor that guy Jefferson was trouble. He just wouldn't listen. First my car. Now this—I can't believe—" He broke off.

"Your car?" Mike frowned at April.

"He took my car while I was in Europe. When I got back last week he told me the car had been stolen off the street. I tried to convince Tor to fire him right then."

"Who are you referring to, sir?" April asked gently.

"Wally Jefferson, Tor—Mr. Petersen's driver. My head is bad. I need a doctor."

"Yes, sir. We can call one right away."

"And call Jason Frank. His wife was with them, with Merrill and Tor. Emma's not—?"

"No, she wasn't with them." April had been feeling hot and dizzy and a bit confused herself in the warm apartment. Now she relaxed a little. They had a suspect. Liberty seemed to think the chauffeur who had stolen his car might have been the killer. That was a start. She was also comforted by the fact that Jason Frank was Liberty's doctor. April narrowed her eyes at him. So the former football player was seeing a shrink. In her eyes that made him suspect of something, but she wasn't sure what. It could mean Liberty was depressed, or mentally unbalanced in some other way. Maybe violent. Interesting about the headaches. Certainly Jason Frank would know. April had influence with Jason Frank.

Mike's hand brushed April's arm. She knew what the gesture meant. Everything in their lives had changed, and yet here they were again, back on a case together—she, Mike, and Jason Frank. The ghost of Merrill Liberty was like the wing of a butterfly fluttering against April's cheek. Her heart thudded so loudly in her chest she could almost hear it.

5

"Well, what do you think then?" Daphne Petersen directed her question at Sanchez, who seemed to expand a few inches under her gaze. The new widow was an intense young woman with big blue eyes, the fairest skin, hair even inkier than April's own, and a voluptuous body clearly visible under her tightly belted satin robe. She spoke with a strong English accent and seemed to enjoy the reaction she was getting from the visiting detective.

"Ah . . ." Mike stalled. Paired with the pose she had taken, the question seemed to confuse him.

April made a little disapproving noise through her nose. The victim's wife was supposed to be in shock, not the detective breaking the news. Daphne Petersen, however, was nowhere near shock. She was hardly surprised to see them, nor did she seem to mind being roused before dawn to hear about the death of her husband during the night. She responded to the news with a somewhat detached interest, as if the deceased had been a neighbor with whom she had shared a driveway.

"What do you mean?" Mike got out at last.

"Well, do you think it's some sort of drug thing, a hit of some sort? A buy gone wrong? A jealous *husband*?" She tossed her head of black curls that didn't look as if they'd been disturbed by sleep. They bounced back to their former position. The curls framed a face that, at 6:17 in the morning, was not by any means devoid of makeup.

As April examined her, she wondered if the English

lady of the house already knew her husband was dead, and if she had not been alone in the bedroom when they arrived. Daphne Petersen was probably around thirty, some fifteen years younger than her late husband.

The only feeling the new widow exhibited for the situation was to shudder at the word "hit." Then she sought immediate relief in a package of Marlboros. Unlike Liberty, she expressed no shock or denial. She almost seemed to have been expecting them. April wondered if the woman's detachment might be a cultural thing. From what she had read about the English in the newspapers, it was pretty obvious that they didn't care much about anything. April turned her expressionless face to Mike to see what he thought.

He was scratching the side of his nose, considering her list of suspects in her husband's death. Drugs, hit men. Jealous husbands. Interesting.

"Did you know who your husband was with last night?" he asked gently.

She shook her head. "Who?"

"Merrill Liberty," April said.

Daphne's breath caught on a gulp of smoke. "Is she—"

April nodded.

"She's dead, too? Jesus!" She looked out the window.

Outside it was not yet light. The heat was just coming up in the Petersens' Fifth Avenue living room, which faced the fountain still ringed with Christmas trees in front of the Plaza Hotel, the huge menorah on the park side of the street with all its lights ablaze, and the section of Central Park bordering Central Park South. There were so many arresting views available that April hardly knew which way to look. Mike wasn't having any problems on that score. He was concentrated on the widow.

Daphne's breasts were several cups too large to stand up as high as they did with no visible means of support. April guessed they were not as nature had formed them. She also guessed the robe cost more than a sergeant's salary for several months. But there was no way of estimating the value of the ruby-studded, heart-shaped pendant the size of a plum that dangled from a heavy gold chain just above Daphne's cleavage. Mike raised his crooked eyebrow at April. *The second trophy wife in the case.*

April nodded imperceptibly as she watched Daphne stub out her cigarette and take a second from the package. *Yeah, and this one is the survivor.*

"What do you mean, jealous husband?" April asked.

"I don't know. I was being smart. I didn't know he'd get mad enough to *kill* them." Daphne studied the cigarette, then lit it with a match from a give-away matchbook.

"Who?"

"Well, Liberty, of course." She put her hand to her mouth. "They were very close friends—it's hard to—"

"Liberty and your husband?"

"Well, the three of them. Tor was best man at their wedding."

"Did you know where your husband was going last night?"

Daphne lifted a shoulder. "I wasn't here when he went out."

"Where were you?"

She tossed her head. "In church."

Mike hid a smile.

"Which one?" April asked.

"Saint Patrick's."

"What time was that?"

"How would I know? I wasn't here."

"What time did you go out, Mrs. Petersen?"

"Ten-fifteen. A.M."

"And that was the last time you saw your husband?"

She nodded. "How were they killed?"

"We don't have a cause of death on your husband

yet," April said. "He may have died of a heart attack—"

"What? Really?" The woman blew a cloud of smoke out of her nose. Confused, she tapped the cigarette on the side of a crystal ashtray already full of butts. "I thought you said he was murdered."

"Did we?"

"Yes, you said—" She scowled at April. "He wasn't murdered? Then what killed them—drugs . . . ?"

"Was your husband involved in drugs?" Mike asked.

"What do you mean 'involved'? You mean selling?" Daphne shook the curls. "He was rich. He didn't need to." She scowled some more. "He did like his snowflakes though, didn't he?"

"Your husband was a cocaine user?"

"Oh yes, and woman user, too." Daphne fondled the heavy ruby heart between her breasts. "He loved rubies," she murmured. "What about Merrill? Did she have a heart attack, too?"

"She was stabbed in the neck," Mike said bluntly.

"Oooo." Shocked, Daphne clutched her throat. Then she inhaled with a wincing noise. "Oooo."

For the ten thousandth time April thought people were weird. First the well-dressed black man with the terrible headache. And now the trophy wife with the artificial boobs who reacted more to the death of Merrill Liberty than to that of her husband. Weird. April felt a tickle at the back of her throat and fought a desire to sneeze. The tickle didn't come from the cigarette smoke. It came from her suspicious nature.

Mike coughed delicately. "Did you expect your husband home last night?"

Daphne shrugged. "With Tor, one doesn't expect. One takes things as they come. Most of the time he does come home eventually," she conceded. "What time did he die?"

"Sometime last night."

"I was here all evening, if you want to know. All night in fact. Anyway, I'm not powerful enough to give people heart attacks. But Tor was. He gave them all the time." She stubbed out her cigarette, splitting the paper and shredding the tobacco.

"Would you mind identifying his body later today?" Mike asked suddenly.

"Oh, is that absolutely necessary? I'm afraid it would make me sick to my stomach."

"You only have to look at his face through a window," Mike told her.

"Couldn't you arrange something?" Daphne pleaded. "Send his lawyer or something?"

April bristled as the cleavage became more pronounced. Of course they could. Mike would see what he could do. April rolled her eyes and made a note to kick him later. The two detectives stayed, asking the dead man's wife questions until the sun rose. Then they went out for breakfast.

6

Jason, the last thing in the world I want to do right now is go in that room by myself and lie down." Rick Liberty shot Jason an angry look. "What do you think I am?"

Emma saw Jason check his watch and gave him a pleading look not to abandon them.

"I think you've had a terrible shock," Jason replied calmly. "And you're going to have a really rough day." He glanced at Emma to assure her he would stay as long as he had to.

"A shock! My wife and best friend go to my own restaurant with my own people all around. Now both of them are dead. No one can tell me what happened. And you want me to lie down!"

Dr. Jason Frank, psychoanalyst and professor of psychiatry, was a man well accustomed to hearing other people vent their grief and rage. He ached for his friend and didn't argue. His own wife was still alive. She sat on the white sofa clutching one of Merrill's sweaters and holding Rick's hand as if he were a child. Emma had been Merrill's best friend, a bridesmaid at her wedding. She'd left the two victims to come home to him only minutes before they were killed. He ached for Emma, too.

Jason stood with his back to the window and the dawning day. Over the years as a psychoanalyst, he had seen a lot of illness both physical and mental, and a lot of self-destruction played out in a wide variety of ways. He'd seen death come in many forms. The endless repetition of tragedies and sorrow that constituted the human condition had always affected him, but until a year ago he had never experienced the catastrophe of a vicious crime against anyone he knew.

He had grown up with a basketball in his hands, a street kid in the Bronx always looking for a pickup game. He'd carried a knife in his pocket and been in fights, but he'd never cut anybody and nobody had ever cut him. Until he was in medical school he'd never seen a gunshot wound or a knife wound or a battered body. Since then he'd seen a number of them, but none of the violence had been connected with him. He was a thirty-nine-year-old psychiatrist who wrote scholarly papers and taught medical students and psychiatric residents and now even Ph.D. candidates how to think about the mind. His had been an orderly life, and though he would never have admitted it, a cerebral one.

He was also a collector of antique clocks. He would have liked to meet the person who invented the first mechanical device to measure time. He himself was ruled by time, obsessed by it. For many years his only fear was that his own time would run out before he was finished with his life's work. But a year ago he'd learned there were many worse fears than that.

A year ago Emma had starred in a film that triggered her kidnapping. Until then, his only connection with the police was as a source of directions when he was lost. Now he was so close to several NYPD detectives that he had actually been relieved when Rick told him an Asian woman called Woo and a Hispanic with a big mustache were in charge of this case. That meant every step of the way Jason would know what was going on. That gave him some comfort.

Jason checked his watch again, wondering when he could get in touch with April. It was the first Monday of the new year. Jason's day was completely booked with eight patient hours, an hour and a half of teaching, and thirty minutes with the psychiatric resident he was supervising. He had canceled his first four patients and was now debating canceling the class. He was still hoping he could get Rick to take something to calm down before having to view Merrill's body at the medical examiner's office.

"Do you know how many needles were stuck into me so I could run down that field?" Rick demanded angrily. "Sometimes an eye or my nose swelled up—twenty degrees outside—and I could feel the blood on my face so hot it burned." He shook his head at his old life of the killer instinct: eleven broken bones, countless sprains, and constant physical pain. He turned his back on Jason to stare out the window.

The spectacular city view of the present embraced lower Central Park from the west. The high-floor apartment faced east, and the three of them could have watched the sun rise at 7:03 if there had been one to see. But there had been no visible sunrise that day. The light had come slowly, almost painfully slowly, and only revealed a morning as bleak and silent as the night had been wild.

"I took so many painkillers. . . . God, by the time I was eighteen, nineteen, no one had to tell me anything about what was going on inside of my body. I knew it all. I could hear things happen. Does that sound weird? I could *hear* the injuries. And there was a lot of screaming going on, a whole lot all around me, from the coaches, my family, every human being who had ever been a slave in all of history."

Liberty paused, looking back on himself and the burden he'd carried for every slave in all of history. "I knew they would get together and kill me if I stopped. I *knew* if I stopped, if I cried, if I said anything, my life would be over. I had to play the game, because it was the game of life. You know what I'm talking about? Everybody was nice to me. I heard nice things, you know, but I knew I had no friends. I was alone. I couldn't *do* anything else but take the needles and play ball. I had no choice."

Jason was surprised to hear this. They'd talked about football before, had even watched games together, but Jason had not heard him talk like this before.

"Maybe I shouldn't tell you this," Rick muttered, glancing nervously at Emma as if he feared he'd just ruined his image.

"You forget that I know you from then," Emma reminded him. "I know who you are."

The two friends made an interesting contrast. Emma was like a ghost, bleached white, with her blond hair a little darker than usual for her theater role and her deep blue eyes now dulled with shock. Beside her, Rick Liberty was a warm medium brown. Both white and Indian blood showed in his cheekbones, his jaw-line, his lips and nose. Everything about his speech, his gestures, the confidence and grace with which he moved, bespoke a man who had grown up not far from where he sat right now. Nothing about him seemed tutored or strained. He was like a white man with brown skin, a man who never talked about his color, and didn't want to be asked. Jason suddenly thought that pretending there was absolutely no difference between them except exceptional athletic prowess had probably been a very bad thing for them all.

"You know you can tell us anything, Rick," Jason said.

"Then don't think I'm proud of myself. Everybody used to tell me I should be so proud of what I've accomplished. That's bullshit—" Rick held his head with the hand not restrained by Emma's.

"No one should be proud of begging to be anaesthetized so they can hurt themselves some more. You know, I used to tell them to give me the max. 'Gimme the damn max,' I used to say." He snorted derisively. "I had a knee injury once they didn't pick up for a year. They stuck me so full of shit sometimes I didn't feel my legs at all. Everybody says I was so fucking fast in that game against the Cowboys. So fast, I ran with the ball farther than anyone in history. Well, I still don't know how I even stood up that day. I wasn't there. Part of me just wasn't there. The other part was doing what it always did—looking down the field, looking to get through that wall of defense to the other side. Just looking for a hole.

"Hell, it didn't matter to me. I just kept going even when there was no hole. I didn't care if I died, and that's the truth. If I'd died then it would have been over. I used to hope for it. I used to hope every three-hundred-pound linebacker would pile up on me at the same time and crush me to death. But I was a valuable player. They wouldn't let it happen." Rick's face showed pure rage. "Shit, man, I'm not taking any more pills to hide from anything."

"How's that head?" Jason asked.

Rick ignored him. "And don't tell me about the good part, the adrenaline rushes, the thrills, the cheers, the money. Truth was I just didn't give a shit. I wanted to die and end it."

"How's the head?"

"I don't know. It doesn't matter."

Jason raised his hand to scratch the three-month-old beard he couldn't seem to get used to. He was worried that Rick would collapse soon. And Emma was not in any better shape. When she'd come into the apartment several hours ago she'd been trembling so badly that Rick offered her one of Merrill's sweaters to put on.

No! Jason almost grabbed Rick to stop him. Possessions of the dead are powerful things. Each object resonated with meaning. Jason knew many families that had been torn apart over a few dollars no one needed but someone didn't want to give up. Or a vintage car, a table, an antique chair, a crystal necklace, a china plate. Some of the most precious memories people have live on in objects. Survivors often have no idea how much feeling they have invested in a certain something until the person who owned it is gone.

Rick went into the bedroom and returned with a tan chenille sweater with black trim. He was holding it to his face as he offered it to Emma. "Here, she loved this one. It smells like her."

Emma took it with a sob and buried her face in the sweater, holding it in her arms for a long time, her cheek pressed against its softness. Jason, the shrink who couldn't stop analyzing everything, knew he had no control over what would happen next. He was surprised that the scent and the feel of the dead woman's sweater eventually calmed Emma, and she put it on.

"You know, Rick, you were an inspiration to watch," Jason said softly, knowing they were discussing Rick's career to avoid dealing with his wife's murder.

"Well, the truth was I was depressed, Jason. I was so depressed I didn't know life existed. I'm telling you I kept hoping one day they'd all pile up on me and break my neck so it would be over. I didn't know any better."

Jason gave him a crooked smile. "You were a great football player. You accomplished more in those years than ninety-nine percent of the population. And look what you've accomplished since. You're quite a guy and a lot of people love you."

"Uh-huh. Well, he let me stop."

"What?" Jason asked.

"Tor. It was Tor who showed me life outside. Tor and Merrill. They showed me I could have a life. I could do something without hurting myself. They made me even—equal. Do you know what that means? I stopped being a black boy who could play ball. They gave me my *life,* man. They were the only ones who loved me. And now they're dead. I swear to God. Jefferson is going to pay for this."

The phone rang. "You stay here. I'll get it," Jason told him. He went into the gallery to pick up. It was a woman from a tabloid-sounding TV show, wanting to set up an interview. Jason told her none would be forthcoming. When he hung up, the phone rang again. Jason repeated the same thing, then checked his watch. It was 9:07. The switchboards of the world were open.

7

"Well, *querida,* ready to do battle?" Mike pushed his chair back from their window table at the Anytime Diner on Eighth Avenue and tried a smile.

"Not yet." April glanced at her watch, then resumed turning the pages of her Rosario. "We have a few minutes," she murmured.

"Mad at me?"

His question made her look up. Her eyes felt puffy and dry, as if the part of her that was supposed to make tears had been claimed by the night's victims. She could hardly see a thing, and now she'd be on duty until 4 P.M. These all-nighters on turnaround days really stank, especially when one was a boss and had to follow up on everybody's ongoing cases, as well as organizing new ones. Now she had some sympathy for her former supervisor, the once-despised Margaret Mary Joyce, who had two children, nine detectives, hundreds of cases to oversee, and a former husband who divorced her for getting ahead.

She yawned behind her hand and tried to focus. "How could I be mad at you? I can't even see you." She squinted at him. "What's your name again, Sergeant?"

"That's good. I didn't know you could tell jokes, *querida.*"

"I can't." She soured her face so he wouldn't laugh too hard.

"Yeah, you're mad. I can tell. Look, I got the call. I didn't know it was your case, okay?"

"I'm not mad. I'm tired. I accept the lie that your presence here is a big accident. So forget it."

Mike eyed the potential leftovers on her plate. "You going to eat those potatoes?"

She pushed the crisp hash browns in his direction, shaking her head.

"You should eat more, *querida*. You're always sorry when you don't. I'm glad you're not mad." He reached across the turquoise linoleum tabletop for the ketchup bottle, then dumped a lake of crimson in the middle of her plate.

"God, if I were a lady, I'd swoon," she muttered.

"My table manners a problem, or does this trigger something important?"

April blew air out of her nose, thinking of some of the delicate habits of her people. Before she'd left Chinatown, she'd assumed that rotting garbage on the street and a dozen people speed-eating from the same plate were normal. Her family and friends dug into the communal serving platters with their chopsticks. They hoisted succulent morsels across great expanses of table to their own rice bowls, then lifted the bowls to their faces and shoveled food into their mouths, making great slurp, slurp, slurping noises with an urgency that might lead an outsider to think this was the last meal anyone would ever get.

This, however, was not the case at Mike's mother's table. At Sunday lunch six weeks ago, the one time April had eaten there, Mike's mother, who was as well fleshed and smiling as Sai Yuan Woo was skinny and scowling, had worn a purple dress that looked like taffeta and was cut low enough to show off her ample bosom. Maria Sanchez served fastidiously. She filled all the plates with the different foods from the platters in the center of the table, using a separate serving spoon for each platter. When everybody's plate was piled high with food, the four people at the table ate slowly. They put their forks and knives down frequently to savor the tastes and talk in the manner of people who had eaten not long ago and would soon eat again.

No, the ketchup had given her a flash to the body of Merrill Liberty lying in the bloodied slush. When April had seen her, not even a half hour had passed since the woman had died. Her body was still so warm to the touch, it made April think her soul might not yet have departed, might still be hanging around there trying to tell them something. April figured Merrill Liberty had been standing when it happened. Her blood had pulsed out of the hole in her throat with the last of her heartbeats, soaking the front of her dress before she fell. April felt a pricking sensation behind her eyes.

Patrice had said it must have happened almost the minute they left the restaurant. He told April he usually went to the door with them. Sometimes he walked with them out to Mr. Petersen's car. Yes, he knew the car well. He knew the driver. Sometimes they gave coffee or food to Mr. Petersen's driver. The driver's name was Wally Jefferson. Patrice said he didn't know why Wally Jefferson hadn't been outside the restaurant waiting for them last night.

"Didn't you wonder where the driver was?" April asked.

The question renewed Patrice's weeping.

"I didn't know he wasn't there so I didn't have any reason to think about it," Patrice replied. And no, he hadn't known how bad the weather was. How could he know? He was busy taking care of customers. That's why he wasn't at the door with them. He'd been very busy. It must have been a mugger crazed for dope money, he insisted to April.

A few things the maître d' said didn't play for her. Restaurant people always knew the weather. The weather accounted for the number of customers. Not only that, rain soaked people's shoes and made tracks on the floor. People wore raincoats when it rained, carried umbrellas. They dripped all over the place. Coats were wet or dry. No way Patrice could not have known. When a person lied about one thing, it was hard to believe anything else he said.

And as for his crying, you couldn't tell anything by tears. Sometimes people screamed, really shrieked. In Chinatown, relatives of victims sometimes went nuts, made enough noise to bring the house down. But one woman she'd informed of the suicide of her last living child, a son of twenty-six, had gone to the gym that very afternoon because she didn't want to change her schedule and disappoint her trainer. And of course the big-breasted widow of Tor Petersen might now be sobbing brokenheartedly over her loss. You never knew.

"You didn't answer my question," she said.

"What question? I forgot." Mike was working on the ketchup-laden hash browns.

"Are you keeping me company for the food, or are you in on this? I have to go back and get organized."

"What makes you think I know?"

"Back at Liberty's you went to the men's room more times than you had to go. The phone is back there. I figured you were making some calls."

He dabbed at his lips with his paper napkin, crumpled it, and dropped it on the table. "Very good. Watching me like a cat. I like that."

April shook her head. Her hair had grown out into a bob that framed her face and sometimes got in the way of serious conversation. "Uh-uh, it's my job."

"Gee, and I thought you loved me."

"I don't do work-and-play combinations, Mike, you know that." In their last case Mike had almost killed a suspect who'd insulted her. Later he told her that was when he realized he loved her. It was also when she realized he could be dangerous. But he was still more powerful in the department than she was, and if he wanted in on a case in her house, there was nothing she could do to stop him.

She smiled, had to be smart about this. "You drove through a blizzard to help me out. Thanks, *chico*."

"Ah, it's my job." He smiled back.

"Uh-huh. I get the feeling you don't like the ADA on the case. What's the problem there?" She reached for the shoulder bag by her feet. Time to go. The lieutenant would be in. She didn't want to anger Iriarte by not reporting everything right away. She put the bag on the table and reached for her coat.

Mike caught one of her hands and held it with both of his, squeezing her fingers just enough to give her the shivers. "You like him?"

"He seemed to know what he was doing." She did a quick survey of the diner, looking for a spy from the precinct who could make something of this. No one she knew was around. She suddenly wished Mike's hand would travel down her neck and into her sweater. Weird. She figured she was overtired.

"Uh-huh, and your lieutenant, he know what he's doing, too?" Mike was asking.

"Iriarte? He dresses well, wants women to be women. Has a short mustache like your mother's boyfriend." April was distracted.

"Is this a professional assessment of his competence?" Mike brought the tips of her fingers to his lips, tickling them with his mustache.

The gesture got her in the stomach. No, no, and no. Flushing, she grabbed her coat and scarf from the back of the chair, making a face at the smell of wet wool as she put them on. "I take it you're coming with me."

"To the ends of the earth, *querida*." Mike gave her a knowing smile.

"That would be nice, *chico,* but I'm not going that far."

"Uh-huh. What kind of hole do you have for people who work on special cases?"

"Oh, a real nice closet, has a phone and everything. Just outside my door."

"*Bueno*." Mike tucked his stiffening leather jacket under his arm and reached for the check. "Well, let's go meet the boys."

April glanced at her watch again. It was 9:13. They really had to hustle now. She had to put in a call to

Jason Frank. Funny, the food must have helped. She was wide awake now.

At 9:29 Lieutenant Iriarte gestured with a cupped hand, inviting April and Mike into the already too crowded space of his office. Today he wore a glen plaid suit in almost mossy tones with a pale amber shirt and bold-patterned orange-and-khaki tie. His suit jacket was buttoned, and a thin stripe of long underwear ribbing peeped out from under his shirt cuffs.

The cheerless trio arrayed around his desk included the woebegone Hagedorn, who warmed his chubby hands on a cup of precinct bilge that smelled a week old; Tom Creaker, a fierce-looking giant with a number of battle scars visible on his close-cropped skull who claimed he was three quarters Native American and one-quarter Irish; and April's favorite, Billy Skye, a diminutive man whose biceps were so large they threatened to split his sleeves every time he moved his arms. The four men had been working together for years. No one offered Woo or Sanchez a chair.

"How ya doin'. I'm Mike Sanchez." Mike looked them over, taking the temperature in a friendly way.

Iriarte's office was deep in the bowels of the second floor. No windows fronting the street leaked in frigid air or gave a view of the prevailing weather as in the Two-O. But even so, there was no doubt about the season. Skye and Hagedorn had sweaters under their sport jackets, disproving the oft-told lie that the radiators in the building were working well.

"Mike." Iriarte held out his hand. Mike leaned over the desk to shake it. "You've met Charlie Hagedorn. And you know Tom Creaker, Billy Skye." At his name, each man lifted a hand in a modified salute.

"I got a call you were coming." Iriarte sniffed at the air like an animal with a new scent, then glanced at April with a raised eyebrow. *You have something to do with this?*

She shook her head.

The lieutenant returned his attention to Mike.

"Well, good to have you with us, Mike, in your new position. How's it going?" Iriarte tapped a finger on his desk and consulted a portion of puckering paint on the ceiling over his head.

"It's going well," Mike replied. "How about you guys?"

Iriarte nodded. "I like a team that cooperates. Want a cup of coffee?"

Mike glanced at April. "Thanks, we just ate."

Iriarte's eyebrow came up at April again. *You sure you weren't the one to invite your old partner in on this?*

A spark ignited in her boss's eye that made April nervous. She'd only known Iriarte for a few weeks. The lieutenant could have been a real bastard to her, could have withheld the kind of everyday information that would have made doing a good job almost impossible. But so far he'd been fair. He hadn't coddled her or made nice, but he'd been fair. April couldn't ask for anything more than that. He could still make life miserable for her, though. Anytime he felt she wasn't on his team, he could chop her up into little pieces and feed her to his three ugly musketeer henchmen.

As the lieutenant had done only a second before, April sniffed the air and smelled Sanchez. Sanchez really complicated things for her. He edged even closer to the door now, smiling at a scenario he was beginning to get used to, that of the outsider who, depending on his mood, had the power anywhere he went to make things more chaotic, or less.

April decided to take a chance. Some cops talked to each other really well without saying a word. On the street, communication was everything. A cop could have peace or war just by his body language and the tone of his voicc. The idea was to get the suspect to give up his hands for the cuffs, not reach for his gun hidden in some unexpected place and blow everybody away. One had to know how to keep the competitive macho thing on both sides of the badge as low-key as possible. April didn't know if Iriarte had ever been on the street, but she cocked her head in the same engaging little way she used when she told some disgusting dirtbag thief or rapist—who thought it would be easy to kill her because she was an Asian, or didn't have her gun pointed at his head, or was a woman—and smiled as she said, *"Come on now, put that gun down. You don't want to spend the rest of your life on death row for killing a* lady *cop, do you?"*

Now she raised her own eyebrows, such as they were, back at Iriarte. *Can we talk about this later, sir?*

Still fair, he gave her a little nod. "Okay, what do we have here? You talk to Liberty yet?"

"Yes, sir." April decided to show Sanchez she was taking the lead here.

"What's the story there, he our killer?"

April drew breath and exhaled slowly. "It's early days to rule it in or out," she answered. "He was supposed to go to the theater with his wife last night, but at the last minute he went to Chicago."

Hagedorn sniggered. "Chicago, huh? That sound familiar to anyone? I'd bet a grand it's the black bastard."

"You don't have a grand," Skye sneered.

Creaker agreed with Hagedorn. "Nine times out of ten it's the husband."

"Could have been the wife," April threw in. "Petersen's wife has a motive and no alibi."

"One woman, two victims? Does that sound likely?"

"Nobody said she didn't have help. The woman has a lot of rivals, including our victim, and a lot to gain with hubby out of the way."

Iriarte ignored that. "So when did Liberty go to Chicago?" he demanded.

April checked her notebook. "He said he took the two p.m. flight, had a meeting, flew home, and returned to his apartment at the Park Century around midnight. The doorman at his building verified his return at between midnight and twelve-ten."

"Which is it?"

"Definitely after midnight when the building's porter stopped by to give him some coffee before he went home and before twelve-ten when he double-locked the door and left his post to go to the john."

"Libery come out again?"

April shook her head. "He says not. The doorman says not."

"How about the back door?"

"The back elevator is shut down at six p.m."

"How about the fire stairs?"

"Anybody who opens the gate on the main floor sets off an alarm. I think we'd better look in another direction. Liberty says Petersen's driver—Wally Jefferson—took his car without his permission while Liberty was in Europe a week ago. The car has disappeared. Jefferson claims it was stolen off the street."

"Where are you going with this, Woo? You think this Jefferson had something to do with it?"

"I don't know, sir. Jefferson was Petersen's driver. He knew where they were. He had opportunity."

"I thought you said he was Liberty's driver," Iriarte said impatiently.

"It seems he drove Liberty freelance. In any case, he borrowed Liberty's car without permission, and it's missing."

"Where's the motive for a double murder with him?" Hagedorn muttered.

"We don't know he wasn't there waiting for them. He could have been there, killed them, and left after it was over."

"What's the fucking motive, huh, Woo? A stolen car?"

Mike flushed but kept silent. April was grateful for that.

"Liberty said he told Petersen his driver was a thief and urged him to cut the man loose. Maybe Petersen took his advice and Jefferson was pissed."

"Because he lost his job?"

"In the postal service, employment beefs end up in mass murder all the time," Creaker joked.

"Good ballplayer," Iriarte commented about Liberty. "What say you, Mike?"

Mike chewed on the ends of his mustache. "It doesn't look to me like one person made the two hits here. That's what's bugging me. There might have been two killers. If they'd been thirsty crackheads, they would have taken the time to grab the purse and Petersen's wallet. Nothing would have stopped them from getting the money. No one took their money. It wasn't robbery."

"Maybe someone's after a lot more than pocket money."

Iriarte stared at Skye and Creaker. "Garbage time," he said. "Start with five blocks all around. What are we looking for, April?"

"For the lady, the ME said possibly an ice pick. Maybe a double-edged knife, thinner than a switchblade. Maybe some specialty item." April shrugged. "Possibly a switchblade. We don't have a COD on the male yet. The ME said he may have seen the woman being attacked and had a heart attack."

"Jesus. Okay, go over the scene again, see if daylight turns something up." The lieutenant glanced over at Mike. "Hey, big shot, you got a plan?"

Mike moved away from the door so Creaker and Skye could get out. "I've always got a plan."

"Well, put it up on the board. I like my cases up on the board, every step of the way. I like to see what we know and what we don't know. I like to see the holes plugged, you know what I mean? April will tell you, Mike, I'm a detail man all the way."

Mike coughed. "That's great, but not in this case."

"Oh, yeah, why not?"

"Because the press is all over this one."

"The press is all over all of them."

"Yeah, but we're going to look really dumb if we're the last ones to know how our investigation is going."

"Yeah, that's exactly what I think. Hagedorn, show the sergeant here where his desk is, and make sure he has everything he needs. Out." Iriarte turned his attention to April. "Anything else?"

April shut her notebook. "That's all we have at the moment."

"All right. Go find the driver." Iriarte contemplated her silently for a moment before adding his final thought. "That's your puppy out there, Woo. You'd better keep him on a leash."

"Excuse me, sir?"

"You heard me. If your boyfriend fucks up the case, your ass is out of here."

"Yes, sir." Was this childish or what? April turned on her heel to hide the flush, spreading over her body like a fatal disease. She didn't bother to insist that Mike wasn't her boyfriend. Iriarte didn't care and wouldn't have believed her anyway.

8

The office where Jason saw his patients was next door to his apartment on the fifth floor of an old-world building on Riverside Drive. At three minutes to four in the afternoon he came out of his office and walked five feet down the hall to his apartment. The day had a surreal quality to it, and he felt almost dizzy from changing dimensions so many times. He'd gotten up early, missed breakfast, spent much of the morning with Liberty, was in too much of a hurry to have lunch. After seeing four patients back-to-back, he was exhausted and desperately hungry. Outside it looked like the middle of the night again. And he had only twenty minutes until his next patient would be sitting in his waiting room counting the seconds until he returned. He needed a break, needed to check on Emma.

He turned the key in his front door lock, opening the door as quietly as he could in case she was asleep. Inside the apartment the lights were on and some of the nine clocks in the living room and hall had already started to chime the hour. They were mechanical, pendulum clocks, all old, less than precise, and it would take a full seven minutes for them to finish their racket. So much for quiet.

"Emma?"

"In here," she called over the noise.

Jason passed the untouched stack of mail on the hall table and turned right. Now he could see Emma in the living room, on the phone with her address book open in front of her. A tray with a teapot and milk jug sat on the coffee table. The cup near her hand was half full of milky tea. She waved at him, her face registering surprise at seeing him so soon.

"Yes, it's a terrible loss. Look, I have to go now. I'll call you later." She hung up and put out her hand to him, tears welling in her eyes.

He took her hand. "How are you doing?"

"Jason, thank you for staying with Rick and me. It meant so much to both of us."

"What's going on?"

"Rick's apartment is filled with people now. I had to leave. Oh, Jason, I love you so much." She kissed his hand, dragging him closer.

"What's this for?" he asked, the darkness in his heart easing a little at the unexpected sign of affection.

"It's so terrible to lose someone you love. I don't know what I'd do if I lost you." She pulled on his hand until he was sitting beside her on the couch. Then she folded herself into his arms.

"You tried to lose me once and couldn't, remember? I don't lose easily." He hugged her tight. In his embrace she felt fragile, smaller than usual, as if she'd lost some of herself since yesterday. Underneath the scent of her floral perfume, he could smell panic.

"How's Rick doing?" he asked.

"Not well. But neither would I in the situation." She mashed her face into his shoulder, wetting his shirt with her tears. "Jason, thanks for being there for us."

"What?" Jason was shocked to hear her thank him for so little. "God, Emma. You make me feel like a shit."

"No, no. I don't mean it like that. I mean—well, I know you never really liked Liberty."

He pushed her away so he could look at her. "Hey, that's not fair."

"Well, you didn't like him." She blew her nose.

"That's not true and not fair. I just didn't know either of them very well. You were the one who spent time with them."

"You were always too busy working," she reminded him.

He didn't want to hear how alone she used to feel, how he didn't like her friends. He shook his head, didn't want to go there at all. She changed the subject.

"Jason, was this how it was for you?"

His stomach growled. He stared at the teapot, needing food. When she was kidnapped? "It was worse. I didn't know whether you were alive or dead. And if you were alive, whether I could save you. I was crazed."

"Did you love me that much?" she asked. "As much as Rick loved Merrill?"

"Oh, Emma," he said softly. "I still do."

First her shoulders shook, and then her whole body. "Jason, I've been so selfish. I'm so sorry." She huddled against him, sobbing again.

"Hey. Let's say we've both been a little single-minded."

"I don't know what I'd do without you. I can see that now."

"Um . . . Emma?"

"Hmmm?"

"You're getting my shirt all wet, baby, and I have to eat something."

She detached herself and reached for the tea tray. "I'll make you a sandwich. Listen, Jason, what do the police think?"

"Here, I'll take the tray." He led the way to the kitchen. "Have you talked with April Woo yet?"

"She called and asked if she could come over later. But I didn't know what time you'd be free."

Emma started pulling plastic bags and containers from the refrigerator. Jason watched, thinking the detective would want to talk to Emma, not him. She was the one who'd been with the victims just before they died. "What did you tell her?"

"I told her to call you. Do the police have any leads?"

A sandwich took shape under Emma's trembling

fingers. She thoughtfully filled a baguette with all the cholesterol Jason wasn't supposed to eat, all the stuff she loved and sneaked whenever he wasn't around. The sandwich she made consisted of salami, brie, pâté, roasted peppers, arugula, and tomato. In earlier days, he would have complained of her insensitivity, taken it apart, and removed the bits dangerous to his heart and arteries. Now, he accepted her offering with pleasure and gobbled it hungrily, savoring every poisonous bite.

"Emma," he said cautiously. "April doesn't want me. She's going to want to talk to you. You knew them both better than I did. You were with them last night."

Emma's mood worsened. "I didn't see Rick last night," she said.

"Rick? No, but you were with the victims last night. Merrill and—"

"Tor." Emma wrinkled her nose.

"What about that? Did they have a relationship?"

The wrinkle turned into a frown. "I don't think so, but I don't know."

"Were they involved?"

"I said I don't know." Angrily, Emma removed a plate from the table, then banged it on the edge of the sink, chipping it. "Shit."

Jason watched her, chewing thoughtfully. He swallowed. "I'd guess you're worried about it."

"No."

"Turn around and look at me, baby. I know you're worried. I can feel it."

She turned on the water. "You'd worry, too," she said with her back to him.

He sighed. "They're going to ask you to tell them everything you know about Merrill, and Rick, and this other person, Tor—"

"Petersen, just about the richest and craziest man in America. I can't believe they're dead. I can't believe it. They were so alive last night. They loved my play."

Jason finished the sandwich.

"And I don't know what to tell them."

"You'll have to tell them the truth."

"The *truth*!" She spat out the word. "The whole idea makes me sick. What if the truth doesn't have anything to do with who killed them?" Finally she turned around and stared at him. "Jason, do you know what I mean about this?"

"You mean you don't want to share the secrets of your closest friend. You don't want her life exposed. You don't want yourself exposed. You don't want Rick exposed." He sighed again. "What's your part in it?"

"They picked me up at the theater. We had dinner together. I left before dessert. I came home to you, Jason. I didn't want to keep you waiting." Her eyes teared. "We made love, remember?"

She'd been in high spirits, as she usually was after a performance. Jason had been exhausted, had fallen asleep. She'd woken him up to be with her, but it had been worth it. "I remember," he murmured, then, "Emma, Merrill's dead. The only thing that matters now is to find out who killed her."

"Jason, you do it."

"Do what?"

"You work with the police," Emma entreated him. "You find out who killed her."

Jason checked his watch. Ten past four. He'd eaten a huge sandwich, full of cholesterol, in four minutes flat and would suffer for it later. He groaned. "I'm a psychiatrist, not a detective."

"It's the same thing. Come on, do this for Rick, no—do it for me. Find out who did this."

"Then you'll have to tell me what you know. Try it out on me."

"It's probably nothing useful," she muttered.

"But still, you're afraid. Look, I have to go." He got up from the table to embrace her one last time before getting back to work.

She put her arms around him. "I'm afraid," she admitted.

"Well, you're safe," he told her. "I won't let anyone hurt you."

"It's not myself I'm worried about," she said softly as he left.

When Jason got back to his office, his patient—a young psychiatric resident who didn't know Jason lived next door—was sitting in the waiting room, tapping his foot impatiently. The man stared at the wet spots on Jason's shirt, and then his face, clearly trying to figure out where Jason had been in the dead of winter, and what he'd been doing, without his jacket or coat. Jason excused himself for a moment to go into his office and try April again. She still wasn't in.

9

Rosa Washington heard the phone ring in the suite where her office was located. She ran down the hall to get it before the secretary picked up and whined to whoever was on the line that no one was there. No one at all. Everyone was sick or dead, and the place was falling apart. The woman was a bit of a loon even for the morgue. Rosa thought they must have gotten her from Bellevue's psych bin down the street.

"I'm here," Rosa called as she jogged into the suite, her white coat flapping around a fresh scrub suit. "Is it him?"

"He." Elinor Dunn corrected her boss's grammar with a shake of her graying head.

Rosa scowled at the thin, wispy woman, nearly twice her age, whose disapproving face always gave Rosa the feeling that she herself was a fake, always on the brink of making some ghastly social or grammatical faux pas.

The nasty woman punched a button and held the receiver away from her ear as if it had lice. "It's a Mrs. Petersen. She sounds English," she hissed. "And you have company." She jerked her head at two detectives standing inside the door of Rosa's office.

Rosa gave them a small smile and removed her cap.

"Himself did call twice, since you asked." Elinor made a point of checking her notes as to what Himself had said. "He said to hold off on Petersen and the Liberty woman. He's coming in tomorrow for sure."

Rosa didn't let her face show her disappointment as she turned away. Her two prizes had been on ice since four this morning. Already it had been a twelve-hour wait to open them up. There was no excuse for this. None at all. They didn't have a full house at the moment, and there was certainly nobody who couldn't wait. These two babies were hers. By anybody's rights they were hers. She'd been arguing this to herself all day. Hadn't she been there and seen them in situ? Hadn't she, in fact, been practically the first one on the scene? You couldn't get more conscientious than that. In her mink coat, no less. She was proud of the mink coat. It could take anything.

"Hi, guys, what's up?" She smiled at the two cops, covering every negative feeling she had. She tossed the cap on the desk and pointed at April. "You're April Woo, right?"

As far as Rosa knew, there wasn't another female Chink detective. She turned to the Hispanic. "Who's this? Oh, yeah." She smacked her forehead. "I couldn't mistake that bit of facial foliage, now could I? You're Sanchez, Two-O, right?"

"Wow, I'm impressed at the good memory, Doc. But I'm in Homicide now."

"Well, good for you, we'll be meeting more often, then. What brings you two over here?"

"What's the schedule on Petersen and Liberty?" April said. "We're under some pressure here."

"Well, have a seat and relax." Rose threw herself in her chair and swiveled back and forth. "You know I can't believe this. I've got those two babies down there waiting for me. And I can't open them up."

"What's the problem?" Mike asked.

"You haven't heard? Dr. Abraham is home sick."

"Oh, yeah?" Mike said. "And?"

"And, he doesn't want the cameras on anybody else."

"Too bad," Mike sympathized.

"Was I not there first?" Rosa demanded of April. "Not that I'm complaining, of course."

"Yeah, you were there first. In your mink coat. Nice coat."

"You like it?" Rosa beamed.

"Who wouldn't? How did you get the call? Someone beep you?"

"No, I was off last night." She laughed. "But who of us is ever really off? No, I like to know what's coming down. I have a beef about these non-MD inspectors going to the scene. You know how much training they have? Believe me, it may seem cheaper in the short term. But the public is going to suffer in the long run. These guys miss a lot, that's for sure. No, I pick up what's on the scanner. If I'm in the neighborhood, I'll hop over."

The pretty Chinese woman had a closed face. She sat on the end of her chair. She wasn't relaxed. Rosa wished she'd lighten up. "And I thought I got lucky last night. No way these two babies aren't mine. Am I right?" she asked April.

"Sure. So, what's going to happen now? We need a death report."

"Blinky's out sick, too," Rosa went on.

"Who's Blinky?" April asked.

"Blinky's the other deputy. He's got a drooping eyelid, so we call him Blinky."

"You mean George?" Mike asked.

"Yeah, Blinky."

"Is that why he's out sick? The eyelid?" The Chink was still deadpan. Not exactly a barrel of laughs, that one.

Rosa laughed anyway. "Oh no, he's out because one of his babies infected him with hepatitis A. I'd call that pretty careless, wouldn't you?"

Mike nodded. "It kind of gives you the willies about playing with other people's blood, doesn't it?"

"You have any leads yet?" Rosa got serious and tapped her desk with a pencil.

"Early days," Mike said. "Give us a call tomorrow. I'd like to be present."

"Fine, I'll let you know." She stood up to show she was done with them, then changed her mind and took them to the door. Then she walked down the hall with them to the elevator. But after all that they still didn't tell her anything worth knowing.

10

"Yes, sir, he told me to go straight home from the theater." Until this point in the interview Wallace Jefferson, Jr., had held Mike's eye without wavering. Now he looked down at his big-knuckled hands, clenching the natty cap he held in his lap. "I'm sorry I did. If I'd been there to pick them up, that fine gentleman and lady would still be alive."

And how could they be sure of that? April was feeling less than patient with this one. Her exhaustion was returning after a second wind that had lasted most of the day. Now it was nearly six, and she was in a hurry to get out of there and meet with Jason and Emma, who'd left a message saying she could come to their apartment at six-thirty.

Okay, there it was. A patch of white showing in Jefferson's apparently downcast eyes, as if he was actually trying to look up at her and Mike from his half-closed lids to gauge their reaction without the appearance of doing so.

"They were fine people. I will miss them," he intoned, speaking like a worshiper in church and not a suspect in a grubby precinct interview room.

"Did your boss often send you home to fend for himself in the middle of snowstorms?" Mike asked.

"He was a thoughtful man. I live in New Jersey."

"Doesn't it seem contrary to the point of having a chauffeur, though?" Mike mused.

"Sir?"

"Isn't the point of a chauffeur to have him around in the worst weather?"

Jefferson's eyes came alive at this. "I do—did—whatever Mr. Petersen asked me to do. Whenever he sent me home he had his own reasons."

"What reason do you think he had last night?"

"What reason?"

Wally Jefferson seemed acutely respectable with his dark suit and dark driver's cap, his manner of almost exaggerated gentleness, and his voice that was soft, reverent, and well spoken. To April he seemed old-style African-American in the same way her mother was old-style Chinese. Everything hidden behind a predetermined formula for expression that could be altered neither by flattery nor torture.

If he was nervous in the interview room, he did not show it. Jefferson was a broad slab of a man of about five nine, weighed something over two hundred pounds, was the color of roasted coffee beans. They'd run him through the computer. He had no priors. Still, there was something about him that April did not trust.

"What was his relationship with Mrs. Liberty?" she asked.

"They were in the same social set," Jefferson said easily.

"Is that a way of saying they were friends?"

"I'm sure I don't know. I just drive the car." He raised his hand to his mouth and coughed delicately.

"Were they possibly more than friends?"

"I wouldn't know."

"What was your work schedule?" Mike changed the subject.

"You mean with Mr. Petersen?"

"Yes, what days did you work?"

"It wasn't the same every week. Mr. Petersen traveled a great deal. When he was here, I sometimes worked every day until midnight, one a.m. When he was away—" He shrugged.

"You drove other people."

"Not really." Jefferson looked wary.

"How about Mr. Petersen's wife?"

"Oh, yes, I drove her."

"What about Liberty?"

"Well him, too. Sometimes."

"Why was that? Doesn't Mr. Liberty have his own driver?"

"He did when Mrs. Liberty was working. But she isn't working—wasn't working anymore. He likes the walk to work. So now when they need someone, they call a service for a driver." Jefferson poked under his collar to scratch at the skin on his neck.

"Or you drive them."

"Yes." Jefferson turned his attention to his knuckles. They were thick and crooked, almost deformed.

"Did Mr. Liberty call you to drive him to the airport yesterday?"

"No, he didn't."

"Why not?"

Jefferson reached for his nose and pinched it between two fingers. "I really couldn't say."

"Is it because he didn't have a car?" Mike leaned forward in his hard chair, shrugging his shoulder holster a little.

Jefferson seemed particularly interested in the gun. "Sir?"

"Liberty's car? What happened with that?"

"Oh, yes. Mr. Liberty's car." Jefferson nodded solemnly.

"It was stolen, right?"

"A bit of bad luck."

"How and when was the car stolen?"

Jefferson hunched his shoulders, shaking his head, as if the whole thing were a sad story he'd heard.

"Come on, now, Wally. We know you took Mr. Liberty's car."

Jefferson was stunned. "Mr. Liberty didn't tell you that!"

"Oh, yes, he did. He said you stole his car."

"Oh, now, that just ain't true. Let's correct that right now. I had per*mission* to use that car. Ask the boys at the garage. I could take it out anytime."

"You had permission to take the car out of the

garage when you were going to drive him. Just as you could take Mr. Petersen's car out of the garage for *his* use."

Jefferson shook his head. "I could use the cars."

"Both of them?"

"Yessir."

"Well, what happened to Mr. Liberty's car then?"

Jefferson shifted his position. "His inspection sticker was expired. Before he went to Europe he asked me to take the car to a service station and get a new one. I did that." He shook his head. "I left it there. The car was gone when I came back for it."

"It only takes a few minutes to check a car out. How long did you leave it?"

"Three days."

"You left Mr. Liberty's car at a service station for three days?" Mike said incredulously.

"I had the flu. Mr. Petersen can confirm that."

"No, he can't. He's dead. And Liberty was in Europe."

"Well, Mrs. Petersen can confirm it."

"Wally, where did you go last night after you dropped Mr. Petersen and Mrs. Liberty at the theater?"

"I took the car and drove home. I've been home with my wife since then. You can ask her."

"We will ask her. Thank you, Wally. I want you to write down here on this pad the name of that service station where you left Mr. Liberty's car. Then I want you to sit here for a while and gather your thoughts about all the things you've told us. Maybe your memory will improve a little over time. In a few minutes we're going to send in a detective to go over all this with you again. We want you to make a full statement about the last few weeks, as well as the events leading up to the murders last night. You've got some explaining to do, understand?"

"The car was not in my possession when it was taken," Jefferson said flatly.

"Well, Wally, I don't think a judge would see it that way. Liberty certainly doesn't."

"But he didn't press charges against me, did he? And if he didn't press charges, I guess that proves I didn't do anything wrong."

Wrong. April glanced at her watch. She'd had enough of this.

"And I was in New Jersey with my wife when poor Mr. Petersen, and Mrs. Merrill, were killed," Jefferson went on. "Bless their souls, I'll miss them."

Feeling sick, April got up and left the room.

Fifteen minutes later she was on her way uptown in an unmarked unit. This time she'd decided to forget worrying about having someone drive her. Once again, it was dark outside and the weather was bad. All the way up to Jason's apartment, she worried about when his next patient was scheduled. Unless there was a major crisis, Jason would not cancel an appointment. That meant if she got there too late, he'd cancel her. What was it with these mental cases that made them so special that all life had to stop when they were with their shrinks? Jason's inaccessibility really annoyed her as she slid around ice-encrusted construction sites and skidding taxis, trying to keep calm behind the wheel. She did not think about her refusal to have dinner with Mike because she had to get some rest, or about the problem that Wally Jefferson presented them with a wife as his alibi. He was clearly lying about a lot of things.

The only good thing about the lousy weather was the decrease in traffic. Problem was, the lousy taxi drivers from hot countries who didn't have any experience with snow or ice were the only ones left on the hazardous streets. Her parking effort was to ram the car into a snowbank in front of a hydrant. She knew she was going to have trouble getting it out later.

By the time she was in the cage elevator in Jason's building, jerking slowly up the five floors to his apartment, she was panting with anxiety. She swallowed, breathed eight counts in, held her breath for six counts, exhaled for eight counts, and did it again a few times to slow down her heart. Jason opened the door almost before she put out her finger to ring his bell.

"Hi," he said, looking her over.

About to meet the famous Emma Chapman again, April felt shabby and double ugly in the new navy wool coat she'd bought only a few weeks ago, the long navy-and-maroon-printed scarf wrapped several times around her neck, and the Chanel-copy shoulder bag that Emma Chapman would certainly know she'd bought on the street in Chinatown but that was strong enough to hold anything April wanted to put into it.

"Hi. Sorry I'm late. I got tied up."

Jason smiled as she removed her leather gloves and extricated herself from the scarf. "No problem. Come on in."

"Thanks." She followed him into the hall where the table with the glass dome covering a large clock made to show its works was piled with unopened mail.

April didn't know any people who lived in apartments like this. The living room was large with windows facing Riverside Drive and the Hudson River. Many books and clocks covered every surface. Neutral colors on the walls and furniture were chosen to soothe, as were the large upholstered club chairs and sofa that April knew from earlier experience were deep and soft. She longed to sink in for a long winter's nap. From the dent in the sofa, it looked as if recently someone might have been doing just that. No sign of Emma now, though. She probably took off when she heard the downstairs buzzer ring.

April knew that Emma didn't like her and could understand why. Years ago, Ja Jien, April's best friend in high school, had gotten pregnant by a white guy. Her family had been murderously angry, had told Ja Jien she would die if she had an abortion. The doctor would blunder, he'd kill her, or do it wrong so if she lived, she wouldn't be able to have more children. At the same time they'd said—didn't matter if she lived, might as well be dead since she was ruined anyway. Ja Jien had the abortion, changed her name to Jennifer. Afterward she didn't want to see April, who had supported her during her ordeal. The two friends drifted apart. Later, when Jennifer became successful as a beautician and opened her own salon, she made it clear she didn't want to cut April's hair, didn't want her in the shop. Didn't ever want to know her again. April had seen Emma Chapman as a naked hostage, her whole body and face painted, her stomach in the process of being tattooed. Emma would not forget that.

Jason gave April one of his penetrating looks. "You hungry, want something?" he asked.

She was starved. She shook her head. "Not at the moment, thanks."

"Yell when you want something." He took her coat and hung it on a doorknob.

"Emma around?"

"Yes, she's coming." Jason went through the opening into the living room. "How's the investigation going?"

April ignored the question. "Liberty mentioned your name when we went to inform him of the death. I gather you've spent some time with him since."

"He's an old friend."

"From the way he spoke about you, I got the feeling he was your patient."

"He's not."

"Oh, really, then you might be able to help us," April murmured.

Jason nodded noncommittally.

April moved into the living room and picked the chair she'd sat in the last time she'd been in the apartment, sank into it gratefully. Her last visit had been in November before she'd made sergeant. She wondered if Jason knew about her promotion.

Emma Chapman strode into the room, wearing soft black trousers and a black sweater. Looked like cashmere. Probably was. As Emma took the chair opposite, April wondered what it would be like to have long legs, peach-colored skin and blond hair, to wear such expensive things, and walk with such authority and grace.

"Ah, Sergeant Woo, congratulations on your promotion," Emma said with a brittle smile.

"Yes, congratulations," Jason threw in.

"Congratulations to you, too, for your new play. I see your name in the top place at the theater every day. I'm downtown in Midtown North now," April explained.

"Your new phone number confused me," Jason said. "Someone told me you're a supervisor now."

"Yes, it's true."

"Well, you'll have to come and see the play—and bring your friend. What's his name—Mike . . . ?" Emma made a face, trying to remember the name of the cop who'd saved her life.

"Sanchez," April said softly. "He's in Homicide now."

"No kidding? Then who's left to take care of us in the Twentieth?" Emma asked lightly.

April thought of Aspirante and Healy. "No one," she said. Her stomach gurgled. She put a hand over it to silence it. Time to go to work. "I'm sorry about your friends," she began, taking her Rosario out of her purse.

"Thank you." Emma twisted her wedding ring around on her finger. She glanced at the notebook, then at Jason. He had his bland shrink face on. April had her cop face on. The actress had her . . . actress face on. April wondered if she'd be able to get past it.

"Let's start with your relationship with the—uh, with Mrs. Liberty," April suggested.

"I've known Merrill for—a long time. We went to acting classes together more than ten years ago. That's how we met. We both wanted to be actors. Merrill made it first. She got a part in a soap. I did voice-overs for a long time. We were very close, even after she married Rick."

"Rick?"

"That's what Liberty's friends call him."

"So the three of you go way back."

Emma took a bite out of an unpolished thumbnail and spoke impatiently. "We all go way back. Rick and Tor were friends the way Merrill and I were friends. This is a devastating thing. Just horrible." She glanced at Jason, sitting silently beside her, then reached for his hand. "For Rick especially. I can't imagine losing both my husband and my best friend at the same time."

April felt a twinge of jealousy at the way Jason was looking at his wife. It triggered a thought, then she lost it. "Did Merrill and Petersen have any enemies?"

Emma chewed on her nail. "Well, of course. I'm sure they did. Successful people always have enemies."

"Can you think of anybody in particular who might want to kill them?"

"Tor just fired twenty percent of the people in his company last week. A lot of people were mad at him. He was a charming man, but he could be ruthless, you know."

April wasn't acquainted with people like Petersen, so she didn't know. She waited for Emma to go on.

"Maybe the killer was someone he'd fired. Sergeant, do you think Tor was the target? Or both of them?" Emma frowned.

"Please call me April. Why do you ask?"

Emma shook her head. "It doesn't make sense."

"What doesn't?"

"It was an accident that they were together last night. Merrill and Rick were supposed to come to see me in my new play. I didn't know Rick wasn't coming until after the show when Merrill showed up in my dressing room with Tor. I have to admit I was surprised."

"Why?"

Emma smiled weakly. "Rick is a fan."

"Is Tor a fan?"

"Oh, I don't know. I hardly knew him. I don't think he even knew who I was before last night."

"You're too modest. So what changed the plans?"

"Rick had to go to Chicago on business. Tor took his ticket. For him it was a last-minute thing. Nobody even knew he was going to be there."

That triggered another question. April made a note. "What about his wife?"

"Tor's wife? I've never met her. The gossip was they were breaking up."

"Maybe she knew where they were going."

"That's—horrible. How would she even pull it off?" Emma shuddered.

"Maybe she had help," April said softly. "And Liberty knew where they were. Either could have—"

"No!" Emma said explosively. "I know Rick couldn't hurt anybody."

"What kind of marriage did Liberty and his wife have?"

"Devoted," Emma said firmly.

"There must have been stresses."

"Every marriage has stresses," Emma said vaguely.

"Merrill was a beautiful woman. She must have had admirers. Was her husband jealous?"

"Rick?" Emma took another bite of nail, ripped it, and winced. A spot of blood appeared at the quick. She dabbed the blood on her handkerchief, staining it. "I don't think so."

April glanced at Jason. His mask was still on. He wasn't saying. "Are you thinking about it?" she asked Emma.

"Yes! I'm thinking about it. I just don't think he's the jealous type," Emma said firmly.

"Not an Othello," April murmured.

"You've read Shakespeare?" Emma seemed surprised.

"I saw the movie. How did he seem that night?"

"Tor?"

"No, Liberty."

Emma looked confused. "I didn't see Rick that night. He was in Chicago."

"What about the phone call?"

"What phone call?"

"He called the restaurant. What was Petersen like?"

Emma started on the other thumb. "We were drinking a bit. Tor was excited—" She stopped short.

April guessed the man had come on to Emma that night, not to his date, Merrill, and that might have been the real reason Emma had left the restaurant before dinner was over and missed hearing the phone call. Maybe she kept looking at Jason now because she didn't want him to know something. April wondered what it was.

"Were Tor and Merrill involved romantically?"

Emma sighed. "Jason asked me that. I—really don't know. I guess they'd spent more time together recently. I know Merrill held his hand whenever he had marital problems." Emma shook her head.

And maybe Liberty was tired of the hand-holding. April changed the subject again. "What time did you leave the restaurant?"

"I don't know. Maybe around midnight. Maybe before." Another check with the watchdog husband.

Jason shook his head. All those clocks everywhere, and he didn't know either.

"Why didn't Petersen send you home in his car?"

"I don't know. The car wasn't there. I think he sent the driver on some other errand."

"An errand? What kind of errand?"

"I don't know. I just know the car wasn't there. Tor mentioned something, but I forgot."

"How did you get home?"

"I took a cab. A woman was getting out a few doors down, so I got lucky, I took her cab."

A surge of dizziness swept over April. "Could I have a glass of water?" she asked faintly.

Jason got to his feet. "When did you eat last?" he asked.

"I'm fine," she said. "I just need a little water."

"I'll get you some juice." He left the room.

"It's nice to have a doctor around," April murmured. Then she put down her notebook and asked Emma what she really wanted to know.

11

Mel Auschauer glanced at the figure retreating through the kitchen door of Liberty's apartment, then attempted to lean forward in a conspiratorial manner. His anxious eyes darted around the room as if to make sure no one was listening who shouldn't be listening. Then he tried again to sit up and bend in closer to his host. Mel's midlife belly, fed for many years with the very best of Manhattan restaurant offerings both at business lunches and social dinners, had a different plan. It listed to the left, pinning his bulk to the soft down cushions and giving him the distinct appearance of a beached whale. Still, his message was chilling.

"Rick, have you thought about getting a lawyer?" Mel said softly, darting more glances at each of his other partners.

Mel and Daniel Rothhaus, the two men with most authority at James Dixon, the brokerage house, sat on the section of white sofa in front of the windows overlooking the Park. Rick Liberty and a third partner, Christopher Richardson, sat on the section that curved into the room. Beside them was a huge Dogon mask with a raffia skirt.

"A lawyer?" Rick was taken aback.

Rick had been watching Mel's eyes follow Patrice as he went into the kitchen for more desserts and coffee and didn't like what he saw. But he knew he was particularly sensitive to nuance at the moment. His whole body hurt as if he had been in a rough game and just had a ton of linebackers use him for a playing field. His flesh felt bruised in places he hadn't known existed.

But maybe the bruises didn't exist. Rick couldn't tell. All day he had had trouble identifying the sources of his pain. This was new. As an athlete, he had had to know where it hurt so he could compensate and go around the end zone of his physical weak spots. Now he couldn't tell whether the pain he felt came from his body or his mind, which made it difficult to know how to handle it. He had that queasy feeling that came after a really crippling migraine, when his clarity of thinking had returned but he was aware that some crucial period of consciousness was missing. At such times, he wasn't exactly sure what had occurred when the system broke down, and he was afraid nausea might make him vomit without warning, or crash out again.

He kept turning to Merrill, wanting to tell her how awful it was without her. He couldn't believe she wasn't coming back in a minute, breathless and apologetic for taking so long. But she wasn't coming back. Someone had killed her. Someone had reached into the very center of his life and ripped his heart out. The police said Merrill had been stabbed in the neck. It was inconceivable. It made him sick to think about it. He couldn't imagine how such a thing could happen. He just couldn't envision a situation in which Tor was not in control. Tor had been in control of everything. Rick had seen him in tight spots more than once. The threat of a mugger, even one with a gun, would not have caused Tor to lie down and die. There had been no mention of a gun, or a struggle. Why not? Something was wrong, and they weren't telling him the real story. But why not? Rick didn't get it. He felt dead, destroyed—and yet he was alive—dazed and puzzled at the same time.

Jokingly, Merrill used to tell him that dazed and puzzled were the two reactions actors had when stinking reviews came in. He and she had received some pretty stinking reviews when they got married, but the hate was never murderous, never struck at the heart.

Snide remarks on either side of the color line were like graffiti on city walls. It was everywhere. They saw it, they didn't like it, but it wasn't going away. So they'd had to get used to it.

They had told each other having to defend their reasons for being together made them stronger. What had made them vulnerable was the inability to have children, for which no doctor could find a medical reason. That flaw in their life was what had kept them from feeling normal, from feeling right as a couple. Rick had believed it was his fault; Merrill had believed it was hers. Now they would never see their love mirrored in other faces. All Merrill's battles were over. Rick thought about that as his partners stared at him with disbelief.

"Don't you know what's going on? Haven't you seen the news?" Mel echoed incredulously.

Rick shook his head. Two cops had given him the news at four in the morning. He didn't need to hear the uninformed versions.

Chris Richardson, a man who had his suits and everything else including his underwear made at Sulka and who trained in a gym for three hours every day after the market closed, was still slim enough to bend at the waist. He leaned forward and put a hand on Rick's knee. "This is going to get ugly," he said ominously. "Really ugly."

Dan Rothhaus was a small wiry man with intense blue eyes, curly white hair, and a long thin nose the nostrils of which he constantly teased with a pinkie. Rothhaus radiated anxiety. Rick shot him an inquiring look, then stared at his other two partners as if he had never seen them before. Both were wealthy, well-fed men whose only adversities were having to endure spoiled first and second wives, spoiled and aimless children, and frequent turbulence in national and world markets.

Now the three men were galvanized with what they seemed to see as a real problem, were catching each other's eyes and isolating him with their concern. Rick took a few moments to get a grip on himself. It was going to get ugly? It was already ugly.

He drifted back into his own thoughts. Earlier in the day, Patrice had given him the feeling Merrill's murder hadn't been a random act. Now he was distracted by the word "ugly," and other, familiar irritations like the way his partners made a point of waiting for the restaurant staff to leave before saying anything of importance. All four men in the room had a stake in Liberty's Restaurant—all had a part ownership. But the other three considered it Rick's thing. They considered some of the patrons, and all of the staff, aliens, from another planet. Rick had the feeling that secretly they believed blacks were Martians. He had to stop thinking about that.

He thought about Merrill's face when he'd gone to identify her body. It seemed to rebuke him with its emptiness. Her eyes and mouth were permanently closed, had no comment about what was going on, couldn't tell anyone what happened to her. Now, hours after he had left her there, he found himself trying to remember something else about Merrill other than her color.

For the first time, her color seemed an unbearable offense. She had been frighteningly white at the medical examiner's office, as were the walls of the closed viewing room that he hadn't been allowed to enter. Rick had seen his dead wife through a window and was shaken by how white and alone she was. When he touched the window, that, too, was cold.

"I want to go in," he'd said. He didn't want to leave her there with no crowd of mourners, to be dissected alone. It was so cold, so very cold. He was shaking all over.

"Is that your wife?"

He didn't look to see whose voice was asking, could not have said afterward which cop it was. He just knew the white corpse on the table wasn't his wife. No. His jaw and fists clenched. He looked at her for a long time. No, it was not his wife. Not Merrill. Then, finally he nodded.

He did not encounter Daphne Petersen, was not

shown Tor's body to identify. He felt as if the two were set apart somehow. He wanted to see Tor but was afraid to ask. No police person told him what really happened last night. Rick wondered if they would ever tell him. It hit him at that moment that he would not be able to rest until he knew exactly what happened. And then he was hustled out. They wouldn't let him go in and say good-bye to Merrill. Someone said something about everybody's having to suit up before getting anywhere near the dead these days, wear masks with respirators, as if all corpses carried the AIDS virus or TB, or something even worse. Or were they afraid death itself was catching?

And everything had been white. A white sheet was tucked up around Merrill's ears so he couldn't see any more of her than her face, white under the harsh lights, unmarked in any way, frozen in an expression he'd never seen. It almost felt as if she'd been killed by whiteness itself, bled of her spirit, bleached into nothingness. He noticed that the large diamond studs she always wore were not in her ears. He had heard that the police stole jewelry, watches, and money of victims, also the property of people who were arrested. But Rick didn't think to ask about Merrill's diamonds.

He was too shaken, for white had never been the color of death to him. He'd seen the dead, many dead in his childhood. His mother, grandmother, sister, and he used to visit all the families of the dead in their congregation. They'd prayed over the dead in church and sung them into heaven. The women probably still did. The dead went to heaven in golden chariots, sung there by the choir. They crossed the river to the other side. They were sung all the way on their journey to Jesus, who'd always loved and cherished them no matter who they had been or what they'd done with their lives. The lives may not have been very precious, but the souls were golden treasures to Jesus. That was what they believed. And the treasures were always black. Rick had never seen a dead white person until he saw his wife on—he couldn't even tell what she was lying on. She was covered with a sheet, and there was another sheet under her, draped to the floor.

He admitted the body was hers, but nothing about the thing he saw through the window was like the Merrill he had known. And what was there was not going to heaven in a golden chariot. Merrill was going to be cut up with saws and scalpels and her tissues examined under a microscope. Sitting now with his partners in the home he had shared with Merrill, Rick's body was tense, but his eyes hid his fury. It was already very very ugly.

"Listen to me, Rick," Chris said earnestly. "You have to focus. Do you know what they're saying on TV? Do you know what's going on downstairs? Downstairs there are half a dozen of those vans with star wars on top. Two of those crews almost knocked me down, fighting to get a microphone in front of my face."

It's never too late for salvation. Sing for Jesus, sisters and brothers. Rick had no congregation now, no one anywhere near to sing for Merrill. "Lord save us," he muttered.

Merrill's family was waiting for her body so they could have a funeral. They wanted the funeral in Massachusetts where she'd grown up, and he'd agreed that was best. His family was on the way. After her body had been cut up and examined, they would take her back to the New England town she came from and bury her there. He sucked his breath in, trying to keep control.

"What?" Mel said, cupping his ear.

Rick shook his head, not replying.

"Rick, I know you don't want to think about this right now, but you never know which way these things are going to jump. It's a madhouse out there."

"What do you mean 'jump'?"

Christopher looked apologetic. "You know how Tor was. Who knows what sort of garbage these fucks will come up with?"

"What do you mean *jump*?"

Chris jerked his chin, irritated. "Don't make me spell it out for you, Rick."

"I'm slow," Rick said evenly. "Spell it out for me."

"You're a celebrity."

"So?" He knew what they were getting at and still he couldn't help pushing.

"So, you've lived with publicity. You have to manage the situation all the time, present your own image. They see what you tell them to see. You have to do that now big-time, you know that. You're an expert." Chris scowled at Dan, prompting him to pitch in.

"Yeah." Dan finally opened his mouth. "You've always been great at managing them."

"So what does managing the press have to do with getting a lawyer?"

Mel shifted his stomach. "You know how we feel about you. We want you protected in every way. We don't want you getting hurt."

Rick stared at the three men, his partners. He was already hurt. "Are you worried about the firm?" he asked softly. "Are you scared I'll taint the firm?"

"No, no," Dan shot back angrily. "You don't get it, do you? The vultures are going to tear at your life, pick at your bones—*schadenfreude*. You know what that means?"

Rick shook his head, but he got the picture.

"It means taking pleasure from other people's troubles. Joy and pleasure from eating you alive," Dan persisted. "This is going to happen. It's guaranteed to happen, and we want to control it."

Mel threw his two cents in. "We don't want to see it get out of control here, you know what I mean?"

Rick clenched his jaw. "They won't find anything to pin on me, if that's what you mean."

Dan shook his head. "Don't be a stupid fuck, Rick. They always find something. You—"

Abruptly he stopped as Patrice pushed open the door and bore down on them with a tray of rich pastries and a sullen expression. Rick turned to him, frowning, and their eyes locked.

12

"What you doing?" Sai Woo screamed at her daughter.

April stopped so short she almost felt as if she'd been halted by a bullet. What she'd been doing was trying to sneak up the stairs to her part of the house without an encounter with her mother. Mike told her she always worried about the wrong things, like her mother's feelings and not her own. Almost thirty years old, and she was still so worried about what her mother had to say that every little verbal foray felt like the beginning of another battle in a long and bloody war that April could never win. Hearing her mother scream now, April held in a deep sigh.

The snow and sleet had stopped that morning. The temperature had held at around freezing all through the day, but started dropping again in the early evening. The streets were so icy that the mayor had gone on the radio warning people to keep their cars off the streets and particularly to stay out of Manhattan. April had heard his voice give the same command repeatedly on her hazardous trip home in the white Chrysler Le Baron that she sometimes felt she would still be paying for at the turn of the century. The last thing she wanted was the confrontation her mother had clearly been waiting for all day.

"Where you shreep rast night? Where you been aww day?" Sai Woo demanded.

Reluctantly, April turned around and made eye contact with Skinny Dragon Mother whose eyes had narrowed into slits of war.

"At work, where do you think, Ma?"

Long ago Sai Woo told April about the meaning of dragons and April knew her mother was one. Dragons had demon eyes, the ears of a cow, the neck of a snake, the belly of a clam. On its camel head is a lump, a "gas bag" that allows the dragon to fly through the air swooping in from the sky to bring rain and snow and all manner of storms to undeserving human worms, exactly like April. Of its 117 scales, 81 are good-influence scales (yang) and 36 are bad-influence scales (yin). Sai said there were several hundred different kinds of dragons, but they all had the same kind of power and ruthless personality. When one of them swooped down out of a golden cloud, it was anybody's guess whether the good-influence or the bad-influence scales were going to be dominant.

Tonight, as usual, this particular dragon was in disguise as her mother, now beautifully dressed in black peasant pants and a thick silk padded jacket, turquoise, sprigged with cherry blossoms. The dragon lump on her head was hidden under two inches of freeze-dried seaweed that looked like, but was not, in fact, a wig.

April stared at the jacket, wondering where it had come from. "Nice jacket, Ma. Is it new?"

Sai shook her head and the hair didn't move. "Owd," she announced. "Velly owd." She stroked the sleeve, stroked the tiny French poodle that was sitting on her lap. The dog, Dim Sum, did not lift her head at April, though her apricot fuzzball of a tail made a feeble attempt at a wag. "Where you shreep, no rie. I can terr."

"I worked all night," April said, glad that it was true.

"No bereave."

"Well, it's true." And she had worked through the day, too, except for a few minutes at lunchtime when, exhausted, she'd broken her own rule by sacking out on a bunk in the detective dorm. With Mike camped out across the hall in the office marked SPECIAL CASES, and everybody on edge because of the unusual aggressiveness of the press, it had been a strange day.

"What can I tell you, Ma?" April could not break the force field that insisted on contact with the demon eyes of her mother.

And there was no way to avoid it. The house was set up so that April had to come through the front door to get to the stairway leading to her apartment. There was an arch in the wall dividing the hall from the living room. Skinny Dragon Mother was in her command post in the living room, framed by the arch and looking like the photo of the all-powerful nineteenth-century dowager empress she wished she could be in Queens, New York.

Skinny Dragon Mother sat on one of the carved hardwood Chinese chairs that was a copy of the kind noble families had in old China. There were two of these black chairs in the living room, one for her father and one for her mother. They had no cushions on them and were the symbol of the classless society of America to which Ja Fa Woo and Sai Yuan Woo had fled half their lifetime ago. They had come to a place where anybody could become rich, buy a brick house in Astoria, Queens, and sit in a throne with a thousand-dollar French poodle on her lap that no hungry neighbor would ever be able to get his hands on and eat.

Despite the paper label under the seat that said MADE IN TAIWAN, Sai should have been a happy woman. She had almost everything she wanted. She believed that the chair in her living room had once belonged to a great silk merchant with many wives. And this illustrious, best-quality chair that she now called her own had been the seat of power of the first and most important of his wives, which was now her.

The truth was Sai was the descendant of peasants so poor they routinely abandoned their female infants to the elements, or sold young daughters as slaves and concubines to those who could better afford to feed them. This fate had nearly been hers. But instead, she had some other unspeakably terrible experiences before coming to America. These she referred to frequently (without actually revealing what they were) to shame her daughter into some semblance of obedience.

Sai was not the happy woman she could be because her daughter refused to come up in the world in the same proportion she had. Her shame was that April had not turned out to be the kind of daughter a Chinese mother would want. April was a policeman, stayed out all night chasing the worst kind of human scum, occasionally going so far as to wrestle with them in the street. Sometimes she came home smelling of death. The rest of the time she spent with men of questionable character—oh yes, she knew all about corruption in the police department from TV and stories in the Chinese newspaper.

She thought April had no shame and had no honor, for if worm daughter had either, she would quit her terrible job, marry a Chinese doctor, and produce many children for her to brag about and properly discipline. This was a grievance she addressed every day and intended to correct in time. She stroked her baby the dog, frowning at her daughter.

"*Boo Hao, ni.* You rook bad."

"I'm tired," April admitted, standing in the arch. After her nap, she had gone into the women's locker room and showered when none of the officers was around. She'd felt bad having to do this, but it was better than using the bathroom for the public. She'd changed into the rumpled jacket and pants she kept in her locker for those occasions when close contact with a malodorous corpse clung to her relentlessly, refusing to go away lest she forget to do her duty. Not that changing her jacket and sweater could purge the smell of death from her hair follicles or her sinuses.

Sai's face softened. "You change crows. Notha muda?"

April nodded. Yes, there was another murder; and even though the bodies had been outdoors in winter for a very short period of time and contaminated her not at all, she had changed her clothes. Skinny Dragon was right on both counts.

"Know awleddy," Sai said with satisfaction.

"I'm sorry I didn't call. I didn't have time for anything. It was a bad day."

Sai nodded. "Know awleddy. You boss. Priece no can do nothing. Oney top boss Apra Woo can do."

April smiled in spite of herself. "Thanks, Ma. I appreciate your good opinion."

"No good pinyun. Oney say tooth." Sai spat out the shell from a pumpkin seed into her hand for emphasis, then put it in a dish on the table in front of her. Her mood changed abruptly.

"I velly sad, *ni*. Rike Elicka velly much. Velly solly brack man kirr. You allest?"

April moved through the arch into her parents' space without actually meaning to. "What are you talking about?"

"Tawking about Elicka Frinree," Sai said angrily, as if April were playing dumb with her on purpose. "Know awleddy you woking Elicka Frinree case. Happen rast night. Leason you no come home. You good girr, *ni*. You catch kirra."

Baffled, April stared at her mother. "Who's Elicka Frinree?"

"Big sta. Watch elly day."

Oh, now they were talking TV. This happened frequently. Skinny Dragon couldn't keep the lines clear between reality and outer space where the dragons and ghosts lived. April dealt with crazies like her every day. What one had to do was kind of social-work them into silence. Only then would they let you go to bed.

"Someone you watch on TV," April prompted.

"No mo." Sai shook her head angrily.

"You don't watch anymore," April translated. Could she go to bed now?

"Watch TV, no watch Elika."

"What show is this, Ma?"

"This TV show. You know."

April did not watch TV. She didn't know.

"You *know,*" Sai hissed. "Don't be douba stupid."

"What did you see on TV?" April asked, trying to soothe down the hysterical yin scales.

"No see you. How come you boss, not on TV?" she demanded angrily.

"You mean as a spokesman for the police?"

Sai nodded. "You make mistake?"

"I don't make mistakes, Ma."

Sai snorted and spat out another pumpkin shell. April frowned. She hadn't seen a new seed go into her mother's mouth and wondered how the second shell had gotten there.

Sai snorted some more and lapsed into operatic Chinese. "You make many mistakes," she screamed. "You didn't marry Dr. George. He liked you, you could have married doctor. Big waste, now marry doctor himself."

April didn't bother to comment on the likelihood of chubby George Dong marrying plump Dr. Lauren Cha anytime soon. This subject reminded her that she had spent part of last night with a Chinese ADA and liked him quite a bit. She wondered what her mother would have to say about a Chinese lawyer.

"Police say husband killed her because she make monkey business with best friend." In more operatic Chinese Sai changed the subject.

April sucked in her breath. "Who said that?"

"TV say police say."

April let her breath escape. "What show are we talking about?"

"Sarad Day."

April's heart beat furiously. She felt lightheaded with frustration, chewed on her bottom lip to keep from screaming back. Sometimes she actually had the evil thought of drawing her new 9mm on the dragon disguised as her mother and blowing it back to China where it belonged. "You're not talking about the news, are you, Ma?"

Sai clicked her tongue with disgust, put the dog

down on the floor, then stood to her full height. Maybe four ten on a good day. "TV say brack man kirr. What you say?"

April got it at last. "Merrill, her name was Merrill Liberty. Not Ericka Findley. Ericka Findley was a soap opera character, not a real person. Merrill Liberty was the real person, and we don't know who killed her."

"Brack man," she insisted.

"I'm going to bed."

"Spanish kirr girrs same." She was talking about jealousy. Now the dragon was really hitting close to home. "So, what you say now, *ni*?" Sai screamed.

April sighed wearily and let the fury go, if only for the moment. Another opportunity to slay the dragon passed without incident. Once again her mother won a battle in her own mind. April went back through the arch and headed home at last. "I say you watch too much TV," she called over her shoulder.

13

At 8:20 A.M. on Tuesday Daphne Petersen cracked open her apartment door and frowned at the Chinese detective who stood outside.

"You're from the police," she said, stating the obvious.

"Yes, that's what I told your doorman."

"What do you want? I can't see anyone now." The woman patted her lacquered black hair irritably. "Monica," she screamed. "Where the bloody hell are you?"

"I need to talk to you," April said.

"I just told you that isn't possible. I answered all your queries yesterday. That should do." Daphne tried to close the door. April's booted foot swiftly moved into the doorjamb to stop it.

The door whacked April's foot. She gave it a push, but the widow Petersen pushed back, determined to keep her out. Through the tug-of-war over the door, April could see a portion of Daphne's shiny silver-blue dress. "Look like silk," Sai liked to brag of her polyester bargains. Here the satiny sheen was very real. With some people, class and privilege made April feel humble and small, shy about asserting herself. This was not the case with Mrs. Petersen. The widow of a day didn't budge, and April felt the sneer behind her emphatic dismissal.

"Don't be alarmed, Mrs. Petersen. Often people have to speak with the police more than once." She took the calming approach.

"I don't see why."

"These things take time. Please open the door. I don't want to hurt you." The woman was begging for a cross-body block.

"Why bother with me when it's clear who killed them?"

"Well, before we make that important arrest, there are still a few details that need clearing up."

"Oh, my . . ." Daphne checked the scene in the room behind her, showing off the back of the complicated hairstyle that featured two tightly sprung black coils dribbling down her back. ". . . It's absolutely not convenient right now. You'll have to telephone for an appointment at some other time."

April opened her bag for her identification. "I'm sorry to intrude on your grief," she said smoothly, "but we're in the middle of a homicide investigation here. That's a matter of some urgency, wouldn't you say? I don't have time to make an appointment."

"I know who you are, and I know what you're doing. And I'll have you know I'm just as concerned about this as you are. I happen to be involved with the issue at this very moment. You'll have to wait downstairs until I'm ready for you."

"I'm afraid that won't be possible, Mrs. Petersen. I can talk to you here, or you can come with me to the station now."

"To the station? Who do you think you're talking to? I can't go to the station. Do you have any idea what's going on? There are people from the press all over the place."

April inclined her head. She hadn't noticed any in the immediate vicinity. "Maybe you can tell them you're helping the police with their investigation. I need to know a few things about your husband's habits, his schedule, and what you know about his driver."

"Wally?"

"Yes."

"Actually, I'm just giving an interview right now." The pressure on the door eased just a little. April gave the door another little shove, but by this time Daphne had made her decision and backed away, causing April to lose her momentum and fall into the room.

"What's going on, Daphne?" A large woman with bright red hair rushed to the door. "Sorry, didn't mean to abandon you, I was in the loo," the woman whispered. "Sick tummy." Then she gushed to April, "I'm Monica Abeel, who are you with and *what* can we do for you?"

April showed her ID and pushed farther into the room. The thick ice blue living-room rug was now snaked with fat black wires for TV lights. Some of the furniture had been moved and a love seat had become the focus of an instant TV set. A crew of three lolled around on the furniture eating doughnuts and drinking coffee from Styrofoam cups. The interviewer, a dark woman in an unbecoming lemon yellow suit, was on the phone.

"Oh, my," the redheaded Monica said. "Didn't you tell the officer we're working here?"

"She didn't want to listen. Deal with this, will you."

Daphne Petersen walked away.

April flashed to Steve Zapora and the mirror in Bed-Sty. *You, in the slutty blue dress. You with the bad hair. Yes, that's right, you. Stop.* She smiled and followed Daphne Petersen into the already crowded room as Monica Abeel clearly contemplated, then thought better of trying to physically detain her.

"Oh, my." Monica flapped after April, changing course toward the woman in the nasty yellow suit. "Oh, my. Cinda dear. Can you take a short break, darling? Daphne has just a *tiny* little chore to attend to in the other room. That's right, relax. Call out for some Chinese or something. Ooops. Come this way, Daphne, be a dear now and cooperate. This is all so difficult. Miss—"

"Sergeant—" April began. Across the room the TV crew looked alive.

"Never mind," Monica cried. "Come this way, dear."

"A cop?" The woman called Cinda drifted over.

Monica grabbed April's arm. "You're very pretty, aren't you? Do you have an agent yet? I've never seen a Japanese cop before."

April stared. "I'm Chinese," she said.

"Well, that wouldn't hurt sales either. Look, don't say a *word* to anybody without a contract." Her hand snaked into her pocket and came out with a business card, which she handed to April.

"I wouldn't dream of it," April murmured, taking it and thinking her mother would love this.

At 10 A.M., April was filling in her notes on Daphne Petersen's views on Liberty's violent temper, his abusive behavior to his wife, and Merrill Liberty's ten-year affair with her dead husband, Tor, when Hagedorn pushed open the door of her office. A huge grin transformed his pudgy face.

"Yeah, Charlie, what you got?" She glanced up at the detective and was reminded of a moon-faced bully she'd known in grammar school, who was now running half a dozen sweatshops in Chinatown that paid illegal immigrants starvation wages. The bully sweatshop owner had a complicated evasion system that nailed his partners every time there was a shutdown and allowed him to get richer and fatter every year.

Charlie leaned against the open door, one hand gripping the knob as if to keep it from getting away. He was wearing a green jacket, a yellow shirt, and a thin black tie. His girth was too big for the shirt. It gapped at the lower buttons. His jacket pockets bulged. His trousers hung dangerously low on his hips. Energetic for a change, he was punching the air triumphantly. "I thought I remembered something about this guy Liberty," he began.

"He was a famous football player," April suggested, wondering for the ten thousandth time just how dumb Hagedorn could possibly be.

"Uh-uh." Hagedorn continued grinning. "Something else."

"He's a stockbroker, makes a million dollars a

year." April tapped the phone, willing it to ring and transport her to another subject. "That's a lot of money."

"What are you getting at?" Hagedorn's eyes narrowed with suspicion. "What difference does that make?"

"No difference whatsoever." Except that Iriarte had told her he wanted them to go very gently on this one. Was that the reason he'd chosen gentle Charlie to do the deep background profile on Liberty and her to check out Petersen's will, and the close friendships and recent activities of his charming widow?

"No dumb mistakes," the lieutenant had told her before going home last night. He had thrust a finger in her face adding, "And watch that Sanchez."

April glanced at her watch, annoyed and suspicious of everyone. Why did she have to watch Sanchez? Was he up to something, or was Iriarte just nervous and wanted her to mess up, lose face and possibly her entire career on this thing? Mike hadn't phoned her last night, hadn't turned up yet, and hadn't bothered to call in with his plan for the day. So maybe he was up to something. She seethed at his coming in on this case and then going off on his own, pissing off Iriarte and keeping her in the dark. Why couldn't they get organized on this thing? She had thought they had a plan, but were they working to plan? Were they organized? No, they were not.

"What do you remember, Charlie?" she prompted cordially, as if she had a high opinion of him and actually wanted to know.

"Oh, I remember we had problems with this guy before." Hagedorn continued to clutch the doorknob, still undecided about whether it was safe to advance further.

"Problems with—?"

"Liberty, who else?"

"Ah, Liberty. What kind of problems?"

"Complaints from the neighbors."

"What about?" Hagedorn was so slow getting his

stories out that April yearned to
her knuckles.

"Screaming, yelling, domestic dist

"And—?" She kept her face dead

"And an officer went to the scen
dispute, possible domestic violenc
grinned. *So there.*

"An officer went to the scene. You have a name on that officer and the report, Charlie?"

"I suppose I can find it." His triumph deflated.

"Thanks."

"It could be significant." Belligerent now.

What was it with this guy? She flashed to the advice of a supervisor she'd had once: *When faced with a suspect trying to bash your head in with a tire iron, or stab you with a switchblade, don't, I repeat, do* not *unholster your gun and shoot the bastard even if the law says you don't have to wait for the glint of steel to do so. What you do, officers, is widen your perimeter. Why widen your perimeter? Because the asshole can't hit you if you're out of his range.*

April did as he'd advised and widened her perimeter.

"How many such reports, Charlie? Was the wife bruised? Was she in need of medical treatment? Did she go to the hospital? You want to check that out?"

He wanted to check that out. He nodded. "I'll get you every single incident in the bastard's life."

"That's great, Charlie. Do it."

He let go of the doorknob and turned to leave, then he turned back. "Oh, and one more thing."

April had already picked up the phone. "What's that?"

"Well, that phone call Liberty made to the victim. At the restaurant."

"What about it?"

"I checked it out. He didn't make it from the plane, or the limo coming into thc city. That call came from the phone in his apartment. He was already home. Twelve-fifteen."

...orn let that item hang in the air for a minute, ... turned on his rubber-soled boots and stomped ...way, leaving April's door open. Out in the squad room, a male in the holding cell started screaming in Greek.

So, Liberty and his wife had altercations that were so noisy the neighbors called the police on maybe more than one occasion. On the night of the murder Liberty had returned home and made a call to his wife in the restaurant where he knew she was dining with his best friend. But they'd already known he'd gotten home by midnight. Was it enough time for him to jog twelve blocks and wait for the two to come out of the restaurant? Did the chauffeur really go home as he claimed? Did Liberty know the chauffeur had gone home?

Eighty percent of homicides were committed by people who were related to or knew the victim. Only twenty percent were stranger killers. It was probably one of the three of them: Daphne Petersen (to make a fortune), Wally Jefferson (because he was a thief?), Liberty (because he was jealous). In any case there had to be somebody who saw something. It hadn't been snowing at midnight.

She dialed Jason's number. He picked up on the first ring. "I need your input here, Jason. What's your schedule?"

"Morning, April," Jason said. "I'm with someone."

"Thanks for picking up. When can we talk—?"

"I'm with someone right now," Jason repeated. "What about twelve-thirty? I can arrange a meeting then."

"You want me to come there?"

"Yes. See you." He hung up.

April called Dr. Washington to find out what was going on at the medical examiner's office. The phone rang ten times before voice mail picked up. April left a message and hung up the phone. Because it was outside the squad room area, there were two solid doors, a wall, and a hall between her and the Special

Cases office where Mike would return soon or not, depending on his mood.

Damn him. April dialed his beeper number. Five minutes later he called her back.

"Yo, *querida,* what's happening?"

"I could ask you the same thing. Where are you?"

"ME's office. We're in the middle of an autopsy here."

"Thanks for letting me know. Anybody I'd be interested in?"

"Yeah, Merrill Liberty, and guess who's with me?"

She sucked in her breath and had her fourth or fifth homicidal moment in the last twenty-four hours. Son of a bitch. For a second she was so mad at Mike she couldn't think of an appropriate reply. Then she said, "Who?"

"Your boss, Iriarte."

"That's great, Mike. That's really great. When are you coming in?" she asked coldly.

"Miss me?" he teased.

"Don't start that. You know I don't like being kept in the dark."

"Lot of things you don't like, *querida.* If I worried about everything you don't like, we'd never get anywhere."

"We aren't anywhere."

Mike sighed. "*Es verdad.* You took off on me last night. It's just like old times, isn't it. Ah, well. I'll be back with a preliminary in an hour."

"I may be gone by then, *chico.*"

"Oh, come on, April. Don't be petty."

"You could have called."

"So could you," he snapped back. The line crackled with New York static. "Just opening her up. Gotta go."

14

Jason was disturbed. By the clock on his desk, it was 12:35, but it seemed a lot later. He swiveled back and forth in his desk chair. "I'm not sure what you want me to do, April," he said, scratching at his beard as if he were truly perplexed.

"At the moment we have three possible suspects: Petersen's driver, Daphne Petersen—and your friend Rick Liberty."

"Fine, take the driver first."

"Wally Jefferson. He's a shady kind of guy. Liberty uses him occasionally, too. There's something off about the relationship. I'm not sure what yet. Liberty claims he stole his car. Jefferson says he had permission. Anyway, Liberty's car is missing."

"How is it relevant?"

"That's unclear."

"Okay, go on."

"The driver took Merrill and Petersen to the theater. That we know. We're not sure about the rest. Jefferson says Petersen told him to go home around 7:45. He claims he took Petersen's car and drove home to New Jersey. His wife swears he was home by ten-thirty and didn't leave her side until the next morning. We're checking with the neighbors to see if anyone noticed the limousine outside. We might find a way to shake the wife's story. . . ." April shrugged. "But so far we don't have a strong motive for Jefferson to kill his boss and Merrill Liberty. He doesn't have either the demeanor or the past history of a killer, not that that proves anything. Number two: Petersen's widow had a lot to gain and a strong motive. He's worth over two hundred million dollars. I think she'd kill her mother to get it."

Jason whistled. "Emma told me he was about to divorce her."

"At eight-thirty this morning, she was all dressed up for a TV interview in her living room. Tonight she'll break the exclusive story of Merrill Liberty's ten-year love affair with her husband. It makes you wonder where he got her."

"Lot of buying and selling of love going around."

"Do you think Emma was holding a little something back about Merrill yesterday?"

Jason frowned. "What do you mean?"

April flipped back the pages of her notes and read. "She said Merrill and Petersen were just friends, and Rick wasn't the jealous type."

"I remember." Jason didn't comment further.

"Daphne Petersen has a different story about them. She says Rick was extremely jealous and that he beat Merrill frequently."

Jason shook his head. "April, if the woman's a suspect, she would say that."

"Maybe."

"Anyway, it's hearsay."

"Not if there are witnesses to Liberty's abuse."

"Come on, April. This is garbage. You know that. Emma would have told me if she had seen evidence of abuse. And Merrill wouldn't have put up with it."

"What if she was fearful and ashamed?"

"No."

"We have a record of a 911 call about a domestic disturbance at the Liberty apartment," April went on unperturbed.

Jason's stomach growled. It had been a long morning. And this was news he didn't want to hear. He didn't want to believe this of Liberty. "You hungry, April? I have about forty-five minutes. You want to get something to eat and talk about this some more?"

April shook her head. "Sorry, I can't." She let him stew for a moment. "Jason, I need your help."

He heaved a deep sigh. "April, April, what am I going to do with you?"

"You're going to help me."

He shook his head. He knew whatever he indicated, his no meant yes, and she knew it, too.

She argued anyway. "Don't you want to find the killer?"

"I'm not a cop."

"That's never bothered you before."

"Well, it bothers me now."

"Look, all I want is for you to talk to Liberty, explore his violent fantasies a little, his true feelings about women, especially his wife. Find out if he could get mad enough to kill. You can uncover that."

Jason smiled. "I know how to do an evaluation, April."

"I know you do."

"Why don't you just give him a lie-detector test? That should do it."

"If it turned out he had opportunity, I'm going to need a psychiatric evaluation. Come on, Jason, you're talking to him anyway." April had her notebook in her lap. Her booted foot was vibrating with impatience. Jason stared at it. April was wearing a different kind of outfit than he'd seen on her before. Suddenly he realized that she was a different person now. She was all dressed up and a department big shot.

"He's still in denial, April," he murmured.

"Oh, yeah, what's he denying?"

"He can't believe they're dead yet."

"Could he look like a woman getting out of a cab?"

Jason laughed. "I think Emma would have known if she'd seen Rick that night. Have you searched his place?"

April shook her head. "We don't have a warrant yet."

"What makes you think the person whose cab Emma took was the killer? Didn't she leave sometime before it happened?"

"The killer could have been waiting for them to come out."

"Have you worked out your time frame for Rick's arrival and everything?"

"Working on it."

"Is a search warrant for his place forthcoming?"

"It's possible. Will you talk to him?"

"If you want a formal evaluation, my fee is a thousand dollars." Jason said it deadpan, but his eyes twinkled at April's shock.

"Jason . . . I'm not authorized to spend that kind of money."

"And you wouldn't anyway," Jason laughed.

"No, I wouldn't anyway. Why let money ruin a great friendship like ours?"

Jason smiled. A cop was telling him they had a great relationship. "What about my friendship with Liberty?" he pointed out.

"I'm not asking you to be an informer. This is not a formal thing. You probably wouldn't have to testify in court or anything."

"You're putting me in a difficult position here. I could get subpoenaed to appear in court."

"Look, it's getting late. I have to go. If you don't want to do it, just say so." April slammed the notebook into her purse. "It's not a big deal."

It was a big deal. Jason owed her. And so did Emma. He sighed again. Yesterday Emma had the night off because the theaters were dark on Mondays. Tonight she'd have to go back to work. He didn't like either of their positions. He and Emma were going to have to betray the secrets of a friendship to save a friend and repay a debt to a cop.

"You have the autopsy reports yet?" Jason asked.

"They're in the middle of Merrill's right now."

"Will you call me with the results?"

April looked surprised. "Anything particular you want to know?"

Jason pulled on his ear. "Cause of death, bruises, old injuries, condition of female organs—tox results."

April jumped up, excited. "Thank you, Jason." She grabbed her coat. Jason got up and came around his desk to help her put it on.

"Okay," he said. "I'll talk to Liberty. But I can't give you my results without his permission."

He was gratified by her many expressions of gratitude.

Still, he didn't rush to make the call. It took a few hours for Jason to dial Rick's number. When he did, the phone rang ten times before Rick's machine finally picked up.

"This is 555-8830. No one is available to take your call. Please leave your message after the beep." Beep.

"Rick, this is Jason Frank. If you're there, please pick up." Jason waited for a few seconds, then spoke again.

"Rick, this is Jason. It's four-thirteen in the afternoon. I'm between patients right now. How are you doing? Let's keep in touch. I want to talk with you about what's going on. Do you want to have some dinner with me later? If you're busy with your family, I could drop by for a few moments. How's your head? Let me know. I'll be screening my calls. . . ."

Finally Rick replied. "Yeah, Jason, what's up?"

"Ah good, Rick. You're there."

"I'm here."

"Thanks for picking up. How are you doing?"

"A lot of people are asking me that dumb question. I don't have an answer for it."

"Well, try. I can translate."

"I'm going crazy."

"Oh, yeah. What's happening?"

"I pace around and can't feel anything. It's nuts. I don't know what to do. I keep turning to Merrill and she isn't here."

"How's the head?"

"I have a hundred clients. Every single one has called me. They're hearing things about me and Merrill. There are these bulletins on TV. Every hour.

They're saying I'm suicidal. They're speculating about Merrill and Tor being lovers. It's crazy. She didn't even like him. He was my friend—"

Jason said, "Look, I'm going to have to go in a minute. Can I call you in an hour?"

"What are the police saying? What was the cause of death? Do they know what happened? Do they have any leads on who killed them? I can't stand this. I have to know!"

"I may have some news later. Do you want to meet?"

"Yes, but I can't get out of here. There are—"

"—Yeah, I know, press everywhere. They don't know me. I'll come there." Jason told him he'd be over around seven and hung up. For the next few hours he tried to convince himself he was doing the right thing.

15

April always tried to learn from other people's and her own mistakes. On the evening of the murders, she had been dressed in her usual uniform: a turtleneck sweater, jacket, slacks. Functional, not classy. The next day she had worn the same outfit most of the day until she had the chance to change into the wrinkled pants and jacket she kept in her locker for emergencies. Sometime during the night in a random dream about the ADA on this case, she suddenly felt that it was time to improve her image. She knew lawyers thought themselves many steps up from cops. She knew they thought cops were uneducated bullies who beat people up on the street, then lied about what their victims had done to deserve it. To appeal to a man like Dean Kiang, she knew she had to make herself look better than a cop.

Her former supervisor, Sergeant Joyce, had always worn suits with skirts to work. At six that morning, April decided it was time for her to wear suits with skirts to work. She prepared for class warfare with a slim, calf-length burgundy skirt with a slit to the knee, a powder blue turtleneck sweater (that looked like but was not cashmere) with a long silk scarf that incorporated both colors, and a short burgundy jacket that was just loose enough to disguise the gun bulge at her waist. She wore boots that did not hide the small size of her feet or slimness of her ankles. She wore makeup and small jade studs in her ears for good luck in all ventures, but especially in love. She knew from the way he smiled that Jason Frank had noticed.

When she entered Dean Kiang's paper-strewn downtown office, she was glad again that she'd made the effort. The Chinese DA was drop-dead handsome by anybody's standards, and she was smitten anew. He was taller and better educated than her former lover, the scrubby and manipulative night-watch-in-Brooklyn Jimmy Wong. He was more elegant and self-assured than the chubby and permanently disappointed-in-love (by a white girl who'd jilted him for a Pakistani in medical school) Dr. George Dong, the Chinatown eye doctor April's mother still wanted her to marry. He was more appropriate and had a higher status in life than the steamy but all-talk-and-no-action Sergeant Sanchez. For a minute April forgot about the victims in the case and stared at him openly.

Kiang was a tall man with a slender build but not the skinny, almost emaciated appearance of some Chinese like her father, who could not convert even the best diets to healthy muscle and fat. Kiang's features were bold and open, classical. April figured he had north Chinese, but not Mongolian, ancestors because of his height and build, his excellent nose and mouth, almond eyes. She thought she could feel the power and intelligence emanating from him.

Both shrewd and clever, his eyes pierced the air. He was a Chinese who didn't even try to seem like the perfect model of Tao teachings, the modest being with downcast eyes who let the wild winds and storms rage around him, deriving power by appearing passive and weak and never saying a word to betray his ambition or true intentions. Here was a prosecutor who could deal with the system and set things right. He was a lawyer in a well-cut gray pinstripe suit, white shirt, and red-and-blue-striped tie.

The elegance of Kiang's appearance was nicely offset by chaos in his professional space. Stacks of files were everywhere so that there was hardly any place to sit. April decided that Kiang was a flexible person, not the rigid and controlling type of man who had to have everything just so (including her) that she'd known in the past.

As April stared at him, assessing his looks and character, Kiang shuffled around the mess to create a place to seat her. Finally he moved his square briefcase from the chair closest to his desk, moved the pile beneath it, placed the chair even closer to his own, then gestured for her to take it. He stretched his long legs between stacks of files. Electricity crackled in the small space between their knees and hands. Dean's long legs in pinstripe, his beautiful face and body, even his law degree were attractive. April's lips were dry. She worried that meant that she had been staring at him with her mouth open. Delicately, she licked her lips and dropped her eyes.

"Well, you're the best-looking detective I've ever seen." Sitting opposite her, Kiang took his turn to look her over, and he did it by aiming his view as if through a rifle sight from the top of her head down the length of her legs all the way to his own right shoe that was close enough to nudge hers. "But then, I've never worked with a Chinese detective before."

"Thanks." Released, April looked up, beaming. Sanchez was always telling her that professional didn't mean she had to be absolutely stony all the time. Now she took his advice and smiled, assuring herself through the giddy flush of pure female pleasure at being admired by such a handsome man that she was still a cop, still a sergeant, still on the job. Still grinning, she turned her attention to the office and searched for a photo of Mrs. and/or baby Kiangs. She didn't see one, smiled some more.

"And I've never worked with a Chinese prosecutor," she murmured.

"This should be interesting then." Kiang was also speculating. His eyes traveled to her left hand where he looked for a wedding ring and didn't see one. "Married?" He found a pen under a pile of papers and carefully set it down beside a new yellow legal pad as if he might take a note on her answer.

"No."

He shrugged. "Not that it matters. Boyfriend?"

April shifted uneasily in the chair, not sure what the right answer was. She had the possibility of an inappropriate boyfriend, one who did not always call and keep in touch as he should. One who only talked about being hot for her. On her side, it was true she often thought about what Mike would look like without his clothes, aroused. How compelling he'd be like that. What he'd feel like touching her, kissing her. What she'd do back. But they always ended up wrestling the bad guys to the floor, not each other. Did such a candidate count? "Who has the time?" she said finally.

"Exactly. That's it exactly." He picked up the pen and made an exclamation mark on the yellow page. No time. April gathered that he was unencumbered and gave him another warm smile.

He returned the favor. She was absolutely certain she'd sleep with him, and for about a minute there was a break in time. The appropriate thing on such an occasion of instant attraction was to get right to the important matter of exploring family trees and ties, aunts, cousins, sister cousins, young and old uncles, as well as Chinatown and other connections. Likes and dislikes, and hopes for the future. For sex to be exactly right, it was necessary to determine if there was compatibility in these other vital areas.

April was too shy and Kiang was too polite to make these inquiries, however. This overlooking of her connections made April think that Kiang's must be vastly superior to hers. His father must be a doctor or an engineer or a very rich businessman. His mother could well have many children, all boys, all professional men who went to top colleges, made much money, and wore pinstripe suits every day to their offices like Dean did. This truly excellent family would no doubt disapprove of a cop girlfriend for their golden son and brother. On this dismal thought, time began again.

"How about lunch?" Dean asked abruptly. "We should get to know each other better."

An hour and seventeen minutes later Kiang was in court and April, with a glow on her face and a delicious Chinese lunch in her belly, caught up with Rosa Washington in the medical examiner's office.

"You can talk if you walk. But shake a leg, I'm in a hurry." Rosa Washington was still drying her hands as she swept out of her suite, forcing April to jog after her. She was wearing a fresh scrub suit but no cap. Her black hair was in a pageboy, and she was all business.

"Any leads on the killer?" she asked.

"Yes, some," April said.

"Well, give. What do you have?" Rosa arrived at the fire stairs and opened the door.

"You first," April said. "What did you find in Merrill Liberty?" Rosa started down the stairs, again compelling April to follow her lead.

"Didn't your partner tell you?"

"Sanchez? He's from Homicide. He's not my partner," April told her back. Rosa knew that.

"He didn't put you in then." Rosa skipped down the first flight of stairs.

"Put me in on what?" April spoke to Rosa's back as she trotted down the stairs.

"The loop. God, those guys will screw you every time." Rosa spoke to the air in front of her.

Guys in general, or cop guys? "Slow down a minute, will you?" April asked.

Rosa showed no sign of hearing the request. "Why did your buddies hold out on you?"

"They didn't hold out. I've been in the field all morning. That's why I wasn't present at the autopsy myself."

"I wondered why you didn't show. I thought nobody told you."

That too.

Rosa hit the next floor still running.

"Maybe you'll keep me informed on the next one," April suggested.

"We're doing the next one now."

"Petersen?"

"No, Abraham's still home sick, but thinks he's coming back for Petersen tomorrow."

"I gather you have your doubts."

"Yes, I do." Rosa slowed down suddenly the better to deliver her good news. "His voice sounds like a dying cat. Worse than yesterday. My bet is Malcolm ends up in the hospital tomorrow. You know, you could help me out. We could help each other here, two little minority girls and everything."

"Oh, yeah." Which one of them was little?

"How about getting your buddies in the puzzle palace—and the DA's office—to pump up the pressure on getting the autopsy results. If Abraham gets too many phone calls on Petersen, he'll have to give in and let me do the job. He hates negative publicity even more than having a deputy hog the limelight." She turned and resumed her charge down thc stairs. "Anyway, it's my turn."

The puzzle palace was police headquarters. April smiled at the thought of having buddies in that place where a bunch of mortal ghosts she didn't know could elevate or destroy her with the stroke of a pen. She considered herself neither a girl nor a minority. Certainly not a little minority girl. She'd never heard anyone talk like that. Most minority girls like herself and Rosa acted like they were normal people. Like the rainbow pals on TV sitcoms.

"I'll see what I can do. What about the results of Merrill Liberty's autopsy?"

"I heard you just got promoted." Rosa hit her third set of stairs, still jogging, not panting a bit.

"I did."

"So, you know how it is when it's your turn."

"Yes, Doc. I do."

"You can't let those guys keep you out of the loop."

"No, you can't."

Rosa laughed. The sound was pleasant, like soft water on stones. "You don't have much conversation, do you?"

"I was just thinking about the case. What about the Liberty woman?"

"Okay, okay . . . There were no bruises on the face, or body. Just the one wound in the neck. Neat, precise. The killer knew what he was doing, was not an amateur. What do you think of the DA?"

"He's cute," April said.

"You think so, really?"

"Sure, for a prosecutor."

"You think he could talk to his boss?"

"I don't know, Rosa."

"Ask him. And then I'll call you when I do Petersen. Here we are. You want to come with me? You might learn something on this one. It's a burn victim. She smells like barbecue."

"Ah, no thanks. Can you fill me in a little more on the Liberty woman?"

Rosa sighed and stopped in the hall outside the swinging metal doors. "She had a tipped uterus. You know, people used to think you couldn't get pregnant without surgery to fix it. That's baloney. She did have some scarring in the uterus, though. Probably couldn't have children."

"Botched abortion?"

"No way to tell. Might have been surgery for endometriosis. She had some endometriosis in an odd place, behind the uterus where it would have been hard to detect. She probably experienced quite a bit of pain, but who knows?"

"What else?"

"The disc between the fourth and fifth vertebrae in her neck was badly compressed. A few of the others also showed signs of degeneration. She probably had sciatica that affected her right leg."

"How do you know that?"

"Her right calf was half an inch smaller than her left. That meant she wasn't exercising it, had been favoring her right leg for quite a while. The muscles had begun to atrophy slightly."

"So this wasn't a recent injury."

"Probably wasn't an injury at all. She might have had arthritis. She had some deformation in the bones in her feet, particularly her toes. She probably took a lot of ballet classes when she was a kid. She might have had the sciatica for a long time, years."

"Anything else?"

Rosa thought for a second. "Everything else was pretty normal. I'll get a report to you in a day or two."

"Tox results?"

"Same. Look, I have to go; you sure you don't want to see this one?"

"No thanks, I'm not fond of human barbecue."

"Very funny, Woo. You're not so bad, after all."

April didn't think that was funny. But she was pleased to be liked.

"And remember to call your DA boyfriend for me. I need all the help I can get." Rosa pulled a green surgical cap out of her pocket and put it on, tucking her pageboy carefully around her glasses and into the cap without needing a mirror. Then she tied the strings under her chin and smiled at April a last time to show what buddies they were and how enthusiastic she was about her work.

16

A hard icy rain fell steadily at seven-thirty when Jason pushed through the small stakeout of reporters still encamped in front of Rick Liberty's building. There were fewer than the night before, but they were just as persistent under their umbrellas and tents. Several called out questions to Jason, but he didn't even turn to see who was talking, just shook his head.

Upstairs in the apartment, Patrice from the restaurant was serving drinks and food to several of Rick's friends, but it was Rick who opened the door. "Thanks for coming," he said. He took Jason's coat and stepped around some recent florist shop deliveries to hang it in the closet.

"Wow, this is something," Jason murmured. The large space was crowded, filled with plants and floral arrangements, some not even opened yet. Most of those that had been set out on the floor and tables were white. Lilies, tulips, roses, baby's breath, carnations, bonsai of azalea, blossoming branches. A stack of gift and condolence cards sat on a table. It was a stunning display.

"Yes, isn't it crazy?"

Voices drifted in from another room. Jason noticed the buffet set up in the dining room and a well-stocked bar on a living-room table. He longed for a drink. "Am I interrupting?"

"No." Rick waved his hand at the doors to the library. "There are a few people here. They're eating and watching TV. I haven't the heart for it. Come in here."

Jason followed him into the living room, sat on the long white sofa, and put his briefcase down on the floor beside him.

"How about a drink?" Rick asked.

"Club soda. I can get it."

"No, no. That's my job. How about something to eat? Do me a favor and eat something."

Jason shook his head. "Not right now, thanks."

"You're too easy." Rick went to get the drink and returned in a moment with a heavy crystal glass for Jason and nothing for himself. "Jason, the police are going to release Merrill's body tomorrow. Her parents want to bury her in Massachussets on Thursday. I know it's a hassle, but will you and Emma be able to go to the funeral?"

Jason did not show his dismay at another workday lost. "Of course we'll come. I know Emma wouldn't want to miss it."

"Thanks, it means a lot to me." Rick frowned as Jason took a new spiral notebook out of his briefcase and opened it.

"What's that for?"

"I wish I could say it's my security blanket, but I'm here partly on business."

"Business?"

"Yes." Jason took a swig of club soda and wished it were a scotch. "The police have contacted me about you."

Liberty stared at him. "No kidding."

"Rick, I want to tell you right up front that I know and trust and respect you very much. I also care about you a great deal. To Emma and me you are family."

Rick gave him an ironic smile. "Thank you, Jason. I love you and Emma, too. Why did the police call you?"

"I also happen to believe that you are a victim of some kind of bizarre, kafkaesque web of terrible events."

Rick's eyes stayed on the notebook. "What's going on, Jason?"

"The police have asked me to do a psychological profile of you, Rick."

Rick barked out a surprised laugh. His discomfort gave it a hollow sound. "What for, do the police always dig around to this degree?"

"I have the impression that the police do an in-depth check of every suspect in a crime they're investigating. It's like working up a business plan."

Rick shook his head. "But why you?"

"There's a connection between me and the investigating officer, April Woo. And also between her and Emma. You know, Emma was abducted last spring."

"Yes, Merrill and I were out of town when it happened. But I have an idea how bad it was for both of you." He looked as if he wanted to say more, but stopped there.

"April was the detective who saved her life. I owe her."

"Jason, would you like a real drink?"

"I would, but I won't. . . . April came to my office today to ask for my professional opinion of your character. I told her I could give my personal opinion, but I could never do a professional assessment without your approval."

Rick rubbed his chin and seemed shocked to find unshaven stubble there. "All this astonishes me. I don't know what to say."

"In spite of my bias in favor of you, I would be working as an agent for the police. The disadvantage of the bias is that eventually, the police may ask someone else to do another. The advantage of my doing one now is that the alternative will most certainly be someone who may not have the warm feelings for you that I do."

Rick flashed another ironic smile. "Well, with such a recommendation I don't see how I could refuse. How is it done?"

"You've never had psychological testing before?"

"I've had intelligence tests, neurological tests, X

rays, even an MRI scan of my brain. I did that for Merrill."

"Oh, really, why?"

Rick hesitated. "I suppose you're going to ask about brain injuries, concussions, blackouts. My—so-called temper, all that?"

Jason nodded. "And incidents of violence in your childhood."

"There were none."

"I'm going to ask you for your whole family history, which will include questions about any family member who heard voices, broke down, or was ever institutionalized or hospitalized. I'm going to ask about substance abuse, violence, if anybody's gone to jail." Jason sighed.

"I don't know about my father, so I can't answer all your questions about his side of the family," Rick said quietly.

"You may not think you know a lot of things, Rick, but you'd know if someone in the family went to jail for killing a man in a bar fight. You'd know about physical abuse. You'd have seen or heard it."

"I had an aunt who committed suicide," he said softly. "My grandmother was raped by a white man when she was thirteen. I'm not supposed to know it. But I do. She wasn't yet fourteen when my mother was born."

Jason wrote it down. "And I'm going to ask you about your headaches and your temper. Let's start with your grandmother."

17

Mike concentrated on the medical examiner preparing for the autopsy of Tor Petersen. She was like an actor, dominating the stage. He guessed all doctors were like that, even doctors of the dead. He glanced at Ducci standing beside him, all anticipation. Why was the dust and fiber expert so hot to be there today? Mike chewed on the ends of his mustache, mulling things over. This was Mike's second autopsy in as many days, and part of him felt as if he were wasting precious hours in the ugliest part of this squat blue brick building, just spinning his wheels. Autopsies took a lot of time. He watched the preparations, trying to let go of the conversation he'd had last night with his mother about April Woo.

"This is the body of a well-nourished, well-developed white male measuring six feet one inch in height and weighing approximately one hundred and ninety pounds. He is wearing a gray knitted sweater—hmm, cashmere, and gray slacks with an alligator belt. Slip-on leather shoes, gray and red tweed socks." Rosa Washington switched off the recorder and moved away from the microphone and the autopsy table to let the photographer take one more picture of the dead man clothed as he had been at the time he died. Flash. "Finished?"

"Yeah."

"Okay, boys, your turn." She gestured to the techs to come in and undress the corpse and moved to where the green-suited Sanchez and Ducci stood gloveless, with their masks pulled down around their necks, each casually using the bottom of his metal throw-up pan as a writing support.

No part of the ME, however, was visible under the green surgical pajamas, green cap, rubber gloves, glasses, and mask with a respirator. Clearly the woman did not like getting splashed with body fluids and did not want to breathe in any contaminated air with the potential to fatally infect her. For a few minutes she was silent, as off came the dead man's shoes, labeled and dumped by two burly assistants into the box Ducci would take away with him to examine later. Off came his socks. Into the box. The dead man's alligator belt was already undone, his mud-and blood-splattered pants already unzipped. The two techs lifted the body at the hips and tugged off the damp, stained trousers. Underneath, the shorts were soiled with urine and feces. The odor soared above the pervasive formaldehyde stench. Off came the shorts. Mike put on his mask.

"Only the shorts, please," Ducci said sharply, as if the techs might add a turd to the box as an extra.

The dead man's penis popped into view. The ME glanced at it, then turned away. "Hey, Ducci. Haven't seen you since Nashville." Through the mask her voice sounded strangely mechanical, like the voice of telephone operators.

"Yeah, don't get around too much anymore." He watched the techs pull off the dead man's sweater. Nothing under it. The dust and fiber expert's thick gray-flecked eyebrows went up at that, and he pulled on an ear.

"Something?" Washington asked about the corpse, but kept her gaze on Ducci. "What brings you here?" She adjusted her glasses on the bridge of her nose.

"Cut on his chest?" Ducci pointed to a tiny irregularity among a sparse furring of chest hairs below his sternum.

The ME moved under the light to look at it. "Looks like a little nothing," Rosa murmured, running a gloved finger lightly over the area Ducci indicated. "Maybe a pimple, I don't see any blood here."

"Mark it and measure it," Mike said.

Flash. The very first picture of the naked body was the chest area photographed with an arrow pointing to the spot of Ducci's query. "Very thorough." Rosa nodded her approval and turned to Ducci again.

"We're honored to have you with us, Freddy. What brings you into the light of day?" she asked again.

The macabre autopsy room—gruesomely fitted out with electric saws, carts of cutting instruments in all sizes, aspirators, containers to save tissue and fluid samples from many sources, and the ageless metal dissecting table, ducted and plumbed for the draining and sluicing of body fluids—intensely flood-lit as it was for the best possible investigation of the examinant of the moment, was hardly the light of day.

"Very funny." Ducci guffawed politely at the joke. "Gotta make sure you guys do your job right, don't I?"

The ME laughed politely herself. "You know I do my job right." Even distorted, her tone held the sharp edge of defensiveness.

Ducci made an offering. "I liked your talk in Nashville."

"Well, it's a damned shame autopsy is becoming a dying art. No one's doing them anymore. Insurance companies won't foot the bill in hospitals. Families don't want them." Rosa widened her audience to include Mike. "With all the lab tests, MRI scans, X rays—everybody figures they already know what killed their loved ones. Nobody wants to learn any more." Angry at the loss to science, she glared at them through her glasses.

"Lot of good work being done," Mike said soothingly of the forensic field in general.

"Maybe in some areas, but a lot of people out there who should know the difference between the bruise from a fall and the battering from a club don't know.

A lot of people out there are getting away with murder. Makes me mad."

"Well, not here in New York, Rosa. That should be a comfort to you."

"No, it isn't. Those ignorant coroners in the big field look at a female body or child's covered with bruises—scars accrued over months, years maybe—husband, father says, 'She fell off a ladder. Can I bury her now?' idiot buys it, doesn't even do X rays. People beat and kill every day and get away with it. Makes me really mad."

A thousand times Ducci had heard the complaints from MDs about coroners in the great Midwest. MDs called the Midwest "the big field" and said it was the best place in the country to commit murder. There, coroners were elected. They were untrained in medicine, certainly untrained in forensic medicine, and they had no idea how to assess the questions and answers on the death reports thcy filled out. Everybody had a soapbox. He glanced at Mike and changed the subject.

"I'm surprised Malcolm isn't here doing the honors himself." The chief medical examiner, Malcolm Abraham, was a well-known celebrity hound who hated to miss an important body.

Flash. The photographer started photographing the rest of Petersen's naked body.

"Believe me, he wanted this one. He's in the hospital, high fever. They're not sure what it is. Lucky for me. I got to do the girlfriend yesterday. Malcolm wanted to wait another day for this guy, but you know how it is. You can't fight City Hall. Lucky for me." Rosa snorted at her luck, then turned back to the dead man. "Well-built fellow, looks like no one abused *him*."

Mike scratched his neck as they turned the corpse over to photograph the other side. The ME was right. He didn't see any other mark on the body anywhere. No sign of struggle, no defensive wounds. Unbroken manicured nails. Mike looked away as the techs washed the body.

When they were done swabbing, Rosa moved back to the table and switched on the tape, began talking into it as she picked up a scalpel and carefully made the Y incision that cut the late Tor Petersen open from each shoulder down to the pit of the stomach and through the pelvis. For a second the whole of his lower body cavity was visible. Stomach gases and feces further sickened the air. Fluids began gushing into the area faster than they could be suctioned out. Mike breathed in and out through his mouth, pinching his nose in his mind.

Ducci remained motionless, seemingly oblivious to the stench as Rosa Washington clipped the dead man's rib cage apart from bottom to top, dividing it into two sections. Clotted blood and other fluids reeking of iron covered her rubber-gloved hands. Clamps cracked the ribs apart, and the lungs and liver were revealed. Mike swallowed, swallowed again. Body fluids spewed out, splashing the sleeves of the ME's surgical gown and filling the channels on the table. A tech turned on the tap to wash down the table.

"How's it going?"

Mike was startled by the familiar voice behind him.

"What are you doing here?" He gaped at April, who hadn't made it yesterday, then swallowed again, gagging a little in spite of himself.

"I got a message from the doc here to join the party." April offered him her vomit pan. "You know the rules. You use it, you clean it."

Mike waved it away with his own. "I'm fine."

"Shush, please. The microphone picks up everything." Up to her elbows in stinking gore, Rosa Washington peeled away the lungs, lifted out the liver, weighing it in her hands and exclaiming over it.

"Just what I would have guessed. Must have been a big drinker, look at the size of this." She told her recorder the liver was enlarged, examined it carefully, took some sections for further examination under the microscope, and dropped it on the scale with a splat. Very enlarged indeed.

Then she dug into the chest cavity for the heart and dissected it free with a series of swift cuts. This, too, she held up to the light in her two hands like a trophy she had just won.

"I think we'll find this to be the heart of the matter," she told them. "You noticed, of course, the amount of blood when I opened the chest area. Hello, April Woo, glad you were able to make it. I like to have the detectives on a case with me. It isn't often I get the pleasure of really conscientious ones, however. You all right?"

April had sneezed into her mask. "Yeah."

"Where was I? Oh, yes. The heart of the matter. I think we'll find a perforated infarction here." The ME put the heart and pericardium down on a separate table and began to dissect them.

"What, you ask, is a perforated infarction? Possibly a ruptured aneurism caused the blood to flow out into the pericardial sac until the pressure was elevated to a point where the heart can't beat anymore under natural circumstances. The heart dies so fast it actually perforates—tears. Yes, yes, it's perforated. Here's the hole."

She fell silent for a long time, forgetting her audience as she examined the heart, then told her recording machine in technical terms what she found. Finally she moved on, methodically, removing each organ, examining and weighing it and taking tissue samples for slides. She opened the stomach and examined the contents.

"What's your take?" Mike had been fidgeting.

"He'd just finished quite the hearty meal. Nothing's digested here. Looks like chicken, cooked apples. Rice. Beans, greens. Hmm, bananas. Looks like soul food."

"I mean, is there anything for us to stay for?"

"Oh, we've got a long way to go. Got to x-ray, got to do testes and aspirate his bladder for urine samples. We got to open his head and take a look at his brain. More than once I've missed a cause of death until I opened the head. Once there was blood all over the place, but I couldn't find a point of entry on the corpse anywhere. It turns out the guy had been shot in the mouth with a twenty-two. Bullet was lodged in his skull."

"Oh, yeah, the jumper," April said.

Dr. Washington ignored the remark.

"But that's not the case here," Mike said quickly, shooting April a quizzical look.

"Oh, no. This guy died of a heart attack. Doesn't mean I won't find he had prostate cancer or something else, though."

"Well, I've about had it, then," Mike said. "How about you, Duke?"

"Yeah, thanks."

April accompanied the two men to the door, then peeled off to the ladies' locker room. "Don't you dare leave without me," she said. "I'll meet you in five."

"What'd she have to go and bring up the jumper for?" Mike muttered.

Ducci laughed. "Probably has her reasons."

Mike gazed after her, wondering if his mother could be right about April after all.

The dust and fiber department in the police lab was a long narrow room with three windows on one side and sea green porcelain tiles halfway up the wall on the other. The floor was a grungy gray-green linoleum that hadn't known a shine since the day it was laid. Years ago, the room served as a dust and fiber lab for one scientist. Now there were supposed to be three dust and fiber people to cover all the felonies in New York City, but one had retired six months ago in fear of losing his vision after twenty years of focusing his whole being into the eye of a microscope. He hadn't been replaced.

These days Fernando Ducci, who'd started as a patrolman thirty years ago, and Nanci Castor, a thin-faced civilian with a good blond dye job who'd just hit forty and didn't look it, manned the microscopes alone. Since very few crimes could be committed without the perpetrator taking something from the scene away with him and leaving something of himself behind, Ducci and Castor thought theirs was the most important job in law enforcement. They had to identify and match those physical traces that could prove a suspect had been at the scene of a crime: a snag from a victim's jacket in the backseat of the suspect's car, a spot of oil from the suspect's basement on the murder victim's sleeve, a clump of asphalt from the suspect's driveway on the robbery victim's front porch. A hair with an unusual dye found in a cap by the body of a murder victim that matched the hair of a suspect who said he'd never been near the murder victim.

Ducci and Nanci went through the items collected by the criminologists in the Crime Scene Unit. They searched for connections that were more subtle than fingerprints and DNA, for the means to make a match between disparate people who might live far away from each other but who were somehow linked by a deadly crime.

Nanci was out when Mike, Ducci, and April returned from the ME's office only a few blocks uptown. Mike picked up the skull on Ducci's guest chair and examined it briefly before setting it on the desk. The skull sitting there the last time Mike had visited Dust and Fiber had had a bullet hole in it and buck teeth with many cavities. This skull had no bullet hole and perfect teeth.

"What happened to Roberto?" Mike asked, meaning the old skull.

"Someone stole him. He was a gift, you know, from the Guatemalan police." Ducci's slicked-back, shiny black hair did not move as he shook his head sadly at what the world had come to. Then he sank into his desk chair. In a dark suit, black-and-purple silk tie, blue shirt with white collar and cuffs, Ducci was an anomaly. His mouth was small and puckered with concern. His face was round and unlined. Except for the winged eyebrows flecked with gray, he still looked like the choirboy he'd been forty-five years ago. He opened the side drawer of his desk that was filled with Snickers bars and took three out.

"How about some lunch?" He offered the first to April. She shook her head, still very quiet.

"Queasy?"

She shook her head again. Just not hungry. Mike gestured to the chair. "Sit down."

"So who's this?" he asked about the new skull.

"I think she's Asian, look at that set of teeth. Now, there's a woman who didn't eat sugar. I think I'll call her Lola." He peeled open the paper on one of the Snickers bars.

Mike's mustache twitched as the scent of chocolate suddenly mixed with the chemical and death smells that recently had lodged in his sinuses.

Ducci pushed a candy bar across the desk. "Come on, I'm paying."

"Uh, no thanks."

"You two. Can't enjoy a party." Ducci took a huge bite of his and chewed happily. "Don't ever say I don't buy you lunch," he said with his mouth full.

"If you bought us a *food* lunch, we'd eat it, right, April?" Mike glanced at April. She didn't look good.

"Oh, come on, this is food. Take. It'll do you good." Ducci finished the first bar, shrugged, started on the second.

Mike swallowed a rising tide of stomach acid. "We've gotta go in a minute," he muttered. "Any thoughts before we leave?"

Ducci threw the candy wrappers in his wastebasket and brushed his hands together, cleaning up for business.

"Well, remember Rosa said the Liberty woman was struck just once. The site of the wound was barely above the clavicle. There were no hesitation marks on the neck or chest. Her injury was a direct hit to the carotid artery, and the victim bled to death. Probably fairly quickly."

Ducci put his hand to his mouth and rubbed his pink lips with his fingers. "We're still drying out her stuff. I haven't even got all his things. So it will be a while before I've done my analysis. The thing is, I can't picture what happened." Absently he stroked Lola's uninjured skull.

Mike sucked on his mustache. "No hesitation marks. So she wasn't threatened or tormented. No bruises, nothing under her fingernails or his. So neither fought back."

"Maybe there wasn't time," Ducci murmured.

"Maybe they weren't afraid," Mike said. He glanced at April again. She wasn't talking.

"Someone they knew."

"Yeah. Quite possibly it was someone they knew." Mike tapped a pencil on the desk. "April, are you all right?"

"Sure."

"Mike, I get the feeling it was an accident," Ducci said.

"Oh, yeah? How do you see that? You think a friend showed up, just happened to be carrying an ice pick. And this person who just happens to be carrying an ice pick meets his two pals coming out of the restaurant on a night when their driver was not waiting on the street. So what's the scenario, Duke? This friend greets them, then strikes the woman a lethal blow. And this blow occurs in a very special place—"

Ducci nodded, demonstrating the sites with his hands. "Higher in the neck the thyroid and trachea cartilage is in front of the carotid artery. A person would have to slit the throat with a knife or a razor to get to it. Where this guy strikes is where the carotid artery has turned the corner and is in the very front, the most exposed place. No knife or razor was necessary."

Mike scowled. "Then how do you see accident here?"

"It was too direct a hit, but not a professional hit. A professional wouldn't use an ice pick, too uncertain.

He'd have to get too close to the victim and would never go for one and not the other. Nah, this person struck once and took off, probably in terror. . . ."

"How about somebody saw him?"

"Well, that might be your man Patrice. But accident keeps coming to mind. You know what jealousy and rage is like. They lose their minds, keep stabbing away, killing the victim over and over. This just isn't that."

"One homicide, one bum ticker. The DA's going to go crazy with this, huh, April?"

"Yes, he is," she said, opening her mouth for the first time.

"You're looking for someone who knew them real well," Ducci said.

"How about the wife?" April said.

"Why would she kill Merrill Liberty if her husband was already dead of a heart attack?" Mike said.

"Petersen didn't have the heart attack until the killer arrived. Maybe Daphne intended to kill him, but he died of shock before she got to it. Stranger things have happened."

"Imagine the prosecution trying to prove that she scared him to death."

"She'd scare me to death," Mike muttered.

"Daphne Petersen still has the most to gain," April pointed out.

"Ah, I don't know. What about Liberty? What's his profile? Is he a man of iron control—a person capable of studying medical books, planning a job like this, hitting her in just the right spot?" He shrugged again. "He ever hurt people before, off the field, I mean? How cold a guy is he? Most of them kill the boyfriend first, and then the wife. They don't kill the wife and leave the boyfriend to die of a heart attack. A little too pat, somehow, isn't it?"

"I'm having someone do a profile on him."

Mike turned to her in surprise. "You didn't tell me that."

"We haven't spoken recently."

Ducci tapped his pencil. "That's good. I'm wondering if maybe Liberty knew he didn't have to kill the boyfriend. Maybe Petersen was incapacitated already."

"In the restaurant?"

"Yeah, in the restaurant. That would ring, wouldn't it?" Ducci said.

"That would ring." Mike patted the skull.

"Doesn't ring to me," April said.

"Why not?"

"You're talking about a big strong guy who could snap a neck like his wife's with two fingers. Why kill her with an ice pick? Well, I've got to go." April grabbed her coat.

"I'll come with you. See you, Lola," Mike murmured to the skull.

18

On Monday Rick Liberty was taken to identify the body of his wife in the morgue but was not allowed in the room to touch her. The rest of that day and the next day he stayed at home, receiving his and Merrill's friends as was appropriate for one in deep mourning. He provided a splendid spread of food and drink, but did not dress up or make much of an effort to speak with his guests. No one but his partners seemed to expect it. On Tuesday evening he spent several hours reviewing his personal and family history with Jason Frank for the police. The interview required a great deal of reflection and forced him to think about things he had pushed out of his mind for a long time. Throughout the interview, he managed to preserve a facade of calm and restraint, but the experience triggered a deep rage. Rick did not sleep at all on Tuesday night. By dawn on Wednesday morning he could no longer bear the inaction of waiting.

Early in the morning Rick decided to test the waters outside his building. He did not know that today would be the day of Tor Petersen's autopsy or how much was at stake in what the medical examiner found. He figured that people from the press would again gather around his building to see if this would be the day for him to come outside and break his silence. He knew that the police already considered him a suspect. He figured they, too, must have their representatives watching the building. Before making his move, he wanted to talk to Jason again, but he was afraid to call him.

He now had a three-day stubble that was thick and surprisingly gray for a man of only forty. He was glad he'd always been so very particular about his appearance. No one had ever seen him tattered or with a three-day growth. Now he was glad to look as ugly as he felt. There was a doorman, but no elevator man, in Rick's building. He took the elevator to the basement. Before eight o'clock, no one was around. He traveled through the dark halls to the storage bin assigned to his apartment. He dialed the combination, unlocked it, and went in without turning on the light. After only a few minutes of rummaging around, he found what he was looking for: a rusty-colored parka, stained and dusty from years in a cardboard box that had not been properly sealed. Near it was a pair of lace-up snow boots, with their sides flopping over. He put on the snow boots and cut off part of the laces with the knife on his keychain so the tops would continue to flop. Underneath the jacket he wore a sweatshirt. With the hood of the sweatshirt up he looked dangerous. In his neighborhood, people would not make eye contact with dangerous-looking black men. He relocked the storage bin and went out the building on the Fifty-sixth Street block. No one was looking for him there.

At 11 A.M. Rick walked into the Persian Garden on Ninth Avenue and Forty-eighth Street, where Wally Jefferson was waiting for him in the empty restaurant. Jefferson was sitting with his back to the wall at a table for two, drinking coffee and reading a racing form. When he saw Rick, he dropped the paper and got up.

"Mr. Liberty, I'm sorry for your loss," he said. His cap was in his hand. He hung his head to show his respect.

"Sit down, Wally."

Wally sat down. "You okay, man?" he asked solicitously. "You look bad."

"Let's talk about your well-being, not mine." Rick sat down in the outside chair, pinning Jefferson in.

When a tiny Asian woman came over to take his order, he waved her away.

"Look, I said I was sorry about your car. It was one of those things. You know how it is." He looked at Rick strangely. "You okay, man?" he asked again.

"I don't steal people's cars, Wally. So I don't know how it is." Rick clenched his fist.

"I didn't steal the car. I told you I—"

"You stole the car."

"Now wait, that's a cold way of looking at things. I was a little strapped. I needed it for a day. I'll get it back."

"Wally, you listen to me. My wife and best friend are dead. I don't give a damn about the car."

Wally looked scared. "No sir, I didn't have nothing to do with that. I swear." He was nervous. His eyes darted toward the door. "I swear it, man. Nothing to do with that."

Rick's fist hit the table. His knife jumped off the edge and struck the floor, making a loud clatter in the empty room. "You're a liar!"

Wally eyed the knife. "No, man. He sent me home, I swear it. I don't know nothing about it."

"What do you use the cars for?" Rick's fist hit the table again. The tiny Asian woman came out of the kitchen. "How about you order," she said calmly.

"Coffee," Rick said without looking at her.

"Espresso, cappuccino, latte, Turkish? What kind coffee?"

"Regular coffee."

She went back into the kitchen.

Wally shook his head. "You don't look good, man. Maybe you should see a doctor."

"I want you to understand me, Wally. I need to find out what went wrong here. You understand. You're not going to shit me. I'm going to know."

"I told you—"

"No, you didn't tell me."

"I can't tell you nothing about no killing. I don't

know about that. They were fine when I left them." Wally looked at his hands guiltily.

"Then what do you know about?"

"I got two kids. I don't know nothing about nothing." He gave Rick the goofy smile of a dumb person catering to a smart one.

Rick studied the grin for a long time, holding Jefferson's gaze until the Asian woman brought the coffee. Then he got up, dropped a five-dollar bill on the table, and left the restaurant.

Through the window, Jefferson watched him head downtown. When Liberty had passed from his view, he pulled a cell phone from his pocket and called Julio. "You have to get that car back for me. I'm coming out to Queens to get it now," he said and hung up before the Dominican could argue.

19

At six-thirty on the morning of Merrill Liberty's funeral, Mike called April at home to offer her a ride into the DA's office in lower Manhattan where they were meeting Dean Kiang at eight.

When she picked up after two rings, she was panting. *"Wei?"*

"*Wei,* yourself. It's me."

"Oh, Mike. What's up?"

"What are you doing?"

"What do you think?"

"You alone?"

"What do you want, Mike?"

The voice coming at him had started cool and was getting cooler with every exchange. He didn't want to let her know it bothered him. "I thought we might make a formal date, have dinner tonight."

"Oh, I don't know. Let's see how the day goes." She sounded weary now.

"That's pretty evasive."

"Well, I've got a lot to do. I may be busy."

"Still evasive. I get the feeling things aren't going too well with us."

"I don't know where you'd get that idea," she replied, downright frosty.

"You're not talking to me, *querida.* We may be working the same case, but you're out there, flying away from me. I can feel it."

"And that's the right way to go." April finally exploded into the phone. "Mike, you call me *querida* in front of everybody. I'm not your darling. I've never been your darling. You humiliated me for a whole year at the Two-O, and now you're starting all over again at Midtown North. If you mess me up here, I get dumped out on the street with a big thud. Do you understand what I'm saying here?"

"Hey, what's going on—?"

"This is not a question of face for me. I'm telling you, don't play with me anymore."

"What are you talking about, I never played with you."

"Oh, come on, you know you did. You get off on making everybody think I'm your girlfriend."

"I want you to be my girlfriend. I love you."

"But I'm *not,* Mike. You're creating an illusion of something that isn't true. I'm just trying to do my job here. I don't want to take the heat for something I'm not doing."

"Jesus, April, I love you. Why make everything so complicated?"

"It's only complicated when you don't get it. This game is over."

"Oy, that was cold. I told you I love you. I don't say that a lot."

"It's like being on the take, or drinking on the job. You shouldn't say it at all, Mike. Just drop it."

"Do we have to talk about this on the phone?"

"Yes, I don't want to talk about it on the job."

"April, you're all mixed up about this. Loving you is not like being on the take."

"Well, maybe it is for me. Maybe I don't want you to love me. Maybe it's a complication I just can't afford."

"Fine, I called you on business. I was thinking, we don't need to take two cars all the way downtown. How about I just come by and pick you up, simplify things."

"You can't pick me up because we won't be coming home together, Mike."

"Okay, I got it. Message delivered." Mike hung up and sat looking at the phone. She was driving him nuts. What was with this woman?

Two nights ago Mike's deeply religious mother had

asked Mike about his relationship with *la novia china.* He assured her that April Woo was a moral woman, like her, his dearest *mamita,* and that his love for April was pure. He thought that would be a pleasing thing for his mother to hear.

Instead Maria Sanchez was troubled by it. "*No amor ardiente?*" This didn't sound like her son.

"This one is different," Mike explained.

"No one is different, *m'hijo,*" she said, flashing him a sly little smile.

"What's that supposed to mean?"

"Even good women have *amor pasionante* these days, *m'hijo.* Even old ones," she added, and she smiled again.

The smile was both shy and daring at the same time and stunned him with its directness. Mike had never seen his mother as modern or daring in the least. Just a few months ago she'd worn only black, claimed she was an old woman of past fifty, finished with life and ready to fly up to heaven to meet the dead husband who was the only man she'd ever known. Now she was wearing rouge and hinting that celibacy was a thing of the past even for women of her ripe age.

"*Mamita,* what's happened to you?" he asked, shocked.

Maria Sanchez didn't even blush. Her son was a famous policeman who'd seen the most terrible things and been written up in the newspapers. But he still had a few things to learn, a few things she could teach him. "*Embrazala,*" she suggested.

He frowned. No, it didn't work that way with April. She was too tough. He tried to explain that it was no easy matter to kiss someone carrying a gun, who could shoot you instead of kissing back. But Maria wouldn't hear it. Kissing was the only way, she insisted. It made him sick with worry how he might carry it off.

"And don't wait too long, *m'hijo,*" she warned.

April was already in Dean Kiang's office when Mike got there at two minutes to 8 A.M. He could see her foot as he came down the hall. The foot, in its new boot, was jiggling up and down. Another thing he'd never seen before. As he got closer, he saw that her right leg was crossed to the left and she was leaning forward to the right, talking animatedly to the DA. The DA's hair had fallen over his forehead and he had a smug look on his face that Mike wanted to punch into his skull.

April was wearing her jade earrings and a new deep green jacket. Her cheeks were pink. With a deep pang, Mike realized that she was excited and happy. Mike had only seen that spark in her a few times, and both times she'd had a few beers and her guard was down. He knew it meant that she was opening up to this guy, was vulnerable, and he tensed to defend her. He could feel the heat of her excitement and his own rage ignite at the same time. Determined to get her back to business where she belonged, he burst into the room smiling a big fake smile.

"Sorry I'm late."

Kiang looked up. "No, Sanchez. In fact you're early. Way too early."

"What's going on?" Still smiling, he glanced at April, but she didn't look at him. Kiang made a noise as he breathed out.

Oh, it was going to be one of those days. Fine. He took Kiang's briefcase from the third chair and let it drop. He looked surprised at the smack it made when it hit the floor, then sat in the chair with his coat on but open, his knees spread apart. He was aware of his gun holstered under his arm, knowing full well that the sense of power it gave him in situations like this was a false one.

"What have you covered so far?" He gave April another searching glance, but she'd shut her face on him.

Kiang ignored the question. "Why don't we start with a status report."

"Fine. After you." Mike bowed to April.

She shook her head at him, warning him with her

expression not to be an asshole. He decided he would if he felt like it. So much for maturity.

"We don't have a full death report on either victim, but preliminary findings indicate Merrill Liberty was stabbed at the base of her neck once. One time only," she emphasized.

"We knew that on the scene," Kiang said.

"Now we know it for sure."

"So?"

"Indicates she wasn't expecting it, wasn't afraid. She let the perp get close to her. Could have been a stranger if it was someone who wasn't threatening to her, but it seems more likely that she knew her attacker. The second victim died of a heart attack."

"So that rules out Petersen's wife and anyone else who had it in for him. His death is a natural."

"Not necessarily," April said.

"Oh?" Kiang tapped the pen on his knee, staring at her.

"The ME hypothesizes the heart attack was triggered by shock, or stress. However, the tox results might show something different. . . ." April glanced at Mike and he nodded.

"Any reason for that?" Still staring at her, Kiang dropped the pen and started tapping his foot.

April shifted uneasily under his gaze. Mike knew what she was thinking. The ME's office had discovered poison in the body of the last heart attack victim they had investigated, which turned a routine unnatural death inquiry into a homicide investigation. She put it another way.

"Who would attack a woman standing right next to a companion over six feet tall and built like a linebacker? It doesn't make sense."

Kiang smiled. "That clinches our killer."

"How do you figure that?"

"Liberty was well known to both of them. He came from his home, waited in the dark for them to come out."

"Why go for his wife and not Petersen?" April

asked. "Why stab her once and walk away? What kind of guy does that?"

"A cold-blooded killer." Kiang retrieved his pencil and punched the air with it. "Maybe he intended to kill the wife and keep the friend."

"So he jabs his wife with an ice pick in front of his friend and then strolls when the friend has a seizure?"

Mike shook his head. "Odd profile of a violent killer, wouldn't you say?"

"Who said violent? This is a sophisticated guy. He doesn't have to be excessively violent to get his way."

"Give me a break, Kiang."

"So maybe the friend's seizure was planned, and that was why Liberty could kill in front of him and walk away as he died."

"That would make it a conspiracy," April said.

Kiang nodded. "Yes, indeed. Maybe Liberty had something going with Petersen's wife, and they were in it together."

Mike stroked his mustache. "Sounds a little far-fetched to me."

"Stranger things have happened, Sanchez. All right, let's get down to business. What do we have on motive? April, how's your shrink doing on Liberty's profile?" Kiang demanded.

"Dr. Frank told me he'd have something for us to look at end of today or tomorrow the latest. He has to type up his notes."

"Did he give you any specifics?"

"No, he didn't tell me anything but what I've just told you."

"Is he going to be helpful?" Kiang asked.

April shrugged. "Jason? Depends what you ask for."

"What else on Liberty?"

Mike spoke up. "We have extremely conflicting reports, what we might call an unclear picture."

"Oh?"

"Yeah, Daphne Petersen is adamant that Liberty's a violent and dangerous guy. She says Liberty flew off the handle all the time for no reason. He was verbally abusive. Did you see her on TV last night? It was in the paper this morning she saw Liberty punch and kick his wife on at least three occasions in the last year. I wouldn't give that too much credence," Mike said.

"Emma Chapman, Merrill's best friend, said he's a pussycat, wouldn't hurt a fly," April added. "Patrice, the restaurant manager, says he's the kindest man in the world. Direct quote, 'He adored her.' "

"Maybe those two are lying."

"I don't know about that. I spoke to her parents on the phone. They said Liberty was a doting husband. They're certain their daughter would not have tolerated an abusive relationship—"

"We've heard that line before."

"Oh, come on, Kiang. The parents wouldn't protect him now if he was a violent type," Mike argued.

Kiang cut him off. "Next item. What else have you got, April? Have you run the route and confirmed Liberty could have done it in the time frame?"

"Not yet."

"Anybody see anybody fleeing from the scene?"

"Not yet."

"Anybody see Liberty leave his apartment or come back?"

"If anyone did, he isn't saying," she murmured.

Kiang's foot stopped tapping. "Someone will," he predicted. "Any way a person can get in and out of the building without being seen?"

"No confirmation on that yet, either."

"Jesus. What have you people been doing with your time? Okay, go try it. Run the route, see how long it takes. See if Liberty could have done it."

Mike saluted. "Yessir."

Kiang ignored the gesture. "If you can fit Liberty in the time frame, we'll have motive and opportunity—probable cause to do a search of his place. Meanwhile, keep him talking all day, casually tell him what a trial will do to him, see if you can get him to confess. It would make things a lot easier." Kiang was finished with them. He checked the gold watch again. "See you later."

"We don't have a motive for this guy. What an asshole," Mike muttered as they left.

"And Liberty won't be there," April murmured. "Today's his wife's funeral."

A few minutes later a wrathful April stalked up Mott Street with Mike striding beside her.

"Come on, April, talk to me."

The temperature had dropped to nearly zero. Zero in New York was really cold. The unappetizing, weary-looking leaves and stems that Chinatown grocers clipped from their produce and threw in the gutters were now frozen still lifes in black ice. Mike crunched over them in his cowboy boots. The boots were new, black and white snakeskin. With thick socks, they kept his feet warm and dry. He wondered what April was up to. Chinatown was pretty shut down in weather like this. All the little stores that hung their merchandise in the doorways and stacked it on flimsy tables on the sidewalks in good weather had moved operations inside. Only the Chinese newspapers were stacked outside on the tables today. April's face was muffled in a long scarf. As animated as she had been with Kiang before Mike arrived, she was shut down now. He figured it was time for a showdown.

"Where are you going?"

April stopped her uphill trudge on Mott for a moment and lowered her scarf. "Do you have any idea what you looked like in there, Mike?"

"What?" Mike was wearing his new black leather, three-quarter-length coat, heavy enough for any weather, new snakeskin boots, a slick gray jacket with a silvery shine in the weave, charcoal trousers, and a black shirt with a green knit tie. He'd taken great care with the combination, had deodorized, perfumed himself, combed his hair many times to get it just right. He'd even trimmed his mustache so it didn't look too wild for the occasion. He thought he looked his best ever.

"How could anybody tell the bad guys from you? You're crude. You talk and look like a dealer."

Mike was called worse nearly every day. But not by anybody he cared about. He was taken aback for a moment, then he made a huge effort and smiled. "Nah, I don't look that good. No gold, no rings, no bracelets. I'm a poor honest cop." Mike took it a little further and laughed. "Yo, you think I should let my hair grow and wear a ponytail?"

He knew where April was coming from, figured her feet in the prissy little East Side boots were completely numb by now. The cloth, Upper-East-Side-lady coat and tailored skirt were a dead giveaway. She was not dressing for the job. She was dressing to attract the DA. Yep, he could see that her feet hurt and she was freezing. She blew a cloud of steam out of her mouth, started walking again. She was so stupid that he feared she actually liked the guy.

"You're steaming, baby, you getting primed by the DA?"

"Trust you to have a filthy mind," she spat out. "We're working a case, remember?"

"Hey, you can't fool me. You've got the hots for that dumb DA. You slept with him yet, *querida?*"

The muffler was up again, but April's eyes could not disguise the erupting volcano behind it. "You acted like an asshole in his office, and now you're acting like an asshole with me. What's your *problem?*"

"Hey, I may be a dumb cop. I may not wear a monkey suit and loafers with little tassels like your little *pendejo* lawyer. But lady, you better watch who you're calling an asshole."

"You were out of line in there. You call that smart?"

"You think suits make a man, huh? Tassels, *cojones?*"

"Pubic hairs and balls, very cultured, Mike. I'm impressed with your style." April plunged her hands deep in her coat pockets.

"You brought it up."

"Well, I guess you don't understand what any of this is about." April stopped in front of a dirty window with displays of ugly dried twigs and leaves and powders. Chinese labels on different colored pieces of paper, but the prices in dollars and cents.

"Oh, I understand what it's about. You don't care if a guy's an asshole. You just want the asshole to wear a suit."

"Hey. It's not that."

"What is it then? He's Chinese? He's sexy and I'm not?"

April didn't answer.

"Oh, great. This is great. I've always been straight with you. You wanted respect. I respected you. I met your parents. I took you to meet my mother. I didn't just throw you over my shoulder and take you to my cave, show you how a real man makes love, so you don't think I'm sexy. This is a switch. I didn't grab you, so now you think I'm dumb and crude." God, he was loco, a gored bull. His face burned with the pain.

Hers was white. "Look, I like you. Why don't we leave it at that."

Like you. "Like you" meant she didn't find him sexy. That meant he saved her face all these months only to lose his own.

"I have to go in here. You all right?" Her voice was soft now, seemed to quaver in the frigid air.

Chinese apothecary. Sold disgusting powders made of insects, dead animals, mold, ghosts and dragons, fish guts and bone, leaves and twigs. For every ill known to man and woman. Not sexy, not lovable. Ugly and crude. Mike's heart was splitting. He turned to go back down the hill to find his car.

"Meet you at the Park Century in half an hour?" April asked anxiously.

He called over his shoulder, "That's where I'll be. Hey, and while you're in there, why don't you check out if they have anything to cure assholes."

20

Wally Jefferson did not find Julio that day in any of his usual hangouts in Queens. He found him in the Magic Club off Broadway in West Harlem at 9:39 in the evening. Julio was leaning against an unpainted side wall, drinking a Corona from the bottle. From the way he was standing it did not look like the beer was his first. But the five or six other men weren't standing at all. They were sprawled on chairs scattered around the otherwise unfurnished room in various states of nodding off. Only one grizzled grandfather was watching the basketball game on the TV in a corner, smoking a cigarette and talking to himself.

As Wally gave the signal to the one vigilant man at the door and was let in, Julio turned away from him. He wore a scarf with three knots tied on his head. Wally knew the knots were some kind of code for bad. He'd been frightened by Liberty and chilled from his daylong search and Julio's lack of acknowledgment. He wasn't in the mood for a display of bad dude. He crossed the space between them on the tips of his toes like the boxer he used to be.

"Hey, man, I told you I needed to talk to you."

Julio's eyes were dead. He shrugged. *"Diga me."*

"Don't give me any of this Spanish *mierda*. I need that car back. And I need it now."

"Why need?"

"Because my boss is dead and so is Liberty's wife."

"So people die."

"These people are *muy importante,* Julio. You have Liberty's car. He reported it stolen. His wife is dead and because of the damn car he thinks I had something to do with it."

"Thees is no my *problema.*"

Wally bunched his broken hands. "This *is* your problem. The car has to go back."

"Why?"

"I told you. He and the police think I killed them. I ain't going to prison for killing no woman."

Suddenly Julio smiled. Seven gold teeth flashed at Wally. "Man, wo-man, what difference?"

"Hey, I didn't have nothing to do with this killing."

"No se nada."

"Don't give me that shit, man. They're going to tie this all together, they're going to tie you into it. You're not safe if that car doesn't go back to the garage."

Julio laughed. "Thees is no my *problema.* Is yours."

"Okay, you want to see it that way, just tell me where the car is. I'll pick it up."

"Thees is the *problema.* I don't know where the car."

"What do you mean you don't know? You used it. Where did you put it?"

"Other guy take."

"What guy took it?"

"Don't know name."

"The guy took the car?" Wally was stunned.

Julio nodded. His hollow eyes held a glimmer of amusement. "Took limo."

"You let him take my car?" Wally couldn't believe it.

"Not your car."

"Jesus, are you crazy? The guys in the garage know me. They know me on the street. Why'd you let him take it?"

Julio shrugged.

"What happened? Did something go wrong?"

"Yeah, went wrong."

Wally looked around and took a deep breath. No one was interested in their conversation. Wally's buddies were all too wasted to join a fight on either side. Julio was a small man who owed him a car and a lot of money. "Went wrong" didn't sit well with him. He considered busting Julio's head, then decided to be smart.

"I want the car and my share of the money."

Julio shook his head. "Don't know about the car, but I'll get you some money. You take off. Okeydoke?"

Wally nodded. "Fine, but don't shit me. I want the whole amount."

"Okeydoke. I'll get."

"When? Don't make this hard," he warned.

"Sabado."

"What the hell is that?"

"Saturday."

"How about tomorrow?"

"Saturday."

Wally chewed on his lips, looked around at his wasted buddies, then nodded. He didn't want to push this Julio too hard. The little man was known to carry a machete under his jacket. Saturday it was.

21

As the elevator door opened, Rick Liberty could see that the reception area was empty just as Marvin had promised it would be. The door to Marvin's office was open. He sat alone at his enormous desk, his head bent over some papers. Rick pushed back the hood covering his head and the lower part of his face. He unzipped his down jacket that covered the laptop he clutched close to his chest. Underneath the parka, he was dressed in the same well-tailored gray trousers and sweater he'd been wearing for four days.

By rote he'd taken the clothes off to shower several times when he tried to cleanse his mind and find a way out of the tunnel. But the showers didn't help. He was deep inside a pit of darkness and couldn't find a way to go. The stock market had taken a huge dip of 350 points in the last two days on the threat of a rise in interest rates. The market fall looked like a major correction. His clients' portfolios were lined up like soldiers in his laptop computer, demanding his attention and review. But he didn't care about the market.

Other thoughts disturbed him, and he wanted to hide away like a wounded animal. Tor and Merrill were dead, and Rick Liberty knew there was something wrong with him. In the instant of their death he'd been robbed of himself. The famous Liberty, who'd always known how to turn a bad situation into a good one, was suddenly completely at odds with the world, too ashamed to face it.

Marvin looked up and gestured him in. For some

reason the gesture frightened Rick. Suspicious of some kind of trick, he quickly pulled the door toward him and looked behind it, then felt stupid to see the space was filled with a Health Rider. Something new in the lavish private office of Marvin Farrish, president and chairman of the board of FCN, the largest black-owned cable-TV network in the country.

"Come in, Rick. Don't worry, no one else is here." Like a cat stretching, Marvin unfolded his compact body from the tilt and swivel orthopedic chair specially designed to ease his lower back pain. The chair and the Health Rider clashed with the massive brass-and tortoiseshell-inlaid French Empire desk and the rest of the priceless antiques. Everything fought for attention in the huge and ornately decorated office that had its own kitchen and private elevator to which only a few of Marvin's closest associates—and his bodyguard—had access.

Marvin Farrish liked to tell white folks that because he had not been tall enough to be a basketball player, dense enough to be a football or baseball player, musical or funny enough to be an entertainer, or handsome enough to be a movie star, he had had to invent some new little thing for a man, black as coal, to be. The white folks usually laughed uneasily when he said this, not sure exactly where the barb was aimed.

"We missed you at the funeral." Marvin opened his arms and crossed the room, eyeing his famous friend as uneasily as white men sometimes regarded him. He tried to give Rick a hug but was prevented from getting close by the computer Rick still held to his chest as if it were the only thing keeping him alive. Drawing away, Marvin waved a hand at one of the two huge armchairs placed in front of his desk.

"Go ahead, sit down. You look like you need a drink."

"I need more than a drink, Marv." Rick sat in the chair, making it look small.

"You sure? I have everything." He waved at the liquor cabinet hidden behind closed doors.

"I know you do."

"Okay." Marvin sat in the other chair, making it look large. "What did you do to your hair?"

Rick reached for the top of his head. "Nothing. What's wrong with it?"

"You've gone gray, man. What happened?"

Gray? Rick was startled and lost his train of thought, didn't know what to say. There was no sound in the office but the ticking of a clock that told the time in six major cities around the world. The ticking clock reminded Rick of the shrink, Jason Frank.

"You're going to need time, a lot of time to deal with this, Rick," Jason had told him. "There are a lot of stages people go through after a death, before they begin to feel better." Jason had never sounded so clinical to Rick before. Since his interview, he now understood where they were going with these questions, what he was looking for. He hadn't told Jason everything. How could he?

Rick listened to the clock and knew his time was running out. As Merrill was being buried in Massachusetts, the police had been in his building all afternoon. The Chinese and the Latino rode up and down in the elevator, timing the trip from his apartment to the basement. From his bedroom window, he had seen the two cops cross the garden that had won so many design awards to the matching building facing Fifty-sixth Street. He'd seen them exit through the gate to the street at a walk, at a run. He'd heard from the doorman that they'd also tried the underground routes through the basement and the garage. There were at least six ways out. He'd heard they tried them all. Then they interviewed the people in the building about his and Merrill's habits, even people in the neighboring buildings. By now they would have found out about the fights and Merrill's screaming. One of the maintenance men and a garage attendant apologized to him for having to tell bad things about Merrill.

"I'm sorry for your loss," Marvin said to break the silence. "She was a good woman."

"Yes, she was," he said with no hesitation.

"It looks bad when a man doesn't go to his own wife's funeral."

"You did a nice job covering it," Rick said. "I appreciate it."

"Her folks are good people." Marvin grimaced and rubbed the small of his back. "It was a long ride to the cemetery and back. . . . It took me all day to go, my friend. You had a lot of friends there. We needed to show that, didn't we? Wouldn't be good for the community not to show respect."

"Well, I appreciate it."

"You're looking real guilty, man."

Rick was startled. "What are you talking about?"

"Merrill's folks believe in you, Rick. Why'd you let them down?"

Rick shook his head. "I spoke with Merrill's parents several times. They agreed that under the circumstances my presence would be more inflammatory than soothing."

"I'm not sure that *I* agree."

"You can be assured that I will visit them as soon as I can. It's a private thing."

"No, it's not a private thing, Rick. You're Liberty, understand? You're public property. You belong to this community. You've got to do what's right. You can't let your friends and your community down and then expect me to protect you."

"I don't need your protection, Marv. I didn't do anything wrong."

Marvin looked around his crowded office, his whole face a question. "Then what you doing here, man?"

Rick was engulfed by hellfire. He could feel it licking at him, teasing him with eternal damnation. He squeezed his eyes shut. "Okay, I do need help." He had to grit his teeth to say it. "I need help, okay?"

"Oh, now you need help. Why not go to your partners? Won't they help you now that you're not Mr. White Nigger?"

Rick's jaw worked on his fury. He didn't want to let go and kill a friend. Involuntarily, Marvin moved his chair back. Rick knew how scary he must seem.

"Oh, they'll help me. But I don't want that kind of help."

Marv made a church and steeple with his fingers. "Give me a hint. What kind of help?"

"I don't want to hide behind a criminal lawyer."

"Really? Why not?"

"Because I didn't kill my wife."

"You think I'm a dumb nigger?"

"Shit, don't start that nigger stuff with me. I hate it. Can't you ever let it go?"

Marvin's first slammed down on his beautiful desk. "No, I can't."

"Shit. You're as bad as they are. Makes me sick."

"Fuck you, asshole. You done a lot of things wrong here. Maybe *you're* the dumb nigger. You didn't answer my calls. What do you think I am?"

Now Rick pushed his chair back. "Where are you going with this, Marv?"

Marvin glanced at the laptop in Rick's arms, then gave him a hard look. "Why did you let your friends and your community down?"

"I'm the victim here!" Rick's voice rose in fury. "Don't you get it? I'm being set up. The net is closing in. The police are all over my life. You understand? People I haven't seen for ten years have left messages on my machine telling me the cops called about incidents"—he raised his hands—"things that happened—"

"They're doing a background search. So is every TV network, every tabloid." Marv shrugged, then he laughed. "So are we."

"Why? Why?" Rick closed his eyes against the heat of hell.

"Just in case," Marv said. "Just in case." He paused

for a moment, then he said, "What do you want, my friend?"

Rick took a deep breath and exhaled. "You have resources. You know what's going on. You have to find out about this guy Wally Jefferson, Petersen's driver. I know he's involved somehow. He says he left Merrill and Tor in the restaurant on the night of the murders. But Tor promised me he'd bring Merrill home in his car. Tor knew I didn't like her out on the street at night. Why would Tor let the driver go home on such a bad night? It doesn't make sense."

"Maybe you're making too much of it."

"The man stole my car while I was in Europe."

"Your limo?"

Rick nodded.

Marvin stroked his chin. "Hmmm. How'd that happen?"

"I was away. He took the car out of the garage. I don't know what he wanted it for." Rick changed the subject. "I need to drop out of sight for a day or two."

"You want me to use my sacred position in this community, where I'm respected as an honest man, to hide a suspected murderer?"

"Oh, come on. I can't even kill a cockroach."

"You almost killed me a few minutes ago, my friend."

As sudden as a tiger, Rick lunged out of the chair, his fist clenched. From behind his desk, Marv watched him without flinching. Rick stopped in mid-gesture. He fell back into the chair, shaking his head. "I'm under a lot of stress."

"Watch the antiques," Marv said softly.

"Okay, think of it this way," Rick said wearily. "When I'm proved innocent, you'll be the only one in the country with the story. How does that sound?"

Marvin turned his head toward the window, but the magnificent view from the high floor was shrouded by heavy velvet drapes drawn against watchers and the night. "Looks real bad when a man doesn't attend his own wife's funeral," he murmured.

"Doesn't mean I won't love her as long as I draw breath."

"You should try a black woman next time."

Rick shook his head. "It never was about color for me. It was about her, but you'll never get that. You're a dumb nigger. You're as dumb as they are."

"Still, I'm the dumb nigger you came to. You haven't been to my home for dinner in a while. Elsie also missed you at the funeral. She'll be glad to know you're all right." Marvin rose and hit a switch, dousing the lights as they left.

22

At 8 A.M. Friday, Lieutenant Iriarte slammed his fist on the pile of newspapers he'd neatly arranged on his desk. He'd stacked them up like pancakes and looked as if consuming them had been a long and bitter breakfast. He scowled in turn at the five detectives in his office as if each one had personally failed him, the department, indeed, the entire Criminal Justice System.

"What the hell is happening here?" The squad commander was having a cow, and the effort of controlling his temper and losing it at the same time caused a vein to pulse dangerously in his forehead. His cheeks flushed purple.

April had seen that particular facial hue for the first time on a tourist from Des Moines having a heart attack in a Chinatown subway station. It had been only by the sheerest chance that they'd gotten him to the hospital alive. She had a familiar impulse to turn to Mike, find out what he was thinking, but after what happened yesterday, she knew all possibility of closeness between them was over. His behavior proved she'd always been right about one thing. Men and women could work together, but they could not be friends or lovers. To this view she didn't think her own interest in Dean Kiang presented a contradiction. Falling for the right man was business everywhere, even in America. She returned her attention to Iriarte as he raised his voice.

"What do you people think you're doing?" Iriarte had wanted the case tied up by today. The commander of the precinct had wanted the case tied up by today. The police commissioner and the mayor had wanted the case tied up by today. That was a lot of people wanting something that hadn't happened. And who was taking the heat? his voice insisted. He was. "What are you, stupid?" he demanded.

April could feel Mike's eyes on her. Was he stupid? Iriarte slammed his fist on the newspapers again.

"You two talked to him all day. You were supposed to make nice and clear this thing up, Sanchez. I thought you assholes had this under control."

Mike's mustache began to quiver. He was not having a good week. He didn't like being called an asshole. "Are you finished, Lieutenant?" he asked softly.

No, the lieutenant wasn't finished.

"You told me you had this under control. You told me we had plenty of time. I'm reading here in the newspapers this guy has a history beating women, and now I find out he took off. Where was surveillance? Getting a sandwich. Do we know where the suspect went? No, we don't. So you shits don't have anything under control." Iriarte's fist came down on a copy of the *Star*.

The headline read NOT THE FIRST TIME, over an article about Liberty's brutal attack of a white coed in Princeton nearly twenty years ago when he was in college there.

"With all due respect, sir, since when do you read the *Star*?" Hagedorn's face was as pale as his boss's face was red.

"I don't fucking read the *Star*!" Iriarte blasted the tiny room.

"Then how come you got it there?" Hagedorn muttered.

"My wife reads it. It was on the kitchen table last night when I got home. You know they buried that poor woman yesterday. You want to know who was at her funeral? Half of fucking Hollywood was there. Every star you can name. Half the black community—

Was her husband there? No, he was not there. You know what they're saying?"

"Who?" Mike said solemnly.

"Huh?" Iriarte lost his train of thought.

"What who's saying," Mike persisted.

Iriarte scowled at him. "The whole world. The whole world is saying California may not be able to convict, but New York can't even *find* its killers."

"Since when do you care what's on TV, sir?" Hagedorn said.

"I don't have time to watch TV. I get home last night. My wife is crying."

April knew where Mike was going with this. She didn't dare look at him. She tried to focus on the issue and brush the ghost of her feelings for him away. Iriarte's wife was crying last night. Again.

"You know why she was crying?"

"No, sir, why was she crying?" April spoke with a straight face.

"She was crying because she didn't see anything on the news last night about our arrest. You understand? Even *my wife* is asking why we haven't arrested the bastard yet." The venom spurted over to April. "Woo, you tell me why you didn't arrest the bastard yesterday when you had a chance."

"We didn't have enough yesterday, sir," April said softly.

"What do you mean you didn't have enough?"

Mike straightened his shoulder against the wall where he was leaning against Iriarte's blackboard. His expression said he didn't like the way Iriarte was handling this. Maybe Iriarte was the stupid one.

"We don't have the tox reports on Petersen yet. The COD may have been a heart attack, but we're not convinced yet that there weren't contributing factors. We're not convinced yet that Petersen's widow didn't have something to do with his death."

"What the fuck does that have to do with nailing the bastard for killing his wife?"

April raised her own shoulder in a half shrug. This

hysteria wasn't like the commander at all. He liked women to be women and men to be gentlemen. He wasn't one of those commanders who had a girlfriend in the office on the side and thought the rules of the department and the law were different for him. As far as she knew, Iriarte had never spoken like this to her or anyone else. Who was he scared of, the commissioner or his own wife?

"We don't have a clear picture yet of what happened that night, sir," she replied.

"What? What?" The commander grabbed the purple handkerchief decoratively arranged in his suit breast pocket and mopped the shine from his forehead.

"There are some things that aren't clear. There's a lot of lab work to do. A lot of background work."

"I did the damn background work." Hagedorn waved his own sheaf of papers, finally ready to jump in with his two cents. "I have it. I got three incidents that form a pattern going back to the bastard's schooldays. We can nail him."

"I've had it. I'm getting out of here," Mike muttered.

"No, you're not getting out of here until I know what the hell went down yesterday when you went over to the bastard's place."

"Fine," April said.

"Don't you want the background?" Hagedorn whined.

Iriarte threw up his hands in frustration. "All right, let's have it."

Hagedorn was seated in the front row with his harvest of dirt from Liberty's life. From the thinness of the manilla file, it didn't look like all that much. Creaker with the scary-looking scars on his head sat blank-faced and empty-handed next to him. He and Skye, leading garbage-and-questioning-of-neighbors detail, had come up with zip from the streets in the crime scene area. Zip. Nada. Nothing at all. When it got that cold, the street people made fires in metal drums in several of the small parks along Ninth Avenue. No one hung out on the side streets. Creaker and Skye had nothing to say about what went down on the street that night. When an arrest was finally made, people would come forward claiming to have seen everything, then they'd have something to do, check it all out. It happened all the time. After the fact, an army of witnesses would appear. They'd want to tell their stories about what they'd seen and what they'd known all along, and just happened to neglect to pass along in a timely manner. Somebody would have to sift through these stories for a possible real story they could use.

It was a different story about what went on inside the building where the couple lived. The Libertys were not the quiet and loving couple Liberty claimed. Hagedorn opened the file and plunged into the spotlight.

"First incident with white people occurred when Liberty was only fourteen." Hagedorn looked up. "We don't have anything before that yet," he said. "But you know niggers. They wouldn't call the police on him if he killed his own mother."

Somebody farted.

April put her scarf to her nose. The living sometimes smelled worse than the dead.

"Get on with it," Iriarte said impatiently. "What'd the man do?"

"He beat up some kids in his boarding school. Broke one kid's nose, another's arm. The parents tried to get him thrown out, but the school hushed it up."

"Did the police come? Was he arrested?" Iriarte asked.

"No," Hagedorn admitted.

"Anything else?" Mike said, disgusted.

"Yeah, there's something else. He went to Princeton. He beat up a white girl and her date on the street. When the police came, he convinced them he was walking by and saw the guy beating the girl and restrained him. This nigger was such a smooth talker he got the police to arrest the other guy. Princeton football captain. What could they do? They believed him. The next day the girl said it was all a lie. It was the black man who punched her teeth out."

"Was he arrested then?" Iriarte asked hopefully.

Hagedorn shook his head. "I told you this guy is smooth. Some kind of sociopath. He talked his way out of it. Next thing we know he's transferred to Stanford. They got rid of him, see. A pattern emerges, huh?"

"Yes, no, maybe so, Hagedorn. Anything else?"

"Yeah, there's more. There was a Super Bowl incident."

Iriarte flipped through the newspapers. "Yeah, the *Enquirer* picked up that one."

"The Giants were thirty-two points down at halftime. Liberty was pissed because no one was doing the assignments he gave them. He thought the team was fucking up, so he tore the locker room up during halftime and they had to take him away in an ambulance."

"I never heard that," Mike murmured.

"Yeah, well, it was hushed up. Everything with him is hushed up, know what I mean?"

"Anything else?" Iriarte asked wearily.

"Now the good part. Present time, the guy had screaming fights with his wife on a regular basis. Everyone in the building knew about it. The painter had to come up and replaster walls in the apartment three times this year alone. Sometimes neighbors called them directly and the noise stopped. Once the police had to be called in."

"Anything else?"

"Yeah, there's more." Hagedorn consulted his notes. "Uh, I talked to some of the secretaries at this place he works. They all said he gets these headaches sometimes and goes kinda crazy."

"Kinda crazy. That's kinda ambiguous. Can you be more specific?"

"Kinda crazy. That's what I have. 'He gets scary.' " Satisfied with his work, Hagedorn shut the file.

"He's black. He weighs two hundred pounds. For a lot of people that's scary enough," April said. She didn't like the foul odor in the room. "You're right, maybe we should have lynched him when we had him."

"You were there all afternoon. You had every opportunity to get him. And what did you do? You didn't bring him in. You scared him off. I'd call that a cock-up. I'd call that a fucking disaster, Woo. I thought you were good. I had big hopes for you, and what do you do? You and your boyfriend mess up on the big one."

April slung her bag over her shoulder and steadied herself. A couple of years ago before she was transferred to the Two-O and met Mike, she used to lower her eyes in situations like this, put her head down and practically knock it on the floor as Chinese peasants used to do to show their humility to their lords in old China. She used to think the impulse to bow to her superiors in the face of humiliation was a genetic thing that she could not overcome. But Mike had taught her to stand up and fight back when she had to. Now even as her face burned with the shame of public humiliation, she kept her head up and replied in even tones.

"Sir, let's get to the bottom line here. As far as we know, there are only two crimes this guy Liberty is guilty of for sure and certain, and we can't arrest him for either one."

"And what might those be?"

April ticked them off. "For one, he didn't attend his wife's funeral. He was in his apartment most of yesterday when we searched the place and checked the route to see if he could have killed her."

"And you've no doubt he could have."

"Oh, yes, he could have gotten out and in and he could have jogged down to Forty-fifth Street and back within the time frame. No doubt about it. The building complex he lives in is like a sieve. There are two elevators in each building and between the buildings is a courtyard that's locked to outsiders but available to tenants twenty-four hours a day. A basement runs under the courtyard between the two buildings. There's also a garage. Liberty could have gotten out at least four ways." April spoke matter-of-factly.

"So he's our man."

"He could be our man," Mike interrupted.

"But you let him get away."

Mike kept his voice cool. "I said he *could* be. Then again he might not be. We have a little problem here. A little question of evidence. As of yesterday no one saw him leave his building on the night of the murder, or return for that matter. We've checked out the garbage in his building for a murder weapon and bloody clothes. Everything in that building is tossed down chutes located by the service area on every floor. Yesterday we tested for prints on the chute handle on his floor. Someone had wiped it clean. We don't know if he tossed bloody clothes or a weapon down there. Nothing's been found. In addition, we have nothing attributable to him on the scene itself. No murder weapon, no witnesses."

"Well, how did he handle himself in the interview?" Iriarte asked. "What did you think?"

Mike did not look at April. She did not look at him.

"He smooth-talked you, too," Hagedorn sneered.

"Nothing clear emerged," April said pretty smoothly herself. "And just because he wasn't at home this morning doesn't mean he's run away."

"Well, I hope you're right, Woo, because I'll hold it against you if we read in tomorrow's paper he's in Mexico."

Finally, just like old times, Mike jerked his head at April. They'd played nice long enough. "Let's go."

"Just a minute. What's the second thing you're sure Liberty's guilty of?" Iriarte demanded.

April pushed the foul air out of her nose. "He's black," she said.

Iriarte pointed a finger at her. "Is that a problem for you, Woo?"

April shook her head. It was a problem for other people though.

"Then get him."

"We'll find him." Mike turned and glanced at Iriarte's blackboard with the assignments on it. The blackboard was crooked now. He straightened it as he left.

23

Liberty writhed in the dark. Street sounds—fire engine, police siren, people screaming outside and in the hall—instructed his dreams of bloody death.

"You a dead man, fucker."

Whine of a siren. "Weeeaaweeeaaweeaa—"

The sound of someone moving around outside the door dragged him back from hell. It was cold in the room. He pulled at the thin coverlet and realized he was still wearing his clothes, wasn't at home. Groaning, he turned over on the sagging mattress and heard the sound again—boots tramping on a bare floor. He cracked an eye. A sliver of gray light squeezed through the slit between the peeling window frame and the blackout curtains of purple velvet covering the glass. He didn't know exactly where he was, but knew he'd have to get out of there in a few minutes.

He was awake now, his anguish blossoming into a full-blown panic. He looked for his computer. It was still there on the wicker rocking chair beside the bed. In the pale light he could see a fringed piano shawl like his grandmother used to have thrown over the back of the chair. Like hers, this one had holes in the flowers and was minus the piano. He was in a shabby shithole somewhere in Harlem, but the computer was safe. He looked for a phone jack, didn't see one. His shoes were on the floor, by the bed. He closed his eyes to recapture an earlier dream. In the dream Merrill had worn a blue robe with white stars. It looked like the robes the dancers called gypsies in Broadway shows handed down to the winner in their version of the Tonys. She wasn't screaming anymore. She'd won the prize, the robe of heaven.

He whispered to her, "I'm sorry, baby. Come back."

But she didn't seem to see him. She was talking to an audience, telling them in her lecturing voice how black people were in America before the *Mayflower*.

"The first baby born in the New World was a Moor. They had no word for black or white skin then. The baby was baptized William. There were free blacks in the North, right here in New York, long before there were slaves."

The robe Merrill wore was wide in the sleeves and sweeping at the hem. Like an angel, she argued Liberty's past.

"Rick, you could be one of those indentured servants, a trader from the Middle East, a descendant of Cleopatra or an Ethiopian king. You could be a founding father of America. A free man all the way back to the beginning of time."

"Never was so, baby," Liberty told her in his dream. "Uh-uh, my grandmother on my mama's side was the daughter of a slave, black as night." Nothing free about his past. His father had died in the Korean War. He'd been a member of the last segregated unit in the armed forces, the one that was officially branded in the army's most recent rewriting of history as the "Coward's Brigade."

The man his mother claimed was his father looked dark in his pictures, but Rick had never known him. There was no way to be sure that the dark-skinned dead soldier, who was a musician before he was drafted, was in fact his real father. Rick himself had no musical abilities. For all he knew his real father had simply taken off when he was born, or even before. Could even be his father was a white man. It wouldn't be the first in his family. No matter who he was, Rick had always felt abandoned by him, fatherless in the most profound and unsettling way because he could not get solid information about the man who'd sired him. And what he'd been told didn't add up. His grandmother's skin was dark, his mother's was almost white. His own skin was closer to his mother's than her mother's. And somehow it had been easier for his grandmother to accept her daughter's light skin than his. Even when he was a small child, his gramma had studied Rick's fine, nearly Caucasian features with anger and didn't like to touch him. When his mother had given birth to his younger sister, his grandmother rejoiced because she was dark. And although there were always men around in the fringes of their lives, neither his grandmother or mother ever married.

"Honey, let's have beautiful golden children and go to the Caribbean to dance in the sun." Merrill's robe faded to black and she disappeared.

Pain sliced through Liberty's brain. He opened his eyes. The dream was gone and he needed a bathroom. He smelled coffee. His sweater and pants were rumpled and sweaty. He slipped on his shoes, grabbed his computer, and reached for the doorknob. The spindle came out in his hand, knocking the knob off on the other side.

"Yo, what's up?" The woman in the living room turned at the sound and examined him coldly.

Liberty stared at her. Marvin had told him a friend of his hung out here but hadn't said it was a woman. She hadn't been there last night when he'd come in.

"What's the matter wit you? Ain't never seen a sista befo?" The woman's hostility almost sent him back into the bedroom.

He held out the knob and spindle. "Your door handle is loose," he said.

"Yessir, I took the screws out. I ain't keeping no strange nigger in *mah* place widout takin some precautions. Coffee?" she offered.

Liberty turned toward the aroma. The kitchen was a corner without a door that contained a refrigerator, tiny stove, and sink. The woman was sitting at a table in front of it with a cup in her hand. She followed his gaze to a sagging sofa and two more wicker chairs and the milk cartons filled with books that served as coffee tables and bookcases.

"Around here, you better have nothin' worth stealin'," she said coldly. "So I don't."

Rick needed to urinate and wash his face.

She jerked her chin toward a closed door. "Bathroom's in there."

"Thanks." Rick crossed the room and opened the door. The sink was brown with rust. The toilet was old and the tank had deep cracks. It smelled. Rick closed his eyes as he urinated. He gathered his friend Marvin had some message in mind when he'd left him here late last night. Marvin always had a message. The mirror was shadowy with age and had a crack in it. The mirror had a message for him, too. His hair had not one or two gray strands. It had become grizzled, as if he'd been fried in the night and all that was left was ash. His beard gave his face a gray covering, too. He stared at himself, shocked. He thought of the electric chair, but then remembered they didn't kill that way in New York State anymore.

The woman put another cup of coffee on the table and moved back toward the wall, putting the table between them.

"Yo, nigger," she said. "Don't know why you in my place, but I owe Marvin. You register that? I'd do whatever, don't matter what he say. I'd do it, you understand? He wants to hide out some nigger killed a white woman in my place—" She spread the shapely fingers of one hand in the cool sign and shrugged. "Maybe that nigger had a good reason."

Rick opened his mouth at the word *killer,* but she didn't give him a chance to speak.

"These the house rules. No drugs here. No weapons of any kind. No drugs, no weapons. That's it. I can smell it before you can open it. I can smell it in the hall. One sniff an' I'll call the cops. 'Nother thing, dude, you try to rape me or hit me or come on to me in any way—verbal or otherwise—you try to touch me any place on my person I'll kill you. Got that?"

Rick scratched the side of his gray face to keep from smiling for the first time since Merrill died. Here was a militant sister of some kind, wearing a cloth twisted around her head in a turban, heavy boots, several layers and colors of sweaters, vest and skirt down to her ankles. African trading beads and heavy metal necklaces on her chest. Lecturing him about drugs and sexual harassment.

"I don't look like it anymore. But my name's Rick Liberty," he said. He didn't offer to shake her hand.

She shook her head vehemently. "I don't give a shit who you look like or who you be. Don't care if you famous, or rich as Croesus. You touch me and you a dead man."

Rick closed his teeth over his lips. The situation was ridiculous. Black humor in the extreme. Marvin had some sense of humor. He kept his mouth closed, didn't want to insult her by laughing.

"Oh, you think it's funny? Marvin knows I has friends in the community. I has lots of friends. I told him, this nigger touch me, and he's a dead man. Won't have no more problems with his image."

"Are you a nigger—?" Rick said softly, pulling out a chair and sitting. "Ms. . . . ?"

She eyed him suspiciously. "It's Belle. You dissing me, man?"

Rick shook his head. "No, Belle. Nobody in his right mind would dare to dis you."

"What's your point then?"

"Thank you for your hospitality last night. It wasn't my plan to intrude on your privacy."

"Black folk gots no privacy," she said flatly.

Now there was a position he wasn't going to touch. "Well, thanks anyway. I have to go."

"Drink your coffee."

Rick considered the coffee.

"Ain't nothin' about us good enough for you?"

He wasn't going to touch that either. Rick picked up the cup, swallowed the coffee. Who was—the community? He thought of his own community, of Merrill. Numb, he put the empty cup down. "I have to go."

"How you gonna do that?"

"Taxi."

"Ain't no taxis here."

"Fine, I'll call a car."

"With that blockade out there?"

"What blockade?"

"They stop the cars, ask them what they doing here, run a warrant check on the passengers."

Rick frowned, trying to take that in. "The police have a blockade in the street and stop the cars?"

She nodded. "Uh-huh."

"Why?"

"They do it in the buildings, too. Anybody don't belong here gets arrested for criminal trespass."

"Why?" he asked again.

"They sweeping the hood. . . . You got a warrant out?"

"No," Rick said. "I haven't done anything wrong."

"That's what they all say," Belle muttered under her breath.

"What?"

"I gots to go to work. If you hear screaming and arguing in the hall, don't open the door. It's just the police doin' a vertical." Belle smiled for the first time, revealing a perfect set of small even teeth. "I think the guy they looking for is on the six floor. All the arrests stop right here." She smiled some more. "I told you black folks gots no privacy."

In a closet without a door, she found a few more layers of clothes. She put them on without looking at him again and left the apartment.

Rick heard her lock the door from the outside in several places. After a few minutes he found the phone under a pillow on the sofa and set up his computer.

A few minutes later a commotion in the hall distracted Liberty as he concluded a long E-mail to Jason Frank. His heart thudded at the sound of boots on the stairs. He got up to look out the window facing the street. There was no squad car in front of the building. Still, he broke into a sweat when the steps stopped in front of his door.

"It's has to be this floor or the next one," a harsh voice speculated.

"Yeah, this is four B." Another voice, higher. A woman. A third set of boots clomped up the stairs to join them.

Liberty panicked. Was this four B? His mouth was dry. His heart thudded. If they were cops, they could break down the door and throw him out the window. Claim he'd jumped. He read stories in the paper every day about the brutal deaths that resulted when people ran from the cops. No way to find out what really happened. Any fatality could occur when the police appeared on the scene and the world would believe whatever lies they told. His heart felt too big for his chest, as if it had swollen up and was about to burst. He was alone. Merrill wasn't there. Tor wasn't there.

Someone banged on the door with a heavy instrument. Could he jump? Not five floors. He looked around for a weapon to defend himself. There were some books in the cartons, the phone, the chairs. Nothing else. The sound came again.

"Police! Open up!"

It wasn't this door. It was the door across the hall. Still, his heart wouldn't slow down. It pounded harder than it had in any game, as hard as it had back in Princeton when the cops thought he'd mugged and beaten that poor woman. They never bothered to check and confirm that her purse and all her money were there at her feet. He was amazed to find himself trembling and clammy with sweat. After all these years, he'd forgotten what it felt like to be afraid.

"Police! Open that door! Now!"

His heart continued to throttle up as the pounding on the door continued. The tightness in his chest made him wonder how Tor had felt when he knew he was dying. That son of a bitch had been so helpful, had saved Liberty's life years ago only to destroy it now. Liberty let the anguish of Tor's betrayal grow and intensify in his chest until the treachery itself took over. It felt as if double-bladed knives were slashing him open from the inside. Liberty felt dizzy from the image of the knives slicing his arteries, dizzy from the iron smell of blood and the sense that he and Merrill might have been one, after all. It occurred to him that the greatest irony of all would be that his life was over with hers. The tightness and pain in his chest made him fear he was dying. It also made him think that dying of a heart attack in Harlem might well be the best outcome he could hope for.

"Police, open up."

Chains rattled outside the apartment as a door was unlocked. Then a melodious voice sang out, "Praise the Lord." The voice sank to a whisper.

Liberty's eyes drifted back to his computer. He clicked "Send Now" on his E-mail to Jason. Then he began to pull himself together. He had things to do.

24

April finished telling Jason's answering machine she urgently needed his profile of Liberty, hung up, and stared out the window in the top half of her office door. All she could see was the wall above the desks opposite her. The ancient off-white paint, mottled with dirt and cracked in a thousand places, had probably yellowed with disgust long before she was born. In the corner of the ceiling nearest Iriarte's office, craters had formed in the cracks from a water leak that must have recurred numerous times in the last several decades. The next leak would certainly bring that section of the ceiling down on the desk below it, which was Skye's. April couldn't help feeling deeply hurt by the way Iriarte had spoken to her. She wondered if she'd still be assigned in the precinct when the ceiling collapsed.

She had closed the door to recover from the humiliating scene in the lieutenant's office and to study the desk-sized sheet she'd made on Monday to fill in the twenty-four hours before and after the deaths of Merrill Liberty and Tor Petersen. Three days later there still were far too many blanks about the victims' backgrounds and the three suspects they had. The goal was always to have a game plan for an investigation and follow it in as orderly a fashion as possible. But with constantly shifting circumstances, the race against time, and the many variables in the personalities of those working the case, chaos nearly always prevailed. It was often luck more than anything else that determined the outcome. Of the three suspects, it was Liberty who was cracking first. As Mike said, it might mean a break in the case and it might not.

From where April sat she could not see Hagedorn on the phone, but she could just hear his plaintive voice.

"That's all you can come up with? What about Motor Vehicle, anything there? Come on, give me a break. You mean the guy never had a speeding ticket?" His voice perked up. "Yeah, car theft, that's more like it. When?"

He burst out, "The fifth of January! You telling me our man boosted a car on January fifth? How come we don't know about it . . . ? *Getouttahere,* he reported his car stolen?"

April pushed some air through her nose. What a jerk. They already knew that. She couldn't stop thinking about Mike. She wanted to talk to him about yesterday morning, try to explain how she felt, knew she couldn't. Sometimes you had to do the right thing and let go. She flipped the pages of her notebook to get her thoughts back on track. On top of everything else Hagedorn was beginning to seriously irritate her. He'd just get hold of an idea and push it around on his plate until he could find the right position for it, then look for facts to back up his theory. She'd heard that scientists did that, too, so you could never believe the conclusions of any scientific study. Sometimes April thought there was no one in the world who told the truth.

She sighed. A pertinent item had been left out of that morning's temper tantrum in Iriarte's office. A woman jogger had been beaten almost to death during an attempted rape in Central Park last night at around seven. She was the second victim in six months. The first had died of her massive head injuries. This second attack had occurred in the 20th Precinct, behind the playground at Eighty-first Street and Central Park West. A highly populated area even in winter because dog walkers went into the park there. If April were still in the Two-O, she'd be working that case instead of the Merrill Liberty case.

On the other side of her door Hagedorn was still whining on the phone. It made her wonder why Iriarte hadn't given him the jogger case. There was good reason for him to be on it. The victim in the case last summer, by the oddest coincidence, had lived in the Park Century, the building where Liberty lived. That investigation had been handled out of Midtown North. The killer was still out there somewhere, and the detectives in the Two-O wanted the files on that case to see if there was a link to this one. With Margaret Mary Joyce now a lieutenant, Sergeant Sanchez and herself all gone from the squad, April figured the Two-O would now need help for almost anything. But Iriarte had assigned two detectives who'd been questioning street people in the Liberty case and not Hagedorn, probably because Hagedorn was good with computers. April's gaze returned to the crater in the ceiling. She told herself to focus on what had gone wrong with her and Mike's investigation of Liberty yesterday instead of what had gone wrong with them personally.

It had been the day of Merrill Liberty's funeral, and they were surprised to find Liberty at home. He was wearing the same clothes he'd worn on the night of the murders. He was unshaven and seemed dazed. After opening his apartment door to her and Mike, Liberty turned his back on them to return to the area in the great open space that served as the dining room, where he must have been seated alone at his long and gleaming ebony dining table. April had been fascinated by that table. It was a graceful oval large enough for twelve. The surface was as shiny as new Chinese black lacquer. Eight matching ebony chairs with shiny white satin seats were placed at wide intervals around it. Four more were positioned against the wall. Liberty sat at the head of the table like a chairman of the board, a man of expensive black and white tastes. There was nothing to eat or drink on the table, and there were no board members around him now. A solitary laptop computer, sitting in the end curve of the oval, was keeping him company. He had hurried back to it.

When the two detectives followed him through the arch designating the room change from entrance hall to dining room, he punched a button, removing a document from the screen; then he shut down the computer for good measure. April took a position on one side of him. She unbuttoned her coat and glanced at Mike, who stood on the other side. They could see each other, but Liberty could see only one of them at a time. He was vague. He ran his fingers over the keyboard of the computer. The keys made a clicking sound, as if he were typing the answers to their questions. Without looking at them, he'd told them they could search the apartment and do whatever they had to do. He told them what he'd worn to Chicago. The coat was in the closet, the suit was on the chair in the bedroom. The shoes were in the closet. He said he hadn't been watching the clock so he didn't know exactly what time he got home, went to bed. He said he didn't go out after he returned home. He talked about the stolen car and Wally Jefferson. He was convinced there was a tie-in between him and the murders. He couldn't be specific about why.

April didn't know much about football, but she'd seen Liberty on TV once or twice. On TV he was striking, a big, handsome man with black hair, the kind of jawline Jason Frank and the Kennedys had, and a powerfully focused gaze that made the viewer feel he was completely at ease in front of the camera.

Yesterday, he'd looked gray, internally soft, as if the structure of his body were no longer sound and inside he'd melted down to nothing. Still, he'd been annoyed by their running the route from the apartment to the restaurant a number of times. He said it was a futile exercise, since there was a camera in every elevator and cameras in the stairways. If he'd left his apartment on the night of the murder—if he'd gone out either way—the person manning the cameras in the security room would have seen him. He seemed very sure that could not have happened.

And then Liberty's eyes had become very sharp. "Why are you doing this to me?" he demanded.

"There's nothing personal about it," Mike replied. "We do it to everybody."

Liberty tried to stare Mike down with his sharp, intelligent eyes. "Do you believe I could have killed my own wife?"

"You mean, did you have the means and opportunity?" Mike shifted his mouth around in his face as he inhaled and slowly exhaled a few times. Finally the shoulder with the gun under it jerked in a half shrug. "All we're missing here is the motive." And a witness, he didn't say.

"Why do you think Daphne Petersen is accusing me on TV?" Liberty's voice became harsh.

"Why do you think?" Mike replied.

"You don't have to go any further than her for a motive. She had a reason to kill Tor. I don't have a reason to hurt anyone."

"She certainly appears to have a lot to gain with her husband dead. Be assured that we're investigating her movements on the night of the murder, as well as yours," Mike had told him.

"She may not have done it directly."

"We're aware of that."

"So, you don't take the TV appearance at face value." He looked from one to the other.

"Frankly, I don't watch TV. What about you, April?"

April shook her head. "If Daphne did kill her husband, it was a dumb move to point her finger at you. But I don't see why she would have killed your wife, do you?"

"No." He said no, but he looked uneasy.

"Did you ever hit your wife, Mr. Liberty?" Mike asked.

"No." Still uneasy.

"Your neighbors say you fought a lot."

"My wife was very volatile. She was going through a bad period. It happens to the best people."

"You want to tell us about that?"

Liberty's eyes had filled with tears. He shook his head. April made a note to check with Emma again, talk to Merrill's doctor. Mike did not press him on the point.

"She couldn't have children," April said softly.

"How do you know?" He looked surprised.

"Just a guess." No reason to tell him she knew the autopsy report. It had not been the time to ask Liberty about the couple's sexual difficulties. Merrill's doctor might be able to answer that.

The phone rang in April's office. She picked up. It was Ducci, telling her to find her boyfriend and get over to the lab right away. She didn't have the energy to tell him she had a new one now.

April wanted to get to the lab and hear what Ducci had to say, but along with everything else, she had a domestic case on the burner and had to send out a team to make an arrest. Early morning was not when husbands usually got drunk and beat up their wives, but it was a good time to make an arrest. The couple in question had been in trouble before. This time when the wife got out of the hospital, she decided to press charges. There was no way the guy could avoid going down today. Ducci's information had to wait.

April went downstairs to meet Carmella Perez, the officer assigned to domestic cases. Perez was probably a few years older than April but looked about fifteen because she didn't have a lot of beef on her body. She was almost razor-sharp all over except for smoothly rounded cheeks that set off a delicate nose and mouth and soft brown eyes. Clearly her favorite feature, though, was the thick, curly black hair that hung half-way down her back in a shiny curtain.

Since the time last summer when an officer had died trying to arrest a guy in a domestic dispute, nobody was allowed to go in alone on a domestic. Last summer a guy on a rampage had thrown a large mirror across the room at the officer trying to subdue him. A shard hit him, severed an artery in his groin, and the young cop, father of two, had bled to death before he reached the hospital.

It was unusually quiet by the front desk where April and Carmella waited for two uniforms. All the news vans that had been stationed there for several days after the Liberty murder had now moved up to the Two-O to cover the jogger case. So had a number of officers and detectives. Except for Hagedorn, who was stuck to his computer, all the other detectives were out in the field. The dozens of other cases they had were on the back burner, except for Jocelyn Kohlbe, who, in her latest beating at the hands of her husband, had sustained four broken ribs, a broken arm, numerous bruises about the head and neck, and a shattered eardrum.

April looked Carmella over, always more worried about the females in bad situations than the men. April figured her fear for other female cops had to come from really old prejudices little girls were taught about not being able to take care of themselves. Or maybe she had some semblance of a maternal instinct, after all. It pissed off the female uniforms when she screwed up her face to assess their equipment and moods before they went out, just as Skinny Dragon Mother did each time she went out.

There were a lot of supposed-tos and not-supposed-tos in the department. You were absolutely not supposed to go out on the street or on an arrest without a bulletproof vest on. Occasionally they had a problem with a female officer—usually one of the young ones—who didn't want to wear her vest because she thought it made her look fat. It wasn't April's job to make sure they were wearing their vests, had all their equipment, and the batteries worked in their flashlights, but when females were working her cases, she couldn't help looking for violations. When one jumped out at her, she screamed the way a mother did at a kid running out the back door into the rain without a coat on. She didn't like to think she had a maternal instinct, so she assumed she just didn't want to feel guilty for the rest of her life if something happened to one of them on her watch.

Carmella Perez. Too skinny. Possibly didn't eat meat, or anything else. April noticed four or five holes, but no earrings in her ears, no rings on her fingers. So far so good. The watch with a large round dial looked too heavy for her slender wrist. It read 9:07. Carmella wore a red-and-black-plaid flannel shirt with a black turtleneck, her vest and her gun under it. April knew that even if it got really cold Carmella would keep her jacket unzipped so she could get at her gun. They'd talked guns at lunch once, so April knew Carmella still carried the old .38 Chief's Special and took good care of it. She told April she'd tried a 9mm automatic at the range once and couldn't get over how light and easy it was to grip. But then the gun jammed when she pulled the trigger and that was it for her. In the department you still had to buy your own gun, and she wasn't taking any chances laying down big money for a weapon that might fail her when she needed it. She was taking some chances with the hair, though. April wrinkled her nose.

Carmella's eyes flashed. "What chu looking at?" She took the attitude position with one foot splayed and a hand on the opposite hip.

She was an inch or two taller than April, maybe five eight. The extra inches she got with her heavy winter boots put her at about five ten. April jerked her chin up at the hair.

"Anybody ever tell you you could get your scalp ripped off?"

"With Bobby here to protect me?" Carmella laughed as a white uniform about five five with his shoes on chugged up grinning and raised a hand to pet her hair as if it were a friendly animal he hadn't seen in a while. She slapped the hand away.

April ignored the horseplay. "Make me happy. Put the hair up. Our lady may be in a loving mood this morning and feel the need to protect her man."

"Shit happens," Bobby agreed, hitching at his belt as if the rise was too short in his uniform trousers.

"Nah, this one's my buddy. She won't give me no trouble." Now Carmella was grinning.

Still struggling with his balls, Bobby did a quick knee bend and hitched at his pants some more.

Carmella watched, speculating. "You all twisted up again, Bobby?"

"Yeah, you want to help me out?"

Now April was getting annoyed. These two were pushing all her buttons and knew it. Sometimes when you went to arrest a batterer, it was the wife who went berserk pulling a cop's hair, hitting him with a frying pan, biting. Horseplay might calm these two down, but it was dangerous.

Bobby's partner, a guy they called Dodo, showed up. "Ready?"

"Put up the hair," April said.

"Sure." Carmella wrapped a scarf around her neck.

"She says 'sure,' but she'll only take it down later in the car." Bobby grabbed a handful and tweaked the hair.

Carmella punched his arm.

"It's trouble all around. Put it up, and keep it up," April warned.

Carmella's cheerful expression soured, and April knew she'd made an enemy. A perfect Chinese person knew how to get her way without giving offense. A perfect American didn't give a shit. April wasn't perfect in either culture. She turned away, suddenly depressed. "Go on, safe landing," she muttered.

The elevator door opened and Mike swaggered out with his leather jacket on. "I hear you're looking for me."

Where did he hear that? April swung around, irritated that she'd waited too long to get out to the lab without him.

* * *

They took an unmarked gray unit, and April was glad to let Mike drive slowly through the dirty slush. He was thoughtful, didn't offer his opinion of her boss, Iriarte, or the surveillance officer who'd lost their suspect, or anything else about the failures in the precinct where she worked. She was grateful for that. Then he spoke.

"Look, April, I know how you feel about me. I see how it is with your boss. Now I guess it was stupid to think I could charge into your new house, into a big case like this, and there'd be no repercussions for you."

She was touched by his sensitivity, didn't trust her voice to reply.

"Pretty dumb, huh?"

"Hey, it's not your fault. You didn't know."

"Wasn't a hard one. We never liked strangers in our cases."

She couldn't help smiling. "Is this an apology?"

"Maybe. The problem is, it wouldn't look good for either of us if I backed off now. We'd have a mess and no sure way to clear the case. We'd both be fucked for sure, no pun intended. We've got to work together on this one, are you agreed?"

"I agree we have to solve it, yes. Do we have to work together every minute? No."

Mike fell silent. After a while he changed the subject. "I checked with security in Liberty's building. Guess what?"

"Liberty isn't on the videotape going out on the night of the murder or last night, either," April said.

"Worse than that."

"He isn't on the videotape coming in on the night of the murder."

"Nope. Guess again."

"Why do I have to guess? Why don't you just tell me?"

"You're no fun."

"I know." Nothing new there.

"So, there's no videotape."

"Someone took it?" April prompted.

"Uh-uh. There hasn't been a videotape in a year. It was too expensive to run it. There'd never been a robbery in the building, and the constant spying was getting some of the people in the building in trouble."

"Nose picking or affairs?"

"Whatever. The board voted to stop the twenty-four-hour-a-day filming. Now a guy sits in the screening room from eight a.m. when the building opens to six p.m. when it closes. Inside the building complex the residents can go anywhere. But delivery people can't go up in the elevators unescorted after that."

"So security is only for nonresidents. Liberty must have known that."

Mike shrugged. "It's how he got out unseen last night. Must have gone downstairs into the basement and walked out through the garage. He didn't take his car because it was stolen the day before the murder. The garage attendants confirmed that Jefferson took it the fifth, not the week before as he told us."

"We've been looking for witnesses who saw Liberty leaving the scene. Maybe it's time to check for someone who saw his car on the scene."

Mike nodded. He cut the motor, and they left the car double-parked in front of the Police Academy building. Upstairs, Ducci was standing by the wired window, watching the street when April and Mike strode into his lab. Glowering, he pushed up a white cuff on his blue shirt and made a big show of tapping the dial of his heavy gold watch. It was 9:43.

"What took you so long?" he demanded.

"Haven't you noticed we've got weather and traffic conditions out there?" April replied, smiling a little at Ducci's sudden hurry to get them there after three days of putting them off.

"We've always got weather and traffic," Ducci grumbled. He liberated a Snickers bar from his pocket and tore at the wrapper.

"So what's up?" April asked.

"What's up is very big. I didn't want to talk about it on the phone. Have a seat." Ducci chewed off half a chocolate bar, then rolled Nanci's vacant chair over for April.

Mike had to move Lola the skull and a pile of files from the chair next to Ducci's desk, which was piled with bloody clothes from the Liberty case. Mike looked around for a clear surface, couldn't find one, finally put the files and the skull on the floor by his feet.

"You know, they're making these things fat free now," Ducci mused, holding up the rest of the candy bar. "Little bitty things. Now who would go for something like that?" The second half disappeared into his mouth, and he chewed angrily.

Merrill's sweater dress and Tor's cashmere coat and sweater had been carefully dried to preserve the shape of the stains. Now they were spread out across Ducci's desk with their tags dangling. Of all the pieces taken as evidence from the bodies and the crime scene, these were the items that held Ducci's interest at the moment. April guessed it was something about them that made him angry, not the idea of fat-free candy.

Mike's booted foot bobbed impatiently, knocking over the skull.

"Watch that," Ducci growled.

"Sorry, Lola," Mike muttered. He pulled on his mustache. "So give."

"Rosa fucked up." Ducci looked from one to the other. "I didn't want to rush over to Malcolm Abraham with this, you know how he is about Rosa Washington."

"No, we don't know. How is he about her?"

"Oh, you know those Jews and their guilt about the blacks, always pushing for them. He loves her, defends her to the death, know what I mean? He brought her in, brought her along—first black woman deputy medical examiner and all that. I wouldn't say she's *totally* incompetent, but—" Ducci shrugged.

"I didn't get the feeling she was incompetent," April said.

"Neither did I," Mike agreed. "Did she make some kind of mistake?"

Ducci was on a track of his own. "There's no way Abraham won't try to gloss this over. And believe me, what I have here doesn't make you guys look too good, either. This whole thing makes me sick." He opened his desk drawer and reached in for another candy bar to console himself.

"You know those things are going to kill you some day," April said, wishing he'd get on with it. What mistake?

"Sure, I'll die of constipation." Ducci took a bite, then offered them the rest of the bar. "Want some?"

"Mi Dios!" Mike burst out. "You going to tell us the mistake, or what?"

"Okay, okay. Remember, during Petersen's autopsy how old Rosa kept going on about coroners in the Midwest not being MDs and how that messed up all their reports on cause of death, because they'd look at wounds and bruise patterns on a body and not have the faintest idea how they got there or what story they told?"

"So?" Mike demanded.

"Well, look at this." Ducci made a space on his desk and spread out Tor Petersen's cashmere cable-knit sweater, turned inside out.

April and Mike bent their heads to the place Ducci indicated with the sharp ends of a lab tweezer. In the middle of the chest portion of the sweater, he pointed to a hole so small it looked as if it could have come from a single bite of a hungry moth. The hole could barely be seen. They glanced at each other. Ducci was losing his marbles.

"Now look." Ducci held up a magnifying glass.

With the hole in the cashmere magnified ten times, they saw that the broken strands of yarn were stiff, discolored, and salted with white dots.

"Now look in here." Ducci snatched up the sweater

and tossed it aside. First he made Mike and April peer through the microscope in his lab. On the slide magnified several hundred times, the white dots were boulders and no longer white.

Then Ducci marched them into another lab and showed an even closer look through the highest powered microscope. They looked at each other again, no longer sure what they were looking at.

Ducci, however, thought it was big. He held his fingers to his lips, commanding silence in front of the other scientists they had to pass to get back to his lab. His jaw was rigid with tension, his round choirboy's face and tiny mouth set with outrage. He closed the door.

"And I stood there yapping with her. And you stood there yapping with her. And we all missed it." Ducci collapsed into his chair, disgusted with them all.

Okay, so there was a little hole in the sweater. April looked for help from Mike.

Ducci glowered at her. "I thought you took forensic science at John Jay."

"Obviously not enough," she said softly. "What about you, Mike? Do you get it?"

"Yeah, sure," he said vaguely. There was a hole in the sweater.

"All right, I'll lay it out for you dummies." He angrily arranged the photographs of Tor Petersen's body—from the murder scene, then both clothed and naked during the autopsy. Then did the same with Merrill's.

"What's missing?"

Mike studied the photos, then replied, "In Petersen's autopsy, the ultraviolets."

"Yes!" Ducci punched the air.

"Oh, Jesus." April reached for two of the photos. Merrill Liberty naked on the autopsy table after the techs had washed her body and the wound in her throat was clearly visible. And the photo of Tor Petersen naked on the autopsy table. The tiny round spot in the middle of Petersen's chest that Ducci had pointed out at the time was no bigger than a mosquito bite. It was just an indentation that did not even have the redness of a recent injury. In the photo, the spot was marked with an arrow and a ruler.

If there was a hole in the sweater in exactly the same place, and the discoloration in the yarn was blood, then the mark on Petersen's chest was no mosquito bite. It was a puncture of some sort. In the middle of his chest, below his sternum. Odd.

"Jesus Christ, do they still have the body?" Mike asked.

Ducci shook his head. "His wife had him removed and cremated yesterday."

"His wife did? Are you sure? They never release bodies that fast." April frowned. "Who would have given the okay on that?"

Ducci shook his head.

So that's why Daphne called the ME just after Petersen died. This was not looking good for Daphne.

"They burned him. That's all I can tell you." Ducci touched the photo of the dead man with one finger. "Poor guy."

Mike pointed at the rest of the clothes. "So what do you think happened?"

"What happened was Petersen came out of the restaurant first, right? You said the woman went to the kitchen to talk to the chef."

"Yes, both the manager and the chef confirmed that."

"So Petersen comes out. Somebody he knows comes over, says hello. Maybe he's a little drunk, a little stoned. The person sticks a sharp instrument into his heart and down he goes. Out Merrill Liberty comes, sees her boyfriend on the ground, runs over to help him. The killer may be surprised to see her, but doesn't do her in the heart. Why not—?"

"Maybe she's not the intended victim," April said slowly.

"Right. She doesn't have to look like she's had a heart attack. Guy gets scared and efficiently stabs her in the throat. Blood all over the place. Looks like she was the intended victim." Ducci spread out the back of Tor's coat. Right in the middle large areas of blood-stains still retained their reddish tinge. "She bled on Petersen's back. That means he had to go down first."

Next Ducci displayed Merrill's dress, now stiff with the pints of blood that had spilled out on it. "Now, why so much blood for her and only maybe a drop or two of blood for him?"

April opened her mouth to speak, but Ducci held up his hand. "I asked a heart doc I know if there was any way I could stab somebody in the heart without any bleeding outside the body. Know what he said?"

"Piece of cake," Mike said sarcastically.

"Now don't get snotty. He said if he were going to kill somebody, his first choice would be throwing him off a boat in the ocean. No witnesses." Ducci brushed his hands together and smiled.

"Now his second choice is a bit more sophisticated but he was pretty sure it would fool most medical examiners working today. Washington was right about one thing. Not many are really well trained."

"Yeah, genius, so what is it?"

"A very thin sharp instrument carefully inserted between the ribs into the heart. The entry wound would almost completely close up when the instrument was removed. The heart would be pierced and massive internal bleeding would result in almost instant death."

"That's some imagination your friend has. But he forgot one thing. Killing like that would mean he'd have to pierce the lung to get to the heart. A pierce like that would collapse the lung, and Petersen's lung was not collapsed." Mike tried to be kind. "So hey, you think a doctor's involved?"

"Don't make fun. I'm sure there's a way to do it if you think about it a little. Anyway, take a look at the widow. See how she is with pins and needles. If she can't sew herself, maybe her boyfriend's a doctor."

"How do you want to handle this thing with the

ME?" Mike turned to April, but Ducci answered the question.

"Get the killer, then we'll worry about the details." He looked proud of himself. "The real fuckup is this. Rosa didn't turn on the ultraviolet lights. If she had, we would have seen the wound more clearly, with the lint and fibers from his T-shirt stuck in it. Without the ultras, we didn't see it."

"You lost me again," April murmured. "What T-shirt?"

"Petersen was wearing a T-shirt when he got his little body pierce. The fibers from the T-shirt are in the severed yarn of the sweater. Don't you people listen? But there was no T-shirt on his body at the time of the autopsy."

"So where's the T-shirt with the hole in it?"

"That's the hundred-and-fifty-million-dollar question." Ducci's smile was not a friendly one. April gathered he wouldn't mind seeing Rosa Washington take a very big fall.

25

Mike drove uptown on First Avenue, through the Twenties and past the New York University Medical Center complex in the Thirties, where the medical examiner's building was set apart.

"Jesus, it's cold. My hands are frozen." April chaffed her hands. "What a day. What do you think, is Ducci a crackpot or are we in trouble?"

"He is and he isn't. But either way, we are."

"In trouble?"

Mike smiled. "Ducci may be right that Petersen died before the Liberty woman. He may not be right that Petersen was murdered."

"You don't buy the sharp-stick-in-the-heart story?"

"I saw Petersen's body and the Liberty woman's body, and so did you. The hole in the woman's throat was a hole. The wound on Petersen's chest didn't look like a hole. It wasn't red like a fresh injury, and there was no dried blood around it. Not any. It looked old to me."

"But the chest is a different part of the body from the throat," April pointed out. "Ducci said when the weapon was removed from the chest, the skin would close up around it. That wouldn't happen on the neck."

"Maybe. But it looked old. And there's no chance for a second autopsy."

"What about the hole in the sweater?"

"There's a hole in the sweater at the site of Petersen's tiny wound—that could have been made days, weeks, or even months before he died—and in the severed yarn fibers is lint from a T-shirt that the victim was not wearing at the time of his autopsy. So one could argue he was not wearing it at the time of his death. One could also argue that the chest injury—whatever its nature—also occurred sometime in the past."

"Many would argue that," April agreed.

"If Petersen was wearing a T-shirt at the time of his death, the T-shirt would have bloodstains on it—maybe not pints of blood, but some—and there would be a corresponding hole in the shirt that would be hard to miss."

"But he wasn't wearing a T-shirt."

"Or if someone wanted to make Petersen's death look like a heart attack, he'd also have to make the T-shirt disappear." Mike crossed on Fifty-seventh Street where the huge Christmas snowflake still presided over the crosswalk of Fifty-seventh and Fifth, forcing cheer out of a thousand tiny white lights. More white lights sparkled on the bare branches of the trees lining the avenue.

"No matter how this gets resolved, it's going to be bad. Liberty's taken off. Why would he do that if he weren't guilty of something?"

April's eyes burned. She felt lousy because they hadn't gotten anywhere with Liberty yesterday, and because of the way they were being treated by her boss. She was also troubled by the things Ducci told them. "What if Liberty was having an affair with the Petersen woman, they planned the murders together, and now she's trying to get him to take the fall?" she mused.

"Oy, the bitch." Mike turned up Madison, then left on Sixtieth. At Fifth Avenue even more white lights twinkled on the dozen Christmas trees still stuck in several levels of the fountain in front of the Plaza Hotel. The only yellow lights were those that cast an eerie glow from the thirty-foot menorah in Central Park at Fifty-ninth Street, right across from Daphne Petersen's building.

Now April's throat felt raw. Everyone working the case had messed up. Most of all she had. The Chinese god of messing up was hovering over her. She could feel his hot dragon's breath on her neck, in Iriarte's dashed hopes for her, in Mike's too. Dean Kiang would not think well of her either. He needed a solid case to prosecute. She'd be exiled to Ozone Park, put back in uniform. Her mother would gloat and make her life a misery, and she'd never get laid by anybody.

Mike stopped the car.

"Well, look at that." April sat up in her seat.

Daphne Petersen was hurrying up Fifth Avenue toward the spot where Mike had parked. She was wearing a huge black mink coat that swirled around her like a furry tent. Daphne was talking animatedly to a tall and strikingly handsome young man in a silver warm-up suit. The guy had bronze hair curling around his tanned neck and face and looked like an underwear ad with his clothes on.

"She looks cold. Let's take her for a ride," Mike suggested.

"Good idea." April opened the car door and got out, heedless of the traffic surging around her.

Mike swore as she headed around the front of the car.

There was a lake at the curb. April hurdled it, landing just north of Daphne Petersen on the sidewalk. The woman gave a little squeak and sprang back with surprising agility. The minute Daphne sidestepped, the underwear ad took her place, moving in quickly to attack April. Mike was out of the car when the man grabbed April by the arm and swung her around back toward the street. Her feet got tangled up in a dance step she hadn't seen coming, but she had the presence of mind to signal Mike to take it easy. No one was supposed to touch a police officer, and now Mike was coming on like a SWAT team to save her. The man swung April around to take her down in the icy lake on Fifth Avenue. But April shifted her weight at the last moment and tossed him away from her.

The man screamed as his feet left the sidewalk and he landed hard in front of their parked car, splashing filthy water on Daphne Petersen's leopard-topped boots.

Daphne stamped the boots on the sidewalk, yelling at April. "Are you mad?" Her piercing English shriek drew the doormen out of the Pierre.

"What's going on?" The one with the top hat tried for some authority.

Daphne ignored him. "Are you mad?" she continued screaming at April, who stood next to her, a little surprised by her ability to send a six-footer flying into the gutter.

"What do you think you're doing? You scared me to death. Giorgio, honey, are you all right?" Daphne put out her hand to the man with his butt in the street but did not advance close enough to touch him or get her feet wet.

He was sputtering in some foreign language as Mike pulled him to his feet.

"Ow, beetch, crazy beetch."

"Hey, watch that, buddy," Mike said. "You just assaulted a police officer." He rubbed his wet gloves together, then smacked one against the other. "You could go to jail for that."

"No way. I didn't do nothing." The man held his hands palms up. "She—"

"You assaulted a police officer. I saw you."

"Oh, for Christ's sake." Daphne Petersen turned to Mike. "The woman practically jumped on me. We thought she was one of those antifur people."

"What—?" April demanded.

"Can't you hear? We thought you were going to throw red paint at me."

"Crazy beetch." The handsome man didn't have much of a vocabulary. He was combing his fingers through his hair, managing to appear both peeved and injured.

Daphne shot him a scathing look. "Oh, shut up, Giorgio."

"Who's he?" Mike jerked a thumb at the bronze hair.

Daphne sniffed. "Just my trainer."

Mike stroked his mustache speculatively. "Nice job."

"You need any help?" the doorman tried again.

"Police," April said. "We're fine." She nodded him away.

"You're blocking the street," the doorman pointed out.

"That's what we're paid for," she told him.

"All right, you ruined my boots, you practically killed my friend. What are you doing here?"

"We're investigating a homicide."

"I had nothing to do with it. I hardly knew the woman. Let's go, Giorgio." Daphne turned away.

"Mrs. Petersen, would you mind getting in the car?" Mike said.

The widow swung back, stunned by the request. "What for?"

"We want to talk to you."

"You talked to me before." She eyed April now.

"You didn't tell me anything I wanted to know," April said evenly. "Now we're really going to talk."

"But I don't know anything," she protested.

"Funny, that's not what you said on TV."

The woman's face reddened. She glanced at her friend. "You'd better go now, Giorgio."

He peered at her as if he'd never heard such a command in his life. "Where?" he asked dumbly.

"Wherever you want, honey. You're a big boy."

He gave her a pathetic look, a hunk deprived of purpose, then scowled at the two cops. "Huh?"

"Go," Daphne commanded impatiently.

Giorgio looked at her again, saw that she was determined, then sloped off downtown, his shoes squishing on the sidewalk.

She turned to them angrily. "I don't know where he kept the stuff or who he got it from. I know that's why you're here." She leaned toward them on the sidewalk, speaking passionately. "It's not my problem. I told you he was a cocaine user. I warned him it would kill him one day if he kept drinking the way he did." Her cheek glistened in the light. She raised a white-gloved hand to wipe away the single tear that teetered on the curve.

April couldn't help herself. She glanced at Mike.

"Where were you the night your husband died?" he asked.

She gestured to April with the gloved hand. "I already told her. I was at home watching a movie. I talked on the phone. I have a list of people who dialed my number."

This was the first April heard of that.

"Tor died of an overdose," Daphne went on. "I hadn't seen him since—oh, I don't know, a couple of days." She started shivering inside the heavy coat.

"Who told you that?" Mike asked.

Daphne looked at him as if he were retarded. "Don't you people talk to each other? That's what they told me."

"Who told you?"

"Some woman from the police called and told me the toxi . . ."

"Toxicology," April prompted.

"Yeah, those reports came in, and Tor was just"—Daphne shook her head—"*chock-full* of cocaine and alcohol." She swiped at her face again. "That's what killed him. I asked her to keep it on the QT, you know. It doesn't help to spread that around, does it?" She looked yearningly at her building. "Can I go home now?"

"We'll come with you, make sure you're all right." Mike's face was impassive at the news of more official blundering.

Daphne made a face and hurried inside.

They left the car where it was on the street and took the elevator up to Petersen's apartment where the TV cables were gone, but plants and bouquets of flowers covered all available surfaces. The flowers were mostly lilies, April noticed. Many of them looked dried or hung over, as if the advice on the accompanying card, "Water me," had not been heeded.

In the living room, which overlooked the park, Daphne opened her fur coat and threw it on a chair. Underneath she was wearing exercise clothes—white tights and a pink body suit with a thong. She threw herself into a deep sofa, careful to keep the boots off the silk.

"You know Tor's death was his own fault. So why are you bothering me?"

"Because you haven't told anybody the truth about anything. That makes a problem for us." April tried not to stare at her body. "Let's start with your original statement. You told us you'd seen your husband the morning he died."

"Well, I didn't." The widow looked at them defiantly, tossing her hair. "I didn't know what the story was. I felt silly, you know. He'd spent the night somewhere, and I felt—awkward."

"Awkward?" April cocked her head. The woman's husband had been murdered and she felt *awkward.*

Daphne checked her nail polish. "One doesn't exactly *enjoy* being a jilted wife, you know. I was pretty certain I didn't have much time with him left, and I just—you know, I didn't say anything. I hoped it would blow over. Sometimes they do, you know. It's my own fault, of course," she added.

Mike was sucking his mustache. April could almost hear him think.

"What's your fault?" she asked.

"Marrying him, thinking it would last. Silly me."

April glanced around the lavish living room, full of silk chairs and shiny tables, objects of art from countries and centuries she could not have identified if her life depended on it. Silly Daphne didn't turn out to be so silly. Her straying husband with the dangerous habits was conveniently dead, and she was his final wife, after all. April unbuttoned her own coat and considered the chair possibilities.

"Do you mind if I take my coat off?"

Daphne flicked her a glance that didn't take anything in. "No, of course not."

April took her coat off and sat in a wing chair covered with red leather that sat at an angle to the sofa where Daphne was displaying the sweat stains in her crotch to Mike, who sat in a similar chair opposite her. Lovely girl.

"So, your husband was a cocaine user. What about you?" Mike asked.

"I'm a strict vegetarian," Daphne said, sullen now. "I must respect the divinity in myself."

Uh-huh. "Earlier, you told us you warned him that his subtance abuse was serious enough to kill him." Now April.

Daphne didn't answer. She chewed on the inside of her cheek.

"All the drinking and cocaine use must have made him pretty difficult to deal with," April went on.

"It was sad to watch," Daphne said flatly. "Are we almost done?"

April ignored the question. "You told a TV reporter your husband was having an affair with Merrill Liberty, and that Liberty killed them both in a jealous rage."

"So what?"

"Well, you also said you knew your husband would kill himself with drugs."

"What does it matter what I say? I'm crazed with grief." She appealed to Mike for understanding.

"Well, you accused a man of murder on national TV. That might matter to some people," Mike said. "He might sue you. We might think you did it for us, so we'd go after him and not you."

"I watched a movie and went to bed. Even if I had killed him, how could you prove it?" Daphne circled her head around her shoulders, loosening up those tight muscles.

"Why did you say you thought Liberty killed them?"

She scratched her cheek. "Maybe I thought so at the time. The interviewer thought so, too," she said defensively.

"And now?"

Daphne made a face. "Well, Liberty had no interest in women. I don't know if he and Merrill even made it together. He might be a fairy, you know. But he might have been upset if Tor wanted his wife. That's poaching, isn't it?"

Oh, so now Liberty was gay. "This is the first I've heard of that," April murmured. "So, do you think Merrill Liberty was having an affair with your husband?"

Daphne's face hardened. "I don't know. She was boring. He liked more—exciting women. And he didn't like blondes."

"Then why did you say it?"

"They were old friends. They were together a lot lately. You know how old friends stick together." Daphne glared.

"So you were a little jealous of the friendship." April changed tack. "You've made a lot of speculations." April pretended to search through her notes. "But you left one out."

"Are we done?"

"You left out the jealous wife."

"Oh, here we go."

"You had more motivation for murder than anybody."

"It was probably his girlfriend," Daphne said abruptly.

"Who?"

"The woman Tor was seeing."

"Do you know her name?"

Daphne shook her head. "But I know her smell. Want to smell her?" She jumped up without waiting for an answer. April realized that she was tall, five eleven with her boots on.

Mike watched Daphne's bottom and legs progress across the room. April frowned at him. He didn't seem to mind. Daphne returned in less than a minute carrying a purple bag with a dry cleaner's name on it, reached inside, and handed a man's large burgundy cashmere sweater to April. "Smell."

April sniffed and wrinkled her nose. She handed the sweater to Mike.

He put the soft knit to his face. "Vanilla musk." His crooked eyebrow went up as he examined the sweater. Inside, like a lining, was a white T-shirt. It smelled of deodorant and the same woman's perfume.

Daphne reached out and pulled something off the hem of the T-shirt. "See," she said, holding up a four-inch length of black hair that was inky like Carmella's but straight. Both detectives examined it. Then Daphne took it back, put the sweater and the T-shirt and the hair carefully back in the plastic sweater bag as if they were still bits of evidence she might need in a divorce case.

"Maybe she killed him with bad stuff," Daphne offered.

"Why would she do that?" April asked.

"Maybe he was breaking up with her."

Mike shook his head. "From what you've told us earlier, Mrs. Petersen, it sounds more like your husband was breaking up with you."

Daphne started to shiver again. "I've never touched cocaine in my life. Tor didn't get the stuff from me. He could have gotten it from that woman, or Patrice—I heard someone was selling at the restaurant. Or it could have been from his driver, Wally. He and Wally were very close. *He certainly didn't get it from me.*" She'd raised her voice and was shouting now. *"I didn't kill him!"* She stopped the tirade abruptly, her face red.

"You made me say that," she said, for the first time frightened by something that had come out of her mouth. "Tor wasn't even murdered, and you made me say that." She shook her head. "You'd better go now."

"Maybe the information you got on the phone this

morning was premature," Mike said. "We'll need you to come down to the station to make a formal statement."

"What?" Alarmed, Daphne reached for her coat.

"Not right this minute, Mrs. Petersen. We'll call and make an appointment." In the meantime, they would check out every corner of her life.

"Oh, do you mind if I take this?" April reached for the sweater bag Daphne had dropped on the table.

"What for?"

April wrote out a receipt. "Oh, who knows, it might prove useful." She handed over the slip of paper and reached for her plain navy wool coat. Daphne seemed too tired to object. Maybe it was all that exercise.

"Thanks, you've been a big help." April smiled. Next time she'd ask Daphne about her calls to the medical examiner's office and how she'd gotten her husband's body cremated in record time.

The two detectives started for the door. Before they got there, Mike turned back to the widow, who had wrapped the coat around her shoulders and was now shivering uncontrollably in her mink. "By the way, Mrs. Petersen, did your husband always wear a T-shirt under his sweaters?"

Deep in her own thoughts, Daphne responded without hesitation. "Always. He thought it was unhealthy not to have cotton next to his skin."

"He wasn't wearing a T-shirt when he died. Where do you think it went?" April chimed in.

Daphne stared at them too stunned to answer.

26

The wail of sirens was almost continuous during the morning hours. Many times Liberty crossed the room to peek behind the parade of orange-and-black giraffes on the African print fabric secured over the window facing the side street. All he saw each time was a group of ragtag males more old than young. They hung out on the front steps of a brownstone identical to the ones on either side. Each time the sirens wailed, two or three of them would drift off in different directions, leaving the same lone man sitting there with a pail and a mop by his side.

The pail and the mop and the man with a flat backpack and bulging side pockets never left the brownstone stoop. He sat there in the cold as Liberty read his E-mail. Sat there in the middle of the block, without coffee or gloves to warm him. Sat there, lost in some space of his own, impervious to cold as his buddies drifted in around him and then dispersed like a school of aimless fish. Sat there loose-limbed and semi-awake, tuned in somewhere else, waiting.

There he sat, like a benchmark signifying Liberty's own downfall, the man his mother and grandmother feared even before he could toddle or talk that Liberty himself would somehow become. The man with the mop and the pail he didn't intend to use was the bogeyman of Liberty's childhood. He was the black bum, the fatherless, motherless, black everyman. He was all the soulless nobodies, unwashed and unwanted at the table at Christmas or Easter or the Fourth of July. He was the signature of failure in every respect, the one for whom no one was left to mourn each day of his empty, worthless, no-good, self-destructive life. The drinker, the drifter, the wastrel, the thief. Loose-limbed, loose-lipped. Greatest pride and best handiwork of the devil himself. Conspiracy of the Confederate legacy, the federal government, and all the forces against God and decency combined. The anxiety had been there in Liberty's childhood every day of his life, an unarticulated prayer in his mother's heart—Oh, Lord, don't let my boy end up like that. Amen, Jesus.

And there he was, rooted to the spot outside Liberty's window, mocking everything he'd become. Behind another curtained window in another dimension of cyberspace was Liberty's E-mail. It sat there in its own place waiting to ambush him with more opinions he didn't want to have. He was receiving a single message over and over: A lot of people thought he murdered his wife simply because they'd always felt there was no other way the story of a pretty white woman and a nigger bastard could end.

Liberty replied to a few and initiated a dozen or so of his own, assuring his partners and friends that he was safe and seeking legal advice in a timely and orderly way in just the manner they had advised him. He called Wally Jefferson half a dozen times, but Wally's wife said he wasn't home. He called Marvin, but Marvin was out of the office. He stared at a cockroach climbing the wall in front of him and flashed to the two cops "interviewing" him in his apartment yesterday.

"If you have something to tell us about the night your wife died, now would be a good time." The one called Sanchez had looked at him in a friendly manner, as if he had nothing against people killing their wives and would be totally sympathetic to a confession.

"I told you everything I know." Liberty remembered the heat jolting through his body like lightning as he talked.

"I know you said that, Mr. Liberty. But there are a lot of ways we can go with this."

Liberty moved back in time to that first terrible point of reference, the "harmless hazing," as the administration at his boarding school had called it when five of the boys on his floor told him he had to be their slave, to kneel, touch his head to the ground, and say "Yes, massa," no matter what they told him to do or when they told him to do it.

The boys didn't understand that five of them were not enough to force him to kneel. Nor ten of them, or indeed the whole school. When he refused and they piled on him in an attempt to lower him to his proper place so they could urinate on him, one got a broken nose that bled all over the room, another got a broken arm, and a third a fractured jaw. The other two escaped with bad cuts and bruises. And the whole community rose to expel him from their midst. No one had told the fourteen-year-old Liberty the rule. The rule was white boys could hurt him but he could not defend himself. The parents of the boys in question, the student council, and the town paper called for his dismissal despite an investigation that absolved him of any wrongdoing. And when he begged to go home to end the confrontation, the administration, for reasons of its own, and his mother, who didn't want him to turn out a bum, had refused to let him.

Liberty was a rich man now. He traveled first class, had the best of everything. People asked for his opinion, wanted him to go on television, took his picture wherever he went. But it seemed that nothing really had changed.

"You asked me every question a dozen different ways. I flew to Chicago and missed the play. If I had been there as I was supposed to be, my wife and friend would still be alive." Liberty said it with no emotion, trying not to let go of his soul.

"But you were in the city. Your doorman and the driver of your car service said you got home around midnight. You knew where your wife was."

"Yes, but I didn't leave the apartment. I'll have to live with that for the rest of my life. If I'd gone to get her, no one would have attacked her." Liberty lowered his head, taking the blame for the situation.

"How do you know?" the Chinese cop asked.

Liberty turned his head to look at her. "Would you take me on?" he asked bluntly.

"Is that why your friend had a heart attack?" Sanchez was the one to reply.

"I don't understand the question."

"Did your friend Tor take you on?" The Chinese woman was standing on the other side of him, watching him with the cold indifference of a sphinx.

"Me?" he'd replied, puzzled.

"Yes. Were you jealous of your friend's relationship with your wife and—?"

He shook his head. "I didn't leave the apartment."

"Why would anyone want to hurt your wife?"

"Why would anyone want to hurt anyone? Why would you want to hurt me?"

"We don't want to hurt you, sir. We just want to know what happened January sixth, the night your wife was murdered. Why don't you tell us. You know we're going to find out in the end anyway."

Keys ground in one lock after another. Liberty had fallen asleep and was dreaming of Merrill, bleeding to death on the side of a mountain and himself struggling to bail her blood back inside of her body faster than it was pumping out. He could hear the police on the stairs and screamed as the apartment door burst open.

"What are you doing? What's going on here?"

No sound came out of his mouth. He was screaming in his mind.

"Hey! What's the matter with you? Can't you hear me?" It was the sandblasting voice of the crazy sister who wrapped her head twice its size. He took a deep breath, shuddering at his dream.

For a second she reminded him of his great-aunt Belle who'd been as tall as this woman, but big as an apartment building. That Belle had thought the world was all right until the civil rights movement came along in the sixties and personally stole her self-respect and set her back a few hundred years to a place nobody in his right mind would ever want to be, a sorry slave from another land. In Belle's world, color had been everywhere and color was fine. Color put no limits on the thing, was neither good nor bad, just was, sweet and bitter like birth and death. But the Movement took the sparkle, the highlights, the savor out of color, drained the nuance of the human palette in all its glory from Aunt Belle's life and made her Black.

"What's the matter wit you?" This Belle talked to him with a voice that streaked graffiti through sound waves.

Liberty saw that his computer power light was on, but the screen was blank. It had gone into hibernation. He must have been sleeping for a while. He hadn't finished the coffee the woman had made many hours ago. His mouth was dry. He couldn't remember the last time he'd eaten.

"Hey, man, I axed you a question. You got some kind of hearing problem?"

"No ma'am."

She took a few threatening steps into the room. "Then answer me when I talk wit you."

"Is that one of your house rules?" Liberty asked.

"What you talking about?"

"Your house rules, remember?"

"Uh-uh."

He raised a hand in peace. "Never mind."

She sucked in the side of her face, scowling. "You some sorry bastard," she said after a minute of staring at his hair.

"I'll agree with you there."

"You got any pills? Marvin said you ain't got no pills."

"I don't have any pills," Liberty said.

She cocked her head. "You gonna kill yourself?"

The woman moved in as if to protect him from himself. Now he could smell her. She didn't smell the way she looked or sounded. Smell was one of the first things he learned when he went to boarding school, how the rich smelled different from the poor. Clothes made the caste of a man, and so did smell. A person couldn't look good to the right people unless he smelled good to the right people, too. Very early on Liberty had learned how culture and color determined smell, and what one had to do about it.

Merrill had smelled like a field of berries. Raspberries and strawberries lived in her hair, in her skin. Liberty's stomach churned. This woman's chin jutted the way his sister's used to when she was defiant and knew she was in the wrong. And Belle didn't smell right. Something was wrong about her. Liberty had a sudden paranoid suspicion that she was a cop or an FBI agent, even a reporter, because she didn't exude any one of the heavy African spice potions of the sisters he knew. True homegirls went for deep and musky, earthy oil-based perfumes guaranteed to drop a brother in his tracks at a hundred paces. This girl smelled light and floral, with an undertone of orange peel.

He scratched his forehead. "What do you do for a living?" he asked abruptly.

She glared at him, the chin advancing even further on the battlefield. "None of your business."

"Miss Belle, do you happen to be the dealer in this building the police are looking for?"

"I told you I don't got no shit. If you gotta have it, you can git outta here now. There's lotsa shit out there." She pointed to the door.

Liberty shook his head. "I never liked the stuff. It makes you stupid."

She humphed through her nose.

"What's that mean?"

"Nothin'."

"It means you don't believe me. Well, we're even,

then." He punched a few buttons to shut his computer down and stood up, stretching.

"What you doin'?"

"I've invaded your privacy long enough. I know this has been a huge inconvenience. I apologize, and I'll be on my way."

Belle hoisted the canvas bag she'd been carrying to the table. "What for?"

He didn't answer.

"I axed you a question." She opened the bag and started unpacking the lunch she'd brought.

Liberty's stomach growled. "And I asked you one. If you don't have to answer, I don't have to answer."

"Jeesus," she muttered. "Is this important?"

"Trust is important to me. I prefer to know the people whose houses I hide in."

She stopped setting the table and parked a hand on her hip. "You wanna know who I am?"

"Yeah."

"What's it to you?"

"I don't know you. It's nothing to me, but if you're a dealer I don't want to be here when you're arrested. If you're a cop, I don't want you to turn me in."

A genuine laugh lit up her face. "What makes you think I'm either?"

He glanced at the merriment softening her features, then eyed the food, determined not to touch it. "Miss Belle, your accent comes and goes, and you don't live here."

"I thought ballplayers were dumb," she muttered.

"I haven't been a ballplayer for a long time."

"I guess you'll want a napkin."

He surveyed the meal a last time, then shook his head. "No thanks, I'm not staying."

"I made it myself."

"I have to go see someone."

"You'll have to wait till later." Belle picked up a fork. For a second Rick thought she was going to reach over and stab him with it. But she used it to fill a plate. She set the plate down in front of him.

His stomach growled again. He'd never liked bossy women, was sure he didn't like this one. She stood there, a bag of rags, pointing the fork at him.

"Your friend Tor was deep into the shit, man. Deep into it."

"I know that. It had been a problem in the past. I thought he was over it."

"No way, man."

"What about my wife . . . ?" The question hung there.

If Belle understood the question, she didn't show it. "Your wife was killed by a black man, that much we know."

"A black man, you sure?"

She nodded. "Could have been you." She gave him a hard look.

"Or Wally Jefferson."

Belle nodded, then switched her attention to the food on his plate. "Nothing runs on empty," she said.

"I've got to find that bastard."

"How about eating something first." Belle looked at the food. "I made it myself."

"All right." After a moment Rick sat down and took a bite.

27

April hurried down the hall to the prosecutor's office, her scarf flapping. She checked her watch: 12:33. She had hoped to catch Dean Kiang at his desk, but now hesitated. His door was three-quarters closed. What if he was with someone, or out to lunch? Suddenly she was unsure that she'd done the right thing by driving all the way down here to see him in person without taking the time to call him first and say she was coming. An hour ago she'd been certain that the great sage, the judge of proper feelings and behavior (in whom Skinny Dragon Mother believed, but April did not) would say there was no fault in her actions. So why the sudden attack of nerves that caused her coat and jacket to feel like a sauna set on high?

April had talked to prosecutors dozens, maybe hundreds, of times. And this particular prosecutor had already called and missed her twice today. Why then did she find it easier to handle a bloody homicide than to be a fragrant flower for an interested Chinese bee? April thrust her gloves in her pocket and tugged at her coat, sweating freely now. God, she hated winter.

A cop was supposed to be professional at all times, wasn't supposed to be attracted to anyone. April had the deepest contempt for the constant flirting, teasing, and fooling around that was a permanent fixture of precinct life. She fluffed at her hair with nervous fingers, then knocked on the door. No answer. She was double stupid, should have called first.

Kiang must be across the street in court. No, the judges always adjourned for lunch. He could be anywhere, could have gone to a crime scene or a precinct on another case. She knocked again, telling herself she shouldn't be disappointed, then poked her head in Kiang's tiny, cluttered office. It was empty.

She stood in the doorway for a second, her heart pounding. What now? Should she go to the medical examiner on her own and ask a few hard questions, as Mike had told her not to do? Should she leave Kiang a note, telling him she'd been there? She debated with herself for a moment, staring at the messy piles of papers on Kiang's desk.

Suddenly an arm draped across April's back. She flashed to a sergeant in the tactics house. The sergeant had played a bad guy acting like a good guy, who happened to have a Glock in his handshake. In an instant that sergeant had shot April dead to demonstrate how you never knew who had a razor blade between his teeth or a gun under his chin. Now, she whirled around, her hand instinctively reaching for the gun in her waistband.

"Well, hello, gorgeous," Kiang said, squeezing the arm going for the gun.

"Dean." An embarrassed flush flared across April's cheeks as she let her hand drop.

Kiang grinned. "Thanks for coming, babe. Can't do lunch, though, I have . . ." He checked his watch. "Ten minutes." Smoothly, he led her into his office and closed the door.

April took a seat, still blushing. People had called her a lot of things in her life, but no one had ever called her "babe," or thought she was looking for a date. The sage says a perfect person does not show anger or hurt. A perfect person is like the earth, accepting of fire and thunder, earthquake and flood, uncomplaining. Surviving all. She did not protest being called "babe," which she believed was the name of a pig in a movie. Remembering Skinny Dragon's advice, she gave him a weak smile back.

Kiang sat down at his desk and put his feet up. He was extremely good-looking even with his feet in her face. Taken for an idiot, April felt her heart banging away in her chest a lot faster than it had to. She wished she hadn't come.

"What can I do for you, sweetheart?" He made a telescope of his fingers and took a look at her through it.

Was it a Chinese thing for him not to admit he'd called her that morning? Or was it a male thing? April had come all the way downtown, past Chinatown, to the courts and prosecutor's office to talk to him. Kiang was the person with the greatest knowledge of the law, a higher authority than Ducci, than Mike, or Iriarte—even the CO of her precinct, whoever the new person was. But now that April was here, she didn't know where to start telling him her concerns. She'd met him over a dead body less than a week ago. Was she his sweetheart already? With men, sometimes it was hard to tell.

Suddenly Kiang put down the telescope and came down to earth. "I hear Liberty's taken off. What's going on?" he said seriously.

"Yes, he shook his surveillance sometime last night. We're trying to locate him." Ashamed of a failure that wasn't hers, April looked down at her hands. "But I didn't come about him."

"What then?"

"Sanchez and I had a meeting with Ducci this morning."

"So?" Kiang's face went blank at the mention of Sanchez.

April took a deep breath. "He's concerned about some irregularities coming out of the medical examiner's office."

"Yeah, like what?" Kiang twirled a pencil around two fingers.

"Someone from the ME's office called Mrs. Petersen and told her the tox reports on her husband."

"How do you know it was the ME's office?"

"The widow had the report before we did."

"What do they say?"

"I haven't seen them yet. They haven't come in. But somebody told Daphne Petersen that her husband had high enough levels of alcohol and cocaine in his body to cause his heart attack." April hesitated.

"Okay, I'll get someone to talk to Dr. Washington about the dripping faucet." Kiang glanced at his watch again, then dropped his feet to the floor.

"That's not the only thing," April murmured. "Dr. Washington didn't use the ultraviolets during Petersen's autopsy."

"So—?" Kiang shrugged and began shoving files into his briefcase.

"Well, Ducci says the victims' clothing indicates that Petersen died first. Petersen collapsed, and Merrill bled on his back. Also, there's a tiny hole and traces of blood on the inside of Petersen's sweater."

Kiang dropped the briefcase with a thud. "What are you telling me, that Ducci thinks Petersen was a homicide?"

April inhaled sharply, thinking of Daphne Petersen and her bronze-headed stud. "It's not impossible that the killer made Petersen look as if he'd died of a drug-induced heart attack, and Dr. Washington missed—"

"Oh, give me a break, April. The killer made a bloody mess of Merrill Liberty. I saw the photos of Petersen. No wounds, no blood. Unless the labs come up with two DNA samples from what they've got . . ." He glanced at his watch a third time.

April made a face at Dean's hurry to get out of there, wondering why he wasn't interested in the fact that Petersen had fallen first. She doubted this was a moment to bring up the question of the lint in the cashmere sweater from a T-shirt that wasn't on the body. Somehow, in this context, it might appear weak.

Kiang gave April a quick smile. "Hey, relax, baby. MEs make mistakes. You make mistakes. We all make mistakes. That doesn't mean we should complicate things unnecessarily by pointing them out. Frankly, this is the kind of conjecture that leads nowhere. It would confuse a jury and quite possibly lead to reasonable doubt in a cut-and-dried case."

"What if it isn't a cut-and-dried case?" With her index finger April worried a hangnail on her thumb.

Kiang started packing again. "Did you know I have an ulcer?"

"No. And frankly, I can't rule Petersen's wife out as the killer. She admitted he was planning to divorce her. He had another woman. She had a lot to gain."

Kiang nodded. "I saw the will, but we don't have a cause of death consistent with your theory."

April was silent as he clicked his briefcase closed.

"Look, this is the case of your life, baby. If you do this right, maybe you could get assigned down here, be a prosecutor's investigator. How about that? We could work together all the time." He reached out and patted her arm before leading the way out of the office.

"Show me your stuff. Bring in Liberty, huh, and then we'll have something to talk about."

They went downstairs in the elevator together. Then Kiang went off to court.

"Call me later, will you? Maybe we'll have dinner."

The wind was sharp and the air bitter cold as April turned to walk the two blocks south to One Police Plaza and the brick monolith that was police headquarters, where she'd left her car. Even in the cold, it was a long time before her sweat dried and her face stopped burning.

28

"Oh shit, man, a visit to Staten Island? That's all I need today," Mike groaned when he got the call that Liberty's stolen Lincoln had turned up in such an inconvenient place.

"You want to see it as is, you go where it is. Otherwise we haul it away and you see it in the lot after we've finished with it."

"What's it look like?"

"A mess. Somebody got wiped in it. Trunk's splattered with blood and cocaine. Must have been quite a party."

"Body?"

"No body."

Mike sighed and looked at his watch, figuring up the three hours it would take to drive downtown, take the ferry to Staten Island, be picked up by a detective there, driven to look at the car, take the ferry back to pick up his own car in lower Manhattan, then return to the line he'd been investigating before the call about the car came in. What he'd intended to do was drive to Brooklyn to have a little chat with Patrice, Liberty's close associate, to see if Patrice knew where Liberty was, and if Liberty and his wife were dopers, too.

An hour and a half to get out there, and the car was indeed a mess. Brains and bits of bone all over the front. It looked to Mike like a gunshot wound to the head of the passenger in the front seat, but what was left of the head and the rest of the body was missing. In the trunk, more gore, and in the corners of the trunk, little spilled piles of white powder from what must have been a large stash.

"You look in the water for the body?" Mike asked the detective, a skinny Hispanic who looked about twelve. "Easiest to get rid of it out there." He pointed to the rocky shore past where the car was parked on a lonely stretch of road.

"Yeah, we looked, didn't see anything. Maybe in five, six days in this water it'll pop up for us."

"It's pretty cold for that time frame."

The detective shrugged. "Seen enough?"

Mike nodded. Now he had to change his plan. He suddenly thought there was a slight leak in one of his tires. When he got back to town, he picked up his car near the ferry and drove up Twelfth Avenue to visit a friend who used to have a little sideline at one of the big dealerships. Somehow the bits and pieces of newly stolen cars would end up in his possession for a brief period of time. Roger Pickard was part of a network that broke cars down and distributed the parts along to body and audio and car part shops in prime locations around the tristate area.

Within a matter of hours, a stolen car would be in pieces, headed in a dozen different directions and virtually impossible to trace. When a rash of cars stolen around the city, and even as far away as New Jersey and Westchester, were linked to new leases sold at the dealership where Roger serviced all models of the five makes of cars available there, Roger had insisted grand larceny was not in his line. He was encouraged to prove it by fingering some people who scared him a lot, but apparently less than Mike did. Roger now worked in a garage that serviced limos. He had been very helpful last year providing background material on the habits of some limo drivers whose murders Mike had been investigating.

The beefy mechanic was stuffed behind the wheel of a white superstretch Mercedes, playing with the audio wires when Mike drove into the garage too fast in his grubby-looking Camaro that hadn't been cleaned up in a long time. He stopped just short of clipping the Mercedes. Pickard stuck his big head out of the window but didn't attempt to get out of the car.

"Long time no see. I almost feel neglected. What's going on, Sergeant?"

"Hey, Roger." Mike got out and casually walked around the Mercedes. The car didn't have a nick or a scratch on its four miles of milky surface. He opened the back door and took an inventory of the inside. Four sofas, a couple of TVs, a bar. A sunroof that opened so that a dozen occupants could stand up and wave at admiring crowds. Two control panels for audio and visual with lots of buttons. The thing looked as if it could seat a football team. Mike finished walking around the Mercedes and glanced at the other limos in the garage. This took him a few more minutes.

"What can I do for you, ma man?" Finally Roger emerged from the driver's seat. He was a big man, thick all over with teak-colored skin and hair cut too short to curl. He smiled. "We're always looking for reliable drivers. Maybe you're interested."

"Maybe."

"You're still driving that old wreck. Looks real bad, man. Maybe you'd like a new car." Roger's grin widened.

"Maybe."

"What's up, man?"

Mike glanced around again. Roger seemed to be working on about a dozen cars. Town cars, stretch limos, a few exotics. The smell of lubricants, gas, oil, and leather intoxicated the air. "You all alone here?"

"Ah, Pancho is around somewhere." Roger didn't turn around to look for him.

"I've got a slow leak." Mike pointed at his right front tire. "Could you take a look at it for me?"

"It's an honor, man." Roger snickered as he rolled over a jack.

"You been following the Liberty case?" Mike asked casually.

"Who hasn't?"

"What can you tell me about it?"

Roger sniffed some air through his nose. Reference to nose candy, the dead white wife, or the pictures in the newspapers of the funeral without a grieving husband? Mike waited as Roger removed the nuts from the wheel and rocked it off.

"He came to fathers' day at my kid's school a few years back."

"No kidding."

Roger lifted the wheel and eased it into a tub of water without making waves, then slowly rolled it around.

"What do you want to know?"

"What kind of shape was his car in?"

"What makes you think I know?"

"You know everything about limos, Rog, ma man. You know which cars come with the boys to blow the gay gentlemen, and which ones supply the tarts. You also know who's got the medicine cabinets, and where they park for the parties."

"Nooooo, man, I don't know nothin' about that."

"I heard Liberty is a gay gentleman, what do you know about that?"

"I don't see no bubbles here. You sure about that leak?" Roger turned the tire over in the water.

"What about it?"

"No sir, no bubbles coming out of here. The man's straight as they come. I'd know that. I can *smell* it a mile away." He smiled. "Like I can smell you, man."

"What about snowflake?"

The smile faded. "You should have heard how he talked to those kids. He told them, 'Once you lose control of your body and your mind, you got nothin' left. Nothin'.' " Roger straightened up and lifted the tire out. "You didn't need me to tell you that."

"Liberty's car was nicked last week, just after New Year's. It showed up this morning with someone's brains spattered all over the front seat."

"Lord save us." Roger bounced the tire to the

ground and rolled it back to Mike's jacked-up Camaro. "You know who that somebody is?"

"I thought you might know."

"No, man. That's ugly stuff. I don't know nothing about nothing like that."

"I keep hearing that. You know Wally Jefferson?"

"Yeah, man, I know him." Pickard busied himself replacing the tire.

"He's the one who took the car out of Liberty's garage. He said he had permission to take it. Liberty says he's lying."

"Yeah, well, some drivers do that when the owners are out of town. One time a garage attendant took a limo home to impress his girlfriend, drove her around, did her in the backseat, had a few drinks from the bar, and totaled the thing an hour later." He shook his head.

"Now the other guy is a different story," he went on, suddenly voluble.

"What other guy?" Mike watched the wheel return to his car.

"That guy Petersen who died. Everybody knew he was deep into it. I heard on the news he died of a heart attack. I wouldn't be surprised if it turned out to be bad shit." He gave Mike a shrewd look. "I wouldn't be surprised if it's all hushed up. Now what else do you want to know?"

Oh, just the names and addresses of Jefferson's friends and known associates, the exact nature of the coke connection to Merrill Liberty's death. Where Liberty's Lincoln had been on the night of her murder, what it had been used for, who the other dead person was, and when he (or she) had died. Mike also wanted to know how Liberty himself fit into it all.

"Who's Petersen's source?" he said finally.

"You got me," Roger said. He finished putting the nuts back on the wheel and let the front end of the Camaro whoosh down to the ground. "You come on back if you have any more trouble with that tire," he said. "And I hear Wally has a girlfriend up on a Hundred Thirty-eighth Street and B-way. That Petersen car is up there allllll the time, know what I mean?"

Out in Brooklyn at 4:05 P.M., Mike Sanchez was back on his original track, looking for his cocaine source and brooding about April Woo. He drove along a quiet street, searching for the building where Patrice Paul lived, feeling really peeved. Dealing with a cop was always a sketchy thing. No matter how well you knew one, how closely you worked together, you never really knew what a cop was up to. April hadn't said where she was going when they parted, so she could be anywhere, following up on any one of the several bombs dropped on them this morning. What if Petersen had in fact been murdered by his wife and the ME missed it? What if Liberty was gay and had a white woman as a cover? What if they were all dopers?

Mike cruised the street slowly, looking for signs of illegal activity and brooding about April. He guessed she'd gone over to see Rosa Washington, but that was just a guess. He'd seen all the messages on her desk from Kiang. It was just as possible that she'd yielded to Kiang's pleas to come downtown and see him. That bastard Kiang called her five times a day. The man happened to be the dumbest prosecutor in New York, and because there were a lot of dumb prosecutors in New York, that was saying something. Mike gave April the benefit of the doubt. Maybe she didn't know how dumb Kiang was. On the other hand, maybe she wouldn't think he was because her mother had always told her, "Chinese people are best people." What kind of bullshit was that? Mike scowled.

Out in Brooklyn, the snow of Sunday night's storm was still very much in evidence in spite of some rain in between. A low wall of snow blocked the cars that hadn't been moved before the plows came in to clear the streets. He watched a discouraged-looking line of kids with their hoods up straggle home in the early dusk. The snow was crusted hard on top from the melting and freezing of the last few days, too unappetizing for the most determined snowball fighters.

Okay, so he was getting a little messed up about this April Woo and Dean Kiang thing. Okay, so he didn't want to make any disparaging remarks about females taking shortcuts by sleeping their way to the top. But Mike had noticed over time that most women, no matter what their culture or class, tried to make their way up the success ladder on the horizontal first. And only when sex was not an option for getting ahead would women resort to actually working for their promotions. It didn't bother him, it was just a fact of life. In the department, female uniforms came on to detectives, sergeants, lieutenants, captains, whoever's attention they could get. And higher ranking females came on to the highest ranking male officers. Not April Woo, though. Not until now. And now she was coming on to the dumbest prosecutor in New York just because he was a Chinese lawyer in a suit. It made him sick. All his sensitivity, his respect for her independence and her feelings. For nothing. Showed how much he knew about women. He drove along slowly, feeling lovesick and bruised.

He scanned the street looking for drug trade, didn't see any. This was a pretty good area, quiet. There was not much going on. A few people were trying to dig their cars out. But there were no suspicious clots of idle men standing around. Looked as if the people in this area were employed. Were at work. Kids going home from school. It was another block or so to Patrice's building.

The tire seemed okay now. Maybe it never had a leak, after all. Patrice Paul lived on the fourth floor of a modest brick building eight stories high. He answered Mike's ring by buzzing him in. The door was open when Mike got off the elevator. The tall light-colored Haitian, dressed in jeans and a gray cardigan, stood by his door watching Mike's approach down his hall like a foot soldier holding his fire on an enemy charge until he could see the whites of their eyes.

When Mike got close enough he saw that Patrice had surprising golden flecks in his eyes and was afraid. "Sergeant Sanchez," Mike said, identifying himself. "Mind if I come in for a minute?"

"I was just having a cup of tea, would you like some?" Patrice Paul's voice was low and musical.

"Uh, sure." Mike was startled. It wasn't the reception he'd expected. He went into the apartment first.

It was a three-room apartment that had been decorated with a lot of thought. The living room had a number of Caribbean-type throw rugs: Two were thrown over the highly patterned sofa. Two fan-top chairs like the kind in the restaurant. Probably came from there. Through the kitchen door, utensils for fancy cooking were visible on the wall and stove. Two doors on the other side were closed. One was probably a closet, the other a bedroom. A pottery teapot sent fragrant jasmine tea steam up into the air above the coffee table that was positioned in front of the sofa. Beside the teapot were a matching milk jug, a plate of large round yellow cookies studded with macadamia nuts, and two cups as if someone had been expected. Their eyes met.

"Sorry to interrupt," Mike said.

"It doesn't really matter." Patrice looked anxiously at the bedroom door. "There's no hurry."

So, Patrice was the one who was gay. Mike hadn't picked it up the night of the murder. He opened his leather jacket without taking it off and sat awkwardly on one of the fan chairs. Usually, he felt kind of peculiar when he was alone with a queen, but Patrice was so demure and resigned that he suddenly had a wild feeling of elation, as if he'd cornered the squirrel who'd killed Merrill Liberty, or the squirrel was behind the bedroom door. Nah, couldn't be.

Patrice lowered his bottom to the sofa and drew his knees together as if to protect his manhood from the policeman's violation. Then he carefully poured the tea without spilling a drop.

"You know about Liberty's missing Lincoln?" Mike asked.

Patrice looked surprised. "I think I heard something about it. Liberty was upset."

"He's going to be more upset now. Do you know where he is?"

Patrice looked worried. "No, he didn't call me last night. Why will he be upset?"

"We found the car."

"I don't think he cares much about the car anymore."

"He may now. Somebody died in it."

Parice made a face and crossed himself quickly. "How, mon?"

"He was shot in the head."

"Aww that's bad."

"You know where Liberty is?" Mike demanded.

Patrice shook his head. "This is really bad."

"We need to find him before he gets hurt, you know what I mean?" Mike picked up his teacup, looked at it, then put it down. He looked toward the closed bedroom door, was going to have to go in there and check it out.

"Is he in danger, mon?"

"He knows a lot of things he hasn't told us about. Now three people are dead. You don't want him to be next, do you?"

"No, mon, I don't."

"Then give me some ideas where I might find him." Mike took a cookie and bit into it, looking away as Patrice teared up.

He ate another cookie. Patrice shook his head, didn't want to tell, then slowly he nodded.

29

A blue-and-white squad car pulled up in front of the precinct as Jason was trying to pay his taxi fare. Two chunky white cops got out of the front seat, opened the back door, and began encouraging their passenger to get out of the car. When the passenger didn't get out, they resorted to a team effort. It took both of them to wrestle out of the backseat of the car a struggling black man covered with blood, who jerked back and forth as if electrically charged.

"Fucking *pig,* fucking *pig*. You *know* I didn't do nuthin'. Fuck *you,* fucker! Geez, man, whatchu doin' this for?"

"Come on, Harry, be a good boy, you don't want to fall down and hurt yourself, do you?"

"No, fucker. I'm not goin in *there*." He was a tall, thin man, emaciated even, wearing pink-and-green-plaid pants with oily-looking stains in the seat and crotch. Navy zip jacket, its front shiny with freshly spilled blood. The man leaned away from the two cops, who were both smaller than he. He braced hard against their tugging like the kind of tree that doesn't bend in the wind, the kind that gets uprooted in a bad storm.

"Jesus, first he stinks up the car. Can you beat that, and now the turd is trying to break a leg. Now stand up, Harry. You're resisting a police officer."

"Fucking *pigs,* fucking *pigs*." The man's voice rose to a wail. His wrists were cuffed behind him and his whole body leaned away from the two uniforms as if he could become a rubber band and extend himself across the street. When that didn't work, he suddenly let his knees crumple under him. He sank to the sidewalk, trying to lie down and scrape his face on the cement. The two cops didn't let him get that far.

"I'm not goin' in *there,*" the man wailed.

The cab was stopped for a long time as Jason fumbled with singles and quarters. He nervously watched the two cops haul the bleeding, screaming man to his feet. He tried to concentrate. The fares had gone up recently, but even so the numbers on the meter seemed very high, almost double the price it used to be. He didn't come to Fifty-fourth and Eighth Avenue very often, wasn't absolutely sure what the fare should be. He frowned as the meter jumped another thirty cents after he was sure the driver had already pushed the button.

"Yo hurtin' me, assholes," the black man screamed. And then, as he was dragged across the sidewalk past a number of bored-looking uniformed officers by the door, his blurry eyes focused and met Jason's. "You a witness," he screamed. "I gonna call you as a witness. Lookit all this blood. Po-lice brutalitee."

"Aw shut up, Harry, a dozen people saw you stab your best friend."

"Never saw the fucker befo," Harry muttered as an obliging uniform opened the precinct door and they disappeared inside.

Jason slammed the taxi door on the Arab driver who, all the way down from the Eighties, had performed a loud sing-along with prayerful screeches coming from a recorder placed on the dashboard. Jason was sure the driver had doctored the meter. It was three minutes past six. He had to be back in his office for his last patient at 7:30. So far the trip had cost him twelve dollars and thirty cents and a very bad case of heartburn. The anxious feeling he'd had all day had intensified until now he was almost shivering inside. His chest burned. He checked his watch. It was now 6:04, and he wanted to run from this spot just like the guy with his wrists cuffed behind him and blood on his jacket. If *he* felt anxious and threatened coming to the police station, it was no wonder Rick Liberty would do anything to avoid coming here.

Jason reached inside his coat and straightened his tie before following the prisoner through the door. Two uniforms noted the gesture and glanced at each other. For a second Jason had a feeling that they might tackle him. But he was feeling paranoid.

Inside, a banner read, MIDTOWN NORTH WISHES YOU A HAPPY AND HEALTHY NEW YEAR. Jason announced himself at the front desk, which was high enough to make him feel short.

"Dr. Frank to see Sergeant Woo," he told the pale-faced man in uniform sitting there.

The man drew the corners of his mouth down and glanced at the two people sitting up there with him. They drew the corners of their mouths down as if they had never heard of such a person either. Jason waited, tapping a foot as they discussed it. It was dark as deepest night outside, and the temperature had dropped again. The bloodied suspect had already disappeared. It was quiet. The uniform at the desk finally punched a number on the kind of old black telephone that hardly anyone outside of third-world countries used anymore. There was more discussion and some shaking of heads as the phone rang unanswered.

After what seemed like a long time, the uniform hung up the phone without having spoken to anyone, and April came out of a green door.

No smile at Jason or the people at the desk. "Thanks for dropping by," she said to Jason.

"I'm sorry I couldn't get back to you today. I've been busy. What's this about anyway?"

She gave him a curt nod and headed back to the green door. The door had STAIRS painted on it. Her face was blank, but Jason could tell by her walk and the way she indicated that they would climb the stairs that things were not going well. She didn't say anything as she took the stairs two at a time to the second floor. On the second floor all the doors were closed.

They turned a corner. The sign on the green door facing them read DETECTIVE UNIT. April's eyes flickered as she opened the door.

The setup here was not the same as the Two-O, where Jason had been several times and almost felt at home. This space was more cut up and looked smaller, though April had told him it was a bigger unit.

"My office."

She held out her hand, palm up like a traffic cop to halt him where he was while she headed a few feet right to another office with a window in the door. She moved a few face muscles at the window. Some moments later, a man many inches shorter than Jason came out of the office shrugging on a glen plaid suit jacket over a deep blue dress shirt and a shoulder holster with a big gun in it. The man's hair was short and shiny. He had a pencil-thin mustache and was wearing a tie that looked a whole lot more expensive than Jason's.

"My CO, Lieutenant Iriarte, wanted to have a few words with you," April said.

Jason nodded at her grimly. *Thanks* for telling me.

"I've heard about you," Iriarte said. "Sergeant Woo here thinks a lot of you."

"I think a lot of her, too." Jason returned the compliment.

Iriarte did a quick check of the room. A man was working at a computer. Two others were at their desks; both were on the phone. The suspect Jason had seen only a few minutes ago was now lying on the bench in the holding cell behind him with the bloody jacket over his head.

"This is a very sensitive situation we've got here," Iriarte said. "Let's talk in here."

He headed to the back of the squad room and opened the door to the interview room. It was very small, about the size of a one-inmate prison cell. Inside was a small table and three chairs. Two Styrofoam cups half-filled with cigarette butts were on the table.

Iriarte made a face and pointed at the cups. April picked them up and took them out of the room.

"Please sit down," Iriarte said to Jason, pointing to the chair facing the wall with the mirror in it.

Jason glanced at the mirror, then sat in the chair opposite the blank wall so whoever might be sitting behind the mirror couldn't see his face. Iriarte ran his tongue around the inside of his mouth, considering whether to take the chair Jason had rejected or order Jason to sit in it.

April returned minus the garbage, her face dense as a brick wall. She closed the door and stood by it, eyes cast down in the traditional Oriental pose of demure deference, as she waited for further instructions. The lieutenant's face relaxed at this show of passivity. He jerked his chin at her, directing her to the chair Jason hadn't wanted, then took the chair between them.

"This is a sensitive situation," he said again.

"So I understand," Jason replied.

"Very sensitive."

Jason gazed at him, thinking he must be an obsessive-compulsive to keep his mustache so short and precisely matchstick thin.

"I understand you've worked with us on other cases out of the Two-O." The upper lip twitched as if it knew how Jason had diagnosed its owner.

"Very informally," Jason murmured.

"Your wife was involved in an incident . . ."

Everybody in the world knew that. "She was kidnapped," Jason said with no sign of emotion.

Iriarte dipped his head as if he'd just gained a point. "She has an unfortunate way of getting caught in the middle of things," he murmured, insinuating something Jason didn't want to explore.

"Her best friend has been murdered." Jason sat in a metal chair, his feet flat on the floor in front of him. He had unbuttoned his coat when he entered the precinct. Now he took it off and pointedly glanced at his watch. Six-twenty. He had to leave in fifty minutes or be late for his next patient.

"You know that Liberty has disappeared."

"I am aware that he was not at the funeral yesterday. I admit I was very surprised, since he told me he intended to be there and wanted us to have dinner with him and her parents afterward. Do you have any idea where he is?"

"You interviewed him."

"I was in close contact with him all Monday. Sergeant Woo asked me to do a psychological profile of him. I believe I did it on Tuesday or Wednesday—I'd have to check my notes." Jason glanced at April. Her eyes were still cast down. She was ashamed at the way her boss was questioning him.

"Why don't you tell me the results of that interview," Iriarte said coldly.

"What would you like to know?"

Iriarte ran his tongue around the inside of his mouth again. "The usual things, what his fantasies tell you." He smirked.

"Well, there is a lot of violence in his background. His grandmother was raped by a white man. His father was killed in the Korean War. He was the victim of violence himself many times in his adolescence and young adulthood. But no member of his family has a history of antisocial or criminal behavior, and he himself does not have a violent nature. In his childhood there were no indicators of antisocial behavior."

"What does that mean?"

"He didn't torture animals, bully other children, play with matches, and burn things. Hurting was something he didn't understand. He was and still is puzzled by it. He doesn't understand how people can hurt each other."

"How do you know?"

It was Jason's turn to smile. "I can tell from his fantasies and his heroes. He revered Jackie Robinson, his namesake Frederick Douglass, Richard Wright. He reads poetry. He has no weapons in his home. He thinks about other people's feelings. He's empathic. Killers don't care about the feelings of their victims."

Iriarte passed over that. "What about alcohol and substance abuse?"

"Liberty has migraine headaches. He can't drink and he has strong negative feelings about drugs. He came from a community where drugs destroyed many of his childhood friends."

"That's interesting. His friend Tor was a user."

"That astonishes me," Jason said.

"You think that would be a problem for Liberty?"

"I don't think he would approve."

"What about the migraines? Is that what triggers his violence?"

"People who get migraines are often perfectionists. When little things go wrong, they become frustrated and the pressure builds up without a safety valve. This kind of personality can't go to the gym or play ball to let off steam. And rather than strike out at others, they internalize their rage. The appearance can sometimes be that of a person in torment. Or a person enraged. But the rage is directed at themselves, not others."

Iriarte made a skeptical face to indicate what he thought of the psychobabble. "Someone was killed in his car."

Jason was stunned. "Who?"

"We don't know. The body is missing. We're wondering what Liberty's connection to it is," Iriarte said coldly.

Jason turned to April. What was the meaning of this? She shook her head. "But Liberty couldn't have had anything to do with that. The car was stolen. He hadn't seen it for weeks."

"Well, if he knew the car was the site of a murder and he happened to be a suspect in another murder, he would say that, wouldn't he?"

Jason glared at Iriarte. "He doesn't have the profile of a killer."

"Then get him to come in here and prove it like a man." Iriarte stabbed the air with a finger.

"I'm a physician. I'm no expert in police work, but I don't get the feeling you're regarding Liberty from the position of innocent until proven guilty, which is the position taken by the law of this land. So I could say the same of you—if he's guilty, you prove it."

"Don't get defensive now. I'm just asking for your assistance here, Dr. Frank. You're an expert in state of mind. You and your wife know Liberty as well as anybody, and we believe you know where he is."

Jason shook his head. "We don't know where he is."

Iriarte went on as if he hadn't spoken. "If you are his friend, you will convince him that his best interests will be served by coming in to see us as soon as possible."

"By turning himself in to people who believe he killed his wife?"

"By coming to talk with us. That's all we want to do."

"Is Liberty aware of your wish to speak with him?"

Iriarte flicked a hostile glance at April. She remained impassive. He took a deep breath. "We're in the middle of an investigation," he said. "We told him not to leave."

"I understand that." Jason directed his next question at April. "I gather you spoke with him at some length yesterday."

"Yes."

"What was the nature of your conversation?"

April raised a shoulder.

"Does that mean you led him to believe you think he murdered his wife?"

"He had opportunity. We believe he may have murdered his wife. We don't know if there's a connection with the murder in his car. But we will," Iriarte again.

More acid roiled around in Jason's stomach. He felt ill. Could Rick have killed Merrill, after all? Could his judgment of Rick be so wrong? What could be the motivation for it? Why would he kill her? He thought of the morning after the murder when Rick hadn't wanted medication. He'd wanted to be there, fully alert, because he thought the police had made a mistake and that Merrill was coming back. Rick was no actor, he'd been in genuine shock. But then again, he was a black man in a white firm, in a white world with a white wife. He had to be something of an actor to look so comfortable pulling that off. Jason realized he was holding his breath. He let it out before speaking.

"Do you have any evidence to suggest Liberty killed his wife?" Jason asked carefully.

"I'm not at liberty to tell you, no pun intended." Iriarte smirked at the pun nonetheless. "Have you been in touch with him?"

Jason thought of the funeral that had been so incomplete without Rick there. He thought of Rick's disappearing before the news of his absence at the funeral appeared on every TV and in every newspaper in the country, possibly to avoid arrest, and he thought of the E-mail message Rick had sent him, rambling and incoherent. Did E-mail count as being in touch? He decided it didn't.

"No," Jason said, they hadn't been in touch.

"Are you aware that if you help a criminal avoid arrest, you are a criminal yourself and can be prosecuted as such?"

"Do you have a warrant for Liberty's arrest?"

Iriarte sucked on his cheeks. "Not at this time."

Jason checked his watch. He had to go. "Well, I told you what I know about Liberty. I don't have anything else to add that will help you."

"Thanks for coming in." Iriarte jerked his chin at April. *Take him away.*

30

Hey, pretty one. What are you doing here again?" Ducci hastily filed some slides in a box and stowed it away in his desk. Then he swiveled his chair around to Nanci, making nice all around. "Hey, Nance, you know April Woo."

Nanci looked April over, raking a hand through her good dye job. "How you doin', Woo. I hear you made sergeant."

"I'm in Midtown North now," April said wearily. She shook some raindrops off her coat and glanced at the two guest chairs in the room. They were occupied by files, a skull, and some labeled objects the two dust and fiber experts must be studying.

"Yeah, I heard, detective squad. That idiot Hagedorn still there?" Nanci pushed back her chair, stretching out a pair of faultless legs in black tights.

April nodded. "Still there. How're you doing, Nanci?"

"Oh, overworked and underpaid. And I have to sit next to an egomaniac. I guess it's raining out." Nanci reached into a desk drawer for her purse and a grungy-looking red sweater.

"Better than snow," April remarked.

"I guess."

"Oh, come on. You love every second you spend with me. I taught you everything you know," Ducci said, peeved.

"Oh, sure I do. I have boxes of stuff on this Central Park case, people breathing down my neck on it, and suddenly *he's* got this bee in his bonnet about Petersen's autopsy and T-shirt lint." Nanci rolled her eyes.

"Well, he doesn't get to see many autopsies these days," April said.

"And, he shouldn't." Nanci sniffed. "Wet stuff's not his area."

Ducci still had Tor Petersen's cashmere sweater on his desk with the severed fibers in the chest carefully cut out for his slides. A sleeve hung over the edge. Ducci played with the cuff like a cat with a tassel.

"I was doing blood before you were born. I know fuckups when I see them." Ducci turned to April. "Where's your boyfriend?"

What boyfriend? "If you're referring to Sanchez, who isn't my boyfriend, I haven't seen him since this morning. The car Liberty claimed was stolen turned up in Staten Island with a bloody interior."

"No kidding."

"Might be a drug buy gone wrong. I think Sanchez planned to look at it, then go out to New Jersey to talk to Petersen's driver."

"In this weather?"

"Yes. Mind if I put my coat here?"

"No, no, go ahead, sit down. You want some coffee or something?" Ducci grinned, playing the host.

"Uh-uh, yours is worse than ours." April slung her coat over the back of Ducci's guest chair and moved the skull over to the filing cabinet.

"Couldn't you get the guy to come into the station?"

"We talked to him once. He held back on us." She sat down and let out a sigh. "Now he's gone elusive on us and we've got two suspects we can't keep track of. Makes us look pretty careless, doesn't it?"

"We all have bad days."

"This is more than a bad day."

Ducci pointed to the plastic bag April had dropped at her feet. "You got something new for me?"

She glanced down, startled. "Oh, God, I'm so tired I don't know what I'm doing." She tossed the bag to Ducci. He caught it and looked inside.

"Nice sweater, a belated Christmas gift for me, pretty one?"

"Nah, it's another of Petersen's sweaters."

Ducci pulled the maroon cashmere out of the bag and grimaced at the heady aroma emanating from it. "Vanilla," he said decisively.

April looked surprised. "How can you guys identify smells like that? I could never have put a flavor to that stink."

Ducci laughed, creasing his round choirboy's cheeks. "I know most things," he murmured. "I know your perfume, know your boyfriend's."

"No kidding. What is it?" she asked about Mike's perfume.

Ducci didn't answer. He seemed stunned by the white T-shirt folded into the sweater. "What are you telling me with this?"

April smiled at Nanci. "You know most things, Duke. You figure it out for me."

"Okay, a T-shirt," Nanci said flatly. "So now we know Petersen wore T-shirts—sometimes. I'm going home."

"His widow told me he never went without one, and she was very upset that I asked," April said. "Apparently Petersen thought it was unhealthy to have cashmere next to his skin."

Preoccupied, Ducci pulled a Snickers bar out of his desk drawer. For once he was too absorbed to tear it open. He scratched the corner of his small mouth as he studied the sweater. "Too bad it's too big for me," he murmured.

"Keep eating those candy bars and it won't be for long." Nanci laughed.

"This is for you, Ducci, nobody else. And you, Nanci, if you care to listen. Daphne Petersen called to speak to Rosa Washington the day after the murder. I was there when she called. Rosa wasn't there so she left a message. Today, Daphne was the first person to get her husband's tox report. And then there's the fact that Petersen's body was cremated in record time. She almost lost her cookies when I told her her husband's undershirt was not on him at the time of his autopsy."

"Who are you suspecting, the Petersen woman or our good doctor of maybe more than just sloppy work?"

April shook her head. "I did a little checking on Daphne Petersen. She came to this country twelve years ago, when she was eighteen, worked as a manicurist in several upscale beauty salons, sang in a cocktail bar at night. No priors, no driver's license. She met Petersen when she did his nails. He married her. She was number three and a step down from his usual style of wife. She might have killed him if she thought the fairy tale was over."

Ducci scratched the side of his face. "We still don't have a homicide on her husband, and if we don't have a homicide, we don't have a case against the Petersen woman, you following me?"

"Of course, I know that," April groaned.

"So if you want to pursue this line—and I'm not saying you should or you shouldn't—you have to prove there was a homicide on a body whose death report says otherwise and that is no longer with us for further examination."

"Well, Ducci, you brought it up. I'm having trouble letting it go now."

"I didn't say you should or shouldn't. Just be careful. It's the kind of thing that can backfire." He pointed to the sweater. "Was this just for background or do you want me to do something with it?"

The black hair that Daphne Petersen had insisted belonged to Petersen's girlfriend, but actually looked to April just like Daphne's, was stuck to the ribbing of the sweater. April picked it off and handed it to Ducci, shaking her head. "Probably unconnected."

"What's your hypothesis?" Ducci rummaged around his desk for a plastic envelope.

"The widow claims it's the hair of Petersen's girlfriend. Didn't you find a similar one on his body?" April asked.

"Oh, yeah, it's around here somewhere. Yeah, interesting hair. It was relaxed and straightened." Ducci squinted at the hair April had given him. "Yeah, remarkably like this. You have any more? I'll need to make some slides of it."

"No more at the moment. Why so interesting?"

"Remember that case with the Jane Doe prostitutes?" Ducci found an envelope for the hair, labeled it, and sat back in his chair.

Nanci nodded vigorously. "We did a big study on hair products. Those girls were well kept. Best makeup, hair products. You name it. Turned out they were Russian. We were able to identify them through their hair."

"Their hair was colored," Ducci went on, "then moisturized with Goldwell products. They're German, and so expensive only a few salons in the city use them. The madam of our three dead tarts had made sure her girls had the very best of everything—that is, until they ran into a little trouble with one of their diplomat customers."

"I remember." April took the next step. "So the hair on Petersen's body was colored with a Goldwell product?"

Ducci nodded.

"Are we looking for a Russian tart?"

"Ha-ha. No, models use them. Actresses. Singers."

"People who might once have worked in a beauty salon."

"Right. Get me a few strands of the widow's hair."

"I don't have probable cause to get a warrant for that."

"Then do it carefully. Going home now?"

"I wish I were." April was way off the chart now. Hours past go-home time. Iriarte had hoped they would clear the case in forty-eight hours. By Wednesday they'd failed that deadline. Now the lieutenant wanted it cleared in a week. It was Friday night. April figured she had two days to go before total disgrace.

Impatiently she waited for Ducci to give her the list of hairdresser salons that used Goldwell products. She bet that the name of the salon where Daphne Petersen had once worked was on it. She checked her watch; it was time to get going.

31

Except for the security guard at the loading dock and three or four scientists working late in the top-floor labs, the medical examiner's office building was shut down for the night. At 8:06, Rosa Washington emerged from the elevator. Without bothering to hit the light switches, she hurried down the murky hall to her office. She was wearing an immaculate green scrub suit, still starched and fresh, with matching booties over her sneakers. She had no surgical cap on her head or mask dangling around her neck. No footsteps sounded on the scuffed linoleum floor as she hurried along, absently rubbing her palms together.

No one looking at her would have been able to tell that Rosa felt anxious. Her sculpted features were frozen in their customary expression of unflappable serenity. She always had a set look on her face, the same one every day no matter who approached her with what request or question. The expression gave her the appearance of being on a higher plane than mere mortals, as if she could not be touched by earthly trouble. Some people thought she was arrogant and the distance she kept from the horrors of her job, attitude. Others were certain she was a deeply spiritual person, someone who reached beyond the grave to heaven itself with every dissection she made. And still others were convinced she was not very bright.

Rosa herself didn't care what people said about her. There had been so many speculations about so many aspects of her and her life for so many years she was no longer interested what the latest rumor about her entailed. Many years ago when she was just twelve, she had learned from a song—and from the death of the sixth-grade guinea pig (gutted with a kitchen knife while it was spending a school holiday with the family)—to hold her head up high and find a way of explaining the unexplainable. She also learned to keep walking in the direction she wanted to go no matter what happened. With such a strategy, she'd always been able to outdistance prejudice and envy.

Her office door was partly open. She saw the haven of her desk with its neat pile of files, and the desk lamp angled the way she'd left it hours ago, beaming light on her appointment book and her blotter. She rushed inside, ready to collapse in her desk chair, safe and exhausted after a long, demanding day.

"Hi, I'm glad I caught you. I was afraid you'd left."

The calm, soft voice came from behind her. Rosa whirled around, stifling a scream. "Sweet Jesus, you half scared me to death," she sputtered at the Chinese cop, who was sitting in a chair behind the door on the dark side of the room.

"What are you doing over there in the dark?" Rosa forced herself to slow down as she continued on to her desk. There, a quick check proved that her appointment book still had its rubberband holding it closed. But who knew what the cop would have looked through when she was in there . . . for how long? Rosa hoisted the briefcase that had been sitting on the floor to the desktop and dropped the appointment book inside. She rubbed her hands together, then sniffed them for chemical smell. Without looking at the cop, she allowed herself to collapse in her chair, willing calm and peace into her troubled soul.

After a moment she let her eyes drift over to the cop. What was April Woo doing here? Rosa looked for an answer in the Asian features and failed; April's face was expressionless, as still and empty as that of a corpse recently deprived of life. Rosa didn't see such complete emptiness in the living very often. It felt eerie to her. It reminded Rosa of her mother, who'd been beaten nearly to death every Saturday night of her life by her husband, Rosa's father, without complaining, until Rosa stopped the attacks when she was twelve.

The images of the bruises on her mother's body, the dead look in her mother's eyes, the sound of her mother weeping while she was raped and the groans when she was kicked, punched, and slammed against the wall had always acted as the inspiration for Rosa's work. It was her mother's blank-faced pain that drove Rosa to look unflinchingly at the most horrible of human damage and decay, day after day, so she could tell the world how and when that damage had occurred. Rosa's mother used to tell Rosa the secret of survival was to whisper to herself, "I am still and free at my center."

Rosa took in the long slender skirt, the silk scarf, and the well-tailored jacket of the Chinese detective and wondered what kind she was. She'd known only two Chinese detectives. One had worked in Harlem and was terrified of the dead at any stage of decomposition. She considered him a wimp. The other had been fired for corruption. She didn't figure April for being scared or corrupt.

"So what are you doing here, Sergeant Woo?" she said, smiling and striving to speak as softly as April had.

April sighed. "It's been a long day. We've got trouble with this Liberty case. I need some help."

"I could use some help, too," Rosa said. "You know poor Malcolm is in the hospital."

"Still?" April adjusted her coat over the back of her chair.

It was clear to Rosa that she'd been there long enough to get comfortable.

"Yeah. His doctors can't find out what kind of pneumonia he has. We have better labs here." She snorted with disgust.

"You have a heavy load?"

Rosa glanced down at her hands, rubbed them

quickly together. "Nothing I can't handle. How long have you been here?"

"Five minutes. The guard downstairs said you hadn't left yet, but he didn't know where you were. Not operating, by the look and smell of you."

Rosa's eyes caught the butt of April's gun sticking from the holster at her waist. "No, I always change after every procedure. Can't risk contamination, you know." She sniffed her hands again, couldn't seem to help it. They smelled bad.

"Yourself or the customers?"

Rosa smiled. "My patients, you could say. I'm a bit of a nut about cleanliness. Can't place too high a premium on every level of professionalism, you know." She rubbed her hands, wishing she could wash them again.

"So I've heard. That's why I'm here. Someone from your office called Petersen's widow this morning with information about Petersen's tox report. How come?"

Rosa shook her head. Her hair, hanging loose and unencumbered by a surgical cap, brushed her shoulders. "No one from here would ever give out information before the detectives on the case got it."

"Well, Mrs. Petersen said she was informed her husband died of a cocaine overdose. That was news to us."

"He didn't die of an overdose. The report did come in, and Petersen had high levels of cocaine in his blood and urine. It was even in his hair. But I could have told you that during the autopsy. You walked out before I finished. You missed the head, remember?"

"What did you find, a bullet in his brain?"

"Very funny, Woo."

This was the second reference to the mistake in an autopsy report made by the ME's office less than a year ago. The report was on a man who'd been a flier from a seventh-floor window. The ME's report, hers in fact, gave the fall as the cause of death. The police, however, had found bloodstains all over the room from which the man had fallen. They'd requested a second look at the body. Dr. Abraham performed the second autopsy. He found a bullet lodged in the man's skull. It turned out the gunshot wound, not the fall from the window, had killed him. Rosa's face registered no anger. She'd come to terms with that blunder.

"What I found, Sergeant, if you'd bothered to read my report, was a septum so badly damaged by cocaine use that had the man lived, he would have needed surgery fairly soon to prevent his nose from collapsing." Rosa reported this in her haughtiest voice.

"I have not seen your report, Doctor. It hasn't come in to our office yet. Are you saying now that Petersen died of a drug overdose?"

"I think I stated clearly enough in the death report that Petersen's cause of death was a perforated infarction. A massive heart attack to you." Rosa checked her watch. It was late. She wanted to end this and go home.

"Are you certain the perforation couldn't have been caused by something else?" The cop shifted suddenly to new ground with the soft voice of a practiced interrogator.

Air whooshed out of Rosa's mouth as anger finally overtook her and she furiously rejected the possibility. "Not a chance. Why do you suggest such a thing?"

"I don't know, maybe it was something Petersen's widow said that got me thinking, and this whole question of the cocaine. Could somebody have given him bad shit?"

"Bad shit? As far as I'm concerned, it's all bad shit. You have any idea how badly damaged that guy was? It was amazing he could still walk around." Rosa shook her head.

"The other thing is Petersen's widow stands to inherit something like a hundred million dollars on her husband's timely death. She had a strong motive, and if he was such a hopeless addict, maybe she helped him along."

Rosa laughed. "That ditz I saw on TV?"

"Money can be a pretty powerful motivator, don't you think?"

Rosa finally sank into her chair. "God, this is heavy. I don't know, maybe for some people. We each have our weakness. For Petersen it was the nose candy. He died because of it. For some people it's love of money, for others it's just love. What is it for you, Woo?"

April shook her head. "I wouldn't kill for anything, except to save a life."

"I didn't mean that. I meant what's your weakness?"

"Face," April replied without hesitation.

Rosa smiled. "Me, too. I don't like being dissed by anybody. So you now think you're working a homicide angle here. That would be a pretty big diss to me, you know. That would hurt pretty bad. I don't know how I'd handle that."

"It's just a thought," April murmured. "So, you don't think it's a possibility?"

"Aren't we friends? Don't you realize what it would do to me?"

"This isn't personal," April insisted. "I have only the highest admiration for you. I'm not trying to *do* anything to you. I just want to find out why Merrill Liberty was killed."

"It seems clear enough to me and everyone else associated with the case that her husband murdered her."

"We haven't come up with a why. Without a why we don't have a strong case to prosecute."

"That's not my problem. That's your problem. The guy's taken off. They were friends; maybe he's a doper, too."

The cop shook her head.

"All I can say is *Petersen* was loaded with cocaine. The physical effort of running for a taxi, or even lifting his hand for one, would have been enough to overtax his heart. Seeing his lover assaulted could easily have caused the massive MI." Rosa tied it up neatly. What else could the cop want?

The cop sat in the dark, watching her like a cat. She shook her head some more. "It doesn't play. Ducci says the bloodstains indicate that Petersen died first."

"So what does all this have to do with me?" Rosa was illuminated by her desk lamp. Suddenly she felt at a disadvantage and moved the beam away from her face. She knew exactly what it had to do with her. The corrupt cop wanted to twist the facts. It happened all the time. But she wasn't going to let anybody cast doubt on her work.

"If Petersen died first, *he* might have been the target, and Merrill Liberty might have been an afterthought."

"He died of a *heart attack*. You saw his face. Blue," Rosa insisted.

"Any cyanide in his blood? That also would make him blue."

"Petersen died of natural causes, I'm sure of it."

"I know it seems that way, but maybe someone wanted it to *look* as if he died of natural causes."

"But how? How would it be done? This line of questioning is very upsetting to me. You're implying I could have made a mistake. It's not possible."

"You've made mistakes before," the cop said quietly. "Last time I believe it was kept quiet, and your ass was saved."

"*This* man died of natural causes, I'll stand by my word. I'll stake my career on it," Rosa hissed. "I'll stake *your* career on it."

"Well, I hope neither of us has to." April Woo rose from the chair and picked up her coat. "Anyway, the widow will be happy you feel so strongly about it."

Blood rushed to Rosa's face at being questioned so blatantly, then suddenly dismissed. She was further insulted by the reference to Petersen's widow. What did she care about the widow? Rosa was taller than the cop by several inches. The Chinese woman was thin, didn't look as if she had much muscle. Rosa watched the small woman drape her coat over her shoulders. It was the *office* that occasionally made mistakes. *She,* Rosa, didn't make mistakes. Why should she have to justify herself to a dumb cop? Rosa wanted to say something about how vulnerable the medical examiner's office was with Dr. Abraham in the hospital, how dangerous it would be for the prosecutors, for the police, for everyone involved if doubts were raised about the reliability of an important autopsy report. There would be no case, no trial. The perpetrator of Merrill Liberty's homicide—the black bastard who was her husband—would get off. Abraham would lose his trust in her. It would be a disaster. But she didn't dare say anything more.

"Well, thanks for clearing this all up for me. I'll sleep a lot better tonight." April Woo gave the deputy medical examiner the fakest smile Rosa Washington had ever seen, and then the sergeant left the dark corner where she'd waited in ambush and swept out of the office with a wave of her hand. Rosa got up to wash April off her hands.

32

Wally Jefferson knew the cops were looking for him. His wife told him the detective called Sanchez had telephoned her three times in the last two days. The cop didn't believe her when she told him her husband was not at home. So tonight he'd driven out to New Jersey in the early evening to check out the situation himself. She was hysterical because the cop had asked if he could look around, and she hadn't known what to tell him.

"Wally, are you in trouble?" She called him on his cell phone and started crying at the sound of his voice.

"Did you let him look around?"

"Yes," she wailed. "He went into the garage, into the backyard. What was he looking for?"

"A body. Did he find one?"

She screamed. "Oh, Lord, have mercy. A body. Oh, you're funning me."

"Yeah, that's right. I'm funning you."

"Well, he didn't find a body."

"That's good. He ask you where I was the night Petersen was killed?"

"Yes. He—"

"What did you tell him, hon?"

"I told him you were with me from ten o'clock on, just like you said. Oh, Lord, Wally, what's happening?"

"Some bad things are happening, but I didn't have nothing to do with none of them. Don't you worry about a thing. Do you believe me?"

"But you weren't home that night," she wailed. "Please come back now, I'm scared."

"You got to trust me. You got to not worry, and let me fix this."

"How you gonna fix it? Where are you? I gotta know."

"No. You don't gotta know nothing. I'll call you later and tell you what we're gonna do." Wally hung up his cell phone and dialed Julio's cell phone.

The Dominican picked up and babbled some Spanish into the phone.

"It's Wally, where are you?"

"Where you, man?"

"Don't jerk me, Julio. You wiped somebody in the wrong car. You got to make things right with me now."

"No kill nobody. This guy, he ate his gun. Dumb *hijo de puta*. He want everything."

"Why'd you have to do it in the car."

"I tole you *accidente*. No do *nada*."

"Julio, you fucked my life. I have to get out of here. And I have to get out of here now."

"Where are you, man?"

"I don't know. Somewhere. I need my share of the money."

"Yeah, tomorrow. I tole you."

"Tonight. I need it tonight. You hear me. You give me the money, I'm out of here. If you don't give me the money and I talk to the pigs, I go down for car theft max. Not even possession, man. You go down for murder. *Comprende*?"

"My *ingles* is bad, *pero* tonight I bring. Okeydoke?"

"Same place?"

"*Sí.* One hour, two hour."

Jefferson sighed. He knew he had to dump his car now, rely on public transportation. He hated doing that. He knew he had to change his clothes, too. It was raining again. He'd have to find another car when he got uptown.

33

April had hoped for a little peace, but she returned home to find the air in the family house so thick with incense and smoke and shrieks that she thought at first the building was on fire and her mother was somehow trapped inside it. On closer inspection, April realized it was just Sai Woo taking many forms as, on occasion, she liked to do. Sai was slamming the woks and spoons around on the stove in the kitchen like a crazy human, howling like a wolf, and spitting fire like the dragon she aspired to be.

Skinny Dragon did not stop this performance when April rushed into the kitchen, demanding to know what was going on.

"Aaeiiiie." Sai's answer was the universal cry of distress.

With every strike of the kitchen drum, Dim Sum, the French poodle, gave a little shudder and rolled her eyes. The dog lay on the chair that was Ja Fa Woo's kitchen throne with her hindquarters hidden inside the gloomy-colored patterned sweater that had been one of Sai's less inspired birthday gifts to her husband. The dog's expressive black eyes and apricot head positioned on crossed paws made her seem to be praying for the noise to stop.

"Ma, Ma, talk to me. What's happening?"

Sai spoke in rapid Chinese. "Your uncle Dai had a heart attack. He's in the hospital. Your father is there now."

She was too angry to explain further, then couldn't stop herself from launching a furious raft of complaints. April was supposed to be home at four. And now it was nearly ten-thirty. Sai was upset because worm daughter, who had no sense of duty to her mother, was not at home to drive her to the hospital as April should have been. Because worm daughter was not home, Sai had had to resort to long-distance methods of rallying the ailing spirit of Uncle Dai. The hospital was many miles away, and Sai had no idea if Dai's spirit could possibly hear her.

Not only that, Sai hadn't known April had a new boyfriend, and this new possibility for a husband was *Chinese*! This Chinese (paragon) called three times and spoke to Sai very politely. He said he wanted to meet her soon, Sai reported as she beat metal spoons against the metal stove, screaming at the irony of the gods for bringing her daughter good lucky boyfriends, only to have ungrateful daughter irritate, annoy, and ultimately lose them.

"You no show up," Sai screamed. "Why you no show up? You lose notha boyfriend you triple stupid, *ni*. You ten thousand stupid."

"What are you talking about, Ma? You want to go to the hospital to see Uncle Dai, I'll take you. Put your coat on."

But no, she wouldn't do that. This boyfriend called April on the telephone three times, so Sai would sacrifice her own feelings, even her duty to Uncle Dai, so that April could behave properly and return Kiang's call, maybe have date tomorrow and get married by spring.

"Let me get this straight," April said. "Dean Kiang called here? In this house?"

Sai nodded and lapsed back into Chinese. "I told him you weren't home yet. He said you were supposed to meet him and you didn't come. He was worried, *ni*, nice man."

"He called you here?"

Sai nodded so seriously and sincerely April couldn't help feeling her mother had been upstairs in her apartment again, waiting for her, and that, snooping, Skinny

Dragon had answered April's phone as she'd been instructed never ever to do. "He's not my boyfriend," April said. "He's the DA."

"What DA?"

"He's a prosecutor, a lawyer. He called me for work."

"Didn't sound like work."

April took a deep breath and tried to calm down. Instead she choked on the incense.

"He mallieed?"

"How do I know if he's married. I just met him."

Sai further reported that she'd invited Dean Kiang to dinner and he said he'd be glad to come. Would April please call him back because he said it was urgent?

April left the kitchen and climbed the stairs to her apartment to call the prosecutor back. At 10:53, he was still in his office. April figured he probably wasn't married.

"Hi, it's April," she said, finally falling into a chair in her living room.

"Gee, April, what are you getting into?" Kiang demanded without any preliminaries. "I thought you were smart."

After being yelled at by her mother, April was in no state to answer any questions about her intelligence. Her mouth opened to frame a reply, but her tongue refused to move.

"April, you there?"

"Yeah, I'm here. I gather you called several times."

"Yes, we're getting some heat over here about your visit to the ME's office."

"Oh, yeah, who from?"

"Abraham called from his hospital bed. He says he'll personally see to it that you never see the light of day again if you screw up this investigation. And so will I."

"I have no idea what you're talking about," April said angrily.

"Oh, yes you do. You threatened Dr. Washington.

You accused her of mishandling the case, of improprieties—and I don't know what all. Are you crazy?"

"Dr. Abraham told you that?"

"You've got to cut that out if you want to come down here and work with me. . . ." Kiang paused.

April's mouth was dry. She knew she'd pushed a few buttons with Rosa Washington, and pushing buttons in an obvious way was against her culture and the rules of her ancestors dating back to the dawn of time. Chinese did not accuse each other outright, did not have confrontations. In old China the guilty were skinned alive, pulled apart by horses, their limbs amputated, and their heads stuck on stakes. But good behavior was vital throughout. Mao was known to have his enemies to dinner, feed them the very best food, then blow them up in their cars on their way home. Better to have an enemy die mysteriously on the road than lose face by having to execute him or throw him in jail.

April squirmed under Kiang's attack. It was hardly her nature to get under people's skin and ask hard questions. She didn't like doing it. In fact, it had cost her a lot to make the medical examiner so uncomfortable.

"April," Kiang said. "Is this getting through to you?"

"Ducci says Petersen died first," April said finally.

"I heard, but it doesn't change the facts."

"Oh, yes it does. If Petersen died first, it raises questions about his cause of death and the motivation for killing Merrill Liberty. You should be the first one to agree that we have to clear those things up if we want any kind of a case that will stick."

Kiang made a noise of disgust. "What happens to the nail that sticks up, April?"

"I don't know, what?"

"It gets pounded down."

April didn't thank him for the information.

"You said you'd keep in touch," he complained. "I thought you were going to stop by and see me tonight.

I thought we might have some dinner." He paused as if waiting for an apology.

April remained silent. What did she have to apologize for if he never actually made plans with her?

"Well, I hope tomorrow you'll keep me informed."

"Yeah, sure," April said and hung up. Sure she would. Today she'd kept him informed and where had it gotten her? She moved her tired limbs into her bedroom and contemplated her bed. The phone rang again almost immediately. April hadn't had dinner. At this point she was so tired all she wanted to do was sleep. She was afraid it was Kiang calling back to torture her some more, so she let the phone ring four times before she answered it. "*Wei,*" she said cautiously.

"I got a call, April. What's up?"

"Mike." April exhaled with relief. "Where've you been?"

"I could ask you that, but I gather you're busy getting us transferred to Siberia."

"Look, I just asked a question or two. I wanted to be sure about Petersen's cause of death. How could I know Dr. Washington would be so cranky about it?"

"You accused her of fourteen different kinds of misconduct as well as every fuckup in the book. What did you expect?"

"Mike, that's not true. I didn't mention the lack of ultraviolets that bothered Ducci so much. I didn't say anything about any kind of misconduct." April paused. "I did remind her of one mistake in a cause of death that came out of her office. That's all I did. And you know what?"

"You love me, you miss me. You're hot for my body."

"You don't give up, do you?" April laughed.

"Yeah, I do in fact give up. I was just kidding. What about the tox report?"

"I asked Washington about the leak to Petersen's widow and she said no one in her shop would give out information before the detectives on the case got it. But you know Daphne called her, we heard the secretary take the message. Maybe they made friends. Washington did confirm that Petersen was such a cokehead he needed a new nose. Has Merrill Liberty's report come in?"

"Due tomorrow."

"Did you talk to Patrice Paul?"

"Yes, but there's not much there. Guy's a closet queen. His boyfriend lives with him. They're health nuts so the three of us had jasmine tea." Mike sighed. "That was a treat."

"Very nice. I take it he's not our coke source then."

"Patrice told me he used to be pretty wild, but when a lover died of AIDS at twenty-seven, he flushed the weed, the coke, and all the alcohol down the toilet. He swears he's been clean ever since."

"What about Liberty? Does Patrice know where he might be?"

"Patrice claims he doesn't know. Petersen was Liberty's closest friend. Patrice had no idea who Liberty would turn to with Petersen out of the picture. He was upset because he'd always thought he was next in the friendship line."

"Maybe someone from Liberty's office is hiding him out."

"Patrice didn't think so. He said Liberty's partners reacted to Merrill's death in a way that disturbed Liberty."

"How was that?"

"Patrice didn't say."

"What about the gay thing?" April asked.

"Patrice said he would have known if Liberty was gay. How about your friend Jason?"

"He came into the station around six for a little meeting with the lieutenant. Jason told us his profile indicated Liberty is as gentle as a lamb, and that neither he nor Emma knows where Liberty is. The lieutenant was skeptical about both items."

"What do you think?"

"I don't think Jason lies," April said slowly. "But I'll tackle them both again."

"Isn't it great to work together again, April? Did you miss me?" Mike asked.

"Yeah, I missed you," April admitted. It was now 11:27. Fully dressed, she was stretched out on her bed trying hard to stay focused on the case and not stray into the dangerous territory of love. "What about Jefferson?"

"He's got no priors, but it looks like he was some kind of mule, moving drugs around in the borrowed limos of his bosses. Maybe Petersen found out and threatened him, triggering the incident at the restaurant. Someone died in Liberty's car. Maybe someone can finger him. Oh, and Jefferson was a medic in the army, so he knows anatomy."

"Wow, you had a full day."

"Yeah, but it's not adding up yet. How about you?"

"I feel the same, but it will," April said more confidently than she felt.

"I'm glad you're so sure, April. But there's a lot going on here. Next time look before you leap, okay?"

April made a face at the phone as she hung up, then yawned a few times to summon sleep. By now, though, she was all wound up and beginning to panic about loss of face and every possibility for advancement. Just then her mother started pounding on her door.

"I've got your dinner," Sai yelled in Chinese.

Groaning, April got up and went into the living room to open the door to her mother, who was carrying a tray with two dishes on it. Skinny Dragon, true to form, had managed to find some cold rice and two of April's least favorite foods, no doubt saved especially to torture her on this of all nights. The plate was piled high with cold shredded jellied eel. Serving as garnish to this gourmet treat were three black and smelly ten-thousand-year-old eggs. It was then that April realized that Mike wasn't calling her *querida* anymore.

34

Liberty checked his E-mail and read a message from Jason, telling him they urgently needed to talk. He didn't want to talk to Jason right now, so he didn't reply. There were also E-mails from his partners, telling him that he was being self-destructive and demanding that he surface and deal with his situation. He ignored those, too. As he was shutting down, a news flash came up on America Online: LIBERTY FLEES AFTER POLICE QUESTION HIM ON THE MURDER OF HIS WIFE. A story followed about the reappearance of his Lincoln after he'd reported it stolen upon his return from a holiday in England. Police reports revealed that the car was blood-spattered, and traces of a white powder believed to be cocaine were found in the trunk.

Rick was stunned. He shut down the computer so he could use the phone to call Marvin on his private line.

Marvin picked up almost immediately. "Hello."

"It's Rick," he said warily. "You sure your phone isn't tapped?"

"We sweep for bugs every day. How you doin', man?" Marvin's voice was neutral.

"You're in the media business. You know how I am. My car turned up."

"Yeah, I was one of the first to know. I have a friend with the police, you know."

"If you have so many friends, why don't you tell me what the hell's going on?"

"I'm in the dark, man, same as you. Just trying to keep my head above water."

"What about my head?"

"Hey, you watch your own head. This is what you wanted, friend."

"Oh, no, this is not what I wanted. I want to be off the hook here. I want this over with. Of all the places I could be, Marv. Why did you want me up here in Harlem, with this crazy sister?"

"I thought you'd want to be where the action is, man. Have a look at your people. What could be better than to hide in plain sight?"

"I'm not hiding, man. I didn't do anything wrong."

"Well, that's as may be, brotha."

Rick heaved a bitter sigh. "Marv, I think my people are setting me up. You have any thoughts on why?"

"No, brotha," Marvin said smoothly. "Course not. I don't know who killed Merrill. If I did, the black bastard'd be in jail right now."

"How do you know the killer's a black man?"

"Did I say that?"

"Yeah, you said the black bastard and so did Belle, earlier today. For God's sake, man, don't fuck with me about this."

"I'm sorry. It was a slip, a slip of the tongue. I have no idea who it was, white or black. No idea, man."

"Sweet Jesus. You're fucking with me. You know that crazy sister of yours said that cocaine killed Tor. Was Merrill caught in the middle of some cocaine buy?"

"Could be that's what happened. But Belle's no crazy sister. She's one of my best people. What's the matter? Don't you like her?"

Who could like a person like that? "What do you mean, your best people?"

"Didn't she tell you? She works with the kids, with the borough. She's one of our community liaisons with the police, with the DA's office. She goes to family court when innocent young folk are arrested. Helps battered women find safe houses. You couldn't find better people than Belle."

"Fine, I'll take your word for it. Who's the cocaine source then?"

"The word is it's Wally Jefferson, Petersen's driver, the man you been wanting to see. You hit the nail on the head with that one. I hear he used Petersen's car for buys. Maybe he got the idea to use yours and forgot to put it back. What do you think, man?"

Rick was silent.

"Hey, these things happen, you know that. It's best you get yourself out in the open, man. I get the feeling you're a little scared, a little agitated. Why don't you relax, go out in the hood and take a look round. See the people, have a little chat with Wally if you happen to see him around. Know what I mean? Just watch out for those Dominicans, okay? They can be mean."

"You know where Jefferson is? No one is picking up at his house."

"I know a place he goes."

"Fine, I'll look for him. But call your police friends and get them off my back. Merrill was caught in a drug hit. For God's sake, tell them that."

"You know I can't do that. I don't make no news—I just report it."

"That's a crock. You assholes make pretzels of the truth every fucking day."

"Still, I'm the asshole you came to, brotha." On that note, Marvin hung up.

Rick didn't feel like calling him back. He opened his E-mail again and sent a panicked message to Jason, then regretted it and tried to unsend it. He realized that Jason might have a similar response to Marvin's. Too late: The message was gone. Then he sat by the window. It was raining. He watched the rain splash on the pavement. No one was hanging out on the stoop across the street now. It looked just like a regular neighborhood on a gloomy winter afternoon.

At 7 P.M. Belle returned to the apartment. Without taking off the fireman's raincoat she wore over her many layers, she gestured for Rick to follow her. They were going out.

35

Jason sat at his desk with his clocks ticking all around him and read Rick's latest E-mail. It was clear to him that Rick was becoming disorganized; he was acting crazy and irresponsible. And this crazy behavior made the police want him in custody more and more. Jason would never advise someone to react this way. All his life he'd believed that order was necessary, that people shouldn't run around doing whatever they wanted to do. He believed in taking responsibility for one's acts. And Rick wasn't taking responsibility for himself. He wanted Jason to go over and get Merrill's mink coat from his apartment and give it to Emma. Jason could think of no explanation for such a request except that Rick didn't intend to come back.

After Jason's own experience in the police station with April's boss, he could see why Rick might want to disappear for a while. In his shoes, Jason might feel the same way. Jason wasn't sure if he was right not to strongly advise Rick to return, but he couldn't do it. He could not tell Rick to come back right now.

Jason checked his watch. The day hadn't even begun yet and already he was heavily burdened with anxiety. He dialed April Woo's number at the station. As of last night there had been no warrant out for Rick's arrest. He wanted to see if anything had changed. He wanted to find a safe way to bring Rick home and get him properly represented by a lawyer. Maybe that was stupid.

A sullen-sounding male answered the phone, "Detective Squad, Midtown North."

"I want to leave a message for Sergeant Woo. It's Dr. Frank. Please have her call me."

"Your number?"

"She has it," Jason said. Then he printed out Liberty's message and sent his reply.

36

Saturday was supposed to be April's day off. She had promised to take her mother to see Uncle Dai in the hospital, so Skinny Dragon could use her power to rally Dai's spirit and save his life. He was in a coma now, and needed all the help he could get. But April's day off was canceled. Naturally, Skinny had to scream at April and remind her for the ten thousandth time that she had no sense of honor, no sense of duty to her family and ancestors. Skinny had to threaten that every ancestor would send April bad luck every day of her life and afterlife until the end of time as punishment. No offer of taxi money for the trips to the hospital and back, and no amount of April's explaining that there was more than one kind of duty in life and the police department didn't take no for an answer, could stop Sai Woo's rage at her.

April drove into Manhattan with a bad headache. It got worse when she sat down in her office and saw a message from Jason Frank, who no doubt also intended to punish her for the rest of her life for his run-in with Iriarte yesterday. Meanwhile, the lieutenant must have been waiting for her because she hardly had her coat off when he walked by, aimed his finger like a gun at her through the window in her door, and ordered her into his office with his chin.

April didn't think she was afraid of him, generally speaking, but the curse of her ancestors, lasting until the end of time, was no small thing to have hanging over her head. She had no doubt bad luck was on the way, and he was the one who'd deliver it.

Iriarte began in a hurt voice. "What do you think you're doing, Woo?" He looked at her with sad and puzzled eyes.

"What, sir?"

"I asked a simple question." The hurt took a sharp turn to anger fast, the way hurt usually did.

"I'm investigating a homicide, sir." April tried a simple answer.

"No, you're dancing on hot coals. You want to know how many complaints I got about you last night? You seem to be making quite a name for yourself downtown."

"Did I offend someone, sir?"

"You know who you offended. You can't accuse the medical examiner of God knows how many blunders and expect the thing to pass unnoticed."

"We had some conflicting evidence, sir. I just wanted to clear—"

"The medical examiner said you interrogated Dr. Washington's technicians, accused her of tampering with evidence, even malpractice."

"What?" Iriarte's words struck April's throbbing head like a hammer. She was appalled. How could she accuse Dr. Washington of malpractice? Wasn't malpractice for patients who were alive? Tampering with what? And she hadn't even seen a tech at that hour. They'd all gone home. April stared at her boss. All she'd done was to ask a few questions straight out, the American way, the way she'd been trained and was paid to do. What was going on? What was the big deal?

"Is that all you have to say?"

"No, the DA's office also put their two cents in about my little interview with Dr. Washington last night. Either the woman's nuts, or the ME's office has something to hide."

April stood in front of Iriarte's desk, waiting for him to speak up and defend her. But the man wasn't happy. His face was purpling with rage. Maybe the case was getting to be too much for him. Maybe he'd have a heart attack like Uncle Dai, who wasn't anybody's uncle, or Tor Petersen, who'd sniffed too much coke. On the other hand, maybe the lieutenant would just snuff her out with a stroke of his pen.

"Woo, I'm beginning to worry that you don't have a brain. Don't you know you're looking for trouble here?"

"It was completely inadvertent, sir. I didn't intend to offend the ME. All I did was ask how the toxicology reports were leaked to Petersen's widow before they got to us. I also wanted to tell Dr. Washington about the dust and fiber lab's finding that the bloodstains on Petersen's overcoat indicate that Petersen died before Merrill Liberty. It puts her homicide in a different light. Since Petersen's death report gave a heart attack as the cause of death, it just doesn't—"

"I know, I know," Iriarte said impatiently.

"I wondered if there could be any other possible cause of death in Petersen that might have been overlooked in the autopsy. The body was cremated with unusual speed, sir. I just wondered . . ."

Iriarte rolled his eyes at the ceiling. "Woo, your job is to wonder in *here,* understand? You don't go wondering all over the place with your mouth flapping."

"Yes, sir." April felt like casting her eyes down in the direction of her feet but refused to let herself do so.

"I'm disappointed by your lack of professionalism, Sergeant. I don't care how smart Lieutenant Joyce and Captain Higgins say you are. At this rate you may have a very short career with *us.*"

April knew the fire-belching Gods of Messing Up, summoned by her ancestors all the way from old China because of her lapse in respecting Uncle Dai on his possible deathbed, had arrived to destroy her life. She shuddered. "I'll take care of it, sir," she said softly about the angry ME.

"Good. Do that." Iriarte stuck his arm out and waved her away.

So much for the legendary loyalty of the department to its own. April slunk back to her office with a great deal of guilt heavy on her mind. Only yesterday her greatest fear had been of handling Liberty all wrong. Instead of getting him to crack, as the ADA Kiang had told them to do, they'd threatened him too much and made the suspect run. Yesterday morning Iriarte had said they'd mishandled Liberty. Then Jason had suggested the same thing last night. Now the lieutenant was saying she'd mishandled the ME as well.

Everybody knew what happened when someone in the department messed up or became a political liability. A few weeks would go by and suddenly that somebody who'd messed up would be offered a nine-to-five Monday-to-Friday job working for a borough, the most boring work on earth with no hope of overtime and no way to get out because, like the Chinese, the police never forgot or forgave. The bosses would laugh their heads off the minute the guy was gone because they'd gotten rid of the asshole. April would not forget what Iriarte had said about the one other woman they'd had in the detective squad before her. "She was here for a while. She went into Special Victims up in the Bronx." Then he'd laughed. "We got rid of her."

And April felt bad about Jason. They'd worked well together, had trusted each other as much as a cop could trust a civilian or a shrink could trust anybody. But Iriarte was CO of the unit; he was her boss. If he wanted to talk to someone, he would talk to someone. If he wanted to mess up one of her important relationships, he would do it. Why? Simply because he could. Rank was power.

"You hear me, Woo?"

"Excuse me, sir?" April looked up.

Iriarte stood outside her door. "Just for your information, the tox reports came in on the Liberty woman. She had high levels of cocaine in her blood, too. So nobody was out there trying to kill either of them with bad shit."

"Thank you for telling me, sir." There went one theory.

April still had a strong suspicion that Petersen had not died of a heart attack, but clearly no one else wanted to think along those lines. The discovery of Liberty's car and the hunt for Liberty himself were now the focus of attention.

Mike tapped on the doorframe, came in, and took the vacant chair, scowling. "I heard your boss carrying on. What's up?" He didn't call her *querida* and wasn't even calling her April.

She was hurt. "*Estoy a mal con todo el mondo,*" she muttered, her face copying the Spanish sulk she'd seen so often on the girls in high school. She was in trouble with everyone.

"*Muy bien.*"

"No, it's *muy* awful. What's the news on Jefferson?"

"There's nothing on that situation that will win Iriarte any points with the commissioner." Mike smiled suddenly as he pulled himself out of his chair. "But things are looking up. There were a number of Liberty sightings last night. One in Manhattan, two in Brooklyn, and three in West Harlem. A lot of people are out working on it. See you." Without saying more, he turned on his cowboy boot heel and closed her door on his way out.

"Shit," she muttered softly. Working alone was no fun.

Three-quarters of an hour later, April was sitting in Daphne Petersen's living room watching the widow try to wake up. "I'm going to need some hair samples," she told Daphne.

It was nine-thirty and Daphne was still in her nightgown. Her hair was not so stiffly coifed as the last time April had seen her. It was all over the place. April felt like grabbing a handful.

Daphne lit a cigarette and coughed on the smoke. "You woke me up for a what?"

"I need a hair sample for the lab."

"Whose?" she cried.

"Yours. Not your pubic hair, your head hair. And I need some with follicles for the DNA typing."

Daphne gathered her hair at the back of her neck and held it in her fist as if for dear life. "What are you talking about?"

"The lab needs your hair. I can't be plainer than that."

"What for? My husband died of natural causes."

"Well, it appeared that way at first, but we're checking into it again to make sure. You know how it is."

"No, I don't know how it is. You can't do this." She collapsed dramatically into a chair, filmy fabric billowing all around her. Then she righted herself. "But he's already been cremated," she pointed out. "What can you hope to find?"

"Oh, there are ways to reexamine the evidence. We have very sophisticated methods these days."

"This is bullshit."

"Maybe. All the same I need your hair."

"I don't understand."

"There was a strand of hair on your husband's body when he died."

"On his body? Ugh." Daphne grimaced. "It wasn't mine."

"On his sweater."

"So, there was a hair."

"He was with Merrill Liberty at the time of his death, and she was blond." April shrugged.

"I don't know what you're getting at. The hair on his body was dark. Well, so what if it *was* mine? We were married. My hair could have gotten on his sweater the day before."

"True enough, but you said you didn't see him for two days before he died."

"Look, I'm tired. You're trying to confuse me."

"On the contrary. You've been trying to confuse me. Did you or didn't you see your husband on the day he died?"

"I don't know, maybe." She looked at her nails. "Did the doorman tell you I saw him?"

"Your husband wasn't having an affair with Merrill Liberty, was he?" April changed the subject.

"No. The bitch had been turning him down for years. The only one he couldn't get is what he liked to say about her."

"Was he mad at her for that?"

"Let's put it this way. He could be very persuasive, and he didn't like to be thwarted."

"So he was a man to be reckoned with."

"Yes. You should see the gifts he bought her."

"How did Liberty feel about the gifts?"

Daphnc shrugged. "My husband was an important man. People did what he wanted."

"Would you say he was a dangerous man?"

Daphne hesitated. "Yes, he certainly could be."

"Did he ever hurt you?"

She looked at the wall. "Who told you he hurt me?"

"It was a guess. I saw an item in the *Globe* about his first wife. He broke her arm one night when she didn't want to give him oral sex. On another occasion he assaulted a stewardess he'd met on an airplane. He beat other women, why not you?"

Daphne pressed her lips together. "He liked to hurt people. He was an awful man."

"You married him."

"I worship the divinity in all creatures. I saw only his good side when I met him. I saw only his good side when I married him. I didn't believe the hateful rumors about him. Powerful people always have detractors, don't you know."

"And he had lots of money," April murmured.

Daphne lit a cigarette. "I could never kill anyone."

"Even someone who hurt you?"

"Only Satan is without divinity. And poor Tor was only a weak man, not Satan."

"I see." April wrote that in her Rosario. Not Satan. "Now tell me about Liberty, was he a jealous husband?"

"She didn't cheat on him."

"You said that, but it doesn't always alleviate paranoia about it," April remarked dryly. "How about abusive. Was Liberty an abusive husband?"

Daphne's eyes flared. "He should have been. She was a real bitch. I mean she was vicious. She and Tor were made for each other. And they died together. Weird, isn't it?"

"What did you and your husband fight about that day?"

"I don't know. He was high as a kite. Who could fight with a person on Mars? The man was wacko." Daphne looked away.

Uh-huh. "Did he strike you?"

"No!" Her fist hit the table.

"Why did you have him cremated so fast?"

"What should I have done, have him stuffed?" Daphne shot back.

She didn't tell the truth about anything. April knew she'd have to keep twisting and twisting her to get the facts. She smiled and held out a plastic bag. "I need the hair, please."

"Isn't there some kind of law against this?"

April shook her head. "Just to rule people in and out, you know how it is," she said again.

Daphne pulled three hairs out of her head. "I'm doing this because I don't think anybody killed my husband but himself."

"Thanks. We'll talk some more later."

Daphne swore.

At 11:31 April came through the heavy wrought-iron-and-glass doors of Jason's building, nodded at the doorman who knew her, and went up to the fifth floor unannounced. Instead of going into Jason's office, where Jason would be waiting for her in twenty minutes, she rang the doorbell to his apartment. Almost immediately Emma opened the door.

"Uh, April," she murmured. "Jason's not here."

"Hi, Emma, can I talk to you for a moment?"

"Sure, want a cup of coffee?"

"Yes, I would. Thanks."

Emma put two cups, two bagels, and a container of tuna fish on the table, poured the coffee. April figured she was serving lunch.

"Tell me about Merrill," she asked.

Emma sighed. "In the entertainment business your best friends are the people on your latest project. So Merrill was special for me. We stayed close. She was my oldest friend, my only real friend except for Jason." She glanced at April. "We don't socialize much. He's always working."

April nodded. "You know, I was looking over my notes of our interview the other day and the only thing you said about Merrill and Liberty's relationship was that it was 'devoted.' You know people can be devoted and still have lots of problems." April spread some tuna salad on half of her bagel and took a bite.

"Yeah, like Jason and me."

"So what were the issues in Merrill's marriage?"

Instantly, Emma became defensive. "I didn't want you to think it was race. It wasn't race."

April was silent.

"Merrill had quit working, just stopped acting. She couldn't have a baby, I don't know why, and she'd lost her bearings."

"Did she have a botched abortion at some time?"

Emma looked surprised. "What makes you think that?"

"The autopsy showed Merrill had scarring in her uterus that would be consistent with it. But she also had endometriosis. Surgery for that could have produced the same results."

Emma shook her head. "The things you learn. Merrill refused to have any tests. She said she'd rather not know the cause than risk having Rick feel like less of a man if he—you know—was the one at fault."

"Little bit of deception there. And she was unhappy with her life?"

Emma put her hand to her mouth. "Sounds weak

and selfish, doesn't it? But she just . . . took it out on him. You know? She'd pick a fight, then if she didn't get him going, she'd unplug his computer while he was working so it crashed. Then he'd get a migraine. And she'd scream at him, and he'd start bashing the wall to make the pain stop. Honestly. I think he was a saint. I would have killed her. Oops. Good job, Emma. I didn't mean to say that."

"Emma, do you know Wally Jefferson?"

Emma shook her head. "No. Who is he?"

"He's Petersen's driver."

"I told you last time you asked me that I didn't know Tor very well. Years ago, before I knew Jason, when Tor was between wives, Rick wanted to fix us up, but Merrill didn't think Tor would ever stay with anybody. She knew he wasn't for me. I heard about Rick's car and the cocaine on the news yesterday, what—?"

"Did you know that Merrill used cocaine?"

Emma nodded. "That's another thing they fought about."

"You held back a lot, didn't you? Thanks, Emma. You were a great help."

"I can't feel too guilty, April. You're very smart. I knew you'd find out. I didn't want it to come from me. Snorting is what Tor and Merrill did together. Rick didn't like drugs and neither did Tor's wife. For Tor and Merrill it was like going out drinking. I knew they were high when they came backstage."

"Emma, what happened when you left them at the restaurant? And don't hold back anything now."

Emma was quiet for a moment. She closed her eyes and seemed to go into another place. "I was in a hurry. There was a limo parked outside. The driver was a white man. Yes, he was—white, I'm sure of it. Was Tor's driver white or black?"

"Black. What kind of car?"

"I don't know. He offered me a ride, that's how I know he was white. They do that sometimes when they have more than an hour to kill, you know, to make money off the books. I turned to look at him. I thought about it, but I don't like negotiating with them over price. It's makes me nervous. A taxi was coming down the street right then. There was snow on the street, but it wasn't snowing. A woman got out of the taxi. I got in. That's it."

"Do you know what Tor's wife looks like?"

"I've seen her picture in the papers."

"Could the woman getting out of the taxi have been her?"

"Oh, God, I hadn't thought of that. God, I don't know. Oh, God, April, I was in a hurry. I remember she had black tights on, and she was wearing a black mink coat. I remember it because it was just like Merrill's. God, Merrill had a gorgeous coat."

"What did the woman's coat look like?"

"I don't know—big, swing skirt. That's all I can remember."

"Could it have been Merrill's coat?"

Emma closed her eyes. "Merrill was wearing her suede coat that night, wasn't she?"

"Yes."

She shook her head. "It wasn't Merrill's coat."

"What about her shoes?"

"I didn't see her shoes. I was looking at the coat."

"Could it have been Merrill's coat and a man's feet?"

"Don't ask me these things, April. I don't know." Emma was getting frantic.

"Would you recognize the woman if you saw her in the same coat again?"

"I don't know—maybe."

"Okay, what else did you see?"

"I saw another couple come out of the restaurant. It couldn't have been Rick getting out of the taxi. I'm sure I would have known if I'd seen Rick. I know his walk. I know how his body moves. I know his gestures. I know he wasn't there."

"You think you didn't see him. The eye sees what the mind is used to seeing. Could Rick fit into Merrill's coat?" April glanced down at her plate and realized she'd eaten more than half the tuna salad Emma had set out.

"Oh, God, don't put me in this position. I don't know who was in the mink coat. It could have been anyone. What about the murder in Rick's car? Could he have anything to do with that?"

"Another mystery, Emma. Look, I have to go. Does Jason know all of this?"

Emma shook her head. "Merrill was afraid of Jason. She thought if he knew how unhappy she was, he'd try to get her into therapy. And she was right, he would have."

Jason's face was stony cold as April came into his office and took a chair. "Any news?" he demanded.

Hello and how are you, too. April looked around at the clocks that didn't chime. All that ticking every day would drive her nuts. It was exactly noon. Not even twenty-four hours had passed since she'd seen him last. Since then, however, she'd offended him and everybody else she knew. How many times did she have to say she was sorry for doing what she was paid to do. She cleared her throat, choking on repentance.

"Look, I'm sorry about what happened last night. I didn't know Iriarte would act that way," she began.

Jason didn't reply. His body was perfectly still.

"If you wanted an apology, that was it." April crossed her legs and swiveled back and forth in Jason's analyzing chair. She wondered what it was like to be a patient, having to tell some doctor every single thought that popped into her head. She used to think that by virtue of his profession Jason could read her mind, but now she knew he couldn't. He didn't know she'd just had lunch with his wife.

Jason didn't move. He was playing his waiting game. April knew how it worked because she often played it herself. Jason could make silence as deep and forbidding as the darkest tunnel full of scaly monsters. But April came from a culture that believed the tongue was the enemy of the neck. Better to keep mouth shut than say wrong thing and be hung from nearest tree.

"So, what's on your mind?" She broke first.

"A lot of things, April."

"Want to tell me?"

"Who can trust a cop?"

April blinked. "Who can trust a shrink?"

They sat in uncompanionable silence. Jason played with a piece of paper on his desk. The back of his hand brushed the desktop. "Why don't you fill me in."

April watched a clock pendulum move back and forth. "It looks like Petersen died first," she said.

"How do you know?"

"The bloodstains on his coat. Merrill Liberty bled to death on his back. That means he had to go down first."

Jason frowned. "What's the significance?"

"Petersen may have died of a heart attack, but not from seeing Merrill assaulted. Merrill was struck in the throat, probably from the front because there were no bruises on her body to show she'd been restrained or grabbed from behind. Another thing is she bled a lot, but the wound was very small, very neatly done. It probably took several minutes for her to die."

Jason coughed. "Why are you telling me this?"

"Your friend may be a very cruel killer. Why did you ask me over, Jason? I'm really pressed for time." April watched him play with a piece of paper, watched the pendulum of the clock on his desk. The minutes ticked by. He didn't answer so she went on. "The toxicology reports came in on Tor Petersen. Turns out he was a big cocaine user, so was Merrill—there was cocaine in the trunk of Rick's car."

"Do you know what kind of weapon killed Merrill?" Jason interrupted.

"Some kind of pointed object. I get all the catalogs of knives you can send away for in the mail, and some you can't. There's a whole arsenal of deadly blades out there. But I haven't seen anything that fits the description of this murder weapon."

"How about an ice pick?"

April shook her head. "The ME measured. We measured. Too big, believe it or not."

"Hmm. So you think Petersen died first. Was the cause of death related to complications of a drug overdose?"

"The report says no."

"They're still certain it was the heart?"

"Yes, they say it's the heart."

"But you're not sure."

April hesitated. "I'm not convinced it was a natural. But I don't know how it could have been murder yet."

"Okay. Was Merrill with him when he died?"

"No, she'd gone into the kitchen to say good-night to the chef. She left the restaurant after Petersen. We're not sure if he was still alive when she came out."

"So Merrill came out, possibly saw Tor die . . . then someone killed her with the only thing at hand."

April nodded. "That's my personal opinion."

"A double homicide, after all." Jason scratched his beard. "So, you don't think Merrill was killed in a jealous rage."

"No, I don't think she was killed in a rage, but that doesn't mean your friend didn't kill her. It just means her death may have been an afterthought."

Jason made some angry noises. "Rick Liberty would not have murdered his wife as an afterthought. That's just not sound psychological reasoning. I don't think he would have killed her for any reason—but to kill as an *afterthought,* that's outrageous."

"Jason, I may lose my job on this. The medical examiner found a natural cause of death, and I'm getting very unpopular with this line of—"

"You think Merrill Liberty saw something when she came out of the restaurant that made someone want to kill her?"

"Yes, and I need to talk to Liberty. I really need to find him."

"I don't know where he is." Jason's face was stony once more.

"You said that before."

"It's still true. By the way, did they x-ray Petersen's body?"

"Of course."

"And were the X rays negative for foreign objects?"

April started to sweat inside her sweater. "What are you getting at?"

"Didn't you tell me that Petersen's cause of death was a pericardial tamponade?"

"A what?"

"Perforated heart sac. That's when bleeding in the pericardium stops the heart from beating. In a massive heart attack, the heart loses its rhythm and runs amok, causing an appearance of perforation to the pericardial sac. If the perforation occurs first, the results can be the same."

April blinked. What?

"This reminds me of a case I had when I was a resident," Jason mused.

April watched the pendulum. Time was passing. She had to get moving. "Yeah?" she prompted, tapping her foot.

Jason frowned, remembering. "It was a very disturbed woman. She was brought into ER again and again, having to have objects removed from her body. Once she shoved a lightbulb up her anus, another time a broken Coke bottle up her vagina. She inserted pieces of broken glass in her breasts. We kept patching her up. Then she started weaving bent carpet needles into her skin. One day, she shoved a coat hanger up under her rib cage. We could see it in the X ray. The wire went behind her lung, so it didn't collapse her lung. But it went in so far and was so close to the pericardial sac around her heart that the surgeons were afraid they'd cause a pericardial tamponade and kill her in their attempt to get it out."

"Wow." April raised her hand to the place above her stomach where her rib cage flared out on both sides and there was a soft unprotected spot in the middle. It was the same place where Tor Petersen's corpse had a pimple. She felt a renewed respect for Jason. Even though he was an M.D., she had never thought of him as a real doctor.

"And did they kill her getting it out?" she demanded.

"No, they were first-rate surgeons."

"Jesus," she muttered. "A coat hanger. Look, I've got to go."

"Well, take this with you." Jason handed over the paper he'd been playing with. April read it. When she was finished, she swiveled back and forth, staring at the wall. "So Liberty's been corresponding with you on E-mail," she said finally.

"Only twice. This is the second time."

"What's this about giving Merrill's coat to Emma?"

"I don't know, it's odd."

It sure was. If he'd been wearing it and he was the killer, the coat would have traces of blood on it. April's scalp tingled. "Thanks." She hadn't thought of E-mail. She wasn't exactly sure how E-mail worked, but she figured with a warrant they could tap into the on-line system and trace the phone he was sending from. Jason probably didn't know that, though.

"What did you tell Liberty?" she asked quickly.

"I told him I'd talk to you."

"Thank you for showing me this," she said again.

"You said last night you don't have any evidence Liberty was the killer. No blood, no footprints. No witness who saw him on the scene. So you just want to talk to him, right?"

April nodded, even though the picture had changed a bit since then.

"What about your own suspicions, April? Why would anybody get in trouble for suspecting a double homicide instead of a single one in a very public case?"

April flinched at the attack. "All right, what's on your mind? Do you want to negotiate Liberty's return?" She waved the E-mail in the air. "Is that what this is about?"

Jason hesitated. "I'm not sure I trust the police."

"You can trust me. I'm the police. We need him back, Jason. We need to talk to him."

Jason looked down at the worn Oriental rug at his feet, then glanced at the clock. "Want to go out for a bite?"

"Thanks, I've already eaten." April smiled. With your wife. "But I could sit with you."

"Fine." He made a gesture with his hand for her to get up and get out of there. She did, figuring that for some reason of his own Jason had decided to forgive her.

37

At 3:31 P.M., Rosa Washington was alone in the women's room on the second floor. About twenty minutes earlier she'd finished doing the autopsy of a homeless woman who'd died of exposure in a doorway of a vacant building and gone unnoticed for some four days. Rosa had finished up, showered, and changed her clothes, but now she was on another floor, washing her hands again.

For her, the hardest thing about her job was the smell of the dead. She washed and washed, particularly her hands, but never felt cleansed of the stink. Nothing else about the dead traveled home with her. Not the colors—the greens and purples and blacks of skin stretched to the bursting point, the body fluids that streamed out like an endless polluted river, or the texture of tissue and fat so long dead it had turned into tallow. Neither was she much distressed by half-rotted corpses dressed in the rankest rags, or mummified babies. She attacked each former being with the same zeal, proud of what she could reveal about them from their remains.

She met the larva that was laid by flies in the eyes and mouths of corpses within minutes of death with particularly avid interest. She actually thought of the puffy maggots that emerged from the larval stage to begin feasting only a few hours later as her friends. The maggots reproduced rapidly. By calculating the number of generations thronging into the soft, wet, open places on a corpse, Rosa could count the hours and days since death occurred. The maggots were only one of many clues and signposts that helped pinpoint time of death. The hours since life stopped and the decomposition of body tissues began could also be estimated by the body's temperature falling to that of the surrounding environment, by the patterns of reds and purples on the skin that showed how the blood settled in the body, and many other ways.

There was always a great hurry to establish the time of death. Among the myriad revelations provided by an autopsy, the law cared the most about how and when the person had died and who he was if they didn't already know. An autopsy took from two to six hours, depending on who was doing it and how careful a job the medical examiner did. If the medical examiner's office was overwhelmed with bodies, Rosa could do an autopsy in two hours flat. She was especially proud of the six she'd done in a particularly active summer weekend back in '92.

The only hard part for her was living with the intensity of the smell. It was impossible to describe the stench of the dead, the way it invaded a space, penetrated every porous surface, and persisted despite all efforts to eradicate it.

Rosa dried her hands and glanced at herself in the mirror. She didn't look like a regal African beauty now. Her hair was wispy and wild. Her eyes were red in a face that wore no makeup and offered no other relief from gloom. Oddly, she felt bereft, almost as if she'd just lost her best friend. But she knew that no friend of hers had died. She looked tired, sad, almost beaten. And this enraged her, for she was a success, not a failure. She was one of the world's winners. Her face, beautiful by anyone's standards, told her so. Her education and status in life told her so. But her face also told her she suddenly felt insecure, even frightened for the first time in her career, and she didn't like the feeling.

More than 111 hours had passed since she'd responded to the 911 call and seen Merrill Liberty and Tor Petersen lying blood-soaked in a puddle outside

Liberty's restaurant. For male corpses she had no pity. For Petersen she had felt no pity. But the death of the Liberty woman unnerved her. Merrill Liberty had died only minutes before Rosa's arrival. Her blood was still steaming in the cold when Rosa squatted beside her. That's how close to life she'd been. Rosa almost felt contaminated by the evil of the woman's death.

Rosa had not expected to be lucky enough to do either of the autopsies. Like many medical examiners—those earthly revealers of the sins and secrets of the formerly living—Abraham was a showman. He had to do all the big cases himself. He might not have given in to her pleas if the mayor and the police commissioner—best buddies now that the homicide numbers were way down in New York—had not insisted on getting the autopsies of the two VIPs done immediately, if not sooner. And because no other medical examiner was available, Rosa had done them. Both of them.

But now she felt besieged by enemies. Potential trouble was everywhere. People wanted her to lose her job, and her job was everything to her. It wouldn't be so hard to destroy her, for there was no doubt that things happened when everybody was so damned pressed for time. Procedures went wrong. Tests went wrong. Nobody understood how understaffed they were now that the city had forced so many people to take early retirement. No one knew how hard it was to replace even one or two competent people, much less four or five. Their staff was cut to the bone. Rosa sniffed her fingers. They smelled of soap, but she lingered in the bathroom to wash them again anyway. It was winter, the worst time for her hands. Already her skin was brittle and dry, not moist and soft as it should be.

After she opened the corpses up, Rosa did not know everything about how their former owners had lived, but she knew far more than *they* ever had. She could tell by a person's bones and muscles how they'd walked, held their tools, even what tools they'd used. She knew their filthy habits by the condition of their organs, the discoloration on their skin. She could see the damage done. She knew about their sexual preferences and what illnesses they'd had, and maybe didn't even know they'd had. Rosa knew whether they'd gone to the doctor and the dentist, whether they'd played tennis or golf, or nothing at all. She knew how well they'd eaten, when they'd eaten last, and often what it had been.

The doctor with the most intimate physical knowledge of a person's life was the doctor who examined him when that life was over. Rosa was proud of the specialty no matter who made jokes about how medical examiners were forced into the specialty because they were not good enough to treat the living, and worse in her case, she wouldn't be even a medical examiner but for affirmative action. She knew people said that. It hurt her even now.

From time to time (okay, maybe a hundred times a year) people told her she was too sensitive. As if she shouldn't mind a dumb cop's accusing her of missing a cause of death, as if she shouldn't think the color of her skin was the reason the dumb cop had suggested it. But how could she not make the leap to race being at the bottom of every problem when she couldn't even walk into a department store without a security guard's eyeing her nervously. Sometimes they even followed her around right up to the moment she produced her credit card, thinking every second she was in the store that she was there not to buy, but to steal. Just because her skin wasn't white. Sure, she was too sensitive.

Sometimes Rosa liked to bug those security guards just a little by carrying an item around before she finally paid for it or putting it down and walking away. She liked to tease them with their own doubts about her honesty. But she did not really want anyone to challenge and hurt her, and always had her credit card in her hand just in case.

The truth was she'd done a damn good job on Petersen. The best. But she couldn't help feeling threatened by April Woo anyway. She thought of Petersen's nose so badly damaged from cocaine. It made her furious. He'd been white, rich, and just as stupid and sick as the poorest street kid. The man deserved to die.

Rosa ran her fingers through her hair but didn't stop to comb it back in place. She was going to put a surgical cap over her head and didn't give a damn, anyway. Absently, she washed her hands one last time, soaping well past her wrists. She rinsed, then cursed quietly because she'd already used the last of the towels. She was shaking her hands dry when the bathroom door opened and April Woo came in. The cop put her purse down on the next sink and, smelling like a mandarin orange, she took out a lipstick and refreshed her lips.

Rattled by the person she suspected of trying to destroy her, Rosa frowned into the mirror.

Woo put the lipstick away in her purse and smiled at Rosa's image in the mirror. "Hi, Rosa, I'm glad I caught up with you."

"You came here looking for me?" Rosa's tired eyes ignited.

"Yes, I wanted to apologize for last night."

"You followed me into the ladies' room to apologize?" she said sharply. "Is that your normal procedure, Sergeant, to trap your suspects on the can?"

"Uh, I'll apologize in your office if you'd prefer."

"I have an autopsy to perform," Rosa said coldly. She turned her back to the mirror and leaned against the sink, her heart beating. I didn't do anything wrong, she told herself. Why panic like this?

"Anywhere you'd like," the cop said.

"I don't think you're here to apologize." Rosa surveyed the dangerous adversary. The cop's lips were red. She wore a short red jacket over a black skirt buttoned from the waist to the knee. At her waist was a 9mm automatic. Rosa knew firsthand how much damage those guns could do. At April's knee, her skirt flared open to reveal her legs.

Rosa sniffed. She didn't think much of the looks of Asian women, even though they were highly thought of by both black men and white ones. Very few were genuinely gorgeous. More often, they had broad flat faces with deep-set, snakelike eyes. They were bow-legged and too long-waisted. Their butts were flat and they had no bosom. Asian women were not generously proportioned and open like African women. They were closed and secretive. Rosa knew from the ones who worked in the lab, from the ones with whom she'd gone to medical school, that you couldn't guess what an Asian was thinking. They were tricky and not to be trusted. Rosa didn't think she was prejudiced. She just didn't like them.

Sergeant April Woo looked like some kind of geisha with a gun as she shook her black helmet of shiny straight hair in denial. "You have a great many supporters, Doctor. I got your message. It's clear I was out of line last night. I'm sorry about that."

"Really? Why don't I believe you then?"

"I'm sure you know how much pressure we're under right now to clear this case. It's been almost a week. I guess the urgency to make an arrest was getting to me yesterday."

"What about today?"

"It's still getting to me. We've got three suspects, two of them are missing, and we've got to plug these holes."

Rosa didn't say anything.

"And Petersen's dying first kind of changed the way we had to look at the thing."

"Ducci's an asshole," Rosa muttered.

"We can't change what the bloodstains tell," April replied softly. "Got to work with the evidence."

Rosa made a face. "Okay, you've said you're sorry. What else do you want?"

"Oh, nothing. That was it."

"You have something else on your mind. I can see

it sitting there on your brain, like a tumor the size of an apple."

"Hmmm, you must be good if you can see that without an X ray." April moved a step toward the door.

"Who are the suspects? What's the theory now?"

The cop paused. "Oh, could be Liberty, could be Petersen's driver. We're still troubled about the murder weapon. We haven't found anything yet. As you indicated for us, measurements of the wound show that the hole in Merrill Liberty's throat is smaller and neater than what we'd get with an ice pick. We're trying to figure out what kind of knife blade, or needle, might make a round hole that size."

"I suggest a knitting needle. They come in all sizes. Did the Liberty woman knit? He could have used one of her—"

April shook her head. "If she was a knitter there was no evidence in her apartment."

"He could have killed her with a knitting needle," Rosa said again. She liked that idea.

"That's a thought I hadn't had. Thank you, I'll check it out." The cop turned to the bathroom door again.

"No problem."

Rosa peered in the mirror. She sighed, then spoke again. "Who's the third suspect?"

"Daphne Petersen."

"Don't fuck with me, April. Petersen died of natural causes. It's in my report."

April shrugged and headed toward the door. "It was just a thought."

Rosa calmed down fast. "Anything else you want to know?" she asked, eager to make amends.

Again April paused before she got to the door. "Well, a lot of things. But probably nothing you can help us with."

"Maybe I can. What do you need?"

"A miracle."

"Well, I have a feeling you'll get one today, and

then we can all get on with our lives." Rosa sighed, knowing it was wishful thinking.

"That would be nice. I wouldn't mind a day off," April murmured.

"No, I'm sure of it, and we women have to support each other, stick together more, know what I mean?"

An Asian lab technician with heavy black eyeglass frames and permed hair pushed the door open, forcing April to move aside. She had a cup in her hand, nodded curtly at Rosa and April, then filled the cup at the sink.

Rosa frowned at her. "I wouldn't drink that if I were you, Marsha," she said.

"I wasn't planning to," the technician replied.

"Drink from the water fountain, not from the tap, don't forget," she admonished.

"Well, I've got to go now. Good talking to you." The cop opened the door and hurried off.

Rosa followed her out into the hall, thinking it hadn't been good talking to April at all. She was more tired than she'd been before. And now she had to go back downstairs to the stink chamber. She really needed a rest, but the next one was a five-year-old boy who'd possibly had his neck broken by his father. Rosa didn't want to keep him waiting.

38

Six days after the murder of Merrill Liberty, there were no more reporters hanging around Midtown North. A number of crime junkies from the local newspapers were now parked at the Two-O, bugging everybody in sight for printable material on progress in the Central Park basher case. Downtown at One Police Plaza, a huge crowd of reporters from all the communications gathered each afternoon, where Public Information held a press conference on the state of the Merrill Liberty investigation. The state that Public Information reported did not necessarily bear any resemblance to what was actually going on. Excessive amounts of airtime and page space, however, were filled with background stories on Liberty and Merrill and Tor, featuring the many highlights in their lives. Since all three of them had led very full lives, the saturation point had not yet been reached.

When April returned to the station from the medical examiner's office at 4:37, there was a chilling message on her desk. "Call mother." There were another two from Dean Kiang and one from Mike. In addition to those, there were five more messages related to cases she'd put on hold because of Merrill Liberty. She was looking through the little pile when Creaker leaned in the door.

"What's up?" April asked.

He smirked. "The lieutenant wants to see you pronto."

"Okay. Tell him I'll be right there." April didn't

move. She stood at her desk with her coat on and called her mother.

Sai picked up on the first ring and spoke in a dangerously angry dragon voice. "*Wei?*"

"Hi, Ma, you all right?" April asked.

"No aw light," Skinny screamed. "Velly bad."

"What's the matter?"

"He die. Father no home. No can go."

"Who died?" April bit her tongue. Oh, God, she didn't need this.

"Unca Dai die," Sai screamed. "You worm, *ni*, you no better than ant—" She would have gone on, but April interrupted her.

"Oh, Ma, I'm sorry. What happened?"

Sai switched to Chinese for her account of going to the hospital with April's father (in a taxi because worm daughter wasn't there to drive them). Dai was in intensive care. She couldn't even recognize him he was so full of tubes and needles, Sai said. Tubes going in, tubes coming out. She began to weep. All the relatives were there. All the friends. Out there in the hall, of course. April's father had to wait in the hall. Everybody in hall. The nurses only let special people go in. For some reason she got in. Then, when she went in, she'd only just had time to say hello and remind old Dai how they'd played together as children back in China when he began to jerk at his tubes. His eyes had been closed all the time and he seemed to be sleeping. But when she came in, it was as if old Dai had wanted to get up and join the living again. His spirit was not strong enough, however, Sai lamented. "Old Dai went to the other world before your father had a chance to wish him a safe journey."

Sai went on to describe how Dai had grunted as if he had something to tell her, then suddenly he was gone.

"I'm sorry, Ma," April said again, wondering who'd let her in intensive care and thinking most likely the old man had died trying to tell her to get out.

"It's almost five o'clock. Shift over. Come home now. Pay respect," Skinny Dragon shrilled.

"Ahhh, I'll be home soon."

"No bereave. How soon, *ni?*"

"As soon as I can. We've got a deadline here."

"TV say you double stupid, *ni.* Say you no good, can't find nothing."

"You watch too much TV, Ma."

As soon as she'd said it April knew it was the wrong thing to say. Dragons carry the pearl of life in their mouths and sometimes they breathe fire through it. Skinny picked that moment to breathe fire through her pearl. "You no gimme babies to take cawr, nothing to do, just watch TV."

Why did other Chinese mothers gather together in societies to improve the community in Chinatown and the neighborhoods in Queens? How come they bothered to build and work in community centers? Hah? How come other mothers found useful things to do and Sai Woo could only watch TV and nag her daughter?

With her coat still on, April hung up and went into Iriarte's office. Mike was sitting in his visitor's chair.

"Hi, Sergeant," he said carefully, then stroked his mustache.

Oh, great, trouble. April smiled at Iriarte.

Iriarte glared back. "Well?"

Well, it hadn't been the best day April had ever had. She made a big deal of searching for her notebook in her purse, then getting it out and opening it up. During her handbag rampage, her fingers brushed the paper with the printout of Liberty's E-mail to Jason. She knew she should give it over. But she turned the pages of the notebook, leaving the E-mail printout where it was. She didn't bother to inform anybody that there'd been a death. A pillar of the Chinese community had died. An old friend Skinny had known since the terrible China days. Maybe they'd been friends. Maybe even lovers. Who knew what went on back then? Her mother was distraught and wanted her to come home, which was not entirely unusual. But nobody would care about any of that.

"Let's see, I talked with Daphne Petersen. She told

me some interesting things about her husband's character and that she'd fought with him on the day of his death. She still maintains that although he deserved to die, she didn't kill him because she worships the divinity in all creatures. She gave me a lock of her hair." April smiled then read on.

"I saw Emma Chapman, who told me Merrill Liberty was something of a shrew. The screaming and fights between the couple were pretty much one-sided—Merrill was a coke user and did her partying with Tor Petersen because her husband didn't approve. That was one of their issues as a couple. I also had a long talk with Jason Frank," she said. "He told me an interesting story about a woman who tried to pierce herself in the heart with a coat hanger, and guess what? She didn't have to stab herself in the chest to do it. Dr. Frank also told me Liberty was not the kind of guy to kill his wife, anyway not with a coat hanger. I've just come back from a visit with the deputy medical examiner. We've gotten very friendly. She was so helpful she left me one of her hairs on the sink. I gave all the hairs I collected to Ducci."

Iriarte didn't look too happy with the report so far. "What do you want the hair for?" That was the part that got him.

"There was a hair on Petersen's body. I just want to find a match for it. You know how these little details can complicate a court case." April's bland expression didn't change.

Mike smiled. *Oh, boy, are you looking for trouble!*

Suddenly she smiled back. *So I'll get an afterlife.* "You know what else Dr. Washington told me? She now thinks the murder weapon may be a knitting needle. Did Merrill Liberty knit?"

"A knitting needle?" Iriarte coughed into his handkerchief.

"They come in all sizes," April said, sobering her face even more.

"This is all shit," Iriarte thundered. "You had a whole day to *find this son of a bitch,* and what did you do? You went visiting with a bunch of women and a shrink."

"You wanted me to make nice to the ME," April reminded him. "I made nice to her."

"I didn't tell you to go asking for her hair."

"It was on the sink. All I had to do was pick it up," April said modestly.

"What do you think you're doing—no, don't answer that." Iriarte turned to Mike. "I get a call from the commissioner every hour. You know, we've known each other from way back. He used to like me. You know what the commissioner keeps telling me? He keeps telling me how personally let down he feels because we didn't clear that murder in the park last summer, and because of *us,* that maniac is still out there hurting young women. *Now* we can't clear a simple boyfriend/girlfriend murder. The whole world's watching us, and we can't locate one of the most famous people in the city. We got several people positive they saw the bastard on the street last night when there was an incident involving a possible shooting. The commissioner wants you two to get in a car and go up there and drive around until you get that guy. We've got to make an arrest before the week's up."

The heat rose to April's face. Her week was already up. She'd missed a day off. If you missed a day off, you didn't get to make it up later. She'd worked all day. It was her night off. Her mother was going to kill her. She glanced at Mike. He loved nothing more than driving around in a car with her all night. His eyes crinkled and he smiled like a pirate.

"Look, April, I'd like to talk to you about this in person," Dean Kiang said to April on the phone at 7 P.M. "I don't want to lose touch on this. The boss is getting anxious. He's talking about putting some new people on the case."

So what else was new. April stared grimly out the window in her office door at Lieutenant Iriarte, talking to his men with his coat and hat on. The lieutenant was on his way downtown for a huddle with their big bosses. Each time there was a downtown huddle, the effects radiated outward through the precincts like ripples in a pond. The talk would be followed by a press conference. The press conference would be on all the news programs. And out of the TV would come an announcement that some new important action was being taken that would inevitably make life a little harder and more pressured at the precinct level.

"April, you listening to me?" Dean demanded.

"Yes, I'm here."

"Here's the deal. I think you have potential, and I don't want you screwing up."

She'd heard this before. "I won't screw up," she promised, fairly sure it was too late for such assurances.

"I heard you paid another visit to the ME's office," Dean went on.

"Yes, I went to make nice."

"Well, that's the kind of thing I like to hear. Now tell me what's happening."

"Not a lot. We've got a BOLO out on Petersen's driver, Wally Jefferson. Also on Liberty. Word is Liberty's hiding out up in Harlem." She didn't add that she was still working on the double homicide/Daphne Petersen angle.

"Anything else?"

April considered Rosa's suggestion of a knitting needle as the murder weapon. Damn. She'd forgotten to call to ask Emma if Merrill had been a knitter. If Liberty turned out to be the killer, he could have picked up something close at hand on his way out, something out of his wife's sewing basket. Nice. But unlikely, since she hadn't seen any such knitting basket when they'd gone over the place.

"No, it's frustrating. There's nothing else," she said. Liberty and his wife were having problems. Merrill was a doper. The usual.

A pause, then Dean made a suggestion. "April, why don't you come down and have dinner with me?"

"Ah," April hesitated. She didn't want to say her evening was already booked, that she had an assignment to drive around Harlem in a car for four or five hours. With Sanchez most likely at the wheel.

"This is your night off," Kiang said.

How did Dean Kiang know when her days off were? "Well, not tonight, Dean. I'm working off the chart," April replied.

"I have to be in court tomorrow, but we could have a quick one. How about it?"

April watched the loyal troops wave as Iriarte departed with a flourish. "Gotta go, Dean, my boss calls. Sorry about dinner."

April hung up, dejected.

"Ready?" Mike stuck his head in the door. He'd done some washing up, had combed his hair and mustache. It was clear *he* was ready.

"Give me a minute." April dialed Jason's home number. No one answered. She checked her watch. Of course. It was late. Emma had probably already left for the theater. She dialed information for the number of the theater and explained who she was and what she wanted to three different people before the phone finally rang in Emma's dressing room.

"Hi, it's April," April said when Emma picked up and said hello.

"Oh, God, did you find Rick?" was Emma's quick reply.

"No, not yet. I'm sorry to bother you, Emma, but I have some important questions for you."

"Okay, but I've got to get dressed in a second."

"Okay. One, did Merrill knit?"

"Huh? Knit?"

"Yeah, knit, quilt, do needlepoint? Anything like that?"

"Uh-uh, she thought it was boring. Merrill was a big reader. And she liked to cook. Why do you ask?"

"Oh, I'll explain it to you later."

"The other question," Emma prompted.

"Oh, yeah, did you ever show an interest in owning Merrill's mink coat?"

"God, no. I always told her I wouldn't be caught dead in such a display. You know how many animals have to die to make a coat like that?"

"More than two. Well, thanks, Emma, break a leg."

"No problem. Call me anytime," Emma told her.

April went to the bathroom to wash her face.

An hour later she and Mike were seated in a small Mexican restaurant around the corner from the Two-O, where the owner didn't like Mike to pay, but Mike always paid anyway. April gathered that Mike's father had worked there when he first came to New York thirty years ago and had remained friends with the owner until his death. April didn't know all this for sure because Mike and the owner and the chef always spoke in Spanish, and her Spanish was limited, to say the least.

Two tables away from them a yuppie-looking couple with blond hair were groping each other and sloshing down the sangria as if they'd never have to be alert again. April eyed them enviously.

"What are you trying to accomplish, irritating everybody like this? You trying to suicide or something?" Mike demanded.

April didn't think that was a question that required an answer, so she made a face at him. His response was to give her a deep look complete with sultry smile that caused her cheeks to burn.

Then he said, "Relax," and reached over to cover her hand with one of his.

The contact was limited to a small site, yet traveled through April everywhere in a way she hadn't experienced with a simple touch before. Oh, shit, she didn't need this. She made another face. This was the line she wasn't crossing. Okay, so they weren't working together in the same house. But they were still working together! And he still wasn't Chinese!! Mike's hand continued to stroke hers, squeezing lightly. She felt weak from the touch and confused because she was crossing the line and her heart didn't stop her. Her tongue started to protest another issue.

"I've been up since five, and now I have to drive around all night, looking for someone who's about as likely to be hanging out on the streets waiting for us as I am to fly to the moon. . . ." April fell silent. Under Mike's, her hand turned over so their two palms met. Their fingers laced.

April didn't mention the E-mail Liberty had sent to Jason asking Jason to remove Merrill's mink coat from his apartment, and how they might find him through cyberspace. She was feeling overheated and excited. She'd forgotten it.

"Look on the bright side, at least we're together."

"Uh-huh."

A waiter arrived with their food, and Mike removed his hand, the better to communicate his appreciation.

"Well, this looks almost as good as Chinese," April murmured.

Mike's father had been a chef in a Mexican restaurant. April's father still was a chef in a Chinese restaurant. Mike always said this commonality of the occupations of their fathers made a special bond between them. Now he smiled as he expertly rolled two slices of chicken *fajita*, refried beans, grated *queso blanco*, salsa, chopped tomato, guacamole, and sour cream into a small corn tortilla, then took a bite. None of the contents squished out on his fingers at either end, nor did the tortilla break in the middle, spilling the food back onto his plate. She watched him take a second bite to see if the performance could be repeated. It was.

April looked at her plate of four skewered and grilled shrimps the size of lobster tails, covered with a green sauce, decorated with chilies that couldn't be eaten, and arranged on a plate of squid-ink-flavored rice. She'd had it before and was so impressed by the idea of black rice she'd told her father Ja Fa Woo to try it in the well-known midtown Chinese restaurant where he worked. She thought it might be an exotic addition to his repertoire.

"April—" Mike had finished his fajita and was staring at her with that expression men get when they're full of a positive emotion beyond the reach of their vocabulary.

Her heart pounded so loudly she was afraid he could hear it. No, she wasn't going there. "Ah . . . you asked me why I'm bugging everybody. Well, I'm trying to get at the truth." She shrugged. "You know."

The moment passed and Mike laughed. "You really got Iriarte with the bit about the hair on the sink. What did you do with it?"

"I told you I gave it to Duke, what else? I also told him Jason's story about the coat hanger and the pericardial tamponade, whatever that is. Duke was most interested. He really thinks Rosa messed up and Petersen was murdered."

"Too bad we can't take another look at the body."

"The way I see it, with Petersen's death ruled a natural the field for suspects in the Merrill Liberty killing is really limited to her husband."

Mike nodded.

"But with Petersen's death ruled a homicide, we could open it all the way up. We'd have a ton of suspects."

"Has it occurred to you that Rosa might have been influenced to make a quick and positive determination that the hole in Petersen's heart was caused by a heart attack?" Mike asked.

"Yes, it has. There's a huge amount of money involved here. Rosa Washington was on the scene practically the moment the homicide call came in. Why would an ME come out of a party or an evening out, all dressed up, to show up at a crime scene when MEs aren't doing that anymore? Think about it."

"I'm impressed, April, but Rosa's obviously very passionate about her work. . . . I came out that night, and I didn't have to, either. I didn't even know you were there, and I came out."

Mike called for the bill, provoking the usual altercation. The owner didn't want him to pay. Mike insisted on paying. They argued in Spanish. April picked up her purse and retreated to the front door, where she discreetly studied a poster of a matador waving a red blanket at a bull. This was one occasion where her interference would not be appreciated by either party. Finally Mike showed up and took her arm. "Thanks for dinner," he said.

"No, thank you."

Winter coats came between them. Many layers of protection against all the various ravages of nature. The corner by the restaurant door was small. A draft leaked in around the edges. April's hands were anticipating the cold already. Yet her face was burning. How to warm her hands and cool her cheeks? Mike's coat and jacket hung open. The hand that was holding her arm slid down the sleeve of her coat until it came to her freezing fingers. He rubbed and squeezed her fingers for a moment, then lifted them to his lips to warm them with his breath. His mustache teased her knuckles. His soft lips opened on the tips of her fingers and drew them just inside his mouth.

"Oh." The impact hit April hard enough to make her eyes smart. She could feel his teeth, even the hint of his tongue against her fingernails. The touch was alive and had her in its thrall. She moved a step closer, and knowing she'd hate herself in the morning, tucked her other hand inside Mike's coat, inside his jacket, around his waist until they were clasped in a full-body hug. He murmured something in Spanish and touched her lips with his own. His kiss was the touch of a butterfly's wing, the petal of a rose, with hardly any pressure at all. He held her close but kissed her lightly, brushing his parted lips against the side of her face, her nose, her mouth. Then suddenly it was over. The door opened on a customer coming in for dinner, and they staggered out into the cold to search for a killer.

39

The darkness was complete when Belle returned to the apartment just before nine on Saturday night. Rick was standing behind the curtain at the window waiting for her when he caught sight of the yellow stripes on her fireman's coat down the street. It wasn't raining, but the pavement was wet. He watched her approach the building, then saw her climb the front steps. Finally she opened the apartment door and looked around, as if for drugs or other enemies.

"You know what's going on?" she demanded. She tossed her raincoat on the floor. Underneath, she was wearing some kind of dashiki with leaping gazelles on it not unlike the fabric on the window. Tied around her head was a turban of deep purple. On her feet were heavy lace-up boots with thick rubber soles. She was dressed in so many political statements, it was hard to tell what she really looked like. When she sat on the sofa and crossed her legs to get down to business, the bottoms of a pair of blue jeans peeked from beneath the African skirts to send out yet another message.

Rick had been listening to the radio so he knew what was being reported. "I'm in Maine, Saint Thomas, Miami. The police know where I am and are about to make an arrest. Is that true?"

Belle's full lips tightened. "You're not in Maine."

"Do the police know where I am?"

"Did you kill your wife?"

Rick grimaced. "What do you think?"

Belle shook herself. "Would Marvin ask me to shelter a killer?"

"No telling what Marvin would do," he murmured.

"Fine. I did some more checking about this guy Jefferson."

"And?"

"He's not a very smart man. He's been getting his shit from Dominicans who used to have their factory in one of the buildings a block over. The building was cleaned up a few months back and they moved their setup out to Queens." Belle noticed that her blue jeans were showing and rearranged her skirt to cover the full length of her legs. "He's hanging out, waiting for those Dominicans to come back so he can hook up with them."

"How do you know all this?"

Belle ignored the question. "He needs money to get out of town."

Rick heaved a sigh of relief. "So he didn't get it last night."

Belle shook her head. "They didn't connect. The club got raided."

"How do we know they didn't hook up during the day?"

"We don't. But these people usually go back to their old haunts at regular times. It's stupid, but they do."

Rick reached for his parka. "I'm going out. Are you coming?"

She nodded.

Outside, the temperature had dropped to twenty-three degrees. The streets were icy, and it had begun to snow. Belle looked anxious for the first time. "What are you going to do with this guy when you find him?"

"Oh, I know Jefferson from way back. He's a Tom, you know the kind of guy—always grinning, reading the sports pages, eager to please. I'm not afraid of him."

"That's what they all say." Belle looked up at the lacy blanket of snow in the sky. Millions of fat flakes in tiny clots plummeted down on them, changing to rain almost before they hit thc ground.

Rick rubbed his hands together, then stuffed them

in his parka pockets. Within seconds his feet were cold. Snow smacked his face like a cold rebuke. His eyes stung, but Belle plunged ahead, west to Broadway, leading the way to the club they had not been able to enter because of a police raid the night before. He hurried along, lost in his own gnawing rage. Get the bastard. Get him, was all he could think about. They came from the east, crossing town a block north of their destination. Like the night before, the streets were alive with men, hanging around in spite of the weather. Belle wanted to go the last block down Broadway and mingle with the crowd.

Rick pounded along the wet sidewalk through a tangle of ill-assorted people from the past he'd never wanted to recover. He was looking for Wally Jefferson, a man he had known not well enough for a lot of years. Bland, affable, comfortable in his black suit and chauffeur's cap, Jefferson had always been there at curbside waiting for his charges even when the police were chasing all the other limos away. He had a way about him that made people trust and want to do things for him. He smiled all the time, bouncing on the balls of his feet. He always had a *Post* or a *Daily News* with him so he could follow the sports. He talked about his kids and his ulcer.

A familiar tightening in Liberty's temples warned him that a migraine was coming on. His hood was covered with snow. His feet plunged through puddles in the sidewalk. He didn't see the Chevy Lumina pull up at the corner, across from a phone store where a dozen or more dealers hung out, waiting for calls from customers. No siren sounded on the unmarked police van that pulled up in front of the Lumina. The two vehicles had come down the one-way street the wrong way, blocking traffic. Four uniformed officers jumped out of the van, scattering the men around the phone store like squirrels chasing birds from a birdfeeder.

Belle saw it, stopped short, and grabbed Rick's arm. "Oh, shit, they're going for the same place. They're hitting it again."

Instantly, the fog in Rick's brain cleared and he focused. "Let's go." His voice was a command.

Quickly they changed directions, turned west, and ran across the north and south lanes of Broadway just as the traffic light turned red. Rick dodged a car, pushing Belle ahead of him out of the way. "Get the hell out of here. Now!"

He went ahead, down Broadway. "I mean it, Belle, goddamnit! Beat it."

She shook her head and followed him. But Rick didn't see her refusal. He had moved down the street, fully alert, closer to the action, wondering whether Jefferson was there and if he could reach him before the police did. Rick stopped in a corner doorway.

"Police! Open the door!" The shout from across the street was loud enough to be heard in New Jersey.

Shit. He waited in the doorway, buffeted by the wind and snow gusting from the northwest. The line of cars blocked by the police van got tired of waiting to cross Broadway. A raucous chorus of horns rose in protest. Five cops drew their weapons and surrounded the door.

"Open up, police." The shout came again. If there was an answer, it didn't travel very far.

A moment later a cop broke away and went to the van. He returned with a heavy object. The uniforms made way for him. Rick's heart thudded. He pressed back against the wall, out of the wind. They were going to break that door down. Suddenly a cop spun around into the street behind him, his body crouched as his weapon pointed first at one moving black form and then another.

"Stop now!"

Rick saw a man with a dark handkerchief on his head and a gun in his hand run out of the variety store next to the phone store. The cop, distracted, did not at first seem to see the man duck down between two parked cars.

Then the uniform saw him. "Hey, you. Drop that gun!"

Suddenly all the cops whipped around, their guns aimed at the man behind the car. The lights turned green on Broadway and a line of cars sped through, blocking Rick's vision.

"What's going on?" Belle cried.

He glared at her, surprised that she was still there. "Didn't I tell you to get out of here? I have to do this myself." He felt like pushing her out into the snow. Restrained himself. "Can't you see you're in the way. For God's sake get out of here."

He turned his back on her, stared out into the traffic to see what was going on. In the snowy confusion, he saw the man with the gun. The head scarf popped up. The man raised his gun and fired a single shot.

A woman screamed. "Where's my baby?"

"Man with a gun!" The wall of police moved, pushing people out of the way.

"My baby!"

"Get out of the way."

"Someone's been hit. Someone's been hit." The cry came like a roar.

More shots were fired. Rick couldn't tell who was shooting. Sirens sounded from blocks away as units in the surrounding areas picked up the call and support moved in. Without his being aware of it, Rick's feet began to move. He grabbed Belle's hand and started running west, toward the river away from the pandemonium on Broadway. A block away, beyond the attention of the police, he heard the pounding footsteps of someone running behind them. He picked up his speed, but he was no star quarterback now, no faster than Belle. Someone bumped him from behind, catching him off balance and knocking Belle away from him. As Rick stumbled, a man grabbed him, pushing him down two steps under the stoop of a brownstone, shoved him up against a wall, and jammed a warm gun muzzle into his neck.

"Let him go," Belle cried.

Another man about the size of a refrigerator

emerged from the snowy dark and grabbed Belle and hustled her down the steps into the circle.

"Hey, hey. What's going on?" Rick stared at the gun, more puzzled and angry than frightened. The man who held it wore a head scarf. His front teeth gleamed gold in the dim light.

"Whutchulookinat?" Head scarf jabbed Rick hard in the Adam's apple with the warm steel. Then his mouth opened and he grinned wider, showing off a ridge of gold. "Don't I know you?"

"No!" Belle cried.

The man laughed, jabbed Rick with the gun. He was small, inches shorter than Rick, and had a weak grip on Rick's arm. Rick figured he could take him, but the gun muzzle jabbed his windpipe, knocking his breath away. His knees buckled. He choked, then tried to straighten up.

Belle struggled to get near him. "Baby, you all right?"

"Let her go. I don't know her," Rick rasped.

The big man gave her a little shake, lifting her off her feet.

"I'm not leaving ma man behind. You hear me?" Belle's voice rose.

"Shut up, bitch. You wanna die wit him?"

"Now why talk like that? We didn't do nothin' to you," Belle whined.

"Fucker, you hear that. She says you didn't do nothin'." He laughed.

"Lady," Rick's voice was hard. "This ain't your show. Get out of here."

"No."

The fist came suddenly as the big man swung and connected with the side of Belle's head, knocking her down. In that split second Rick shook the smaller man's gun arm loose, pushing the gun sideways hard, out of his reach. He brought his knee up between the man's legs. The gun clattered to the pavement as the man pitched to his knees, groaning.

"Fucker!" The big man kicked Belle again as he

turned his attention to Liberty. He pulled a long, thin knife out of his coat and held it underhanded as he advanced on Rick. Belle struggled to her feet.

"Gut him, gut him," screamed the man on the sidewalk.

"Oh, man. No." Belle staggered between Rick and the knife. "Oh, man. You can't do that. No."

Still writhing, the man on the ground reached for the gun he'd dropped. Rick ducked the knife and grabbed the gun. The knifer's arm caught Belle with a force that slammed her down onto the sidewalk again. Rick threw the gun out of reach and hurled himself at the man with the knife, taking him on with his bare hands.

Belle screamed as the knife sliced at Rick's parka, shredding the front of it. The knifer struck at him again. Then Belle's shrieks and more police sirens sent the two men stumbling off into the storm. The gun lay on the sidewalk forgotten.

40

April and Mike drove uptown to check in with the detective squads in the 33rd and the 30th precincts. It had started to snow, and both of them were deep in their own thoughts. Mike had moved into action mode. April was still distracted by his kiss.

The 33rd Precinct was pretty quiet for a Friday night. But the 30th had a number of special operations going on and was a zoo. In spite of the weather, the number of arrests made that night was already so high there was no more room in the holding cells for prisoners. Opposite the front desk in the lobby area where roll was called, the folding screen had been pulled for privacy. Barely out of sight, seven bedraggled, angry-looking men were cuffed to chairs, to the wall, even the radiator pipe. Several were carrying on arguments with officers who were no longer in the room with them.

Upstairs in the squad room, only one detective was in. A tired-looking female African-American called Yolanda Brick was typing up a report. She told Mike and April she'd just gotten a call that a man fitting Liberty's general description had been spotted on 108th Street, accompanied by a firefighter.

"Anybody follow it up?" Mike asked.

The detective gave him a cold stare. "We had a couple dozen calls on this today. After the first twenty amounted to nothing, it got kind of busy around here."

"Well, thanks," April told her. This was a high priority. She was sure the commissioner would be pleased.

As Mike and April came down the stairs from the squad room, five uniforms were being pulled together for another operation. In the makeshift holding pen, a prisoner threatened to defecate in his pants if he wasn't immediately taken to the bathroom.

Snow was falling even more heavily as they came out of the building. "Great," April muttered. Now they wouldn't be able to see Liberty if he danced naked in front of the car. "I just hope I don't have to chase anybody. I've got my best boots on, and I'm really stuffed." She wanted him to kiss her again, but he didn't.

He switched on the wipers and pulled out into 151st Street. "I'd bet your chances for that are about nil."

For what? She'd forgotten what she said.

He drove west, plowing through the snow. At Broadway he turned downtown, heading to the location where the unidentified caller to the 30th claimed to have seen a man who looked like Liberty. Accompanied by a firefighter. Now that was a description. He drove slowly down the treacherous street. April scanned the sidewalks. People were heading home. It looked as if the Friday-night dealing game had been called for weather.

Mike switched on the police scanner, where several excited voices were cutting in over each other, calling in a shooting—man with a gun. Man with a knife. Shooting wasn't confirmed. It was confirmed. The victim was dead. He was alive, but seriously injured. Shooting was in the lobby of a three hundred building, in the basement. Request for backup at B-way and 138th Street.

"That's our location," Mike said excitedly.

He didn't have a gumball for the roof, but the Camaro was rigged with a siren. When he heard the address of the shooting, Mike hit the hammer. The Camaro's siren shot out a warning as he accelerated into traffic. The traffic around them had been moving cautiously through the snow. The two cars ahead parted for them at the first red light. The Camaro's tires spun for a moment at an incline in the middle of the cross street. April turned away from the headlights of the cars coming at her from the side street. The first car would slam into them at the passenger seat where she was sitting. And her mother always said she'd die before giving birth.

"Hang on," Mike ordered.

As if she had a choice. April braced her hands against the dashboard. The tires caught, the car shot forward, skidding sideways on the other side. Mike slammed the Camaro into low and regained control, then accelerated exactly the same way into the next changing light.

Take it easy, pal. I want to make it through the weekend, April didn't say. She knew enough not to tell Mike how to drive, particularly in bad weather. She also knew enough not to tell him this wasn't their party. He'd only say they were on duty. On duty, everything was their party. And most cops felt the same way, loved getting in on any operation—as long as they didn't have to make the actual arrest, fill out the damn arrest forms, follow the prisoner downtown. Lose days in the process.

Excited voices on the radio continued. Sirens sounded to the south of them, to the east. Even behind them in the north. Everybody was hot to join. The voice on the radio gave only one item of identification on the shooter. His head was covered with some kind of scarf. April snorted. It was snowing. Everybody's head was covered.

At 145th Street, Mike slowed the car to a crawl. He let the hammer have two final spurts of whine, then shut it off.

"What do you say, east, west?"

"Is it my call?" April asked, scanning the street.

"Yes. Yours."

"You want me to flip a coin?"

"No, I want you to make a call."

April shrugged. "Okay, he'd go west. Hang out under a stoop for a while. Too much activity east of B-way."

"Fine. Remember, you called it."

"Oh, give me a break."

"You called it." Mike turned west, headed down a quiet street of brownstones. A few people were hurrying along. Not many. The snow was thicker now, was beginning to stick. They needed a spotlight to see through the storm.

Mike kept going, through the next light. Two blocks from Broadway at 141st Street everything was nice and quiet. No one out on the street here—except one guy halfway down the block, fiddling with the top of a garbage can. He had a scarf on his head.

"Let's check him out," Mike said. He accelerated the car to where the man was standing, then stopped a few feet in front of the garbage can.

Startled, the man whipped around to look at them. Just as quickly, he gave them his back, let go of the garbage can top, and walked quickly down the street in the opposite direction. April was out of the car before Mike cut the engine.

"Oh, come on, April, no."

In her haste, April planted the heel of one of her new boots in an ice slick in the gutter. She slid into a freezing puddle between two cars, managed to grab the back of one of them before falling to her knees in the wet. She righted herself, splashed out onto the sidewalk, and charged down the street. The guy limped away through the snow, didn't look back at the car with one door gaping open and two people running after him.

"Hey, you. Stop. You dropped something." April ran, slipping with every other step. Mike caught up and passed her.

"Pare alli," he shouted. *"Policia."*

The guy stopped suddenly at the word *"Policia"* and turned around. He put his hands up. *"No tire. No tire."*

April caught up, unholstered her gun. She didn't like the look of this guy. He was whining at Mike not to shoot him, but one hand dropped almost immediately. Bad sign. A big mocking grin on his face revealed an impressive ridge of gold where he should have had top teeth. He was not really frightened.

"¿Ouien es la chica?" he said, dipping his head at April.

Good, she got that. Who's the girl? April raised her gun, covering Mike.

"Policia," she snapped back. It worked for Mike. But the guy didn't seem worried enough about her gun.

"Hey, hey, hey." Mike growled at the hand slipping into the right-hand jacket pocket. *"Arriba los manos."* Mike jerked his head at April.

April got that, too. Raise your hands. He wanted her to cover him as he patted the guy down.

"¿Ayiie, *por qué?"*

"Porqué digo lo." Mike wasn't playing around. He jockeyed the guy against a car, arranged his hands over his head, kicked his legs apart. Very efficient.

April saw a smear on the man's hand. Blood was leaking from a cut on his hand, or maybe his wrist. "Blood," she barked. "He's injured."

The man wiped his hands in a puddle on the windshield.

"Hey, hey, hey. Don't you move. I tell you not to move, you don't move."

"¿Oue hice?" the man whined. He whirled around.

"Get back there." Mike pushed him back against the car.

"No hice nada."

"Then why's your hand bleeding?"

"No hablo ingles."

"The fuck you don't, buddy."

"No hablo ingles," he insisted.

Mike patted down skinny legs. The man's hand held above his head caused the blood to drip down his right sleeve. "Ayiie," he cried. *"Estoy enfermo. No hice nada. No hablo ingles."*

"Did you hear that, Sergeant? This man is sick, he didn't do anything, and he doesn't speak English."

"No hablo ingles."

"We heard you the first time, around we go. Real slow here, keep those hands up. No fast moves." Mike turned the guy around and unzipped his jacket. After a quick forage, he pulled out a mean-looking switchblade. "Well, look at what we have here. A guy doesn't speak English. My partner here loves to shoot people who don't speak English, don't you, Sergeant?"

"Yes sir, my favorite. You want me to put him out of his misery?"

"Aw, come on, I'm hurt here. Don make a big thing. I have cut, gotta go to doctor."

"Oh, I see we do speka de ingles. Didn't anybody tell you you could get hurt playing with knives." Snow whipped Mike's face as he patted the guy some more. "Oh, look at this, another one." Mike sounded peeved as he pulled out another knife, this one sheathed in well-used leather. He gave both knives to April, yanked the man's arms behind his back. "I'm getting cold. How about you, Sergeant?"

Tears stung in April's eyes. "My feet are killing me," she said. "Let's take him in and warm up."

"Oh, no, man, hey. I ain't done nothin'."

"Looks like you were into something. We got a report someone looks just like you shot somebody. We'll take a little visit to the station, warm up a little. See what's up with you." Mike cuffed him with a set of handcuffs he'd stuffed in his pocket before leaving the car. April holstered her gun. One on each side, they marched him back to the car. "What a night," she muttered, shaking out her boots.

"What's your name, hombre?"

The hombre whimpered. "Oh man, no gun. I got no gun. You see a gun, huh? Come on. Some guy with a gun hit *me.* Looka this. Guy hit me. It was that football guy *mato su mujer.* He shoot a guy."

"We'll come back for him." April pushed the guy's snow-covered head down, guiding him into the backseat. "Move over." Damn, there was no guard between the front and backseat. She had to sit next to him. "Gun's probably in the garbage can," she told Mike.

"We'll take him in, send someone out to take a look." Mike slammed the car door. The car was warm. He'd left it running.

The hombre whined. "I didn't have to tell you nothing. I was nice, tole you who made the hit."

"Okay, if the football guy made the hit, then you have nothing to worry about, right?"

"I don't need no trouble."

"Tell it to the detectives."

"Oh, man, I'm bleeding," he complained.

"You bleed on my car, you're a dead man," Mike snapped. He called into the 30th to say they were coming in, then hit the hammer and the accelerator at the same time. The car's tires spun, then lurched forward. Six minutes later they unloaded their cargo at the 30th.

"Oh, yeah, Sanchez. You're the one that called." The name plate on the desk officer's chest read LIEUTENANT TIMOTHY BRAMWELL.

"We need someone who speaks Spanish for this honey," Mike told him.

Bramwell took a look at him. "Oh, it's Julio Don't-Speak-Ingles. Julio, don't you know it's not healthy for you to come back here?"

"Good, you know him, we're out of here." Mike turned to April, who was swabbing blood off her sleeve with some tissues from her bag.

"He bled all over the car, too," she muttered. "Hope he's not HIV."

"I was just visiting a friend," Julio whined. "I got out of my car. This football guy shot someone. I just happened to see it, that's all. Then he run over and smash me with the gun. Jeeeeze."

"What the hell you talkin' about?" The desk sergeant rolled blue eyes, beckoned to a uniform to come and take the guy.

"Better send someone out to look for the gun." April gave the location of the garbage cans.

"Got anything on the shooting?" Mike asked.

"Yeah, the victim's still alive. We don't have an ID on him yet. Any chance this guy is on the level and Liberty was involved?"

"We'll go check it out."

"Hey," Bramwell barked. "Sanchez, you can't just come in here, dump your garbage, and walk out without making a report. You picked him up. You make a report. Forms are right here."

"Oh, yeah, and here's the arsenal he was carrying." April deposited the knives on the desk.

Bramwell looked them over, tsking. Then the phone rang, and they lost his attention. It was forty-five minutes before April and Mike were on the road again. By then April's boots had dried and stiffened with the salt the city used all over the streets, the snow had stopped, and any chance they might have had of catching Liberty anywhere near the scene of the shooting was long gone.

41

On Saturday morning the phone rang in April's bedroom before seven. April rolled over, groaned, squinted at the clock, couldn't make out the numbers, closed her eyes again. Hadn't she just gotten into bed? She kept her eyes closed as she listened for rain, pelting the roof above her. When she didn't hear any telltale rat-tat-tatting, she rolled over to the wall, away from the phone. It rang again. This time she let her eyes slide along the wall to the window where the gray around the edges of her white curtains told her the dawn hadn't come. It wasn't day yet. She decided not to answer the phone.

Then she realized she was awake and started thinking. Skinny Dragon expected a ride into Manhattan and the Chinatown funeral parlor where Uncle Dai was lying in state prior to his funeral tomorrow. Her mother wanted to bring offerings of paper money and fruit for Dai's journey through the afterlife. Sai wanted to light joss sticks, one after another, until there was enough incense to tease Dai's soul into repose. And Sai wanted to sit there with Dai's body for as many hours as it took for a good show of respect. After the "for show" appearance at Dai's coffin side, she wanted to kick up her heels in Chinatown and go shopping—accompanied by worm daughter to pay for her purchases with credit card and to carry her packages. Skinny Dragon had it all planned. The phone rang a third time.

April ignored it. No matter what, she was not going to deny her mother the day's pleasures Skinny had planned. She and Mike had not located Liberty last night. It was out of her hands now. They'd failed in their task. There was no way she was going to clear this case before Sunday, so why not sleep while she could. She'd decided absolutely. She was taking the day off, wasn't answering any phones. Through the fourth and fifth rings she held her ground. But the answering machine didn't pick up. On the sixth ring, April answered the phone.

"Wei."

"There was a shooting in Harlem last night."

"Good morning, Dean. And how are you?"

"You know who was shot?" Kiang demanded.

"No, I don't. Are you in the office?"

"I hear you and your buddy picked someone up for questioning."

"Dean, you know, you have big ears for a Chinese. Don't you ever go home?"

"For a Chinese, April, you don't have much loyalty."

"What's that supposed to mean?"

"I thought you were my pipeline on this case. I thought we had a deal to stick together on this."

"Hey, I'm a veritable pot sticker in the loyalty department. What's your problem?"

"Jefferson was shot last night. He was the one who was shot. Didn't you know that?"

April's mind raced. What did that mean? "Is he dead?"

"Yes, he's dead. You were up there. You were on the scene. You picked up a suspect. Did you call me? No, you did not call me. I'm going up there to question him now. I'll see you in my office tonight at seven. We'll review the case then."

He hung up before she had a chance to tell him she probably couldn't make it.

So another day off was lost. At eight-thirty April checked the squad room before pausing to hang her coat up on the wooden coatrack in the corner of her office that wasn't her office today because it was supposed to be her day off. Everyone, including her opposite number, was in the field. In the squad room, the holding cell and all the desks were empty. She did not peek into Iriarte's office to see if the lieutenant was there. It was now more imperative than ever to find Liberty. Now she understood Iriarte's disgusting respect for the chubby, colorless Charlie Hagedorn.

Iriarte believed technology was the future, and Hagedorn happened to be a computer whiz. Hagedorn could hack into anything. He'd be able to find Liberty's location by Liberty's E-mail activity. They had no choice about locating him now. April returned to the squad room and showed herself outside Iriarte's window. He beckoned her into his office, where the mood was not a happy one. Mike, Hagedorn, and Iriarte sat gloomily in the only chairs in the room. Mike got up and offered her his chair.

"What's the story on Wally Jefferson?" She took the chair Mike offered. "Thanks."

Iriarte scowled and jerked his chin at Mike to tell her.

"Story on Jefferson is they found a Glock on the sidewalk a block and a half west of the shooting," Mike said. "They think it might be the murder weapon. Ballistics is going over it." He sighed. "Looks like some kind of fuckup."

"What kind?"

Mike glanced at the scowling lieutenant, then back at April. "Seems when they raided a club last night someone had time to run in and warn the customers. The door was barricaded. Jefferson was inside. Apparently he had a date to meet someone there. There's a door to the basement of the building next door. When the raid started, Jefferson went out that way. Our guess is that the shooter was waiting for him. When he came out on the street, the shooter wiped him out."

"Was the hit man our little golden-toothed Julio?"

Iriarte made a disgusted noise. He and Hagedorn exchanged glances too. A lot was going on in the room. April had no idea what subjects the three of them had covered before she got there. She dug around in her purse for Liberty's E-mail of the day before, hoping that when Hagedorn successfully hacked into it, he'd get a boost and be transferred into somebody else's computer room. She smiled at her boss. He looked surprised.

"It's not clear yet." Mike answered her question about Julio. "Jefferson was his mule. He could have been involved with the hit out on Staten Island."

"Witnesses?" April asked.

"In Harlem? Oh, you know the scum up there. Ten thousand people on the street. Every single one of them blind. No one saw a thing," Iriarte complained.

"Except one old lady who lives in the building next to the club. She said Jefferson was a regular there. Day, night, weekend, whenever," Mike said.

"So?" Iriarte studied April. He knew she had something. He cupped his hand at himself and waved. *Give it up.*

Sure thing. She pulled Liberty's E-mail out of her bag. Then she laid it out for them. Hagedorn could be the one to locate the phone Liberty was using to send his messages. But she and Mike were the primaries on the case. They had to be the ones to pick him up for questioning.

Hagedorn took the paper and studied it, his face all gooey with happiness. "We got him," he said. "Thank you, God, we got him."

"Now, wait a minute," April said quickly. "I told you. I want to handle this with Liberty."

"Sure, sure, April."

April checked her watch. She had a lot to do. She wanted to get hold of the mink coat at Liberty's apartment and send it to the lab to see if there were traces of Merrill's blood on it. And she had to be home in Astoria in time to drive Skinny to Chinatown no later than three-thirty, four. Had to see Kiang at seven. She and Mike headed out into the field.

At five in the afternoon ballistics confirmed that the

Glock that had been found on the sidewalk a block and a half from Jefferson's shooting had been the murder weapon. But there was a big surprise. Three partials and one thumbprint lifted from the barrel of the gun were identified as belonging to the right hand of Frederick Douglass Liberty. No one beeped Sergeants Sanchez and Woo to let them know.

42

Belle lay on the sofa in her sometime apartment, her eyes closed and a towel full of ice on her head. She had bruises and swelling on her forehead and every half hour Liberty woke her up, concerned that she might have a concussion. He'd had six or seven himself, and didn't want her falling into a deep sleep, not to wake up for a week or two. The man had kicked her hard. The yards of turban she'd been wearing hadn't protected her at all.

"Come on, baby, open those beautiful green eyes."

"They're hazel. Men don't know nothin'," Belle grumbled in her sleep.

The times she didn't respond, he squeezed some water from the towel onto her face and sponged it off, stroking her forehead until the green eyes fluttered open.

"Don't you touch me," she muttered, raising a hand to her hair that was a color hard to pin down. Red-gold, gold-rust. Brown-gold, harvest gold. No, definitely red something. It was good hair and there was a lot of it. Probably drew attention to her, and Belle clearly didn't like that kind of attention.

"Don't look at me," she mumbled.

"I'm not looking at you. Just worried about your health. You have a lot of courage. You got yourself messed up." *Because* of me, he didn't say. She'd jumped in front of a man with a knife, and the man had tried to stab her. What kind of crazy woman would do that? Some kind of urban guerrilla. Now Rick knew why she wore what had to be a thirty-pound raincoat. The coat was useful in case of fire and wasn't easily penetrated by a stiletto. He wondered if Belle also wore a bulletproof vest under all those sweaters and if she'd been stabbed or shot at before. He had a feeling she had.

"Belle, you got a family, a husband or boyfriend, somebody I can call to come get you?"

No answer. She'd fallen asleep.

The night had an eerie quality to it. Rick had three shallow cuts on his chest that oozed into the only other towel in the place, and burned some. He got up and washed them with soap in the grimy bathroom a few times. He was sore, and like other times he'd been hurt and his body was trying to mend, he was hungry. He thought about his restaurant. The restaurant was a place backed by him and his white partners, run by blacks, where both blacks and whites felt comfortable. Anyplace where blacks and whites both felt comfortable was considered trendy. Rick used to be amused by the term. Now it made him sick, as if all along he'd only been part of a zoo exhibit.

When everything was going wrong in her life, Rick's mama always said, "I am still. I am still so God can show me the way." She told her boy that God lived in stillness and only in stillness would Rick himself be able to find his way through this life.

"If God so still, then why the peoples scream and yell so loud in church?" he'd demanded.

"Is, do. Don't you go leaving out those verbs, boy, and don't question. Don't go questioning the ways of God."

But how could he find out what God's ways were if he wasn't allowed to question? Liberty couldn't question the ways of God now. He didn't believe God had a personal interest in him or anyone else. Merrill was gone for no reason at all. Water flooded his eyes, blurring his vision, but he couldn't be crying. "I don't cry," he said aloud. He swiped at his face with the sleeve of his sweatshirt, which was ripped and bloody on the front. He glanced at the girl on the sofa, who was so leery about men. He wondered what had happened to make her that way, and realized she was beautiful.

He thought about the man with the gold teeth and the gun. A dozen people must have seen the man fire. Maybe more. Why had he bothered to cross the street and run a block and a half after him and Belle? Had he known they would be there? How did it fit? The street had been teeming with people. There had been people all over the place. It was possible that even some of the police had seen the shooter with the ridge of gold and the scarf on his head. Rick worried about Belle and couldn't fall asleep.

About eight hours later, at eight-fifteen in the morning, she sat up and rubbed her eyes. "I'm hungry," she said.

Rick looked at his watch. "So am I."

She went into the bathroom and stayed there a long time while he made some coffee in an old pot. Maybe it was the aroma of brewing coffee that made his throat close up around his windpipe and finally acknowledge the truth. Merrill was not at home, waiting for him with her sexy voice and all her troubles and demons. She was not going to agonize anymore over not giving him golden babies in his image. There would be no more heated (and painfully naive) discussions of politics, no more arguments with them against the world about race or anything else. No more screaming fits about cocaine. Merrill was gone. Another one of his lives was over. Rick's eyes were wet, but he was not crying. He now had to make the choice Merrill hadn't been given. He could die and not be buried with her in that bleak New England cemetery that had probably never received a black body. Or he had to become someone new. Again. Neither prospect had much appeal.

The water had been running in the bathroom for a long time. He knocked on the door. "You okay?" he asked.

"Don't come in." The reply was a nervous mumble through the door.

Rick expelled the trapped air in his lungs. "I'm just asking if you're okay," he grumbled to himself. He didn't walk in on strange women in their bathrooms.

"Don't come in," she said again.

Jesus, she was exhausting. He poured some coffee and sat at the table drinking it as the sky cleared and slowly lightened. Finally Belle came out of the bathroom. Rick was careful not to look at her as he handed her a cup of coffee with milk. He hoped her screwy brains hadn't been knocked any looser.

"Thanks." She sounded surprised.

"You're welcome."

"What are you doing?" she asked.

"Drinking coffee. Then I'm going to take you home, Belle. Where do you live?"

She sat down at the table and held the mug in both hands. "My head hurts."

"So does mine, but I can't stay here any longer, and neither can you."

"Why?"

"You got hurt. That crosses the line for me."

"So what, lot of men hit." Belle touched her head. "Kick, too. They think women belong to them, and hurting them doesn't signify much." She studied Rick thoughtfully. "Maybe not you."

"Not me."

"It's so touching when these guys visit in the hospital, bringing flowers. Everybody's crying, and that's what they always say. 'She wanted it. Yeah, we had some fun, but I wouldn't penetrate a twelve-year-old *baby*. I didn't *hurt* her.' Or, 'Yeah, we may have tussled around some, but I didn't put her *eye* out with a *poker*. No way, man. I loved her.' "

Rick bent his head and told himself he wasn't going to let tears fall down his face. "You've been hanging around with the wrong people too long, Belle."

She sniffed angrily.

Well, she might not think much of him, but she'd

used herself as a shield to save him last night. Why did she have to be so tough on him now?

"What?" she demanded as if he'd said it aloud.

He shook his head. Now he knew the reason he'd avoided Merrill's funeral and left his home. He'd run away because he couldn't stand the world's accusation that he was just another one of those black scum who robbed and stole, took drugs and raped women, murdered them when they got too sassy. He simply could not bear the suspicion. All his life he'd worked hard to be clean, clean, clean to the world, clean to the core. So he wouldn't be his mother's nightmare. So he wouldn't end up just another rotten nigger. He finally knew what he had to do.

Five minutes later Marvin Farrish was quiet on the other end of the phone line as Rick Liberty blasted him.

"Marvin, I always thought you were a smart man. I know you've done a lot of good in this world. You have a great TV station, good radio. You're a faithful husband and a good father. I thought your heart was in the right place. But shit, man, this stunt you pulled with me was the stupidest, the most dangerous, God-damned dumbest cock-up I've ever seen. I don't know where your brain is. You know what happened up here last night, you fucking idiot?"

"Hey now, brother," Marvin finally joined the conversation, "that's no way to talk to a friend."

"Friend! You know what happened. Answer the fucking question!"

"Is Belle all right?" The impassive voice tensed for the first time.

"I don't know if she's all right. Because of me, she got her head kicked in by an elephant. I don't have people getting hurt because of me. This has got to stop now."

"Let me ask you again. Is Belle all right, is she conscious?" Marvin's voice became more agitated. "This is important!"

"Of course it's important. She won't call anyone to take care of her. She won't leave me alone."

"She must like you. You sound angry, man. You sound real angry." Marvin heaved a dramatic sigh.

"Oh, I'm more than angry. I'm in a fucking mess here. You understand? You know what's happened to me? I lost the only person in the world I really trusted, and the whole world's come down on me, insisting I killed her."

"That's the way, man," Marvin said softly. "That's the American way. It's show business. Raise a man up high as he can go, make him a hero, let him *feel* the glory so intensely he thinks he's above it all. Then expose his weakness and cut his drooping flag so bad he can't even pee anymore."

"Is that what you're doing to me, Marvin?"

"No, man. I'm telling you how it is."

"Okay, so that's how it is. And I'm a weak son of a bitch because I couldn't handle the cameras—the questions from the police. You know, man, they pushed all my buttons, kept asking me how often I forgot myself when I had a migraine, how often I did things I wasn't aware of doing. I couldn't take it."

"Uh-huh." The unasked question hung in the air.

"Fuck you, Marvin. Your little friend and I walked into a shooting last night."

"Yeah, I heard that chauffeur Jefferson got shot. I'm sorry, man."

"You're *sorry*! You sent us into it. And you know what? For some strange reason, the asshole who shot Jefferson, instead of taking off, crossed four lanes of traffic, with cops all over the place, and tried to kill Belle and me with a stiletto."

"Praise Jesus, Belle just got a kick in the head. You okay, man?"

"Oh, I got a few stab wounds in the chest."

Another great sigh traveled the phone line. "Where are you now?" Marvin asked.

Rick hesitated, then he said, "I'm on my way home. I'm ready to make a statement, Marvin."

"Are you sure about that? What about your frame of mind?"

"I said I'm ready," Rick insisted.

"Okay, I'll set it up. . . . What are you going to say?"

"You'll have to wait to find that out, won't you?"

"You want to do it in the New York studio? We'll have some control over the situation there. And, Rick, I wouldn't advise going home just now. Why don't you take a little rest? Calm down. Write a speech or something. You know, think it through, work it through with Belle. She's done this before. And Rick, I'm going to risk millions of dollars and my whole future to tell you this. Because any lawyer in his right mind would never let you do anything this dangerous. But I'm your friend before I'm a businessman and I have to say it. Maybe you should consult a lawyer before you go ahead with this."

"I don't need a lawyer," Rick insisted. "I haven't done anything wrong,"

"Fine, if that's your decision. At least I asked. Where are you? We'll pick you up, get you cleaned up—"

"I don't want to be cleaned up," Rick snapped. "This is a dirty story."

"Okay," Marvin said quickly.

"And I don't want to go to the studio."

Silence.

"Did you hear me, Marv?"

"Don't be an asshole, Rick. Think about what you're doing. You want to look like a fugitive? Come on, what do you think is going to happen after the interview?"

"I know what's going to happen. I'm going to call the cops. Those two cops who've been bugging me. I'm going to call them up and tell them what happened to me, what I saw last night—"

"What about Belle?"

"I won't bring her into it."

"You promise? You gotta promise me."

"Yeah, I promise, but that woman has a mind of her own. She's—"

"That's all right. I'll talk to her."

"Listen, Marv. I'm a witness to a shooting. Now I do have something to talk to the police about."

"This is good. This is good. The police try to finger you for your wife's murder. But instead of sticking around to take the fall, you go out and try to solve the crime yourself. But the one person who could shed light on the picture is rubbed out in front of your very eyes. Then the shooter tries to kill you. You have the stab wounds on your chest to prove it, right?"

"I'm not taking my shirt off on TV."

"Well, we'll talk about the details later. Rick, this is a big story, a very big one. Trust me, we'll do a good job, a tasteful job, and we'll nail them. We'll nail them for what they tried to do to you. . . . Rick, you with me on this?"

"We still don't know who killed Merrill."

"Yeah, but we can get the police for what they did to you. I like it. I'll set it up. Great, we'll set it up for the seven o'clock news. I'll have a car pick you up at five. Now, put Belle on the phone. I want to talk to her."

43

The sky was still clear, though the light was fading fast at four-thirty when April illegally parked her white Chrysler Le Baron in front of a fire hydrant fifty yards from the 5th Precinct on Elizabeth Street. She glanced at her watch, aware that she had to check in with Mike soon. When they'd parted earlier, he'd taken Merrill Liberty's mink coat over to Ducci in the lab. They probably knew by now if they had the piece of physical evidence they needed to make a case. She hoped things were finally coming to a head.

For a few seconds she forced herself to linger in the driver's seat while Skinny Dragon chattered excitedly in Chinese. April longed to get away from her mother, to jump out of the car and pay a visit to the 5th Precinct, a landmark building in the middle of renovation. She wished she could check out the ceiling in the detective squad room, see if it is still leaked. See if her old boss was still there, or if he'd retired as he'd been threatening to do for the last ten years. She could use the phone to return Jason Frank's call. He'd told her he'd be home about now with some new thoughts about the murder weapon. She wondered how he'd take being proven wrong in a diagnosis.

April was distracted by her mother's shrill excitement over the funeral. She herself was not looking forward to the viewing of Dai's body in a funeral home fitted out to look like the Buddhist temple from hell. Lots of red everywhere, folding chairs, clouds of incense, an altar dazzlingly bright to scare off any evil spirit that might want to come in. And the body strategically placed in front of the altar, face serene for the voyage and dressed in best clothes, with stacks of fake (red) paper money and ritual good-luck food gifts in shopping bags scattered around as sacrifices. But duty demanded that she attend.

Skinny was rattling on about the virtues of the dead man. Sai considered Uncle Dai a great man, a pillar of the community. Always good to his friends. Dai had helped April's father when he first came to America. Dai had come first, in the early fifties, and had never paid a single cent in taxes. A truly great man, not afraid of anything. This last was a snide reference to April's high level of honesty that baffled and annoyed her parents. Sai believed that the gods had played her a cruel trick at April's birth and given her the wrong baby. April worked in a corrupt police department, paid taxes for no reason, ran around all night with Spanish man, didn't honor the ten thousand years of Han dynasty ancestors. Or drive her mother where she wanted *when* she wanted. Today Sai had had a lot to say about the police department and the personal inconvenience she was forced to suffer because of it. She almost went so far as to blame the police commissioner himself for causing the death of her old friend. But she stopped short of *that* in case the gods were listening and heard the insult to April's boss.

It was fully dark now. Sai hauled herself out of the car and breathed the air of home. She turned to look April over as if she were a child making an important appearance at a grown-ups' party, then marched down Elizabeth Street, carrying her two shopping bags of offerings. They passed the apothecary she liked that sold nasty powders of ground insects and plants and bones of mythical animals guaranteed to cure any illness known to man. The rank-smelling store April had visited only a few days ago would still be open when they came out.

Near the bottom of the hill, they turned into the funeral parlor. As April had predicted, the room was cloudy with incense. On one wall, the large cross with a vivid depiction of Jesus Christ's suffering was not illuminated. Nor was the small, kneeling statue of Mary praying at his feet. Sometimes it was a mixed crowd and both Christian and Buddhist rituals had to be observed. Not today. Chinese music played softly in the background. A crowd of some twenty, mostly old people, had drawn the chairs away from the center to better display the coffin—best quality, white with much brass, look like gold. The people sat in two lines on either side of the coffin, talking, and in some cases, screaming at each other.

The room became silent when Sai and April Woo entered. Sai did not greet anyone. Silently, she staggered (the better to exhibit her grief) over to the coffin. She carefully examined the features of the corpse, as if to make sure it was really he. And then she burst into tears, wailing loudly. Three people held out boxes of Kleenex tissues. Ostentatiously she grabbed a handful and blew her nose. Then wept some more. April stood beside her, exactly as she had all those times in her childhood when her mother had dragged her along to funerals to show respect. She felt like a complete fool. Suddenly her mother whispered, "Look good, much makeup." April thought she was going to be all right.

Then, out of the corner of her mother's mouth came the old command, same as it used to be when April was four or five. "Cly, *ni,*" she demanded.

April glanced at the crowd of old people in their best clothes. They were watchful, silent, waiting for her. She knew the only way she was going to get out of there and get down to the prosecutor's office in a building a few blocks south was to make the correct display and save her mother's face. April let all the frustrations of the case wash over her. Her problems with Iriarte and Rosa Washington, Dean Kiang, and Mike's butterfly kiss that she couldn't help thinking about all night. Lumping it all together she managed to summon a tear. Then an actual sob erupted from deep in her throat. She wanted love, sex, a high rank in the department, and a happy life. Why was it so hard to get those things that were supposed to be within the reach of every American? Tears streamed down her cheeks. She hiccuped. Skinny jabbed her hard in the side with an elbow. *Don't go overboard and show me up.*

But the crowd was happy. An approving murmur rose from the mourners as more boxes of tissues appeared. A woman April had known from the cradle, Auntie May Yi, jumped up to congratulate Skinny on her obedient and loving daughter, the cop who could cry. Then everybody started speaking at once, and April's beeper went off, letting everyone know how important April Woo was to the safety of every citizen in New York.

44

The computers in the detective squad of Midtown North were a big step up from the typewriters of years past, but the unit still didn't have a modem. Without a modem Hagedorn couldn't go on-line and reach deep into the system to tease out the secrets of the phone numbers behind the entry codes. Hagedorn had to move downstairs to the main precinct computer room, where Mark Salley, the lean, anal-retentive sergeant who manned it, was not pleased to see him.

"Hey, wait just a little second. What do you think you're doing here?" Salley demanded when Hagedorn marched into his computer room, heavily laden with two Styrofoam cups of coffee, light on the milk, a fistful of sugar packets, and a six-pack of cola.

Hagedorn had come downstairs to the main floor of the precinct, trotted quickly past the open door of the precinct commander's office, where Bjork Johnson, the brand-new commander, was at his desk talking into the phone with some urgency.

"Nobody told you I got a priority assignment here?" Hagedorn asked, his watery eyes opening wide with surprise.

Salley sneered. "I mean that shit there." The sergeant pointed to the drink supply.

"Gotta have sustenance." Hagedorn held the cans by one finger hooked through the plastic harness. He rattled them for emphasis.

"No, no. Not in here, not with my equipment, you don't." Salley shook his head and gave a little whistle. "Outta here."

Hagedorn whined. "Oh, come on. I can't think without my caffeine."

"I don't give a fuck." Salley gave Hagedorn his back.

"What's going on here, Sergeant?" Iriarte trotted into the room, pushing Hagedorn aside.

At the sound of Iriarte's voice, Salley made an quick about-face. "Well, hello, Lieutenant, how ya doin'."

"You got a problem?" Iriarte radiated genial concern at the sergeant.

Salley smiled ingratiatingly. "I hear you need to go on-line. Wouldn't you like me to help you with that? I got the experience from the Kerson case, that fraud—"

"Yeah, yeah, I remember. Good job, Salley." Iriarte flipped his hand at the chair in front of one of the computers, indicating that Hagedorn should take it.

"Lieutenant, excuse me, sir—"

"Computers are the wave of the future in police work, Salley. No doubt about it. You're riding the crest. You'll be right there at the top."

"Thank you, sir. But we have a rule here, no food or drink in the computer room."

"You heard Hagedorn, Salley, he can't think without his caffeine. Now, we've got a special assignment here. The whole country is waiting on us to pick this guy Liberty up. You want to obstruct or help with that effort?"

Salley watched with horror as Hagedorn put the coffee cups down beside the computer.

"So help him out, Sergeant." Iriarte spun on the heel of his woven leather slip-on and left the room. He headed down the hall to brief the commander on the break in the Liberty case.

When Iriarte lingered in the door, Captain Johnson waved him into the office, then kept him waiting for twenty-eight minutes as the commander tried to negotiate with someone at headquarters for a postponement of his first Comstat appearance.

Comstats were computer compilations of the number of crimes and arrests in every precinct every week. They were programmed and analyzed by the precinct commander's aides. Every precinct commander periodically had to go downtown to explain and defend his numbers. The way it looked the new commander would have to take his turn in the hot seat, defending the police work in his precinct for the last month with less than a week on the job. Iriarte tapped his fingers impatiently, but could not get up and leave. When Captain Johnson finally hung up, he immediately reached for his hat. His second-in-command jumped up to help him with his coat.

"I have to go to a meeting downtown, Lieutenant—"

"Iriarte, sir." The lieutenant saluted.

"I'll have to catch you later." He nodded imperiously as he left.

Iriarte went back into the computer room and hung over Hagedorn's neck. "How's it going?"

Sergeant Salley spoke first. "We're lucky. He uses one of the easy services."

"So—?" Iriarte prodded.

"Liberty hasn't generated any E-mail activity today," Hagedorn said. "We can't trace yesterday's numbers. We can only locate the phone he's using if we're in the system at the same time he's in."

Iriarte sucked in his lips pensively. "He was in the area of the Thirtieth last night. We know that. Shot someone. Ballistics tells me we may be able to tie some other homicides to that gun. Maybe Liberty's been a busier boy than we thought."

"There's a BOLO out on him. Everybody's looking for him," Hagedorn said.

"Yeah, but I want to be the one to get him. I want him nailed out of here, out of this precinct, understand?" Iriarte stuck a finger in Hagedorn's back. "We didn't get that raper last summer. If it turns out the same guy hit that woman up in the Two-O, we're going to look like fucking idiots. We've got to get Liberty."

Sergeant Salley smiled. "Don't worry, they always reach out to their mothers, or somebody they rely on, sometime. If he has the habit of E-mailing, he'll do it now."

Iriarte checked his watch. "He'd better do it soon. I go off duty at six."

At a few minutes past five, Liberty E-mailed Jason Frank from a phone in the one hundred block of 110th Street. The E-mail intercepted by the police at Midtown North read, "Jason, everything is going to be fine. I'm going on TV with my story tonight at seven. Watch me on WCRN."

Iriarte flipped. "Oh, man. Oh, shit. We got him." He clapped his hands with excitement. "I'm telling you that is good work. I'll remember you in my will."

"Thank you, sir," Hagedorn chirped.

"Any word from Sanchez and Woo?"

"Not for an hour, you want to leave them a message?" Hagedorn didn't bother to swipe his empty containers into the wastebasket at his feet.

"Nah, get me four bodies, two units, and that address."

"Yessir." Hagedorn was on his feet.

Iriarte grabbed Hagedorn's sleeve and continued talking. "We go up there. No sound and light show. We're talking real quiet and real fast. We have an advantage. Liberty's not expecting us. We have a disadvantage. We don't know where the interview is taking place. If there's a camera crew arriving, we've got to move fast. Go!" Iriarte nodded at Sergeant Salley and left him to deal with Hagedorn's garbage.

45

The kitchen cabinets and table dated back nearly a hundred years to the turn of the century, but the dishwasher, stove, and refrigerator were brand new. The rest of the brownstone Belle called home had been carefully restored in a style Rick Liberty recognized from historic photographs of the lives of wealthy people of color at the turn of the century. The dim light of the January afternoon did not diminish the warmth and glamour of the rooms. Entering such a place in his ripped parka and bloody sweatshirt, Rick had felt like the felon that half the world thought he was.

Belle took him into the kitchen, gave him a cup of coffee, brought him into the living room to drink it, then went upstairs to shower and change her clothes. When she returned fifteen minutes later, she was a different person again. Now her long hair was in a ponytail, and she wore a maroon turtleneck, gray tailored trousers, and a navy blazer. Black alligator belt. This Belle was no child of the slums. The change was unnerving.

"We have to get you some clothes," she said briskly. "Is there anybody you know who can get in and out of your apartment?"

"Sure, but it's probably being watched."

"Fine, I have a friend about your size. I'll get you some clothes. How about a lawyer?" she said casually. "I know a few of the best. But I'm sure you do, too. By the way, what do your friends call you?"

"Rick," Rick said, sitting forward on a rich burgundy velvet chair with a complex braid trim.

"Rick, you're bleeding on my chair," she remarked.

"Thanks."

"What for?"

"You stopped calling me nigger. Do you have any gauze pads?"

"I'll get some. You need stitches?"

Rick shook his head. "Just a messy scratch. I'm sorry about the chair. I'll have it recovered. Who are you?"

"Nobody important. My name is Isabella Wentforth Lindsay." Belle grimaced as if the three words gave her a bad taste. "This is my grandma's house. Granny isn't very well, but doesn't want to leave. So I stay here and watch her home-care nurses, make sure she's all right." Belle looked toward the bow window overlooking the north end of Central Park.

"This house belonged to her father. My father grew up here." She stroked the patterned cut velvet on the antique sofa. "Daddy left here after law school. I grew up in White Plains. My parents live in Westchester now. But I still love the house. Granny let me do the restorations. Do you like it?"

"Very much." The shooting of Jefferson, the cuts on Rick's chest, and the long sleepless night of worry over Belle's head wound and her barrage of insults were all catching up with him. He was having trouble taking everything in. Now he knew who her father was, a prominent conservative black New York State Supreme Court judge. Her mother was a documentary film producer. A white documentary film producer.

Grief swept over him, tightening his chest until he could hardly breathe. He closed his eyes against the onslaught of nausea that severe pain often brought him. Belle's mother was white. Until that moment Rick had never considered the possibility that the children of white mothers might feel anger, even despair, at having to go through life bearing the color their fathers had not wanted to—would not have—married themselves. Belle's skin was honey-colored, as if the sun had warmed her from within. Her famous mother was white. The charge always leveled at him was that when black folk came up in the world and married white, they forgot that their children would be black no matter how light their skin. Perhaps if he and Merrill had had children, they would have felt the same.

"You okay?" She studied him.

"I'm sorry to get you into this," was all Rick could say.

"I do this with adolescents all the time. I do it with battered wives. It's my calling—anyway, I've always thought you were—" Belle broke off. "Why don't I go get you those clothes and stuff?"

An hour and a half later, dressed in borrowed clothes, Rick was waiting for Marvin's van to pick him up when a shriek of sirens brought him to the bow window where he parted the lace curtain. He saw a forest green Chrysler with a light flashing on top and two blue-and-white police cars speed up the wrong side of the street and cluster in front of the brownstone, blocking Marvin's van that was pulling up at the same moment.

Rick watched four uniformed cops and the WCRN news team scramble out of their vehicles. Four cops unholstered their weapons. A man in a gray overcoat and a man in a suit jumped out of the Chrysler and started screaming at the man with the TV camera.

"Get back!"

"Get out of here!"

"Is that camera on?"

"Get that camera off."

"What's going on, Officer?" The reporter moved in with the camera.

"Get back, please."

"Can you tell me your name, Officer?"

Rick watched the scene with horror. A white uniformed officer shoved a black reporter with a video camera. The cameraman shoved him back. The red light on the camera was on. Six officers jostled each other as they climbed up the front stoop to get him. He was afraid, and he was angry. He wanted to tell Belle he was sorry, that he would make it up to her. But he couldn't open his mouth, knew he could not make anything up to anybody.

It occurred to him that Marvin had friends in the police. He could have set this arrest up. Or maybe Belle had set this up. He glanced at her. No, Belle looked as frightened as he. She held his hand, speechless for once. How could the police have found him? The doorbell rang.

"Stay here. I'll go by myself." Rick's head pounded as he went down the graceful circular staircase toward the insistent ringing doorbell. He opened the door. Cops were arranged all around it with their guns pointed at him.

"Put your guns away," he said. "I'm not going to resist you." His hands were by his sides. He did not think to raise them. Belle had followed him down the stairs. She stood beside him, pressed against his arm in case they intended to shoot.

The man in the dove gray overcoat did not bother to ask who Rick was. His first words were, "Mr. Liberty, you're under arrest for the murder of Wallace Peter Jefferson. You have the right to—"

"What—?"

"Remain silent—"

"Wait a minute—wait, you have the wrong man."

"Tell it to the judge, Mr. Liberty."

"Wait—!" Liberty shouted. "Just wait one minute."

Two uniforms jerked his hands together and wrestled his wrists into handcuffs, closing them tighter than they had to be. Rick heard Belle's voice, but couldn't make out what she said. The camera crew filmed him with Belle, then him alone as he was hurried, in a huddle of blue, down the stairs and pushed into a car—protesting so vigorously the arresting detective never got a chance to finish reading him his rights.

46

At five-fifteen, April rapped sharply on Dean Ki-ang's doorframe, then walked into the prosecutor's office. He was leaning back in his chair with his eyes closed, didn't seem to have heard her knock.

"You never go home, do you?" she said, sorry to have to wake him up.

He started, looked surprised, then checked his watch. "April, you're early . . ." He recovered quickly. "But looking very good," he amended. "I'm glad to see you."

"Thanks." April took off her gloves and unbuttoned her coat.

Dean gazed at her appreciatively, smoothing back his hair. Then he got up from his desk to close the door. "Here, give me that." He took the coat, threw it over a chair, then stepped back to look at her as if from a distance, making a telescope with his fingers the way he had the last time they met. "You're a sight for sore eyes. Did I tell you I'm a sucker for female Chinese sergeants?"

She smiled, trying to think of a suitable reply, neither too cold nor too warm. Something pleasantly neutral that wouldn't generate deeper forays into the subject, for she didn't know any other female Chinese sergeants. But Dean moved before she could think, stepping forward into her space and in one fluid move drawing her into a full body hug. April was too surprised to react. The unexpected embrace took her breath away. It was as if she'd been waylaid by someone on the street she'd never suspected.

Things like this happened all the time in the station houses, particularly to unwary patrol officers. April had always managed to step aside, get out of reach, show it wasn't worth it to mess around with her. She'd never been one of the "girls" the horny ones went after.

But this was no cop on a power play. This was a highly desirable suitor. Dean Kiang was a lawyer, a Chinese. He was the kind of person Skinny Dragon told her she must smile at—be honey to his bee: work for if she could get the job, be indispensable to, then clinch the deal, lie back, and do nothing for rest of life. In the case of Dr. Dong a few months back, Sai had gone as far as to advise kissing on command, as necessary, the way the prescriptions on pill bottles read. Just to close that pie-in-the-sky deal for a June wedding and the happy life Sai wanted for her. Just keep up that kissing, and never mind what the man looked like, or whether he was an asshole. Never mind love. Sai liked to say love was like a lily: bloom only one day. Better think of other things.

In one second, less than a second, Kiang's hard wet lips were sucking noisily on her mouth while his hard tongue penetrated the unguarded space between her teeth, diving for her tonsils. His hips ground against her, driving the hard plastic of her gun into her side. His arms wound around her hips like a vine choking a tree. He pushed his chest against her breasts, hunching his shoulders around her. His hands grasped her bottom, pushing it up, pushing her pelvis forward against the hard protrusion bulging from his well-cut, gray pinstripe trousers.

"Oh, baby." He groaned and reached for her skirt, pulling it up, started rubbing the front of her thigh, then reached even higher to her crotch. He was holding on so tight with his other arm she could hardly breathe. Then, as she protested, he plowed into her mouth with his tongue and lips again with another rough kiss as he kept rubbing her, chaffing her as if he actually intended to rip off her tights and plunge into her on the spot.

Think of other things, her mother would advise at such a time. But the things Dean Kiang made April think of were too much garlic in his lunch and too much starch in his shirt, a thin and bony body like her father's. Unpleasant greedy lips and a hard greedy tongue. He reminded her of a goat rutting in a field or oversexed monkeys humping in a rain forest. Kiang's hand exploring her leg suddenly grabbed her crotch and gave it a hard squeeze. The reminders stopped and a rocket went off in April's brain. She was a cop, not a helpless woman. She pushed Kiang away.

"Stop!"

"Uh-uh." He didn't want to stop. He didn't let go.

"Stop. *Now.*" She jabbed him hard with her elbows.

"Oh, baby," he groaned. He didn't seem to care about resistance. He was lost in another place.

For a few seconds she had been lost in another place, too. It was as if her magical Dragon Mother had actually entered her mind and made her forget how to kick, how to punch, how to judge right and wrong. For a few seconds April had actually been paralyzed, afraid of kicking the Chinese prosecutor in the balls and causing him to lose face.

But he didn't seem to be concerned about face, either. When he recovered himself, April was further shocked by his arrogance and her own uncharacteristic restraint. Before letting her go, Dean let both hands once again drop to her bottom and roam around the territory, squeezing at will, front and back, even as she was slapping his arms off.

Then he sat down at his desk again as if nothing had happened. Not a single thing. "Look, you're early. I don't have a lot of time. What's on your mind?" He checked his watch to show how rushed he was.

Murder. Murder was on her mind. She wanted to kill him. "You asked me to come here," she reminded him.

"Well, give, baby." He leered suggestively. "What's going on?"

Flushed and confused by the sudden shifts in his behavior and her own reaction to them, April opened her notebook and coldly told him everything that had happened that day.

"Well, that's good. But we don't need bloodstains on the mink anymore. It doesn't even matter what Liberty was wearing when he stabbed his wife. We've got him on another homicide now." Dean squirmed his fanny around the seat of his chair, proud of himself for his little adventure.

"What homicide?"

"We have a warrant out on him for the murder of Wally Jefferson."

"Huh? No, no. You're getting messed up here," April fumed. "That guy Julio something, the one we picked up last night—"

"Well, you caused me a lot of trouble with that. You picked him up. I questioned him. He wasn't the one."

"What are you talking about? The guy was a—"

"We found the murder weapon. Liberty's prints were on it. It's been confirmed. Liberty killed Jefferson. We figure it's a sure thing that he killed his wife as well." His face said *end of story*.

April's stomach was all over the place. The man made her physically sick. His spit was in her mouth. She was afraid she was going to hurl. "Where's Julio?"

"Oh, we let him go hours ago, but he's a witness. We know where he is. He'll come back and sing anytime."

"Who arrrested Liberty?"

"Your people. He's at Midtown North."

And no one had told her. Ducci beeped her, Mike beeped her, she couldn't reach either of them when she called back. But no one from the precinct beeped her about that. April stood and grabbed her coat.

"Wait a minute, we have to talk."

"Oh, yeah?"

"Ah, I wanted to tell you I can't do dinner tonight. I have to start interviewing Liberty around seven-thirty, eight." He checked his watch again.

"No problem," April assured him. She wasn't available either.

"But maybe we could meet later, you know . . ."

Sure, dream on. She didn't look at him as she left.

There was a great commotion on Fifty-fourth Street when April arrived. During the afternoon the wind had picked up. It was a cutting January knife now, slashing through the excited crowd that had gathered outside Midtown North in the early dark. The special breed of people who drove vans with dishes on top, wore heavy cameras around their necks, spoke heatedly into microphones, and manned minicams like soldiers with assault rifles were there en masse. More of them were trying to move in at Eighth Avenue, and no uniforms were down at the light, directing traffic, or out front to keep the predators away from the station house door.

April double-parked half a block away. As she walked back, she was still trembling with fury at the treachery all around. She inhaled some frigid air through her nose to calm down. The cold made her want to sneeze. Approaching the crush, she started shouting instead. "Move that equipment out of here. Right now. You know the rules. This is a police station. Clear the entrance."

The sharks moved a few inches back. Inside the precinct there was more pandemonium. At the desk April had to raise her voice to be heard over the din. "Sergeant, we need some bodies outside."

"We need some bodies inside, too," came the reply. "Got some coming in."

"Where is he?"

The sergeant didn't have to ask who. His answer was a scowl as his thumb jerked upward. April climbed the stairs, fighting wasteful emotion. As she neared the top, as if on cue, Mike came out of the office he'd been assigned. His face was grave as he waited for her, then drew her into the tiny office and closed the door.

"Are you part of this?" she asked coldly.

"I just got here. I tried to call you. Where were you?"

"It's a long story."

"What did you do with your mother?"

"I asked a friend of hers to take her home. She'll never forgive me. Not if I have ten thousand lives." April longed to grab him and hold him tight. Skinny Dragon said Mike smelled too sweet for a man, but he smelled good to her. She breathed him in. He looked good to her, too. Sexy. Strong. He always knew what to do in every situation. She liked his hair, his mustache. Liked his dangerous-looking clothes and the respect he had for her. He'd never grabbed her no matter how tempted he was. In all her years as a cop no matter what happened, no matter how great the carnage or the violence, or the tragedy of any situation, April had never cried on the job. She could feel the tears coming now.

"They arrested our suspect," was all she could think of to say. He nodded. So they had.

"Did you talk to Kiang?" he asked, changing the subject.

"He's a *pendejo,*" she exploded. A pubic hair. Worse.

"That bad."

"Yeah." April vibrated with emotion.

"Hey, take it easy." His calming tone agitated her further.

"How can you say that when everybody's fucking us over like this?" Eyes blazing, she jabbed a finger at his chest. Hysterical Skinny Dragon on a rampage couldn't have looked wilder. "You realize what's happened here? They—"

He caught the finger and kissed it. "It ain't over till it's over. By the way, did you talk to Ducci?"

"No, what's he got on the coat?"

"I don't know. He wasn't there when I called him."

April shook her head. "Where is he?"

"He left a message saying he'd call back."

A few minutes later they walked into the squad room. Iriarte was hiding behind his closed door, talking on the phone. When he saw them, he turned his back.

Hagedorn was hunched over his desk with the forms. He'd gotten stuck with the paperwork—preparing the arrest forms, the complaint arrest report, the property voucher form, and the On Line Booking System arrest report. The last had approximately a hundred data elements and had to be filled in by hand. He didn't look up when they came in.

"Hey, Charlie," Mike said, casually opening his leather coat and shrugging at his shoulder holster. "Looks like you made an arrest here. What's the story?"

Hagedorn's eyes darted over to the window in Iriarte's office before settling on Mike. "You didn't hear?"

April glanced at the holding cell. It was empty.

"No, man. We didn't hear."

"Gee, I thought—" Hagedorn's pen tapped the desk. He looked for help from Iriarte, but the CO of the squad kept his back to the window.

Mike leaned over and read Liberty's name off one of the arrest forms. "What's going on, man?"

Hagedorn made a slurping noise. "Those guys in the Thirtieth really suck. I bet they told you there were no witnesses to the Jefferson hit."

"So what have you got?" Mike asked.

Hagedorn's body did a little street-boy bob. "We got the shooter." Yeah.

"No kidding, and who might that be?" Mike asked, eyes innocent.

"Don't pull that wiseass stuff on me. You know we nailed the black bastard. Got him for one homicide. That'll do for a start." Hagedorn slapped his knee.

April looked around for a black bastard, didn't see

one. Her body made up its mind. She was boiling. "Where did you make the arrest?" she asked.

He kept his eyes on the paperwork. "The fucker was in a town house on One-Ten Street with some black chick, probably his girlfriend. He E-mailed your shrink buddy that he was going to make a statement on TV."

"No kidding." Mike looked mildly interested.

"We had to arrest him before he could do so."

"Why didn't you beep me?" April demanded.

Hagedorn ignored her. "See, our supposition is that Liberty made the Jefferson hit because Jefferson saw him kill his wife and may have been blackmailing him. As soon as Jefferson was out of the way, Liberty was ready to come out of hiding."

"From what we heard from uniforms on the scene no one saw the shooter. What evidence do you have that it was Liberty?" April's voice was beginning to sound angry.

Hagedorn turned his head to make eye contact with her for the first time. "Liberty's prints were on the murder weapon." He made a fist and jerked his elbow back. Yeah.

"Mi Dios," Mike muttered.

April already knew this, but Mike clearly didn't. "Nice of you to let us know, Hagedorn. So, who's talked with Liberty so far?" April asked.

"Just the lieutenant and me. Chang hasn't gotten here yet."

It was Kiang, but April didn't bother to correct him. "What did he say?"

"Who, Liberty? He said he wanted to talk to his lawyer."

"I'd like to see him," April murmured.

Hagedorn returned to his forms. "Hey, you've got four, five hours before he goes downtown. Why not, you're the primary," he added, then laughed. "He's in the interview room."

April glanced at Mike again. The tiny no-no motion of his chin told her not to break Hagedorn's neck just yet. She turned away to take her coat off in her office, trying to clear her head of usless things. Mike opened her office door. He'd taken his coat off, too, and combed his hair. "You thinking what I'm thinking?" he asked.

April frowned. "It's pretty hard to find prints on a handgun, particularly one that's been tossed around in the snow. How would that—?"

"That's what I'm thinking."

She shoved her purse in the drawer and slammed it. "Let's go talk to him."

They filed through the squad room to the interview room where Liberty waited alone. From the back it looked as if he had his head down and was resting on the table. But when Mike and April got inside, they saw that he'd been cuffed to the leg of the table and couldn't sit up. An indication of what Hagedorn thought of him. Nice. At the sound of the door opening, Liberty turned his head.

"Oh, you two," he muttered. He looked worse than the last time they'd seen him. Now he was pale, exhausted—and much of his hair was gray.

"How long have you been here?" Mike asked.

"About an hour. Where were you? You missed the fun."

"Sorry about that." Mike gestured vaguely.

Liberty rattled the cuffs. "I'm new at this. What happens when a person needs a bathroom?"

"Have you asked anybody?" April asked.

Liberty averted his eyes. "No one seemed interested. Maybe they wanted me to pee in my pants."

Mike slipped a key from his pocket and snapped off the cuffs and jerked his chin at April. She moved aside to let them out of the room. A few minutes later they were back. Still no cuffs. Liberty sat in the same chair as before.

April stuck a fresh tape in the recording machine on the table, pushed a button, and told it what day and hour it was, where they were, and who was in the room. Then she told Liberty the tape was for his own protection.

Mike was the first to talk. "You've gotten yourself in a lot of trouble. Why don't you tell us what happened."

"Thanks for taking off the shackles, but I'm going to wait for a lawyer."

"Did they tell you how long a wait that would be?"

"What do you mean?"

"You might not get to see a lawyer or anyone else until sometime tomorrow. Right now we're the only friends you've got. You could tell us what happened and save a lot of time."

Liberty licked his lips.

"You want a Coke or something?" April asked.

"I called someone."

"That's good, but the legal process takes time. You know you've fucked up big-time. You've got yourself involved in a homicide they can pin on you. You're locked in the system now. There's no getting out." Mike shook his head. "I thought you were smarter than that. Now why'd you go make it harder for yourself?"

Liberty scowled at him. "I didn't want to end up chained to a table."

April moved a chair away from the table and sat down.

"Like a dog," Liberty added.

Her eyes flickered. At central booking she'd seen prisoners chained to the walls so they couldn't even sit down. Liberty's shirt was wet. April could smell his fear.

"Now getting chained to a table is personal. I'd take that as a personal thing, how about you?" he asked.

"They tell you about the evidence they have against you?" The expression on Mike's face was of benign interest.

"I don't blame the media for what they do," Liberty said. "They can make up any stories they want. But you people are supposed to uncover the truth."

Mike sucked on the ends of his mustache. "And?"

"You fuckers couldn't investigate your way out of a paper bag."

"You ducked out two days ago," April said softly. "Did you finally find your wife's killer?"

He turned around to look at her. "Somebody shot the man, I'll never know what he knew or what he did."

"Did you shoot him?"

Liberty shook his head. "I couldn't have shot him. I don't have a gun."

"Uh-huh. What happened?" April asked.

"I wanted to talk to him. I tried to go to the club where he hangs out, but I couldn't even get close. There was a police raid going on. I heard a shot, but I didn't know then who had gotten shot. The cops, everybody, were running around. Two guys came across Broadway at us. One of them had a bandana tied on his head. He had a ridge of gold teeth." Liberty touched his top teeth. His face was gray.

"Us?" Mike said, quickly taking over.

"What?"

"You said us."

Liberty looked annoyed. "A slip of the tongue. The guy with the gold teeth shot Jefferson."

"This sounds like a fairy tale," Mike said.

"The fuck it is. Can't any of you do your job?"

"I'm doing my job." Mike shook his head sadly. "I've always admired you, man. I thought you were intelligent. But even a dumb cop like me wouldn't buy a story this weak. If the phantom with the gold teeth shot Jefferson, how come your prints are on the gun?"

Liberty was shocked. "Huh? Couldn't be."

"That's what they got. Now why don't you tell us about the woman downstairs who wants to make a statement, and how your prints got on the gun that killed Jefferson."

April shot a look at Mike. His expression didn't change as Liberty hesitated, then started speaking. When he was finished April went out for a mug shot of Julio.

47

Two hours later Lieutenant Iriarte's face was affable as he waved April and Mike into his office. Hagedorn was still up to his nose in arrest forms and didn't bother to acknowledge them as they passed his desk. April eased into the office and lowered her eyes so Iriarte couldn't read the situation in them. Mike was almost a head taller than the lieutenant. He was also in better shape. His full mustache made Iriarte's thin one look anemic. He didn't have an angry expression or look a bit tired after twelve hours on the job. Standing in front of Iriarte's desk with his arms by his sides and his cowboy-booted feet apart, Mike looked like a showdown in the making. April dropped the tapes that she'd made of their interviews with Liberty and Belle Lindsay on the desk. The two of them had corroborated each other's story for the last two days, and last night in particular, in all the essential elements.

Iriarte's face flashed annoyance. "Don't tell me he said something," the lieutenant began.

"Who?" Mike asked.

"You know who: Liberty. You talked with him. So, what've you got?"

"What did he say before?" April asked.

Iriarte looked annoyed. "He asked if he could use the phone."

Mike spoke first. "Lieutenant, do you know who's downstairs right now?"

Iriarte shrugged. What did he care?

"Three of Liberty's business partners are down

there talking with McCarthy. Three white guys in suits on a Sunday night. Each one has a lawyer with him and they're in suits, too. All six suits want an apology in front of the TV cameras and Liberty out of here now."

"Dream on." Iriarte shrugged again. McCarthy was second whip in the house since Captain Johnson wasn't on duty this Sunday night. Angry protesters were not Iriarte's problem. His problem was solving the crimes.

"You know who else is here? Judge Lindsay and his wife, you know, the filmmaker—and they are not happy, either. The woman videotaped with Liberty when you arrested him is their daughter. They saw the clip on TV. They went batshit. The house you arrested Liberty in happens to belong to Judge Lindsay's mother. This isn't looking good, Lieutenant." Mike smiled.

"Oh, shit." Now they had Iriarte's attention.

"Jason Frank is here, too," April added.

"What's *he* doing here?"

"I called him," she said. "I had to tell him, and he had something he wanted to show me. What's going on? When Sergeant Sanchez and I left here this morning we thought you were going to bring Liberty in for questioning. We get back here and he's been arrested. You've got him cuffed to a table. What happened?"

"I didn't cuff him to a table." Now Iriarte wasn't looking too happy. "I don't have to answer to you, Woo. We arrested him because the situation changed. We had Liberty's prints on Jefferson's murder weapon. We got a warrant. The DA was adamant about arresting him for the Jefferson hit."

"Well, maybe we'd better have a little talk with the DA about that, because the situation's changed again."

Iriarte rolled his eyes. "Oh, yeah, what now?"

"A lot."

"Well, talk."

April sat down. Mike did not. Mike nodded to April

to go on. She complied. "Before Dr. Frank left here the other day, he asked to see the death reports and photos on Petersen and Merrill Liberty. I showed him the photographs of Petersen's body. He was interested in the pinpointed spot above Petersen's abdomen. The same thing Ducci was interested in."

"Shrinks aren't doctors. Dust and fiber nuts are not doctors. What do they know?" Iriarte grumbled.

"Remember the story about the woman and the wire hanger?" April was unruffled.

"Not that again." Now Iriarte was looking really peeved.

"I asked at the labs if there's any way they can enhance the autopsy photographs to show the exact size and nature of whatever that thing on Petersen's chest is—and whether the injury had been filled in and disguised with makeup so that we all might have missed it during the autopsy."

"What?"

"In Petersen's autopsy the ultraviolet lights weren't on. There was a lot we might have missed, including the lint from Petersen's T-shirt."

Irarte scratched the side of his face. This was getting away from him. "Makeup?" he grunted, ignoring the T-shirt issue.

"You know, like they do in funeral homes to fix customers who've had really bad illnesses, or injuries, to look—"

"All right, I get the picture." Iriarte rubbed his eyes and the bridge of his nose as if he had a headache. "Don't make me guess. Can they perform this photographic miracle?"

Mike was smiling broadly. The makeup idea was his.

"We don't have the answer to that yet, sir. But we have enough other problems with the autopsy to cast serious doubts on the ME's report."

Iriarte inhaled noisily, then exhaled, making the sound of an angry goat. He changed the subject. "What did Liberty and the woman say?"

April gave the short version from her notes. "They

said the guy who shot Jefferson ran across the four lanes of Broadway, recognized Liberty, and threatened him with a gun. There was a second man with the shooter. He punched the Lindsay woman in the head, knocking her down. Liberty went for the shooter, causing him to drop the gun. The other man came at Liberty with a knife, slashing him in the chest. Liberty went down, saw the gun, picked it up, and threw it out of reach. That's how his prints got on the gun. The woman started yelling. The two men ran away."

"Chest wounds?"

"Yes," April confirmed.

"Could the injuries have been caused during the earlier homicides?" Iriarte demanded.

"They're fresh, sir. EMS took a look at them, no infection, no healing—new."

"Shit."

Mike took it up from there. "Both Liberty and the Lindsay woman picked out the mug shot of Julio Andreas Garcia as the shooter and the man who attacked them. Has ballistics come up with anything else on that gun?"

"Yeah, they picked up a floater around the Statue of Liberty yesterday. No ID yet. Hispanic, thirty-five to forty, exotic dental work, what's left of it. He was shot in the head. There are fragments of gold bridgework and only a few of his teeth are left. Probably went in the water four days ago. But he may have died before that. Three bullets in the head match with the gun that killed Jefferson. They're checking with the blood in Liberty's car to see if it's a match with the floater."

"I'd guess the time frame of the man's death isn't going to match up with Liberty's other busy killing and running schedule. What do we have now, four homicides?" Mike asked.

"Three homicides," Iriarte said, still taking the hard line on Petersen.

"You can probably send Julio down for the two shootings, Jefferson and the John Doe."

"No, Jefferson could have killed the John Doe. He was the mule who stole Liberty's car."

"Well, we can credit Jefferson with being the great brain who thought of using Liberty's car for drug exchange. Something went wrong. One of them shot the guy. They abandoned the car. At some point they got scared and dumped the body in the water somewhere off Staten Island. We'll have to check about the currents near where the car was found to come up with a time frame."

"I'm betting no connection with the Petersen/Merrill Liberty homicides," Mike said.

"One homicide," Iriarte insisted.

"I'm betting on a double homicide," April said. "And I think Julio had to get rid of Jefferson last night because he didn't trust Jefferson to keep his mouth shut about their drug activities once Jefferson was a suspect in Merrill Liberty's murder. Julio must have worried that Jefferson would rather go down on a drug charge than a murder charge."

The three were silent, thinking it over.

Finally Iriarte figured out a solution. "All right," he sighed, "we'll handle it this way. Two of these homicides don't belong to us. Jefferson belongs to the Thirtieth. Let them go out and pick up this Julio."

April and Mike nodded. Good plan.

Iriarte licked his lips. "Now about this Liberty thing."

"Jason Frank has been trying to reach me all day. You want to see the little present he brought me?"

"I don't like shrinks. Shrinks aren't real doctors," Iriarte muttered.

April smiled. That's what she used to think. She reached into her sleeve and pulled out a round thin plastic container.

"What's that?"

April opened the container and drew out a thin ten-inch needle with a sharp point on one end and white plastic head on the other. The needle was sheathed in clear plastic tubing. Iriarte grabbed his glasses and read the words on the container. Trocar catheter. 3.3 mm. He put his hand to his mouth, worried.

Finally he said, "Does this little goody match the hole—assuming there is a hole—in Petersen's chest, and the hole in Merrill Liberty's throat?"

"Three millimeters is about half the size of an ice pick. We'll have to get the lab to make the measurements and see. In Merrill Liberty's case, we can dig her up if we have to."

"Where did the shrink get this?"

"Every emergency room, every operating room, every EMS unit has them. Trocars are used to create an airway, or draw fluid, or blood or air to release pressure. Every resident has to practice with them. They come in several sizes: for adults, children, and infants. They're sharp, can penetrate quickly and deeply. Looks like a knitting needle, doesn't it?"

April slipped the unsheathed trocar back in her sleeve, then drew it out, demonstrating to Iriarte how it would neatly slide out to become a lethal weapon, then be easily concealed when the perpetrator left the scene.

"You're going to have to let Liberty go for now, sir."

Groaning, Iriarte checked his watch. It was 8:59 P.M. Liberty had been there for four hours. At 9 P.M. Sunday night the lieutenant was going to have to call the mayor's office, the police commissioner's office, and the DA. Everyone had to hear about the problem with the deputy medical examiner—and the release of Liberty—from him first. It wasn't going to be a good night for him. He scowled at April. She knew her mother's curse would be accomplished, and she would pay for tonight. She glanced at Mike.

No one mentioned Rosa's name.

Iriarte said, "Well, get out of here and go bring her in. I'll have the DA here to talk to her, see how deeply she's involved. He's not going to like this," the lieutenant added in a warning voice, as if the homicides and improper autopsies themselves were all April's fault.

"Thank you, sir," she said.

She and Mike exchanged knowing looks. Once again Iriarte wanted the two of them gone as fast as possible. He wanted to be remembered in the photos, not as the one who arrested Liberty, but as the one who let him go.

48

Rosa Washington lived in Greenwich Village. April was silent as Mike drove Captain McCarthy's unmarked green Ford Taurus south on Broadway. It was a clear starless night, the coldest yet. She stared out the window at the dizzying display of lights. Neon signs selling theater, underwear, watches, sex, sneakers, punched out of the dark, jolting the senses like a drug shot through the veins. Cruising through Times Square, where the golden ball had dropped on the new year only twelve days ago, April felt a slight surge of energy. Outside the car, the air cut to the bone, but there was still action on the streets this Sunday night despite the frigid temperature. January in New York. April adjusted her scarf. Static, more static, then a garbled call jumped out of the scanner. Mike reached over and turned it off. Ducci had left a message: The ultraviolet lights had not turned up any traces of blood on Merrill Liberty's mink coat. But it was definitely Rosa Washington's hair that had been taken off Petersen's body. When it had gotten there was now the question.

"What are we taking her in for?" April asked after a minute. "Intentionally messing up an autopsy or unintentionally messing up an autopsy?"

She had been working for seven days straight, the last three days for fourteen hours at a stretch. Today with the funeral and the fiasco in Kiang's office had been the worst. Mentally, she shook herself, trying to wake up. She was tired, felt flabby and soft as she tried to work herself up to the nervy state necessary for telling the deputy ME she was in big trouble.

"You know her best. What's your call?"

"Here we go again with the your call, my call bit," April complained.

"You did pretty well last time."

"Fine. No plan. We play it by ear." She sank into her own thoughts and didn't glance in Mike's direction until he said, "There it is."

April studied the building at Rosa Washington's address. Nine stories. Red brick. Small windows except on the Hudson Street side, where the middle apartment every other floor had French doors and a narrow balcony for plants. The building was prewar, but not the kind of prewar Petersen's lavishly appointed Fifth Avenue building was—all limestone and brass and marble with huge windows. This kind of prewar was just old, kind of run-down, had an external fire escape. Mike parked in front of a fire hydrant and killed the engine.

"Let's take this real easy." April inhaled and exhaled a few times, trying to take it real easy herself. She glanced up at the sixth floor. The left apartment still had Christmas lights ringing the window, but the inside lights were off. The right apartment was dark. The middle windows glowed. April guessed that Rosa was up.

The front door of the building was open. Inside, the second door was locked. Mike found Washington's name on the menu of tenants: 6B. His options were to ring the super's bell and, if the super was there, have a conversation with him about letting them in. Mike could ring Rosa's bell, ask her to ring them up, thereby alerting her to their presence. Or he could wait for some other tenant to open the door for them. Apparently none of those options appealed to him. He didn't look at April as he casually popped the lock open with a tool from his pocket.

April brushed past him, got into the elevator, hit the button marked six. "Nice and easy," she cautioned again as they moved slowly upward after a few introductory bumps. She realized she was afraid of Rosa.

The elevator door slid open. Mike moved out into the narrow hall first. April followed. Five apartments on the floor; 6B was in the middle of the hall, just opposite them. April took the center position. She glanced at Mike's face, taut now. When he lowered his chin, she rang the bell. She knew he didn't like her position. He preferred to be the target in front of the door, liked her to be the one covering him from the side. She smiled. Macho man. Rosa wasn't going to hurt them.

A crack of light showed under the door, but the occupant was in no hurry to open up. April rang the bell again. Maybe she had company.

Finally a low voice came from within. "You have the wrong apartment."

"It's Sergeant Woo," April said, then added, "and Sergeant Sanchez."

"It's late. What do you want?"

"We want you to open the door." This from Mike.

Rosa didn't reply. She took some time rattling the chains and turning the locks. When she finally opened the door, she was gazing past April at the elevator door. The window in it showed that the elevator was not there. It had returned to the first floor. Rosa stood in front of the entrance to her apartment. "What's up?"

"We need you to come uptown with us." April took in the fine white sweater, the gray trousers, and gold chain belt the doctor wore. The gold earrings and gold watch. The doctor's hair was washed and set, not wispy now. Her lips red. She looked good.

"This is my day off," she said.

Mine too, April didn't say. "Are you going to let us in, or do you want to talk in the hall?"

Rosa's face showed no sign of tension as she backed away and let them enter her surprisingly gracious apartment. The foyer had a parquet floor and a black-painted fence that ran the width of the sunken living room except at the entrance in the middle where two small steps went down. Recessed lights gave the yellow living room a warm glow. Trees and plants lined the windows facing Hudson Street. Two maroon sofas and two club chairs had a comfortable look. A large square coffee table placed between them was laden with books. The focal point of the room were the French windows that opened on the narrow balcony Mike and April had seen from below. Now that they were up here, April could see that the French windows were cracked open.

Dispassionately, Washington watched them examine the place. "You want to sit down?" she asked, inviting them down the steps into the sunken living room.

Mike checked his watch. "We're in kind of a hurry," he replied.

April could see he wanted to get moving. When they'd entered the building, she'd unbuttoned her coat, just in case. Now it was very hot in the apartment even with the French doors not fully closed. If they didn't get going immediately, she'd have to take the coat off. It didn't look as if Rosa was ready to come with them. The woman moved to the sofa closest to the windows and sat down. April considered her options in the coat department, but Rosa started speaking before she had time to make a decision.

"I saw that Liberty was arrested. Good job."

"Yeah. A real stroke of genius," Mike said sarcastically.

"What's the problem?" The doctor looked puzzled.

"You'll hear everything uptown at the station." Mike checked his watch again. "They're waiting for us."

Rosa didn't ask who. She scowled and turned her attention to April. "I took you guys into my confidence. The least you can do is fill me in."

"It's your turn to fill us in," April said softly.

"About what?"

"Oh, a few things need clarifying."

"What things?"

"Your relationship with Tor Petersen. Your relationship with Daphne Petersen."

"Hey, hey, hey. I have no relationship with that bitch."

"She called you on the phone the day her husband died. What did she want?"

"She wanted to know when the body would be released."

"Before she knew the cause of death? Come on, Rosa, the game is up. You have to come clean about this. We know about you and Petersen."

"Well, I can't do it this way," Rosa snapped. "I'm a doctor. I don't go to the precinct. You can send someone to my office tomorrow."

"Doctors come to the precinct to talk all the time," April told her. "Tomorrow is too late. We have to do it now."

"It's been a hard week. I don't work on the weekends," Rosa said stubbornly. "My position requires some respect."

"Rosa, none of us get respect in murder cases. Don't make this hard for yourself." April pursed her lips. She glanced at Mike, standing by the door. He was sucking on his mustache.

Rosa glanced at him nervously. "All right, I may have made a mistake about Petersen," she admitted suddenly. "Let's let it go at that."

"People make mistakes," April said, neutral.

"I thought I could get away with it. We were so careful."

"You and Daphne?"

"I told you I had nothing to do with her," Rosa said angrily. "It was Tor I knew. Isn't that—?" Her face flashed horror as April's mouth dropped open: Rosa Washington was Petersen's secret lover!

Mike picked up instantly. "Guess you weren't careful enough."

"We only met here. Can you believe that son of a bitch wouldn't even take me out to dinner?" Rosa glared at them. "He was afraid his wife would find out and steal his money." Her breath came short. "Oh, he was some piece of work."

The trocar that only doctors knew how to use, Rosa's hair on Petersen's body—on his sweater—the mink coat that Emma saw at the scene of the crime—all Rosa's. That was Ducci's message. Rosa hadn't missed the cause of death; she'd murdered the victim.

Mike opened his jacket and placed himself between Rosa and the door. He jerked his head at April to get out of the way. She moved toward the window. "Why?"

Rosa's face distorted with rage. "No way I'd let him tie me up and beat me. Not for all the money in the world. Once was enough." Her mouth twisted. "I don't let nobody trick me and hurt me like that." She sniffed back angry tears.

"What about Merrill Liberty, did she hurt you, too?"

"I'm a doctor. You understand? I'm a doctor." Rosa didn't move. "I'm a doctor. You can't treat me like this."

"I don't understand, explain it to me. He hurt you, so why didn't you just break up with him?" April asked.

Rosa shook her head. "He wouldn't let go."

April shot a look at Mike. Now one of them was at each end of the room. It occurred to April that Rosa might be crazy enough to try to shoot them. But where was the gun? Not on her person. Maybe behind the pillows in the sofa. Once again Rosa's hands were folded in her lap. She'd calmed down. Now she looked both dangerous and helpless at the same time. Spooky. This was a woman who killed her lover, then coldly dissected him as part of her job. All the pieces that hadn't fit before came together. Rosa had access to Petersen's body in the morgue. She had removed his T-shirt with the tiny hole in it and used waterproof makeup to disguise his wound. Rosa had been so cool when Ducci picked it up during the autopsy. She must have figured, as ME, she was in control. Only later, when April kept picking at it, did she feel threatened. April took off her coat and laid it over the back of a chair.

Rosa turned to her, complaining. "You got me into this by criticizing my work. I was respectful of you, and now you want to destroy me. This is not my fault."

"Rosa, let's not debate it here," April said.

"I'm a doctor. Do you know what it takes to be a doctor? Huh, you little street rats? You know how much it costs, how many years it takes? Ten years of starving and studying and taking tests, working two jobs. Eighty thousand dollars in loans," she screamed. *"Call me doctor!"*

"This isn't about medical school. It's about murder." April watched Rosa's hands.

"Call me doctor," Rosa insisted.

"Where's your coat, Doctor?" Mike asked.

"You got the jock. What do you need me for?"

"You talking about Liberty?"

"Fucking football player," Rosa muttered. "The man's a fucking football player. Let him go down."

"He didn't kill anybody," April said quietly.

"No!" Rosa was shocked. "You didn't let him go! I saw it on TV. He was arrested."

Mike shook his head. "You stopped watching too soon. The eleven o'clock news will have another story. Liberty wasn't arrested for the murders of Tor Petersen and Merrill Liberty."

"No!" Rosa exploded again. "I don't believe this."

"You wouldn't want someone else punished for your crimes."

"Uh-uh. You're not pinning murder on me. I didn't do anything wrong. I only did what I was told. My boss was sick. I did what he and the mayor and the police commissioner asked me to do. That's all." Rosa stood, shaking all over. "My only fault was that I knew Petersen. You can't prove anything else."

"We can prove you killed them." April watched Rosa, giving her a moment to make her decision. The best thing was to get them to confess. But sometimes they came at you instead.

"You're going to have to get me out of this," Rosa cried. "It's your fault. You started this. And now it doesn't look good for anybody. I'll blow your careers. I'll blow all their careers. No one will survive."

April thought the mayor and the police commissioner, and even Rosa's boss the ME, would survive somehow. She and Mike, however, would probably not get a medal.

"Let's go, Rosa," she said. "You can tell your story uptown."

Rosa moved toward the French windows. At first April thought she was going to close them, but Rosa quickly swung one door open and stepped outside onto the tiny balcony. April didn't pause to consider what she was doing. She followed Rosa out the door into the small space where she stood looking down at the street and shivering all over.

"No," April said softly. "That's not the way." April was trembling, too. She could hear her voice crack in the cold. The sidewalk was six stories down, and the railing on the balcony was low, meant for plants, not people.

"Come inside. We just want to talk, that's all. You'll have lots of chances to explain. Just come inside," April urged. "Come on. This isn't the way." She held out her hand. Rosa didn't take it. "Come on."

"I'm not going to the station. You understand me. I'm not going to any police station. I'm one of the good guys." Rosa was crying now. "You're just treating me like this because I'm black. If I die, it's your fault. My blood is on your hands."

"No." April was shaking all over. Her gun was in the holster. She was too close to the woman to unholster the gun. The gun wouldn't do any good anyway. It wasn't April who was in danger.

"Yes!" Rosa screamed. "You just want a black to go down for killing those white folk. How could you do this to me? Don't you know you're colored, too?"

"No, Rosa," April said. "Come inside. We can talk about this later."

"Yes, you are. Chink and spic—colored." She spat out the words. "No better than I am."

"Mike!"

"I'm here. I'm right here." Mike reached out the door and touched April's shoulder, encouraging her to move aside. "Come inside, April."

April shook her head. She didn't want to move and give the hysterical woman a chance to jump. "I didn't do anything wrong."

"Rosa, let me talk to you," Mike said. "No one wants to hurt you. And you don't want to get hurt." He nudged April. *Will you get out of there!*

There wasn't room for three of them on the balcony, no way to each take a side of Rosa and move her downstairs into the car before she was totally out of control. They'd wanted her to go quietly. They'd played nice. But Rosa was screaming now, calling for help.

"Help! help! Police brutality! Somebody help. They're trying to kill me. Helllp!" The noise soared out into the street. Later witnesses would recount the scene. Two against one. Police brutality.

"Okay, that's enough," April said sharply. She reached out to take hold of Rosa to pull her inside. At April's touch, Rosa lunged, grabbing April's arm as she tried to launch both herself and April over the railing.

April dodged, shifting her position to throw Rosa off balance so she could save the woman, take her down on the right side of the abyss. But both women were holding on to each other, and Rosa's weight propelled her over. April lost her balance and her breath as her knees banged against the railing, then caught as Mike grabbed her around the waist, stopping both women from plunging to the pavement below. April's shoulders wrenched from their sockets. A scream caught in her throat.

She tried to pull Rosa back, grunted with pain, as

Rosa dangled by her wrists, kicking against the side of the building.

"Let go!"

"Take my hand."

April couldn't breathe, couldn't think or speak. She heard noises from below, heard Mike say something, but couldn't tell what it was. Some language she didn't know. She heaved on Rosa's arms, but couldn't budge the bigger woman. Sirens rang out on the street below.

"Hold on, baby." This she heard. "Switch hands," Mike said.

Whose? How? April's fingers were frozen. She heard the sound of a fire engine. Had she been there two minutes? Five minutes. How long? Her body trembled. She didn't think she could hang on.

"Switch hands," Mike said again.

How could they do it without the woman falling? Tears froze in April's eyes. She didn't want to let go. Mike moved around to her side and grabbed one of Rosa's wrists, taking some pressure off, then reached to grab the other. Now April and Mike both had hold of Rosa's two arms. They started dragging the woman back. Someone banged on the apartment door, trying to get in. Must be the fire department.

Rosa kicked at the building's brick wall, screaming at them to let her go. People started calling up from below. More instructions April couldn't understand. A ladder was coming up. "Hold on."

Behind them, the door to the apartment crunched.

They pulled, and Rosa's head rose above the railing. Mike adjusted his grip. "Come on, Rosa, you don't want to die."

"Oh, God," April cried. "Help us, Rosa."

Rosa's face was contorted with pain and fury. She let them heave her chest up on the railing. Then, when the tragedy was averted, when April and Mike moved their hands to haul her higher and the firefighters rushed in with their axes, Rosa turned her head and sank her teeth into Mike's arm. He recoiled, letting go. As the firefighters spilled into the apartment to help, Rosa twisted from April's hold and propelled herself out from the building.

A gasp rose from the crowd on the sidewalk as she fell, missing the round trampoline-like contraption that six firefighters held out too late to catch her. She socked into two of the firefighters holding it before hitting the pavement.

Then, upstairs on the sixth floor, something happened that April would be ashamed of for the rest of her life. Overwhelmed with the pain of two dislocated shoulders and regret for not having saved the suspect they'd been charged with bringing in, she did a very uncoplike thing. She fainted in the sergeant's arms.

49

The TV was on most of the time during the seven days of April's recuperation. For the first two days she was stuck in the hospital where her room was not far from that of Rosa Washington, who had survived her fall with more than two dozen broken bones, some so badly shattered the doctors were confident she would never walk again. It was predicted, however, that before the year was out Rosa Washington would be well enough to appear before the grand jury in a wheelchair and be indicted for her crimes.

Through the haze of painkillers, exhaustion, and a bad chest cold, April saw clips of Liberty finally returning to his home at the Park Century. He had nothing to say. She saw Cinda Stewart make an appeal on TV for Liberty to come on *Ahead of the News* and tell of his ordeal. She saw Emma Chapman get out of a car in front of the theater where she was acting. Asked to make a statement for the press, Emma said she was grateful to the police for finding Merrill Liberty and Tor Petersen's killer and clearing Liberty's name. She talked about Sergeant Mike Sanchez and Sergeant April Woo on TV, then said the department, indeed the whole city of New York, was indebted to those first-class detectives for their extraordinary police work. Emma stated she felt they deserved commendation, thus making Skinny a happy Dragon Mother, finally with something to brag about. April, however, had no doubt they would not receive medals. During April's confinement in bed, Jason Frank and Mike Sanchez both visited, called every day and sent flowers. April did not hear from Dean Kiang. But she was not thinking of him. She lay in bed thinking about Mike Sanchez and what a great man he was.

At six-thirty on the morning she was supposed to return to work, April awoke in her own bed. Her shoulders were still aching badly and the cough from her cold was not entirely gone. Carefully, she sat up and punched out Mike's number.

Yawning, Mike picked up after the third ring. "Yeah? Sanchez."

"My car won't start," April murmured.

Instantly, Mike's voice got soft with concern. "How are you feeling?"

"Fine. Great," she lied.

"Uh-huh . . . well, did you try putting the key in the ignition?"

"I don't think that would help. The car's—you know . . ."

"No kidding, it's you know. Well, what time is it?"

"Sorry to call so early. I just didn't want to miss you."

He didn't say anything for a minute. Then he said, "I'll be over in twenty minutes."

Twenty minutes later, Mike stood on the cement sidewalk in front of April's house in his new leather coat, completely oblivious to the rain. The frowning face of April's mother was in its usual place in the front window, watching him with a Chinese curse on her lips. She looked as if her head had been separated from her body and planted there as a warning that she would never forgive him for loving her daughter. Too bad for her. This time April had summoned him. He waved at the head.

"Good morning, Mrs. Woo. Howya doin'?" he mouthed into the wind.

Though she certainly couldn't hear him, a tentative hand came up from below the windowsill in reply. Mike considered the almost wave an extremely good outcome and felt ridiculously happy. Half a minute later the front door opened and April came out. She was wearing black rubber boots and a black slicker with a hood. Burnt cinnamon lipstick. She glanced up at the sky and put up the hood before dashing down the walk to meet him. The rain slowed to a fine drizzle as they got to the sidewalk where the Camaro was parked behind the Le Baron.

"What do you want to do about the car? Want to jump-start it and take it in?"

"Thanks for coming to get me," she said. A flash of lightning behind her eyes caused his breath to catch and the radar in his mustache to quiver.

"You don't want to jump-start it?" He took a deep breath and blew steam out into the cold misty morning.

"Doesn't need it," she murmured. Her inner eye flickered over him again like a butterfly searching for nectar in a flower garden.

¿Mi Dios, existe? Could it be? His heart jumped into his throat and blocked his breathing. Could it be? He'd been watching this woman with his whole being for many months, waiting for a sign. He'd been waiting for such a long time he'd begun telling himself to give it up. Give it up, move on. How many times could a man get that close only to be pushed away at the very last moment with a look determined enough to stop a starving tiger from lunging at a still target? Move on, his head kept telling him. A thousand women wanted it, move on. And then what would he do? He'd move an inch or two away from her, only to lose the ground the minute he saw her again. In the middle of work, he'd be sitting across the desk from her and smell her, feel the whole of her living inside of him as if his body were her home, and he'd yearn to be inside her the same way.

"You want to get in the car, or stand here in the rain? Either way's fine with me," she said.

Jesus. There was the sign. There it was. She loved him. No doubt about it. His scarred eyebrow jumped up as he opened the door for her. He checked for the devil's face in the window. It had disappeared. A good omen. He trotted around the car and got in on the driver's side, glanced in the mirror. His hair and face were dripping. His coat was water-spotted. He looked horrible. The car smelled like wet upholstery. This was not the best moment, but he couldn't let the chance pass. His lips burned. He didn't want to mess up again, closed his eyes and took a deep breath. What was he supposed to do here, ask her to marry him? Ask her to sleep with him, or give her a kiss?

Okay. He opened his eyes. April had put down her hood and was studying him with a wrinkled forehead.

"You all right?" she asked.

"Yeah, sure." He nodded, trying to be cool.

"So?"

"So . . . April, I've been thinking." He scratched his cheek. "We know each other pretty well now. It's been six weeks since we haven't worked in the same shop. What do you say we get married?"

April let her breath out in a whistle. "Just like that?"

Mike shrugged. "Well, it's not just like that. I've been thinking about it for a while now. I think cops should marry each other, know what I mean?"

April chewed on her bottom lip, then glanced out the car window at her house.

"So, what do you say?"

She studied the water dripping down the windshield before answering. "What about love?"

"Huh? Didn't I say I love you? You know I love you. You'd have to be crazy not to know that." He started patting his pocket down now for the car keys, didn't think this was going well and wanted to get away. "I want to marry you, be with you forever, don't I?"

"They're right here." She handed him the car keys.

"So?" He fumbled with the ignition.

After a long moment, she shook her head. "I couldn't marry anyone I haven't slept with, you know, quite a bit. Maybe as long as a year, to see if we're compatible."

"No kidding?" Mike perked up.

"I don't know why. But it seems important to me."

"It's important." Mike cleared his throat. "Shouldn't marry if you're not"—he coughed again—"compatible." He checked his watch. It was 7:00 A.M. He didn't know what time her shift started.

April brushed raindrops off the front of her raincoat, waiting for his next move.

Mike sucked on his mustache, considering. "You hungry? Want to go to my place for breakfast?"

"Sure," she said. "Got any food?"

"Ah, not really. Is that a problem?" Mike looked at her again, checking to make absolutely sure he wasn't missing something somewhere.

"No problem," she said, then smiled, stopping his heart again. *Jesu Christe,* she meant it.

After all this time no problem? Mike plunged the key into the ignition, got the car started, and pulled out with a roar. At 7:33 the rain stopped. At 7:45 Mike and April were in his apartment in their first deep kiss, struggling to embrace around their various weapons when the phone rang.

Mike picked up, breathing hard. "Yeah. Sanchez."

"You in the middle of something, Mike?"

"What's up?" He nuzzled April's neck, wasn't leaving now no matter what.

Hardly wincing at all, April pushed up her sleeves and wrapped her smooth slender arms around his neck. He kissed the inside of her upper arm. Her skin smelled of soap and roses. She pressed her hips against him. He kissed her mouth and tongue. She tasted of mint toothpaste. He could feel her breasts, her heart beating, her thigh nudging between his legs. He felt light-headed, almost dizzy with excitement. All he wanted was to sink down on the floor with her and never get up.

He couldn't hear what was being said to him. "I have a bad cold," he said. "I have a fever. It's my day off."

"You heard me, this is important. Are you coming in?"

April had removed her weapon and now was disarming him. She caught a tender place under his arm and tickled, making him laugh into the phone. And he hadn't thought she was funny! Then she was tugging at his shirt, at the buckle on his belt. He was breathing hard.

"Mike—! Are you coming in or what?"

"No, man, not today," he croaked. He tried to hang up the receiver and dropped it with a crash. By the time he got the two pieces of phone together and the dial tone shut down, April had most of her clothes off. He stopped short, gawking like a kid.

"Jesus, April—"

"What was that about?" she asked.

"Oh, nothing. Um—" He took his pants off, tripping and almost falling on a cuff. Not cool, not cool at all.

"Very nice," April murmured at what she saw. She said "Kiss me a lot" in Spanish. He was pretty much out of his mind with desire, but he did notice that her accent was pretty good. He figured that she didn't really mean kiss me a lot. She meant what kiss me a lot really means. So he did.

If you enjoyed reading *Judging Time,*
be sure to look for Leslie Glass's
powerful new April Woo
suspense novel,

STEALING TIME

Read on
for a special brief excerpt. . . .

A Dutton hardcover on sale
in February 1999

At 5 A.M., on what would turn out to be anything but a routine Tuesday, April Woo saw the glow of morning spread around the corner and down the hall into the bedroom where she was trying to sleep. The light came from the living-room picture window of the twenty-second-floor Queens apartment where her boyfriend had lived for six months and where no curtains concealed the drop-dead view of the Manhattan skyline. Punched out and highlighted by the dawn, the jumble of building shapes hung as if etched in the sky, a monument to the ingenuity of man, that great magician who used the raw power of steel and concrete in bridges and glass towers to dwarf nature and hide himself. Another day, and the city beckoned even before the cop was fully conscious.

April Woo was a detective sergeant in the New York City Police Department and second whip in the detective squad of Midtown North, the West Side precinct between Fifty-ninth and Forty-second streets from Fifth Avenue to the Hudson River. She was a boss who supervised other detectives and was in charge of the squad when her superior, Lieutenant Iriarte, was not around. She was also a person used to sleeping in her own bed. Having grown up in a Chinatown walkup, and living at the moment in a two-story house in Astoria, Queens, April was now in the highest place she'd ever spent the night. She yawned, stretched, and let the soft drone of the news perpetually playing on 1010 WINS filter into her consciousness. A sharp detective listened for disaster twenty-four hours a day.

Hearing a radio report of a crime in her precinct could get her out of bed even if she wasn't aware of hearing it. Now, April urgently needed the story of some catastrophe for her mother, that April could claim kept her working around the clock. She needed the story if she wanted to go home in peace.

Only three weeks ago, on April 25th, April Woo had celebrated her thirtieth birthday, but you'd never know it by the way her parents treated her. It was particularly humiliating to her that instead of bringing her the respect she deserved, her rank in the department and the ripeness of her age only served to pick up the pace of her mother's tirades on the subject of her low-life job and lousy marriage prospects.

In the Chincse culture, dragons can be both good and evil, can appear at any moment and have the power to make or break every human endeavor. April called Sai Yuan Woo "Skinny Dragon Mother" because her mother, too, had the ability to change shape before her eyes, and had a tongue that spit real fire. April was no less afraid of her now that she carried two guns on her person than she had been as a small and defenseless child.

Lately, Skinny Dragon Mother had upped the ante on her disapproval of her only child, calling April the very worst kind of old maid, a worm old maid with an undesirable suitor. The undesirable suitor in question, Mike Sanchez, was a Mexican-American sergeant in the Detective Bureau like April. But unlike her, he was now assigned to the Homicide Task Force. Carefully, April turned her head to look at him, lying on his stomach beside her, sound asleep. One arm was curved over his head, the other cradled the pillow that hid his face. The sheet covered his calves and feet. The rest of him was naked.

The clutch hit her above the heart and below the throat, somewhere around the clavicle. His legs and butt, the muscles in his back and shoulders, the fine tracing of curly black hair on the backs of his arms, more on his legs, seemed exactly right. His waist, though no longer exactly slender and boyish, was proportionately correct for his age and stature. He had smooth skin—in places it was as soft as a baby's—and the hard muscles of a trained fighter. His body was an interesting blend of hard and soft, dotted with a collection of scars from various battles, only a few of which she knew the origins.

The tightness in her chest rose to her throat as she thought of his welcome last night. When she'd gotten there at 1:30 A.M., he'd given her food and wine. Then, in the flickering light of a dozen candles, they'd made love for much of the night. The candles, she'd thought, were an unusually nice touch. She shivered as the dawn slowly infused the room. The idea of her former supervisor as a thoughtful and compelling lover was so alarming that part of her wanted to get off the slippery slope and slide right out of there with the morning, never to return. Another part told her to relax and go back to sleep. She was wrestling with the conflict when Mike spoke.

"Want some coffee, *querida*?" The question came from the depths of the pillow. Not a muscle in his body had moved, but the sound of his voice told her he'd been awake for a while, knew where his gun was, could roll over, hit the floor, and fire at the door or window in less than ten seconds. She grabbed at the sheet to cover herself.

"No thanks, I've got to get going."

"Why? You don't have to be at work until four this afternoon?" He rolled over, stretched his arms above his head and arched his back, showing off his chest and stomach and the rest of the merchandise that was fully restored after very little sleep.

April busied herself tucking the sheet around her neck, looking everywhere but at the goods. "You know my mother," she mumbled.

Mike laughed softly. "We're already acquainted, *querida*. It's okay to be naked."

"Not where I come from."

"Don't you like to look at me?" He nudged her with his knee.

"Yeah, sure," she mumbled some more, wimping out.

"So come on, take that thing off. We can look at each other in the light. Make my day." He reached out to tickle her, but she turned around to study the clock and didn't see his digits coming.

"Oh my God, it's almost six. Gotta go." She jumped when he touched her. "No, no, really."

He withdrew the offending fingers. "Aw, don't pull the guilty number on me. You know you don't have to go home anymore. You can stay here with me. We could have coffee, sleep a little more. If you don't want, I won't bother you." He lifted an edge of the sheet that covered her and pulled it over himself. The action got him closer to her. They were side by side now, touching from shoulder to knee, and the sheet did not succeed in hiding his intent.

She shook her head and laughed.

"What?" he demanded, his lush mustache twitching innocently.

"You know."

He rose up on one elbow to look at her. "Lucky me, you are one pretty woman in the morning, *querida*. Give me a hug."

"Yeah sure, I bet you say that to all the girls." By her calculation, Mike was the good-looking one, and he had a rep. He was like Sarah Lee to the opposite sex: no one didn't like him.

"You're the only girl in my life." He said this with just the right amount of huskiness in his voice, not too hokey.

April swallowed the hook and believed him, but didn't want to get all teary about it. She scrunched down, put her arms around him, and laid her head on his chest. She was trying to go with the flow, but wasn't finding it so easy. From the things Mike said and did in bed, she was aware that her own erotic repertoire was somewhat lacking. It made her afraid that regardless of what he told her right now, he'd be tired of her before the week was out.

He was able to distract her from this pessimistic speculation for a while by kissing her all over and encouraging her to return the favor, which didn't turn out to be so very difficult.

Then he got up, made coffee, and scrambled some eggs for breakfast. She was impressed by his domesticity. At nine, he showered and dressed for the day, collected his gun and his keys from the table, and took off without saying anything about the case that was bedeviling him. April decided to put off going home. What difference could a few hours make, she asked herself.

Time made a big difference in everything, though. If she had gone home either sometime during the night or early in the morning, she might have avoided a whole lot of trouble with her parents. If she had been a few minutes earlier or later in to work that day, or if she hadn't started the evening tour on radio call, driving around with her driver, Woody Baum, newly promoted to detective, new to the squad, and highly desirable to April because he didn't have any loyalties, she might never have been involved in the Popescu case.

As it was she didn't go home. She started work on radio call, and she and Woody had hardly settled into their gray unmarked unit when she got a call from the dispatcher to 10-85 the Midtown North Patrol Supervisor forthwith.

"Possible kidnapping, K," the dispatcher squawked. "Be advised the Midtown North Patrol Supervisor has also requested Crime Scene and Emergency Service Units, K."

"Ten-four, Manhattan North Detective Supervisor on the way, K." April turned to Woody. "That's that fancy building at Seventh and Central Park South. Turn around."

Woody threw the bubble on the roof, hit the sirens,

and did a gut-wrenching u-ie on Fifty-seventh Street, leaving tire marks on the road.

The address of the requested investigation was a glass tower that curved around the corner from Central Park South to Seventh Avenue, sweeping up as much view as it could along the way. A driveway to the building entrance cut through the sidewalk, curving the other way. In front of the driveway was a tiny garden, consisting of a burbling fountain, a Japanese maple full of red leaves, and a thickly planted patch of gold and purple pansies. The building was already locked down. Yellow crime-scene tape was stretched across the entrance. Vehicles jammed the area. Uniforms swarmed everywhere. Three minutes from the 911 call, and the operation was already in full swing. The area was sealed off. The curious were clumped together outside police lines, talking, staring. The media was gathering.

"Park as close as you can and meet me inside." Adrenaline kicked in, and April was all nerves. It looked like something really big.

As Woody tried to pull into the driveway, a tall uniform with a mustache waved at them to stop. Woody jerked to a halt to talk to him as April took out her shield and clipped it to her jacket's breast pocket. The uniform saw it and waved them on without a word, but April had already jumped out of the car and joined the fray. The first thing she did, before going into the building, was to look up. On the roof, she could see two detectives in vests, with double-barrel shotguns, peering over the edge from above at ledges and anything else that protruded. She then saw a familiar face and went to talk to the precinct patrol supervisor, Lieutenant McMan, a steely type with startling green eyes and no lips at all, who had called the special units in after receiving the call from the 911 dispatcher.

"What's the story?" she asked.

"Hey, Woo. Woman's name is Popescu. It appears

she was assaulted in her apartment. Her baby is missing."

"She still here?"

"No, she's in ER at Roosevelt."

"Anybody go with her?"

"Her husband claims he found her." McMan shrugged. "I have two uniforms on them."

"Upstairs?"

"Four detectives trying to get the phones tapped in case there's a ransom demand. ESU's canvassing the basement, roof, elevator shafts, tops of the elevators, trash, trash compactors." He smiled grimly. "The building superintendent freaked out at the heavy tools and the floodlights. He didn't want them breaking down any walls or doors."

"Any sign of the baby?"

McMan shook his head. "Nothing yet."

"What about CSU? Wasn't the crime scene secured for their first shot?"

"Yeah, yeah, they're up there, too. Apartment 9E. You going up?"

"Just for a quick look-see. I want to go over to ER to Q and A the victim right away. What's her status?"

"She was unconscious when she was taken out."

"Hey, boss." Woody bounded up.

"We're going up," she told him, nodding toward the front elevators, two pink-marble-fronted horrors.

"Not those. We got people in the shafts. You'll have to go up the back elevator," McMan told her.

Uniforms were swarming on the back stairs as April walked through. One was also guarding the back elevator. The elevator men and doormen were being questioned by detectives. A clot of tenants, unable to get home, was having a fit. April and Woody commandeered the elevator, stopped at the ninth floor and tried to enter the apartment through the kitchen.

"Forget about it, I'm not even started here. You can look in and that's it," came a voice from behind the door. The unseen criminologist added, "I don't give a shit who you are," in case somebody planned to put up a fight.

"Sergeant Woo. We just want to take a look," April said.

"This is where it happened. One look, don't touch," came the warning.

"Fine."

The door opened a little and April and Woody got a partial view for all of three seconds of some bloodstains on a marble floor. Somewhere in the front of the apartment, another feisty Crime Scene investigator and more detectives were locked in a noisy conflict over contamination of the scene versus the need to get the phones up right away so they could tape all the incoming calls. She'd have to come back later.

April glanced at the garbage can by the back door and repressed a strong urge to go through it. Victim first.

"Okay," she said to Woody. She turned to leave, and realized he'd frozen the elevator on the floor so she wouldn't have to wait when she was ready to go. Good man; he was taking care of her.

Roosevelt Hospital was only a short distance away on Ninth Avenue at Fifty-ninth Street, just a block down from the Manhattan branch of Fordham University. Woody negotiated the car through the streets and April was lost in her own thoughts. Her antennae were up and she was bristling all over. By now there would already be detectives from the Major Cases unit there. They would move in and take over the precinct squad room, maybe even her own desk. They'd be setting up their easels and starting the clocks ticking on their time sheets. It rankled her that no one thought precinct detectives could handle anything important. From now on, until this missing baby was found dead or alive, the precinct squad would be ordered to do the scut work. No precinct squad detectives liked it one bit.

What April always did was to work around the specialized units as if they weren't the hotshots with all the muscle. Right now, she didn't want to vent her feelings about how things were to the new kid. She wanted to manage the case correctly so the outsiders wouldn't make a mess in her territory.

"Leave it here," she said abruptly about the car in a no-parking zone by the emergency room entrance. Then she jerked her chin to indicate that Baum should accompany her inside.

They hurried into the ER entrance. Right away, April picked out two uniforms flanking a nervous-looking man in a blue suit. She decided to take the time to stop at the reception desk before speaking with him. She didn't say anything to Woody. He didn't say anything to her. Good, he was following her lead.

At the desk the harried-looking woman with permed red hair saw the shields, then returned to her computer screen.

"Where's the assault victim? Po-pes—"

"Popescu. It's Rumanian," the woman snapped. She kept typing and didn't look up.

"Thanks, that's the one. Where is she?" She didn't glance at Baum.

"She's in Treatment Room 3."

"I'd like to talk with her."

"She's unconscious."

"How about the doctor?"

"The doctor's with her."

"You have any idea when I could talk with him?"

"No." The woman returned to her typing, pleased to thwart April. She filled out her uniform and then some, had angry eyes, and a patch of fiery red pimples on each cheek. After a pause, she added, "They've finished with the X rays. Shouldn't be too long now."

"Thanks." April turned back to the rows of seats occupied by the motley bunch that formed a little pond of human misery in the waiting room. She didn't want to think about the bacteria and viruses circulating the room. She recognized the uniforms, Duffy and Prince. Both were white, five-ten or so, beefy, a few years younger than she, and not much for taking initiative of any kind. Duffy worked a wad of gum around his mouth without actually chewing. The two cops flanked the victim's husband in an informal kind of way. The obviously upset, dark-haired man sat on a chair between them, wringing his hands. She noticed that his tie had alligators on it, his pink shirt had white collar and cuffs that were stained with blood, and his blue pinstriped suit looked expensive.

"Mr. Popescu?" she said.

His head twitched her way. "Yes."

"I'm Detective Sergeant Woo, this is Detective Baum."

He looked from one to the other. "Who's in charge?"

"I am," April said.

He pulled himself to his feet with an effort. "How's my wife?"

"We don't have a report yet."

"Did she say who did it?" he asked.

"She's unconscious."

"Jesus." He shook his head. "Who could do this?"

"What happened?"

"I want to see my wife." Popescu had a wide mouth and wide-set eyes as black as April's. The voice was cold, the eyes were on fire. He looked about to blow.

April felt sorry for him. It wasn't uncommon for people to get crazy when someone they loved was hurt. "She's with the doctor."

"I told them I don't *want* doctors to touch her without my being in the room."

"That's not possible—"

"I won't have any emergency room doctor playing around with my wife." Popescu's panic screamed out of his voice. "I forbid them to do anything to her, working on her face—or, or . . ."

"Can you tell me what happened, sir?"

Popescu gave her a crazed look. "Somebody broke into my apartment and took my baby." His voice cracked. "He's only three weeks old. I came home.

Heather was on the floor. There was blood all over the place. At first, I thought the blood was the baby's. Then, I realized the baby wasn't *there*—" His hands flew to his face. "Oh God, you've got to let me in to see her. I need to be with her."

"They have to clean her up first. It's procedure."

"She's all right. I know she's all right. It's just a cut on her head. It bled a lot, that's all. These goons restrained me physically. That guy put me in a hammerlock. I almost choked to death." Popescu pointed accusingly at the offender.

April glanced at Duffy. He stuck the wad of gum in his cheek and gave his head a barely perceptible shake. *No way.*

"I don't want her to stay here. I want her to come home with me. I'm sure she's all right." Popescu was raving. April figured him for a lawyer.

"Let's hope so." She took some notes on her steno pad, and frowned at Baum to do the same. The first things people said were often important. The new kid on the block, Baum dutifully followed her example.

Years ago, when she'd first joined the department and worked in Chinatown, she'd jotted some Chinese characters along with her notes in English on the steno pads the DAs called Rosarios. The DA on the case had gone nuts when he asked for her Rosario and saw the Chinese characters she'd written there. He told her nothing she wrote in Chinese counted and not to do it again. Now her notes were pretty much in English even though she missed the calligraphy practice. *Husband reports that when he got home, his wife was unconscious and the baby gone. The stains on his shirt are probably his wife's blood.* He would have tried to revive her, of course. Unless he'd injured himself and some of the blood was his. She'd noticed a cut on his left palm.

April and Baum saw the red-haired lady signal them. She tried to distract Popescu. "You want some coffee or something, Mr. Popescu? Officer Duffy could get you something while you're waiting."

"Where are you going?" he demanded.

"Detective Baum and I will be right back," she told him.

Popescu tried to follow them, but Duffy and Prince blocked the way. Their size and the clanking police equipment hanging on their hips convinced him to stay where he was. April didn't wait to hear what he had to say to them.

Treatment Room 3 was guarded by another uniform. A woman with a clipboard and a white coat over a blue scrub suit came out before April could question the officer. MARY KANE, M.D., the woman's name tag said. The plastic picture ID clipped to her uniform read the same. Dr. Mary Kane had a square jaw, blunt- cut, wheaty-brown hair, the kind of eyes April's mother called "devil eyes" (washed-out blue without lashes or much expression). Dr. Kane looked about twelve, but April couldn't complain about that because both she and Woody did, too.

April showed the doctor her own identification. "I'm Sergeant Woo, this is Detective Baum. What can you tell me about Mrs. Popescu?"

Dr. Kane shook her head. "She's unconscious." She glanced quickly at Baum, then looked April up and down. "Maybe you can help."

"How badly hurt is she?"

"She has contusions, couple of cracked ribs. He must have kicked her. Lump on her head. Her skull isn't fractured. But she's bruised all over. Weird."

"What's weird?" Baum asked.

April gave him a look.

"Some of the bruises are fresh. Others look like they're a few weeks old. And we have a chart on her. She's been here before."

"Did she have her baby here?" This was from April.

Blank-faced, Dr. Kane shook her head.

April pulled out her Rosario to write what the doctor said. "What was she here for on previous occasions?" April was blank faced back. Baum knew not to interfere this time.

The doctor checked the chart. "Third-degree burn, a cut—fifteen stitches on her arm. Sprained an ankle twice. She seems to fall down a lot." Still deadpan.

April wrote some more. "Anybody call the police to check it out?" Heather Rose Popescu wasn't so lucky; but maybe April Woo and Woody Baum would get lucky and there'd be no kidnapped baby in this case. Maybe the mother hadn't been feeling well, had given the baby to a relative for the afternoon and the assault came from the husband.

The doctor's square face took on a belligerent expression. "I couldn't say anything about the follow-up. The chart indicates they were localized injuries—one site each time, nothing major. Not the pattern we would associate with abuse. I'm not aware of any requirement for reporting a cooking burn, a sprained ankle, that kind of thing. There's a note from the husband that Mrs. Popescu has a neurological problem being dealt with by a private physician."

"Did you happen to check that out?"

"You're the detectives, we're ER. You want to try talking with her now?" It seemed as if Dr. Kane was one of those doctors who didn't like cops.

"In a minute. Is there anything else you can tell me?"

"I don't know." Finally she focused on April. "Maybe we've got a mental case here. If she's self-destructive, that would explain the previous injuries on her chart. She could have made up a story about a baby."

"Then her husband is a mental case, too. He says there was a baby this morning, and now it's gone."

"Maybe the baby was adopted," the doctor went on.

"They put it up for adoption? This morning?" April frowned.

"No, the woman here *adopted* the baby." The doctor was getting annoyed, as if April were really thick.

"Why do you say that?" Baum asked.

Dr. Kane pointedly consulted her watch, showing the two cops that she'd given them enough of her time. "She doesn't appear to have a postpartum body."

"Did you give her an internal exam?" April asked.

"For head injuries?"

April glanced at Baum. What was a postpartum body?

"There are other changes that occur in a woman's body after childbirth." The doctor gave April an amused look.

April flushed. "What are they?"

Dr. Kane slapped her clipboard against her hip impatiently. "The breasts become engorged with milk. The skin on the stomach is loose. The stomach itself is soft, enlarged. Not all of the excess weight would have come off yet—a lot of things." She glanced at Baum. He was writing it all down. Probably didn't know a thing about women. But apparently, neither did April.

"And Mrs. Popescu?" April asked.

Dr. Kane turned her attention to April. "No engorged breasts, no soft, distended belly. She didn't have a baby, or she sure got her figure back fast." Clearly the doc didn't think that was possible.

"Her body looks like yours," she added.

Baum smiled. April was a little over five foot, five inches, was well proportioned and willowy. She had an oval face with rosebud lips, and lovely almond eyes, a slender neck, but not with the hollows and protruding bones of a truly skinny person. She also had clearly discernible breasts, though not really ample ones by American standards. Her hair came down to the bottom of her earlobes. When she was away from her boss, Lieutenant Iriarte, she hooked her hair back around her ears so her lucky jade earrings would show. Mike Sanchez kept telling her she was more beautiful than Miss America, and the thought of an Asian Miss America always made her smile.

At the moment, though, she wasn't amused. She

didn't see how Dr. Kane could tell anything by *her* body, since it was covered with loose nubby-weave slacks, a thin sweater, silk scarf, and a cropped whisky-colored jacket. Except maybe, if she was looking really hard, she could tell that April was carrying a 9mm at her waist.

"Maybe you can get something out of her," Dr. Kane said and walked away. April would not have liked to be one of her patients.

"Wait for me," she told Baum. Then she opened the treatment room door.

Heather Popescu was lying on a rolling hospital bed, covered up with a sheet so that only the shoulders of her blue-flowered hospital gown showed. The sides of the bed had been put up so she wouldn't fall off, but she wasn't going anywhere. One eye was covered with a cold pack. Her lip was split and already puffed. Her extremely long, inky hair spilled off the pillow. April was startled, then recovered fast. The unconscious woman, Heather Rose Popescu, was Chinese.

No wonder Iriarte had ordered April sent down here immediately. Iriarte hated her. He'd never voluntarily gave her a big case. He'd sent her here because the victim was Chinese and it would look better with a high-profile Chinese detective on it. April flashed to the husband standing out in the waiting room. A belligerent Caucasian. Oh man, she was in trouble. She didn't like this one bit. Skinny Dragon would think this was a warning just for her. She was going to shake her finger at April over this. "See what happens," she'd scream. "Mixed marriage, woman beaten to a pulp. That's what you can expect when you marry *laowai,*" (shit-faced foreigner).

Oh man. Suddenly April wished Mike, her mother's nightmare, was here with her now. He could take this case in hand. Woody was too inexperienced to be of any help, particularly with the husband. If the husband beat the wife, he wasn't going to like April as his interviewer. April needed the expert partner she'd had in Mike, then lost on purpose because she hadn't wanted to mix business and pleasure. So much for integrity and scruples. Now she was on her own. Thank you, Lieutenant Iriarte.

April studied Heather Rose's battered face. Where were her parents, her protectors? "Heather? Can you hear me?" she said softly. "I'm April Woo. I'm here to help you."

No answer came from the unconscious woman.

"Heather, we need to find the baby. Where's the baby?"

Heather did not stir. April felt the cold brick of fear in her belly. "Come on back, girl. We need your help here."

It was no use. Heather wasn't coming back.

April tried in Chinese. "*Wo shi, Siyue Woo. Ni neng bang wo ge mang ma?*"

No response.

Finally, April turned to leave the room. "Whoever did this to you, I'll get him for this," she promised.

Back in the waiting room, Heather's husband was standing in front of his chair. Baum was talking to him and writing down what he said.

"How is she?"

April gave him a look. "She's unconscious."

"How long will she be like this?"

April studied him, didn't have an answer.

Popescu's cheeks were gray, like a dead man's. He glanced at the two cops who'd stuck by his side since he'd come in. Duffy and Prince lounged against a wall as if they were used to hanging around for long periods of time with nothing to do. A baby on someone's lap on the other side of the crowded waiting room started to wail.

Another brick hit April. If it wasn't Heather's baby, whose was it? Who was this man she'd married, and why was he lying? He said he wanted to go home and she had to let him. There wasn't anything they could do for Heather here.